THE GLAMOUR OF EVIL

THE GLAMOUR OF EVIL

A Maddie Lynch Mystery

by

Michael McKinley &
Nancy Merritt Bell

FIRST EDITION

All inquiries should be addressed to BookGo at
www.BookGo.pub

Cover Design by Khadijah Ali
First Printing, 2025

To our daughter, Rose,
with exponential love, joy and pride.
--Pops and Mumma

"The best and most effective espionage service
that I know in the world belongs to the
Vatican."
Simon Wiesenthal

"And the Lord said unto Satan,
From whence comest thou?"
And Satan answered the Lord, and said,
"From going to and fro in the earth,
and from walking up and down on it."
Job 2

1. New York City.

Christopher Zimmerman has to laugh. The rendezvous spot is not one that he would have chosen, and yet it is perfect. An abandoned church on the far west side of Manhattan, and in Hell's Kitchen no less. It would be the ideal place to trade his secret for what he wants in return. And what he wants is nothing less than the greater glory of God. And some cash to buy it.

The church, St. Martin's, is a beauty. Built in the late Victorian Gothic style with red brick masonry and terracotta dressing, it had housed a dwindling Lutheran community until the early 2000s, and then it shuttered.

What could they expect, really? Zimmerman believes that their failure is payback for that uppity German monk and his hammer and nails a few centuries back.

Martin Luther is to blame here for this abandoned church in Hell's Kitchen and Christopher Zimmerman will be thanked for the reconsecration of it for the one true faith. He will have to negotiate the price. Later. After he has sold what he is here to sell.

She said she'd be blonde and wearing black, and so she is. When Zimmerman spots his contact going into the church, his heart thuds faster. She looks from a distance so much like his Regina. She wears a black tracksuit and has her blonde hair tucked under a black baseball cap. As for her eyes, they are behind black sunglasses. She's dressed as if she is someone famous who doesn't want to be seen on her way to the gym on this cool and cloudy afternoon in mid-April. And not a woman sneaking into a deconsecrated church.

Christopher Zimmerman was surprised when her team agreed to meet him. He thought they might want to rendezvous in some hotel bar in Washington, where deals like he was proposing are made. But no, Regina's team insisted that he come to New York, and to come under heavy cover. So he did. Breezing through JFK on his regular Swiss passport, and not the other one from the Vatican, which would have been even faster, but got tagged at customs as "official business."

He isn't here on official Vatican business. He is here to do something that the Vatican cannot and will not do. He will change the western world for the better. And this woman who looks like Regina is going to help him to do that. The fact that she does look like his Regina is one more sign for Zimmermann that approval of his plan comes down from God Himself.

Christopher Zimmerman crosses West 57th and enters the church. Despite its handsome exterior, the church's interior reflects a characteristically Protestant lack of imagination. No stained glass, no sacred statues, no perfume of incense. The pews have been sold off, and now only a circle of chairs stands next to a table draped in a white tablecloth, a laptop upon it, all before a plain wooden altar in a large white room. The kind of room where you would have to work hard to connect to heaven. If at all.

However, a vision of heaven is standing on the altar today. It's that woman in black, smiling at him.

"Hello, Christopher," she says. Her accent is flat. Not of New York. Not of the south, either, but somewhere in the middle. Zimmerman prides himself on knowing his American accents, and this is the kind you'd have if you never wanted anyone to notice. He smiles. She wants to be seen as neutral. So he turns up the guttural volume on his Swiss accent. He is anything but neutral.

"Hello, Jane," he says, offering a courtly bow. He suspects that Jane Jones is not her real name, but it doesn't matter. So long as she can pay for what he is selling, then she can be called anything.

Jane Jones smiles at him with the smile she knows works on male clients, even the holy ones, a smile of promise. "Shall we?" she says, and gestures to one of the chairs before the table with the laptop.

"So we shall," he replies and then sits, still smiling, even more expectantly.

She sits next to him, and he guesses her age to be about thirty. She has fine pale skin, and a body that is not as voluptuous as Regina's, but she's tall. She's taller than Zimmerman, maybe six feet. She works out, and her smooth unblemished face could be that of a child, save for her eyes. With her sunglasses now cresting her forehead, those eyes are an icy blue gray, like a cold sea where boats capsize in winter winds and their secrets go to the deep. Or, thinks Zimmerman, the same shade as the Bombay Sapphire gin he'll be raising in his first-class seat on his way back home to Rome tonight.

"What is our destination?" Jane Jones asks almost tenderly, as if they are both going on a luxury vacation.

But then she raises the laptop screen that asks for a banking address.

Zimmerman reaches into his inside coat pocket and produces an envelope. “It’s all in here,” he says.

“Excellent,” she replies, and peeks into the envelope. Then she taps in a sequence of letters and numbers, and shows him the account in an Austrian bank. “Very secure. The transfer will happen seamlessly once we’re done.”

Zimmerman almost laughs. If only she knew what he does about Austrian banks. And he watches as the agreed upon amount arrives in the account. It is a fine number: $250 million in USD. That will go a long way to doing what needs to be done, and what he will do: save the Christian world from destruction.

“Excellent,” he says. Then he hands her another envelope.

She takes it but doesn’t even open it. Instead, she logs into her Tor browser which will take them to the dark web, a place that can’t be traced by snoopers who might be in the church ether, and she types in the first of Zimmerman’s URLs.

On the website is a series of folders. One is labeled “Regina Photos”, and the other two, “Regina Correspondence”. His Regina.

Jane Jones clicks on the Regina Photos folder. She doesn’t react to the thumbnails, many of them photos of Regina naked, or mostly naked, and in her early 20s. Then Jane hits delete. She does that for each of the folders, bearing the exact same names as the first set, on the five URLs that Zimmerman has given to her. Each time he feels a fever flashing over his body, his body remembering Regina. Then a hum of relief. It's over.

She looks at each folder before she vaporizes it, and says nothing. Zimmerman watches her, aroused by her non-reaction. Sure, he has forty years on her, but she might catch a whiff of the lather of this mighty transaction and who knows where things could go?

"That's everything?" she asks, after deleting the contents of the last folder, now looking at him with those frozen blue eyes.

"Yes, everything." Which isn't true, because he needs a parachute, just in case they somehow try to screw him. He knows from his own time as a banker in the secular world that you can never have too many parachutes, but he also knows that all he needs is one that works. And he has that.

"You're sure?" Jane continues. "Because if everything is not gone, you will be gone."

She says this with such a friendly, easy manner, he might think she was joking, but her eyes say otherwise. If they have to come to find him, they will kill him. So, he will make sure he cannot be found by the likes of this woman in black.

"Yes. I understand what you need, and you understand what I need. We are complete."

Jane Jones looks at him in her genial way, eyes still freezing cold. "Good." She returns to the bank account website and keys in the transfer of the money to the account number that he had given her on the first envelope.

Zimmerman watches the money flow from her account to his and he nods, well pleased. “That was much easier than I thought it would be,” he says. That isn’t true, either. Zimmerman knows from his time in the Vatican Bank just how easy it is to move money around, if no one is watching you too closely.

“We like to be efficient,” Jane replies. Then she reaches under the table and surprises Zimmerman with his favorite champagne. She has placed a bottle of Krug Grand Cuvée in an ice bucket, and now produces two crystal flutes. “And I think this deserves a toast.”

Zimmerman smiles at her. She has done her homework on him. And he appreciates her style. A glass of champagne in a deconsecrated Lutheran church with this reasonable facsimile of Regina will be a fine way to end a transaction that has benefitted them both.

Jane Jones pops the cork, then hands him a glass of champagne, and pours herself one. “To Reagan,” she says.

Zimmerman raises his glass and replies, “To Regina.” Then he takes a long sip. The champagne is perfect and he sighs at its ticklish effervescence. Jane takes a more modest sip and sighs back.

Zimmerman drains his glass and Jane pours him another. Then she walks behind him, and wraps her arms around his chest. Zimmerman is pleasantly surprised. He hasn’t expected her to try to seduce him. But he will go along, for old time’s sake. For Regina’s sake.

Then he feels a prick on his neck and sees the syringe

suddenly in her hand. "Sssh, sssh," she says, before he can say anything, "you'll soon be where you've always wanted to go."

"Where's that?" he says reflexively, astonished by this turn of events. But his words are slurred, for his muscles feel like they are melting.

"Heaven, of course," she replies, then jabs him with another syringe. The first to relax, the second, to kill.

As Christopher Zimmerman fades away in a deconsecrated church in Hell's Kitchen, his life with Regina flies across his mind's eye, and it gives him one last burst of hope. He has not given Jane Jones everything that he has collected on Regina. He kept a parachute in a very safe place. And Jane Jones will know that fact as soon as the people who are with him on his quest know that he is dead. He might be going to heaven, but he will send Jane Jones to hell.

2. New York City.

Maddie Lynch looks out the window on to 43rd Street and silently curses. The guy on the other end of the Zoom call is not making her life easy, and he seems to enjoy it. Now, in the middle of her pitch to Brett Muenster—"Moonster, not Monster," he jokes—he has vanished from the screen to take a call on his cell. For talking to this asshole, she says to herself, she will upgrade her post-work shot of Jameson's to a fat double. One ice cube.

Maddie takes a breath and reminds herself that, given the state of things, at 29 years old, she is lucky to have this job. And for the most part, her work as a chase producer at the International News Network is a straight line. She books the guests for her boss, Teddy Wright's show, *I'm Wright, with Teddy Wright,* she does the pre-interviews with the guests, and she preps the questions for Teddy. Then she watches as Teddy does her own thing and goes off in directions no one has imagined except for the show's legal team.

Teddy's independence from consistently red or blue politics is what makes Teddy's show the most highly rated on INN's prime time slate, even though INN is about as blue a network as you can get and still be in the blue section of the color palette. Teddy's stubborn take on the political landscape defies color-coding, and that's what makes her so popular. And such a hellish enigma to work for, Maddie thinks. Now Teddy wants presidential candidate Reagan Clark on her show and to do it Maddie has to make nice with Mr. I'm-too-busy-for-you Brett Muenster.

As Maddie waits for Muenster to reappear, she scrolls through Reagan Clark's campaign website on her phone. It features the "I am an American patriot" talking points in bold caps that every conservative candidate needs to have these days, given their claim of the state as a holy church they repeatedly make, but Maddie notices something in Reagan Clark's eyes that defies political convention. Sure, her blonde, blue-eyed wholesome soccer mom look fits into the central casting rotation of Patriot 1 News, but Maddie sees in Reagan's eyes the hints of shadow. She sees something dark around the edges, threatening to ruin the picnic. It is a look Maddie knows well. Her father had it. And she has it, too.

Brett Muenster, on the other hand, looks like a Friday night cop shop mugshot. If Maddie hadn't known he was Reagan Clark's director of communications, she'd have thought this bald, dumpy man in round metal glasses was some minor accountant who fell on his sword for the thieving bosses now in the Caymans. Not so much a bag man, but stubbornly, or stupidly, loyal to a bad cause.

"Hey, sorry about that." Brett Muenster is back, and he isn't sorry. He smiles at Maddie with cold calculation. What is he calculating, she wonders?

"Sure," Maddie replies. "I know you're a busy guy and I appreciate your time. So, as I was saying, we'd love to have Reagan Clark come on the show and talk to Teddy."

Muenster grins. "We couldn't get arrested by you guys this time last year."

Maddie takes another breath, and wonders what would happen if she just tells him to go fuck himself and have Reagan Clark blather her holy America nonsense to Patriot 1 News? But she keeps her temper—the temper that she got from her Italian mother—under control.

She reminds Brett Muenster that this time last year, Reagan Clark wasn't the overwhelming favorite to win the party nomination for president come July. And now, given the sharp three-way cleft in the American electorate, with Them and Us and Undecided, she might even win the presidential election come November.

Muenster chuckles in an ah-shucks kind of way**.** "I'm glad you folks at INN have noticed," he says. Maddie can feel the "No thanks," coming her way from Muenster and she is already framing the rejection to Teddy, who still might throw a water bottle at her head. But then Muenster says, with an unexpected smoothness, "How about I buy you a drink and we'll discuss it?"

Maddie has not expected that invitation. But then he nods at her as if he approves of what he sees: Maddie's long black curly hair, her alabaster skin, and regal nose – also from her Italian mother – her full lips regularly set in a cocky half-smile and her frank, green-eyed stare, which she got from her father. She'd look beautiful to an idiot. She also knows that Muenster is based in Houston.

"Yeah, I'll be in New York later this week. There's a bourbon bar I like in Hell's Kitchen."

Maddie bites her lip. The last thing she wants is to go

drinking with Reagan Clark's director of communications, because if someone snaps a pic of the two of them bonding over glasses of bourbon, it could zap her on social media in a pretty unpleasant way. On the other hand, if it will get Reagan Clark closer to Teddy, then it's worth the cost.

"Sure. I think I know the place. The Three Roses, on 39th. It's just down the street from my office."

Muenster snickers again. "Then I'd say it was destiny. How about 7 PM, Saturday?"

Teddy's show airs at 9 PM each weekday, but it is taped, so Maddie is usually free by 6. But she has a regular Saturday dinner date with her mother. "Would Friday work?" she asks. She will show up on Saturday if she has to, but she wants to gauge his confidence.

"I can do Friday," he says, still smiling. "See you there at 7. And we'll see where things go," he adds a little too confidently. Then he is gone.

Maddie shouts "Fucking hell!" at the window, and this outburst summons her supervising producer, Aretta Zayed, into her small office. Aretta is both Maddie's immediate boss and her fellow traveler on the show, though at five feet, she's about a foot shorter than Maddie and barely weighs in at 100 pounds. She has her black shiny hair cropped short and wears a slash of scarlet lipstick to dramatic effect, its shade of red made even brighter by the darkness of her skin.

Not only is Aretta smart and talented, but she is also gay and Black and Muslim, and that helps INN tick off all kinds of boxes on its diversity checklist. Maddie loves her because they are on the same page politically. They believe that the founders of the country might want a refund if they saw how big money had corrupted their vision.

"You OK?" Aretta asks. Her voice is surprisingly deep for someone so small. She offers Maddie a bag of *chin chin*, a Nigerian dessert like mini deep-fried donut balls. Aretta likes to feed the office Nigerian sweets.

Maddie takes a couple of *chin chin*. "Yeah, sorry. I was just trying to get Reagan Clark on the show, and—"

"And?" Teddy Wright is suddenly looming in Maddie's doorway. Teddy is like that, able to show up like a ghost at the feast. She is staring at Maddie like Wonder Woman, her black silk t-shirt and black leather pants matching her horn-rimmed glasses. Her blue eyes are electric with expectation, and her body, pushing 50, looks as if she has defied time and is at least a decade younger.

Even so, Maddie has seen Teddy look at her with jealousy. Maddie tries to tamp it all down, knowing that even her worn-in jeans and a paisley shirt under a blue blazer, her Italian-Irish beauty, with her black hair and emerald eyes, could somehow be an impediment to continued employment. After all, Maddie's Oxford education is impediment enough.

"And," Maddie says, "I am having a drink with her director of communications on Friday. To iron out the details."

"No, you're not," Teddy replies.

Maddie's pale cheeks flush. She has expected this

moment ever since her mother called in a favor with INN's owner and got her the gig when she came back to New York unemployed and broken-hearted from Oxford. It's the moment when Teddy says, "Favor's up, charity hire! Goodbye!"

But it's not that either. "You're not going to drink with that weaselly, sick-flirt fucker because Aretta is going to drink with him."

"I am?" Aretta will be having soda water on a Friday. A day known to her as Yawm al-Jum'ah. The Muslim Day of Assembly.

"And you, Dr. Lynch, are going to Rome."

Teddy always calls Maddie by her academic title when she wants to show her who's boss.

"I am?"

Teddy smiles at them with sudden maternal warmth, which Maddie has to appreciate as Teddy has no kids. Maybe she would have done if they could have been born fully formed at age 18. And if Teddy believed in love.

She steps into the office and shows Maddie and Aretta her iPhone screen. On it is the headline: "Pope Pius XIII will come to America in August." And a photo of the Catholic Church's first African pope.

Maddie's heart beats a dirge. She knows what's coming next.

"You speak Italian, right?"

"I do."

"And you lived in Rome, right?"

"I did."

"And your mother was a nun?"

"Almost. She met my father before her final vows."

Teddy's eyes shift into the past for a beat. "Your father was a great man."

Maddie feels gravity pulling extra hard, tugging on her sadness: she still misses her father who really was a great man. And her famous journalist dad is the reason why she's here, now, about to get a mission she dreads.

Teddy now smiles like the card player with a full house. "So you're the perfect person to go chat up the Vatican. And get me a sit down invu with the Pope. When he's here."

Maddie knows it's useless to say that Pope Pius XIII is not Pope Francis, who would talk to anyone. This Pope has never given an interview to the media because he has told the Vatican media crew that this is their job, and not his job. He's to mediate between the world's 1.3 billion Catholics and a pretty harsh God, as far as Maddie is concerned.

He is also, as Maddie knows the Church is fond of saying, a traditionalist, who believes that the purity of the Holy Mother Church must be preserved no matter what. Or so the cardinals who elected him thought. But then Pius suddenly went progressive on them, calling for dialogue with Islam and with the so-called liberal wing of the Church that loves gays and women and refugees. Pope Pius, from Nigeria, like Aretta's mom, has turned out to be a surprising guy, which has made a lot of his old fellow traditionalists angry.

And so an interview is impossible. Failure: imminent.

Still Maddie has to say – "OK, I can sort that out."

Teddy holds up a dismissive hand. "Aretta, you look after the details. As for you, Maddie Lynch, just make sure you come back with a, how do you say 'yes' in Nigerian, Aretta?"

"That would be in Hausa. You say 'ee'."

"Eeeeee!" Teddy trills. Then she smiles at Maddie like an executioner. "Just make sure there's a 'y' and an 's' bookending that Eeeee from the Popester before you come back, OK?"

Maddie returns the smile, but she feels her cheeks flush with anger. "Yes, Teddy. Unless he says it in Italian."

Teddy looks at Maddie as if she has just slapped her, but then she bursts out laughing. And walks away, her laughter following her down the hall.

"Wow," Aretta says. "The Pope is coming here. I wonder how his message of Muslim love will go down in the, uh, heartland of America? Where they all think we Muslims come out of the womb as suicide bombers."

"And I bet that's why the Pope is coming here, to get out that Muslim-love message. I just hope his press people have some Teddy-love," Maddie adds. Right now she'd rather drink with Muenster than go to Rome. Which is saying a lot.

Aretta promises to 'adjust' the budget and get Maddie a comfortable seat in business class for the nine hour flight to Italy.

"Are you going to be OK Friday with the 'sick-flirt fucker?'"

"Sure!" Aretta grins. "I am definitely not his type."

"How's Karin?" Maddie asks. She knows Aretta doesn't discuss her private life much, but she did tell her that she was dating another woman who is also Black, gay and Muslim. Being a martial arts teacher as well, Maddie thinks, is worth bonus points.

"I broke up with her. But even so…" Aretta swipes her hands in the air—two people going in different directions.

"I'm sorry." Maddie gives Aretta a hug. Her own heart takes a plunge for her friend; Aretta has a long list of boxes to check. And so meeting someone is hard. Getting a relationship going is almost impossible. Maddie knows.

After Aretta slips away, Maddie sits down, ready to call Muenster and tell him there will be a substitute for their drink. No, that would piss him off and maybe end the chance that Reagan might show up to spar with Teddy. Best to say nothing and go to Rome and deal with whatever shitstorm happens here.

She has not seen Rome since it was home. Behind the memory of the eternal city is one of her father, James Lynch, and the last time she saw him, which was in Jerusalem. He told her then, and he would tell her now, "*There's nothing you can't overcome with a big bottle of Jameson's, a big gun and a big sense of humor. And always remember, no one gets out alive.*" She would count on that philosophy to get her through. As for the big gun, well, that's what got her father killed on assignment for INN. He didn't get out alive. And Maddie has no plans to die for Teddy Wright.

3. Chelsea Piers, New York.

Maddie skates hard down the ice at the Chelsea Piers Sky Rink for her Columbia Chiclets team. It feels good and fresh to be in the cold. And to be with her friends on the team, in their sky blue and white home uniforms, tied with a minute and twenty-two seconds left on the clock. A win tonight against the Fordham Fallen Angels moves Maddie's Columbia alumnae hockey team into the quarter finals.

Maddie taps her stick on the ice to get Emily, her center, to pass the puck over. They have been close since day one at Columbia where they had many of the same classes and the same taste in nuclear-powered espresso. So, Maddie is very sure that when Emily sees a chance, she takes it.

And Emily, tall and broad, sees that chance and skates across the blue line herself, only to have the puck pick-pocketed off her stick by a strapping Fordham defender, who then lays Emily flat on her ass.

Maddie charges after the Fordham defender, and knocks the puck off her stick. She picks it up and skates fast to the corner to the right of the goalie, and pivots, aiming to pass up to the point. But she's screened by the defender coming right at her. It's personal now, so she shifts hard to her left and steps around her, and now has a clear path to the net.

Skating an arc in front of the net, Maddie has the other defender now closing in. Once the goalie has committed to Maddie shooting on her backhand, she hits the brakes, pivots again, and fires the puck from her forehand into the lower left-hand corner of the net.

The Chiclets leap off the bench to mob Maddie, screaming for joy as she wins the game for them with just forty seconds left. She wants to punch that Fordham defender who knocked down Emily, but instead sucks in air and just grins at the woman. Who does not grin back.

Maddie is addicted to the screaming physical pleasure of playing hockey with teammates who are old classmates. They are now in the quarter finals of the New York City Women's Senior Hockey League and the screaming is louder: "Let's go, Chiclets, let's go!"

"You coming for a beer, Maddie?" asks Emily after they have showered and changed back into their street clothes. Maddie has pulled on a Rangers' ball cap over her wet hair, and slashed on some lipstick to make it a look.

With the Vatican Mission hanging over her, and her job dangling from that noose, Maddie could use a drink, but she really doesn't feel like heading to a bar. And yet it's so rare that Emily ever has time to do that kind of thing that Maddie says yes.

"You're not in the office dark and early tomorrow, Em?" Maddie asks when the eight players who make the trek to the bar are settled around a table at the cozy, quiet Westside Tavern on 23rd Street, with real wooden tables and a real fire in the fireplace.

"No, we have a remote training day," Em replies, and raises her pint of Brooklyn Lager to that reprieve and to their win.

"What are you training for?"

Emily takes a long sip and comes up smiling. She has a slender face framed by her silky blonde hair. Her mother is Icelandic and her father is an Israeli and Em, with her tall, broad, blonde self with an open, girlish face looks like a poster child for white supremacy. Which they have laughed at, as Em, despite her Wall Street life, is even more to the political left than Maddie. Thanks also to her Icelandic and Jewish genes.

"I'm doing the training, Mads. Explaining our industry-leading suite of generative AI tools and how they deliver business-grade insights."

Maddie thinks about that. "I need to invest."

Em delivers a wary smile, having heard only the opposite. "I thought you didn't want to get into the market. Ever."

"I think I'm going to need a rainy day fund soon." Maddie goes on to explain that the skies are gloomy now that she is being sent on a suicide mission to Rome, and that it is likely to kill her career because her boss, Teddy, has always thought of her as a charity hire.

"So, this trip to Rome is a test?"

"Yeah, Em, it's a test. I leave Friday night."

Karla, a lawyer and bruising defender, hears that travel plan and pipes up, "And you'll be back in time for our next game, Lynch, right?"

Their next game is in two weeks. Maddie is sure that not only will she be back, she will have time on her hands. She raises her glass. Cheers for her Chiclets.

"Hey Maddie," Emily says, "I can help you with that rainy day fund. Give me whatever you can afford, and I'll work some Wall Street voodoo."

Maddie can afford to part with $1,000, so she writes Emily a check for that amount.

"I'll send you all the official stuff after I have made the buy," Emily says. "And we'll get a stretch of sunshine into your life."

For that, Maddie gives Em a hug and buys the next round. Some sunshine would be good. It has been a long dark stretch since she returned from Oxford. There, for a lovely while, she had found love with a good man, and a career as an academic lying before her, and a golden sun in a soft blue sky.

Then her father was killed in a war that was so far away. Dark clouds scudded over everything, so the only thing she could do was finish her thesis and come home. But she still feels like a stranger in her own land. And until she finds her way back to the light, then a stranger she will remain, to those who want to know her, and to herself, most of all. Maybe her trip to Rome will give her the missing GPS coordinates to her own happiness. Before, Rome had given her nothing but trouble. And now, she suspects, Rome will offer her even more of it.

4. Brooklyn, New York.

Maddie feels the chill of February on this April night as she makes the five-block walk from the 7th Avenue subway to her apartment on 5th Avenue, one of those creaky old Brooklyn brownstone converts, last touched up in the 1970s. She checks her mailbox in the lobby, not that she expects any letters, or even paper bills, but out of a sense of possibility. If her father is still alive, he'll send her a letter.

She knows that's the kind of possibility called miraculous. He was vaporized in a fire fight in southern Lebanon by Hezbollah. No body to be found, said the Israelis. He was reporting on a war and these things happen.

Maddie is thinking about her father tonight because he would have loved the goal she scored. He loved hockey and his love landed on her when he took her to Rangers games when she was in elementary school. "You can't teach that, Maddie," he'd say when Eric Lindros made a pass where the puck seemed to have eyes, or when defenseman Brian Leetch stopped an attack and turned it into an odd man rush with his own superb skating. "It's pure talent, like Mozart, like Shakespeare."

For a while, Maddie thought Mozart and Shakespeare played for the Rangers.

She warms into that memory and lets herself into her walkup on the third floor of her building in Park Slope.

Maddie's apartment is about as basic as you can get and still be inside. It's painted eggshell white with high-vaulted ceilings and a couple of ye olde Brooklyn fixtures, such as the leaded glass windows and the hammer-knock in the radiator.

But there are two luxuries: the 52-inch flat screen TV so that Maddie can watch the Rangers and often with one eye closed, INN. The other is her bed, a miracle of memory foam that seems to be able to remind her how to sleep, which was a $5,000 splurge after her first three paychecks to give herself a good night's sleep. And a place to share with a worthy young man. So far, she has been the only sleeper in the bed, which she also uses as a dining room, eating take-out and watching hockey, when not playing it.

Maddie has just tucked into a Cubano, a miracle of ham, Swiss, pork, pickle and mustard on Cuban bread, when her phone rings. She is prepared to tell the swindler in some boiler room in Bangalore to do something honest, but she sees it's a WhatsApp number. And she knows it.

The number belongs to Cosmo. Whose heart she broke in the wake of her own when she lost her father.

If he's calling her now, when it's two o'clock in the morning in Oxford, it must be urgent. She hopes his parents are alright. She hopes he is all right. So she answers, and she gets her second shock of the day.

"I want it to be you," he says. "We all do. Daddy especially. Please say 'yes'."

It is another proposal from Cosmo. Maybe this time

Maddie will say "Yes". But the past returns, reminding her she said "No" to Cosmo. Then another woman, Elka, quickly said "Ja", and a wedding and a baby very quickly followed. The offer tonight is not to be his wedded wife.

That baby who sped along just after the wedding will be baptized in the college chapel on Saturday. And everyone wants Maddie to be the godmother.

Cosmo takes her silence for a "No" and feels he must explain. "The short notice is because Elka nominated some third cousin somewhere in darkest Bavaria, and she wanted all kinds of promises that we would raise little Mathilda to be a fun-hating killjoy of a Catholic. So I managed to persuade Elka that you would be the best, and she just moments ago said 'Yes', and so I wanted to lock you in, as it were."

Maddie has to laugh. Once again the cosmos is telling her that she's the right choice, and that there's a clock on her.

"As destiny would have it, I am flying to Rome on Friday night. I suppose I can get a layover in London and come up to Oxford to save your new daughter from sin."

"So that's a 'yes'?" Cosmo asks.

"I won't be staying long, but I'll be there for the show."

Cosmo is elated. It's the happiest that she has heard him since, well, since before her father was killed and her overwhelming sorrow killed off Cosmo and Maddie. But now she feels a spark of the old times, and she likes the feeling.

"I don't have to make a speech, do I?" she asks.

"No," he says. "All you have to do is protect Mathilda from Satan."

Maddie thinks about this as she drifts off to sleep. She is going to Rome to try to get a television interview with the Pope, the likelihood of which is about zero. And on her way there, she is going to be godmother for the baby of a man she once thought would be the father of her own children.

Now, she was happy for him. He had created new life. And she feels a small flush of hope for herself: this unexpected offer to do something good for someone she loved makes her feel that she has a fighting chance in Rome. Once she takes care of Satan in Oxford.

5. Brooklyn, New York.

It is just past midnight when the white Ford Escape pulls into the parking lot of the Food Bazaar Market in Red Hook, Brooklyn. The market closed two hours earlier, but that is the point. Brett Muenster isn't here to shop for organic olive oil and artisanal cheese.

Muenster is early, even though he's flown up from Houston especially for this parking lot rendezvous. The trip was wearing and the image in the rearview mirror agrees. He has too many lines raking his brow for a thirty-five-year-old, and the fact his head is shaved bald doesn't help.

With his metal glasses he looks like a dumpy version of like that guy on TV who made crystal meth in an RV. Muenster hates that show. It makes fun of everything that he's about, which is nothing less than the salvation of this country. In the last years, it has been pummeled into a bloodied, weeping mess by hand-wringing do-gooders.

It is because of guys like Brett Muenster that Reagan Clark has a shot at the White House. Imagine that: a conservative and a white woman will get the golden prize – should everything work out as Muenster and a few others have planned.

And everything should work. She is just trailing the incumbent President Marty Klein in the polls. Klein, a man who is so impressed by his own pieties that he believes himself a god. Well, Muenster is all about slaying false prophets and especially those gods with feet of wet, progressive clay. The only place Klein will lead the country is off a cliff.

A black Tesla slides up next to him, and Brett Muenster momentarily loses his calm. Surely, she isn't coming to this meeting that she has commanded here in this Brooklyn hipster parking lot in an Uber? What is the point of being clandestine if you are going to bring along a driver?

Unless, of course, he isn't a driver. He is blonde and fleshy, his unblinking blue eyes boring into Muenster as if calculating how much pain he can inflict before killing him. Yes, this is both driver and muscle in case Brett Muenster is stupid enough to try to cheat her.

"Igor loves driving in Brooklyn," says Jane Jones, nodding at the driver, Igor, who leans on the driver's door, hands at his sides, ready for action, his eyes fixed on Muenster.

Igor? Really? thinks Muenster.

Jane adds, "His family lives just down the road in Brighton Beach."

Igor nods, then lights a cigarette and smiles broadly at Muenster, as if he's the first course at a feast. He has gold incisors and they glitter in the streetlight. That's not dentistry, thinks Muenster. That's some Russian mobster shit, like star tattoos on your shoulders for every kill.

Muenster turns away to get a fix on Jane. He runs her stats in his head. Midwest, army, private contractor, now here with a Russian driver. Probably met him in some hellhole they were both making worse.

Her blonde hair is covered by a blue Brooklyn

Cyclones baseball cap, and she wears no makeup, not that he thinks that she needs any.

Of course, Jane Jones is totally off limits. Especially since this meeting isn't happening, not even when history writes of his triumph.

Muenster beckons her away from Igor and into the shadows. Instead, Jane Jones walks the other way, toward the chain link fence that gives perfect vantage on the Statue of Liberty.

"It's the best time to see her, Brett," she says, gazing at Lady Liberty, who stands surprisingly close across the harbor.

He doesn't respond to that sentimental cue. "Do you have what I need?"

Jane Jones gazes at Lady Liberty like a loving child, then turns to Muenster, her eyes now of ice, and hands him a flash drive. "It's all there. I deleted it all with him sitting right next to me, and then moved the money to his account."

"Which you have moved back."

Jane's wide mouth draws upward in a rare smile. "I'm so touched that you noticed."

Muenster lets the jab go. Hard not to notice $250 million belonging to the Friends of Liberty, but it was, as he knows, the cost of getting that goddamn priest out of Rome and into the crosshairs.

"I see the media haven't figured it out yet," he adds.

"If they do, they'll think this old guy wandered into an abandoned church and had a heart attack."

"Which is what they were supposed to think. But I

have this nagging feeling that our blackmailer didn't give us everything, Jane."

"You still think there's buried treasure?"

Muenster throws up his fat hands and shrugs. It's his nature to be paranoid, but they have combed everything, first the priest's safety deposit box, and now the ether.

"He was a blackmailer," Jane says. "He wanted money, and as far as he was concerned, the deal was done. I was there. And now I want my money."

"Of course. Excuse me while I go get it."

Muenster walks over to his rented car. On the way he flashes a palm to Igor to show that he only has the key fob in his hand and not a grenade, then pops the trunk. He hauls out a shiny silver Halliburton briefcase, like luggage from a spaceship, which weighs twenty-two pounds when fully loaded with cash.

"It will take a while to count it," he says, cleaning off his glasses from the drizzle which has started.

She lifts the briefcase and gives it a jiggle. "It's all there." She has done this before and knows what a million dollars in cash feels like. After all, that's what the Halliburton is built to hold.

Muenster looks at Igor, who watches as if waiting for a signal to attack. Muenster calculated that risk when he agreed to meet here. With a mercenary and muscle in a Brooklyn grocery store parking lot, handing over a million dollars in cash. He is a long way from Cairo, Georgia.

"And next time, Brett, if we happen to meet again," she says, holding the briefcase tight, "I will expect more moolah." She leans toward him, as if to give him a kiss, but just wants to see his eyeballs up close. "You understand?"

He nods. He understands that this win for Reagan Clark is going to cost a lot more than he initially calculated. And so long as it's not his money, he's just fine with that.

6. Oxford, England.

The gray April chill filters through the stained glass, dimming the bright colors of the ancient chapel of St. Jude's College, Oxford. Maddie Lynch stands on the altar with Cosmo Smythe, the man she once thought she would marry, who still looks at her adoringly. And beside him, his redheaded and stern wife, Elka, a novelist, narrows her blue eyes on Maddie with suspicion, as if formatting her next book's villain. Her baby just smiles. Maddie gets her mixed reviews, which she knows she more than deserves. After all, she's here to fend off sin for the baby, having done loads of that enthusiastically with the father.

"A book and a baby before I'm 30," was the mantra Cosmo Smythe had repeated. And now he had both, ahead of schedule, even. Cosmo is younger than Maddie, and won't turn 29 for another month. Maddie will turn 30 next March.

The smiling Mathilda is a beautiful child, like her father. Cosmo's lean, handsome face is balanced with brown, brainy eyes, and a regal nose all topped by a wild shamble of blond curls. The baby's hair is blonde and wavy, like his. Mathilda looks with her bright green eyes right into Maddie, who stands there about to formally enter her life forever, the baby's eyes as clear as those of Cosmo.

The look in his eyes now is one of happiness and an antidote to the tears she saw when she said goodbye. She had to leave to confront her own truth about her wounded heart, a wound inflicted by death. Love alone could not do it.

There is another joyous gaze falling on Maddie, one scanning her up and down approvingly. Luke Macclesfield, Cosmo's best friend, was asked to be godfather. Luke, his auburn curls framing his Celtic oval of a face with its alluring forehead bulge that holds his extra helping of brains, can drink everyone under the table and once seemed to want to get Maddie on top of it. Luke backed off that flirt because Cosmo would have died of heartbreak. Maddie felt a little offended that Cosmo would even think that Luke had a chance. But now Luke is clearly thinking he has a chance. Maddie knows he does not. She is still, she realizes, looking at Cosmo.

Then all eyes are on the priest and they all stand straighter, like students before a teacher, as the priest begins. "Dear parents and godparents," he says in his clipped Oxbridge accent. He goes on to explain the Catholic magic, of how with water and the Holy Spirit, the baby will receive the gift of new life from God, who is love.

He then looks deeply into Maddie's green eyes as if for signs of doubt. "Your duty is to see that the divine life which God gives her is kept safe from the poison of sin, to grow always stronger in her heart."

Maddie feels her cheeks burn with the challenge of the mission. If she is going to bail, this would be the time to do it, but she would lose Cosmo forever. That would be stupid after he has given her one more chance to come back. And she has come back, though she's not staying long.

The priest smiles at Maddie and at those gathered, maybe fifty of them pretending it is a lovely spring day in April instead of a chilly and gray gloom fest. The women sport flamboyant hats topped with tiny, silk gardens of flowers and feathers, and the men bright party neckties, and they are all chomping to hit the reception room with its grand fireplace and warming booze to counter the dank winter that lingers.

"And so, parents and godparents," the priest deepens his voice, "we are now going to renew our own baptismal vows of the faith in which this child is about to be christened. Please answer 'I do' after each question."

Maddie appreciates the irony. Here she is at the altar with Cosmo and about to say, "I do."

"Magdalena Maria Lynch," the priest begins, using Maddie's full name. "Do you reject Satan?"

"I do," Maddie says. She doesn't think Satan exists, but that's not a point to make here.

"And all his works?"

"I do."

"Do you reject sin, so as to live in the freedom of God's children?"

Maddie thinks that saying "I'll try very hard" would not get a laugh with this crowd, so she says, "I do."

"Do you reject the glamour of evil?"

Maddie has always liked that phrase, 'the glamour of evil'. It is one of those counterintuitive requests that

Catholic theologians are so good at. No scaly, fang-toothed evil this. Instead, a voluptuous stunner with a gravitational pull that is hard to resist. So, she says, "I do," loud enough for the priest to flinch, as if he has underestimated Maddie's commitment to baby Mathilda.

And then little Mathilda giggles and the gathered coo in delight as the priest ladles holy water over her brow, intoning, "I baptize you Mathilda Margareta Letitia, in the name of the Father, the Son and the Holy Spirit."

Maddie feels like laughing, too. The child's initials are the same as hers: MML. Just what is Cosmo trying to tell her with this child?

"Nice name that you gave to your daughter, Cosmo," Maddie says, taking a sip of champagne at the reception afterward in St. Jude's Senior Common Room. The fire is crackling, and conversation among the guests has shifted from polite to loud, amped up by champagne and heat. Looking down at them are the portraits of five centuries' worth of college scholars and scoundrels hanging on oak paneled walls, as if relieved to be above it all.

Cosmo blushes. "Yes, it only struck me on the altar, when the priest said your full name, that the two of you have the same initials."

Maddie wants to believe it was deliberate, because then she believes Cosmos still loves her. But is that what she wants? Or is it just nice to know it?

Cosmo catches her wondering gaze, and slips an arm around her. "I am so happy to see you, Maddie. We all are. Mom, Dad, the whole Smythe team."

Maddie sees Cosmo’s father across the room, giving her a small smile. The Einstein-haired, gray-bearded Professor Sir Geoffrey Smythe, then retreats into his resting face, a slightly sour look, as if disappointed in his own company.

Cosmo's mother, the blonde and gentle Lady Penelope, standing beside him, looks as if she forgives him. Cosmo has certainly won his beauty and good nature from his mother. Lady Penelope would often hint how Cosmo's Nordic luminescence would pollinate so handsomely with Maddie's Italian-Irish dark.

She beams at Maddie now and raises her glass, but they aren’t swooping in to chat and catch up. They have not forgotten that Maddie broke their son’s heart, and any healing is for Cosmo and Maddie to do unmolested.

Cosmo’s wife, Elka, is not of that opinion, and strides over, as if to stop any burbling intimacy between her husband and that woman.

“Thank you for standing in for my cousin,” she says, her German accent light, snapping off her consonants with sharp white teeth. “I was happy to know Luke would be godfather. He is a good Catholic. His research even takes him to the Vatican. And you?”

“I’m fully committed, too,” Maddie says calmly, though she would love to punch Elka in her turned-up nose. “I stood up for myself when I stood up for Cosmo’s daughter.”

Elka stares at Maddie, feeling the insult. Cosmo laughs nervously, and offers to get Elka a glass of champagne.

"No champagne. My daughter doesn't like it when she suckles. She only likes German beer. Come, Cosmo, you can find me some good German beer."

Elka takes Cosmo by the arm and away from Maddie.

This gives Luke Macclesfield the opening to sidle up.

"Have to say I was surprised to hear that you were the godmother, Maddie," he says in his buttery Scots accent. "So, let's work out our god-parental job sharing. You'll show Mathilda all the bad stuff. And I'll help her pray it all goes away."

"We'll make a good team." Maddie replies. "Though you might need extra pay for the praying to come."

"No, no," Luke says, apologetically. "I didn't mean it that way. I am delighted we'll be saving the lass from Satan together. I just meant…" and his gaze wanders off to Elka, with Mathilda nursing in her arms, and Cosmo offering a bottle of Becks to Elka in regular sips.

"What do you know about her?" Maddie asks quietly.

"She came to St. Jude's on a post-doc, after you left," Luke says. "But she was writing a novel, which surprisingly, got published, and even more surprisingly, the critics loved."

"What did they love about it?" Maddie asks, amazed Elka could produce anything to cuddle up to, besides the baby.

"It majestically united with their notion that you don't need character or plot. Just unpunctuated dialogue about anything that comes to mind."

Maddie swallows her champagne so she doesn't choke as she laughs. "What's it called?"

"The Seatmate," Luke says as if it's a curse word. "A divorced woman sits next to an autistic on a flight, and he delivers a three hour—unpunctuated—monologue to her about his incredibly boring life."

Maddie laughs. "Well, I hope he's not on my flight to Rome. Next to me." She looks at her phone and sees the time. "I should get going."

"We must get together for a prayer and a pint soon," says Luke, as Maddie presses a kiss into his cheek.

As Maddie heads for the back door, Sir Geoffrey resolutely blocks the way. When he offers his cheek for a kiss, Maddie takes it. She remembers how she first had a crush on the father, her kindly mentor, brilliant thesis advisor, and cheerleader of her academic career. Seeing him is almost as hard as seeing Cosmo.

"Did I hear you're off to Rome?" he asks Maddie. "What's there, besides the Pope?"

Maddie smiles. "That's who I'm after."

"Ah, be careful around the Vatican," he says.

"And what should I be careful of?" Maddie asks.

"Your soul," Sir Geoffrey answers with a wink. "So why are you taking your D. Phil in Middle Eastern Studies to Rome? I know the Pope supports Islam, but…" He holds out his hands the way he did after reading a draft of her first thesis chapter, as if to say, "tell me more…"

"I'm going to see if I can get an interview with the Pope. For my boss."

Maddie and Luke and Sir Geoffrey are now joined by the priest, who has heard enough to be curious. And now

Maddie will have to explain to a growing audience how she works for the Great Whore herself: TV.

"You want to get an interview with the Holy Father?"

"I have to meet with the Vatican's media guys to see if I can get my boss a sit-down with the Pope. I work in TV news." There, she said it.

"Magdalena left a very, very promising career as a scholar to work in television," says Sir Geoffrey, as if beginning a eulogy. "I'm sure you're doing a lot of good."

Not good, but trying to stop a lot worse from happening, Maddie thinks, which is hard as her face is burning and her feet are ready to run for the door.

"So, you want to interview the Pope on American television?" The priest seems to like the idea.

"The Pope is going to America in the late summer," says Luke. "I can see why Teddy Wright would want a chat."

Maddie blushes harder. Luke knows where she works. He has been keeping tabs on her.

"Teddy Wright. Hmm." Sir Geoffrey wrinkles his caterpillar brows in a frown. "Never heard of him."

"Her," Luke continues. "She's a pretty big deal."

"I hear you're not with us for long, Maddie," Lady Penelope interrupts, as she now appears beside her husband, a kind smile matching her gaze.

"Just long enough to take on Satan for Mathilda," Maddie replies. "But I need to go right about now. My flight to Rome leaves at 7."

"I'll send you in one of our cars," Sir Geoffrey says.

St. Jude's is so rich that they have their own chauffeured car service. "Our treat to the godmother."

"Thank you," Maddie says.

"It means you have time for another drink."

Maddie knows this also means Sir Geoffrey has a motive for keeping her here longer.

She watches Sir Geoffrey wander off in search of champagne, then turns back to Luke. "How is Dublin treating you?"

"University College? Yeah, fine. Teaching the history of the Church in the 20th century."

"You must get to Rome a bit."

"I do. And New York as well."

"We could share pints and prayers very soon."

Just as the gleam returns to Luke's eyes as he is about to lock in a date with his new godpartner, Sir Geoffrey returns with two flutes of champagne and mutters apologies to Luke as he steers Maddie away. Hidden in a nook overlooking Martyrs Quad, Sir Geoffrey nods out the window to the square commemorating the three Jesuit priests who were burned at the stake there in the late 16th century.

"Geoffrey, is this a warning to me?" Maddie teases. "I won't end up like those priests. They got burned for proclaiming their Catholic faith. I will not let any such thing happen to your grandchild!"

"I have missed you," he says on a wide smile. "So has Cosmo. I know he has. Or you wouldn't be here today. That was noble of you."

Maddie feels a surge of emotion rise in her throat. She

has missed him and Lady Penelope and Cosmo, too. They were the family of her heart with a home of peace away from her battling parents. So she takes a sip and smiles. "It is an honor, Geoffrey."

"I need you to do me another honor, Maddie. One in Rome."

Maddie is sure Sir Geoffrey will want her to light a candle for his granddaughter at some obscure chapel. Or bring him back some red cardinal socks from Gammarelli, the suppliers of church vestments, a few steps from the Pantheon.

But he extracts a business card from his billfold. "*Bishop Christopher Zimmerman, IOR, Cortile Sisto V, 00120 Vatican City.*"

"Ah ha, the IOR! *Istituto per le Opere di Religione*—Institute for the Works of Religion, also known as the Vatican Bank. My father told me all about it."

Sir Geoffrey smiles at Maddie; she was always his best student. "Yes, I imagine your father knew some characters there."

"And you know Bishop Zimmerman?"

"He's very important to St. Jude's. And he's not answering his phone, or his email. I'd like you to… pop by and see what's up."

"I'll be glad to pop by…" Maddie stops to take in the size of the favor: the president of St. Jude's College can't get a response from a Vatican bishop and now she's the pop-in intermediary. Sir Geoffrey is never so glib. There must be another reason. "What do you want me to say when I see him?" she asks.

Sir Geoffrey looks again at the Martyr's Quad, misting in the drizzle. "Tell him we want to know how our money is doing."

"Don't you get regular statements?"

"It's not that kind of bank, Maddie. It's all done in person."

"So…" She looks into his heavy dark brown eyes, hoping for more.

"So, why don't I go? Because I have a much more attractive emissary in you. And I know that he'll be much happier to see you than to see me."

Suddenly, her car to Heathrow has arrived. But Cosmo is there, and now Elka with the baby and German beer, standing over them like a goddess of hearth and home. They ply her with thank yous as Cosmo opens his arms, ready for an embrace, but then they fall away and he shakes Maddie's hand. He would kiss her, too, if his wife weren't standing next to him. Maddie has a strong feeling that she would kiss him back.

She knows, as she walks to the car on that wet February day that she has just been given yet another chance with Cosmo, thanks to Sir Geoffrey. But will she take it? That will depend, she thinks, on this silent Bishop Zimmerman. She suspects that he is more important to Sir Geoffrey than the Pope. And now, she is going to find out why.

7. Rome.

The sun seems closer to Rome than it does to Oxford, polishing the marble statues, and warming the air with the scent of imperial triumph, and good wine. Even the police, the Carabinieri, look wonderful with their dramatic black capes with red lining as they wave Maddie safely along the burnished beauty of the city, one that slows everyone down to look, see, and be seduced by Rome. It's a sunlight seduction Maddie remembers, as she hurries along with her head down. Rome is not going to do it to her this time.

She strides along the Via della Conciliazione. Mussolini showed his appreciation for peace with the Vatican in 1929 by building the grand boulevard she walks on now by bulldozing ancient neighborhoods to do it. With St. Peter's Basilica rising in holy grandeur at the top of the road, it reminds Maddie of why she doesn't like this city. Its history is one of brutality and betrayal.

At the Secretariat for Communications, she salutes the security guards, whose uniforms are deceptively dull and gray. The guards salute back, and Maddie tells them she has "an appointment with the Cardinal," which isn't true. She knows from her Oxford time that if you step with purpose, swing a briefcase, and flash a touch of entitlement, even the most vigilant guardian will let you pass on the benefit of the doubt. And in this place, on the mention of a cardinal.

She breathes deeply as she waits for the elevator,

hoping to poke an air hole or two in recent life. She warms in the afterglow of the promise she has made to baby Mathilda, and she is also a bit chilled by Sir Geoffrey's odd request. She can handle Satan for the child. She'll give the Prince of Darkness a shadow box, since he isn't real. But this Christopher Zimmerman fellow has her puzzled. If he is such a great friend to St. Jude's, why has he disappeared on them?

Dottoressa Maria Corvina seems very pleased by Maddie's appearance at her office on the third floor. "What an honor!" she says, with the kind of Italian smile Maddie knows so well, the kind that could be followed by a kiss on the mouth, or a knife in the heart. "*I'm Wright* is big stuff!"

She waves Maddie into a seat opposite, in this cramped room that is unseasonably warm. The dark-haired Roman woman across the cluttered desk is in her handsome late thirties, with her crisp white blouse and blue cashmere cardigan buttoned all the way up. Maddie is glad that she also observed the Vatican's dress sensibility by wearing a black suit with a skirt, and low-heeled shoes, though she likes the height of a stiletto. Puts her over six feet. Looking down.

Maddie looks around the tiny room for clues about this woman. She had found nothing on the internet about Dr. Corvina except that she worked here, where they both now sit. All Maddie knows is that she's the media link that Maddie was told to contact. That and the diploma behind Dottoressa Covina's head. It is a doctorate in canon law issued to Suora Maria Teresa

Corvina, O.P. She's not a media person. She's a canon lawyer.

"And you're a nun," Maddie says.

"Yeah, I am. We insist on hanging around." Sister Maria's English is colloquial, seasoned with Britain. She has spent time abroad, Maddie thinks, and she doesn't let on that her Italian is as good as the nun's English. She wants Sister Maria to think that she is the clumsy American, in the hope that her sympathy might at least get her a compromise.

"No, I didn't mean…" Maddie says, holding up her hands.

"It's OK," Sister Maria smiles again, gently enjoying Maddie's surprise. "I became a nun, joined the Dominican order, and they encouraged me to engage with the academic world, so I became a canon lawyer, too!"

"You speak English very well," Maddie says, then realizes how patronizing that sounds. "I mean…"

"That's OK, too. I spent two years in Cambridge, getting an M.Phil. in the history of religion. At Jesus College. You, as an Oxford person, may have heard of the other place."

Maddie smiles, but she's wary. She is sitting in the Secretariat of Communications with a Cambridge-educated nun who is a canon lawyer, defending the laws of a Catholic God on earth.

"I found my calling here, serving in the busy world of communications," Marie Corvina nods at stacks of files on her desk, on the floor, and on the other chairs. "I am glad that you are here to see me. I understand you would like the Holy Father to appear on television with Mrs. Teddy Wright for an interview when the Holy Father is in America?"

"That's pretty much it," Maddie says.

Sister Maria glances over the top sheet of a sheaf of papers in a folder. "And what do you propose to discuss? Another conservative winning the presidency after…?" Sister Maria extends her hands as if releasing a puff of smoke, the Italian gesture for "*craziness beyond human comprehension*".

Maddie laughs. It is true that the autumn is going to be crowded, with the Pope's visit to the US in late summer serving as a prelude to the presidential election. But Sister Maria hasn't said no, so Maddie pushes her luck. "The Pope's thoughts on the next leader of the free world would certainly get everyone's attention. And wreak havoc in Las Vegas."

Sister Maria smiles like a conspirator. "Yes, Pope Pius has certainly confounded the oddsmakers, has he not?"

And she is right. When the College of Cardinals elected a conservative African to sit on the throne of St. Peter, they had astonished the world. Here, Maddie had done her research. The cardinals who elected him thought they'd be getting the type of Pope who would return the Church to its proper authority and tradition, after popes who had sought to change the Church to match the world's needs. They thought they had their man in this Nigerian professor of theology, who had served as the Prefect of the Vatican's Congregation for the Doctrine of Faith. Which, once upon a time, was known as the Inquisition.

The Pope is also a member of the Dominican order, as is Sister Maria, designated by the O.P. after her name. Order of the Friars Preachers, Maddie knows. And the Dominicans are known for their fine preaching, and their orthodoxy.

This pope who stunned the world not only with his election but also by choosing the name Pius. It looked as if the Catholic Church was about to plunge back into the Dark Ages. The last Pius had been Pope when the Nazis unleashed their evil on Europe, and his silence on the slaughter of the Jews resonated still, seemingly made louder by all the other noise in the world, nine decades later.

He was anything but like that Pius. The next day, he was speaking out against abuse and corruption wherever he saw it, including in his own Church. Worst of all, he wanted to reform Vatican finances. Going after the money had truly alarmed the conservatives.

But what got them frothing for a do-over was that this Pius wanted to engage with Islam, and reconnect the Peoples of the Book to a common purpose. Catholics, Jews and Muslims reading from the same page was a radical idea that alarmed the Old Guard, for whom the Crusades had never really ended. This Pope Pius would place Islam at the same spiritual level as Christianity. To them, that was offensive.

By taking the name he took, he would also try to

redeem the legacy of Pius XII. He wanted the world to know what exactly his papal namesake had done to fight the Nazis. So he would open wide the Vatican's Secret Archives with its acres of documents that landed there during the Second World War to prove it. Of course, now it would take years to sift through the records and find, Maddie knows, the smoking gun that proved Pius XII a saint or a sinner. Or maybe a lot of both.

"So why does Teddy Wright make this request to speak to the Holy Father?" Sister Maria asks, as if she really wants to know.

"Well," Maddie begins, "she thinks the Pope is the most important political—and religious—figure in the world. She would like to ask him what he thinks the world needs. To find a way to heal." Teddy Wright has said nothing of the sort to Maddie.

Sister Maria considers this. "Teddy Wright is a Catholic, yes?"

Maddie nods. "She is." She does not add "*but about as lapsed as you can be.*"

"And you are a Catholic, that I know. Your mother was going to become a nun, even."

Maddie flushes with a touch of embarrassment. This nun really has checked her out. Time to drop the clumsy American act, so Maddie switches to Italian.

"Yes, but she fell in love with my father, and made her choice. Which, I have to say, I am glad she did, or we wouldn't be here now."

Sister Maria laughs at both the joke and at Maddie's effortless Italian. It's always nice when an English-speaker can speak your native tongue. She switches, too. "Yes, for sure. How long did you live in Rome?"

Maddie has done nothing but remember those years since she landed last night, and it is a relief to say she moved here when she was nine years old, and left when she was thirteen. She and her mother went back to New York, and her father left Rome for Jerusalem. His job as INN's Jerusalem's correspondent was in war zone, and so they went home, thinking that they would manage as a family. Which they did not. He stayed in Jerusalem for four years, then went to Moscow, then to Beijing, then back to Jerusalem. But never back home.

"You have family still, here?"

Maddie shakes her head. "No, my mother was an only child. Her parents died when I was sixteen."

"In the same year?"

"Yes. My grandmother died in May, and then my grandfather died in June. Of a broken heart."

"I will say a prayer for them, and their love which still lights your life," Sister Maria says with warning kindness. Then she switches back to English. "You know, the Holy Father does not do interviews."

Maddie is ready for this: "That's why this one would be so significant. We would, of course, provide the questions in advance. And we'd stick to those you, or the Holy Father, want to address." Maddie is desperate now, trying to stop the "no" that she feels is a moment away.

Sister Maria looks at Maddie's flailing, and again spreads her tender smile. "OK," she says. "Here's what you need to do. Find someone the Pope knows and trusts, and get them on board with the idea. They could help."

Maddie sees that this is a kind of Vatican “maybe”. “Do you know such a person?”

“There are many,” Sister Maria replies. “And you, Dr. Lynch, with your education, your family contacts, your journalistic pedigree, will find the right person. And then we may have the pleasure of meeting again.” Sister Maria hands Maddie her business card. The meeting is over.

“Thank you for your time, Sister.” Maddie flashes a smile of confidence that she doesn’t quite feel. She opens the QR code on her phone, and offers it to the nun, who snaps a photo of it. “I will be back,” Maddie says.

“This is your direct phone?” the nun asks.

“Yes, it’s my cell.”

Then the nun surprises her by cupping her own warm hands over Maddie’s. “God very willing, we shall meet again soon!”

8. Vatican City.

It is going on noon as Maddie wanders into St. Peter's Square to join the thousands of people already there. School groups of teenagers stare mesmerized by their cell phones, oblivious to the great church before them, and lovers take selfies on their phones, with the church as a backdrop chaperone. Teams of pilgrims warm the square, following guides bearing flags in their national colors—red and white for the Poles; green and orange for Irish; red for the Chinese, who make up the largest pilgrim group in the piazza.

Maddie watches them go through metal detectors and bag searches before being allowed into the Basilica. She remembers as a girl how she could just run inside whenever she wanted to, but those days are over. The Chinese are killing Muslims. Orthodox Russians are killing Orthodox Ukrainians. Christian armies turn up in Muslim lands and kill Muslims. Muslims attack Israel which in turn destroys Gaza and now fights with itself. Global carnage in the name of religion.

Maddie takes in the scene. Africans sell postcards of the Pope along the edge of the white line demarking the Square, just inside Vatican City. Italian soldiers cradle Beretta assault rifles, watching the vendors and everyone else from the Roman side of the line. She thinks that any carnage here will be due to the crossfire of Italian machine gun bullets unleashed upon some attacker.

She leans against a cool stone bollard in front of the

four-hundred-year-old Bernini fountain. She looks at the two giant magical halves, one dripping water, the other catching it forever, and thinks about her own annoying dilemma.

She could text her boss back in New York and tell Teddy Wright that the sit-down with the Pope is more challenging than she thought it would be. Because now it is more possible.

No, Teddy wants a *"Yes!"* Some *"maybe"* text from Rome will speed up what she expects will be next: being kicked out the door of INN and into the unemployment lines.

Either way, she knows she has to prove she belongs in the TV world that she inhabits. So, she will send a cheery *"It's going well"* text and make it come true. She'll also dust off her resumé.

Maddie retrieves her cell phone from her pocket with a stab of sadness. There on the screen is Maddie and her father in Cairo. She looks as if the future will be glorious, and the tall, burly, copper-headed James Lynch looking as he always did, about to have a drink before the war began. The Sphinx, behind them, reveals nothing.

Cosmo had given Maddie the phone as a gift when she was halfway through her doctoral thesis, and he had even managed to get a heavy-duty case for it in St. Jude's colors, green and gold. Cosmo had told her, with more irony than he meant, "It's so you'll call me, baby." Maddie's screen saver was the only photo she had of herself and her father together as adults. And before the year was out, her father was dead.

She is thinking of them all now, of Cosmo and herself and her parents, and of a happier time. She imagines this is what it will be like should she live to 90 years, and find herself alone in the world, staring at a phone that no longer rings. But an elderly Swiss couple wakes her out of her gloom, asking in perfect English, if she will take a picture with their phone. And she does as they share a hot kiss in front of the fountain.

Maddie has to remind herself that she is 29, and she is in Rome, at INN's expense, even if she's the only person in the world who hates the place. She is, in a way, home, for she is half Roman herself.

The last time she was here with family, it had begun so beautifully. Her father James was the newly installed INN correspondent for Italy. Maddie's mother Francesca had been pining for her native Roma, and they lived on the other side of the river, in the ancient city's oldest neighborhood, Monti.

Maddie's pre-teen life was exciting, for at least she spoke Italian and could fend off the inevitable teenage cruelties inflicted on her as the "new kid."

"You'll go to the American School," her father promised.

"When in Rome..." her mother countered.

So Maddie went to Giulio Cesare Middle and High School, about a fifteen-minute drive from where she stood now. It's where Magdalena, of which there were a few in the school, became Maddie, of which there was only her.

And it suited her. She wasn't bullied by other kids or

ignored by teachers or constantly cruised by Italian guys, but she soon felt alone, and it made her angry. Angry at being taken to this foreign country just when she needed to be at home. When she needed her feet on solid, familiar ground. Rome was not her home. And her parents didn't seem to care.

James Lynch was constantly tempted away by assignments in the Middle East, and was often gone. He finally took a job dangled by the Jerusalem bureau, even when Francesca and Maddie both said no, it was far too dangerous, with rockets from Hamas blowing up everything.

James Lynch assured them that he would protect them, but in the end, it was the prospect of a land at war that called him away. And Maddie and her mother went back to Manhattan. To wait for James Lynch to return to his senses. But he never did.

Rome had killed Maddie's family.

Then, All Saints, a Jesuit prep school on Park Avenue, between East 83rd and 84th streets, had killed Maddie's faith. She remembers the day as if it was earlier this week. They were in chapel, before Easter, and the priest was delivering a sermon on how the greatness of God's love is such that he would sacrifice his own son to redeem mankind, and Maddie knew it wasn't true.

How was that love? She didn't even have her own father's love. Had he been sacrificed? No, he had been murdered. How could anyone who loves someone let them be murdered? No, that idea was a "get out of logic jail" faith card play. She thinks about this as she stares at the grand, gleaming Catholic shock and awe that St. Peter's Basilica is meant to be.

Maddie thinks the only thing people seem happy with—and that is largely out of anti-Catholic bigotry—is Pope Pius XIII's washing of the dark and dirty windows of the Vatican Bank. Transparency is now the mission.

And Bishop Christopher Zimmerman, as Maddie had learned, was the Vatican banker who helped to shine light on those murky windows of Mammon.

The sun is warm on Maddie’s face, and suddenly she feels infused with purpose. Dottore Sister Maria Corvina has put hope and a challenge before her. She has to admit she feels a bit closer to her father, having landed in this dangerous city, on an assignment from two sources—INN and Oxford. James Lynch was a masterful teller of stories, and Maddie feels that she can tell them, too. She just needs the chance. And now, she has it.

She punches the coordinates of Bishop Zimmerman’s office address into Google Maps on her Lumia phone and sees that the banker-priest works about a five-minute walk from where Maddie now stands. She will find this elusive Zimmerman and set the new story in motion.

Behind the Apostolic Palace, the Vatican Bank looks more like a medieval fortress, spherical and brick and windowless, until you get to the top floor, where there are windows. And these high windows have bars protecting them, as if to stop rebel angels from robbing the bank.

Most officials have offices just outside the bank’s

cramped rooms, and Zimmerman is one of them, so his business card says. Yet when Maddie turns into the Via di Porta Angelica, a street just opposite the eastern walls of the Vatican, she sees a group of men standing outside the address where she is heading.

Two of them are Roman cops, in uniform, and the third is a stocky guy in a suit, who looks like a detective. The fourth is a priest, a tall, blonde ruddy-cheeked man in wire glasses in his early 40s who looks English. He seems to be the one in charge.

Maddie walks closer, passing by them, eyes on her cell phone, just another tourist on the wander. But she understands what the priest is telling these cops in Italian. To take everything out of Bishop Zimmerman's office and deliver it to him.

Why would they want to empty Bishop Zimmerman's office? Maybe he has committed some crime, and vanished?

Maddie hears the stocky detective say, *"Il Vescovo non c'è e non tornerà."*

And so "The Bishop isn't here, and he is not coming back."

And that's why the police are there. And also why the bishop is not answering his phone. He's gone to ground.

Oxford's connection to Christopher Zimmerman has quickly run deeper and darker than she suspected. And to find out what it is, she has to find out more about this Bishop. Where would her father look now?

He would go to the Bishop's residence. She knows he's not there, but she has to check it out.

Maddie takes out the business card that Sir Geoffrey had given her, and stares at it as if it's an Old Master painting, with layers to be stripped away, to reveal the truth buried beneath. Then she smiles and turns the card over, and on the back, in Sir Geoffrey's spidery pencil, is the name of a building: Palazzo San Carlo.

Maddie opens Google and it tells her that Palazzo San Carlo is a decommissioned Vatican office building that has been turned into a lodging for church worthies. It's about a three-minute walk.

The Palazzo is burnished by the sunshine and looks even more handsome as it stands opposite the Vatican's private gas station. There is a pharmacy and a supermarket, too, where Vatican employees can buy everything from flat screen TVs to single malt, all at a heavy discount. She is betting that this is where Zimmerman, banker that he is, lives.

Entering the Palazzo, Maddie notices the ramps that have been built to ease access to the 17th century palace for those prelates who now travel in the 21st century's version of the sedan chair—the motorized scooter.

Coming the other way are two guys pulling a hand cart piled high with bankers' boxes. They're in suits, but they're followed by a uniformed cop wheeling a dolly also packed high with bankers' boxes. He wears the uniform of the Vatican police, with the blue kepi and blue jacket with "Gendarmeria" emblazoned on it, so Maddie figures the first two guys are Vatican cops as well. One has designer stubble and a sneer, and the other has a shaved head with sunglasses perched atop it.

"Stoppia e Calvo" Maddie thinks. Stubble and Baldie.

Stoppia gives Maddie a look of professional appreciation as he walks on past, and a smile. He has a gold tooth. She pretends not to see any of it and approaches the concierge, a middle-aged guy with a lavish 19th century mustache and slicked back curly hair, giving him the look of an Italy from more than a century ago, when the Pope still had the papal states and not this patch of land, a little bigger than Central Park, in Rome.

"Good day, sir, I am looking for Bishop Christopher Zimmerman," Maddie says in Italian, on a bright smile.

"Ahh, signorina," the man says, using a term for her that is also old-fashioned, "there he goes." He points to the cops carrying the boxes out the door.

"I don't understand," says Maddie. "He is in those boxes?"

The man smiles at her humor, his grand mustache rising. "I expect they hope so, as he has not been here for a while now."

"Do you know where he is?"

The man shakes his head. "No one knows, apparently. But it looks to me as if they don't think he's coming back, no?" He smiles at Maddie in a fatherly way, and shrugs.

She returns the smile, and nods. If he is coming back, then it will be to have a chat with the cops. And maybe that's why Christopher Zimmerman left in the first place. So she asks herself: to where would a Vatican bishop vanish? And why?

9. Rome.

The evening is just beginning to settle in, but because the sun loves Rome, it will take longer to say good night than it would in dank Oxford or chilly New York. Maddie has walked around the city, just thinking, for the past hour or so. She would like to sit at a cafe and enjoy a glass of Jameson's or two. But her head might not be completely clear to think about her next move to locate the mysterious, missing Bishop Zimmerman.

So Maddie returns to her room in the *Il Convento*, a spacious former convent that is now a hotel and run by nuns, just a short walk south from St. Peter's Basilica. She grabs her key from the desk clerk, an Italian guy in his mid-20s, and heads up to the third floor to her room.

But the door is unlocked.

Maddie locked it when she left this morning and gave the knob a throttle, knowing what old locks are like in the old city, then handed in the key. Maybe the maid has been in and forgotten to lock it. Even so, she turns the handle gently, and spins as she enters to confront any attack from behind.

There is no one there. Maddie's heart pounds, even so. She is on full alert, here in this convent hotel. She takes a breath and surveys her room.

The bed is as she left it, unmade, so there has been no room service.

Her laptop is still on her desk, but there is a piece of paper beside it.

Maddie picks up the piece of paper and reads it:

> *"O Divine Saviour! I thank Thee for having perpetuated Thy humble, obedient, self-sacrificing and recollected silence of Nazareth in the* ***tabernacle****. How Thy example puts me to* ***shame****! Forgive me for my bold, self-seeking, and superficial talkativeness.* ***Teach me to understand*** *the words: "In silence and in hope shall your strength be."*
>
> *Bishop Christopher Zimmerman.*

Maddie sits down at her desk. She reads the prayer again, and notes the words in bold: *tabernacle, shame, teach me to understand.* It's an affectation, or a hidden message. And it's from the guy who everyone seems to want her to find. But how did he find her?

Maddie checks every inch of her room, first hanging a bath towel over the mirror above the desk, to make sure no cameras can see her. Then she takes everything out of her travel backpack, and lays everything on the bed.

She carefully runs her fingers along her clothing. She has seen her father do it, so she does it too, to feel out any foreign items inserted in the lining and meant to spy on her. She finds nothing. She checks her bedside lamp, and the crucifix above her bed to see if any spy devices have been planted. No cameras in the lamp or on Jesus.

She heads down to the lobby.

The clerk says she has had no visitors.

"Do you have security cameras operating?"

"Yes, in the lobby and on every floor," he says.

"May I see the camera for the third floor? I think someone has been in my room." She is trembling inside, but her voice is firm and edged with accusation.

The clerk looks at her as if she is going to be trouble, his eyes wide with alarm, which is exactly what she wants him to think. "We don't normally—" he begins but Maddie holds up a hand.

"This is not normal," she says.

He thinks about this for a second and then nods. "OK. I will show you."

He takes Maddie into the small office next to the front desk and calls up the camera for the third floor. "When did you leave?" he asks.

"Early. Let's start there," Maddie replies.

He rewinds the tape and hits play. Maddie sees the time code at 8:30AM, and an empty corridor.

"You can fast forward," she says, and he does, as the empty corridor now flashes by in ten-second time jumps. Then, at 10:30, a nun appears, as if from nowhere, and lets herself into Maddie's room. She wears a black veil and white habit. Maddie guesses she is old by her stooped walk.

"That's not the maid," Maddie says.

"No," the clerk smiles. "That's Sister Nuala. She used to live here when this was a convent. We have a few of them left. She's a little…" and he shakes his hand from side to side. Unbalanced. "She's OK. She was probably lost."

About fifteen seconds pass before Sister Nuala exits

Maddie's room and vanishes down the corridor.

"How did she have a key to my room?"

The clerk shrugs, apologetically. "She has lived here so long, she probably has a key to everything."

"I would like to speak to her," Maddie says. She hears the anger in her voice, and tempers it with a smile. "Just to say hello. My mother was going to be a nun, before she met my father. I have a soft spot for nuns."

The clerk understands. "She is on the top floor, with one other nun. They are just opposite the roof terrace."

Running up the stairs to the top floor, Maddie catches her breath before she knocks on the door. The other nun, younger, opens the door and glares up at Maddie with heavy brown eyes, and answers. "*Si?*"

Maddie explains in Italian that she is looking for Sister Nuala. The nun at the door regards her with suspicion, so Maddie adds that she is a journalist, with INN in America. And her name is Maddie Lynch.

On that news, Sister Nuala appears, and takes Maddie by the hand. And says to her in English, "I was waiting for you."

They sit on the rooftop terrace. Sister Nuala, who is from Casteleblayney, Ireland, has been in Rome since she was 21 years old. She is 83 now, but still has the lilt of County Monahan to her voice. Her face is still freckled and full, making her look younger than she is.

"I knew your father," she tells Maddie. "He was a great man. When I heard you were here, I had to say hello. I left you a prayer."

Maddie thanks the nun as she thinks her father

connects with this nun who connects with Christopher Zimmerman, who she wants to find. Now more than ever. But she begins with her father. "How did you know my father? James Lynch?"

Sister Nuala takes a sip of tea, and her green eyes travel back in time. "I met him when he was doing a story on the priest whose house I kept."

Maddie knows that nuns have been exploited by male clerics since forever. And Maddie knows who this priest is. "Christopher Zimmerman?"

"Yes, the Bishop. I worked for him ever since he came to Rome, in the mid-90s. A long time ago."

"You kept his house? In the Palazzo San Carlo?"

"I was more like his wife in everything but the marital bed," says Sister Nuala, surprising Maddie. The nun laughs at Maddie's surprise, her laugh deep and almost lusty. "And don't think he didn't try it on with me. But I am faithful to my vows, and I was already married. You know what I mean."

Maddie knows nuns symbolically marry Jesus. She nods the nun on.

"I ran the household. I cleaned and cooked a lot, heavy Swiss food, and a heckuva lot of drink. The Bishop loves champagne, and he likes his gin, too. The blue stuff."

"Bombay Sapphire."

"That's it. Your father, on the other hand, likes his whiskey. As do I, from time to time."

Maddie notes the use of the present tense with her father. She doesn't want to upset the nun; the clerk said she was unstable, but Maddie thinks this nun is not cracked, but cagey. It takes even more smarts to know what not to say.

"You know my father is dead," Maddie says.

Sister Nuala closes her eyes, in a quick prayer. "I know. He is in heaven. He was so kind to me."

"How so?"

"He was doing a story on Bishop Zimmerman, and he came one day to find the Bishop had stood him up. The Bishop had a fancy house up in the Cinque Terre, and he'd gone there with some of his priest friends. They knew a good time when they saw it. So your father took me out to lunch. It became a regular date, every Tuesday. The Bishop wasn't happy about my friendship with your father, but there was nothing he could do. Your father had the goods." Sister Nuala closes her eyes again, not in prayer but because there is something she does not want to see.

Maddie wants the nun to tell her more. But she can see that Sister Nuala is upset. "What goods do you mean, Sister?"

"Your father wrote about him, but I don't think he published. He told me everything, though. He was worried for me. That's why I gave you the prayer. To guide you." She takes a deep breath. "Sorry, a touch of the grippe," she says. Then adds, almost casually, "I have something else for you."

"You do?"

Sister Nuala nods, suddenly strong again. "But not here. Meet me by the Pietà tomorrow at 11 in the morning. I will give it to you then."

The old nun heaves herself up and leaves Maddie with a promising wink, then shuffles off to her room.

Maddie's mind is sizzling now with questions about her father, and Christopher Zimmerman. It's as if she has found an undiscovered part of her father's life, and he is alive again. This is the kind of thing Rome does to you. Makes you count on miracles. But Maddie can't rid herself of the feeling that she is counting on a miracle, too. And if she doesn't believe in them, will they still come true?

10. Rome.

It's midnight in Rome and Maddie is on a Zoom call with her INN teammate, Aretta, and with Teddy Wright, back in New York.

"So the upshot is that we have a shot," Maddie says. "I just need to do a little more facetime stuff at the Vatican. It's how business gets done here."

In the Zoom image in front of Maddie on her laptop, she watches Aretta smile. "Great!"

Teddy frowns. "How long do you think it will take?" Teddy likes quick answers.

Maddie knows she has to keep ahead of her own story to fill in the holes before Teddy spots them. "As they say here, the Vatican thinks in centuries. But I will aim to be quite a bit faster."

Aretta laughs at that, and Teddy even manages a smile. "Just so long as you get the Popester, for me and me alone." Then Teddy leaves the meeting, without so much as a goodbye.

"How are you, Maddie?" Aretta asks.

"I'm fine, and you? How was your drink with Reagan Clark's guy?"

Aretta chuckles, her deep voice rumbling. "Let's put it this way. Brett Muenster wasn't expecting a dry, Black, Muslim lesbian. About four more challenges than he was capable of digesting."

Maddie laughs. "Is Reagan Clark going to come on the show?"

"He said he's still negotiating that with you. So, Maddie, the Pope, Reagan Clark, whoever next?"

"Well," says Maddie, "there is this priest named Christopher Zimmerman that everyone seems to be looking for. And can't find."

Aretta thinks on that. "There was a dead priest found on an altar in some midtown church a couple of days ago."

"This guy lives in Rome. And he's Swiss."

"Well," Aretta says, scratching her forehead, "the church was abandoned, and all the guy's ID was stolen."

"How do they know he was a priest, then?" Maddie asks.

"They're guessing. He had a tattoo. Strange one on the inside of his right arm, just above the wrist." She checks her cell phone and comes back with – "SBUIII, with a cross next to it. They figured it was a start."

"Do you know what SBUIII means?" Maddie asks.

Aretta nods as she keeps scrolling through her cell. "From what I'm seeing online, using the double II to mean two, it refers to an organization called the Society of Blessed Urban II. Why? Does that mean anything to you?"

"Not yet," Maddie replies. "Are there any photos of the guy?"

"I'll see what I can get," Aretta says. "Sounds like you're working on another story."

Maddie leans forward with a smile. "I just hope it has a happy ending."

Aretta salutes Maddie and they end the meeting.

Relief brings a thirst that sends Maddie to the mini bar. As spare as the old convent, there is only a small half-bottle of red wine beside a picture of a very sobering picture of Mary grieving for her dead son.

Maddie is just starting her second glass when her phone pings. It's not a photo of the dead priest, but a text from Sister Maria Corvina: *Cardinal Otley will see you tomorrow at 10. Are you free?*

Maddie toasts herself with the rest of the glass and just about spills it, laughing. Cardinal Otley is the Vatican's Secretary of State, the guy who deals with international diplomacy on behalf of this mighty little kingdom. And he wants to see Maddie. Just this morning, Sister Maria had told Maddie to find someone who could put in a good word for her with the Pope to get that interview, and now the second most powerful man in the Vatican is summoning her for a meeting.

Maddie knows what her father would say. It's a set up. If it is that easy, she is being used.

Use me, please! she thinks as she texts back, *Thanks. Where?*

Sister Maria texts right back: *Segreteria di Stato Vaticana 00120 Città del Vaticano. Enter on Via Sant'Anna. It's just next to the Cortile di Belvedere.*

Maddie types in the GPS to Google maps, and sees that Otley's office is a short walk from where she sits. Rome is tiny. She has to meet Sister Nuala at 11, but that is only a six-minute walk from the secretariat. Surely the Secretary of State will not keep her longer than half an hour.

After she plucks her second black suit out of the closet and shakes out the wrinkles for tomorrow, her WhatsApp pings. It is not Sister Maria needing to cancel, as Maddie's nervous heart insists, it's Aretta. She has sent her an image, captioned "heart attack". Maddie opens it and sees that it is a morgue shot; on the cold steel table is the mysterious dead priest found in an abandoned church in Manhattan. Aretta is good.

Maddie goes online and double checks what she already knows: that the photo is of Christopher Zimmerman.

The man she was asked to find by Sir Geoffrey.

The man who wasn't returning his calls.

The Vatican banker found dead of a heart attack in a deconsecrated church in Manhattan.

Maddie feels like she has been embraced by a warm and dangerous wave. Her story, her father's story, Sir Geoffrey's mission, just got thrown into the deep end of something.

Maddie has found Christopher Zimmerman, and he is dead.

What should she do next? Call New York and tell them who they have? Let Sir Geoffrey know where Zimmerman is? It's the right thing to do.

No, she was given a prayer from him, and an Irish nun has more for her. She hears her father's voice. *"Find out who he really was first. And what, even in death, does he want from you?"*

11. Rome, The Vatican.

Maddie arrives early at the Secretary of State, and before she enters, makes sure she is buttoned all the way up. When she steps inside, she sees that her greeter is the rugged blonde priest with the wire rim glasses who she saw directing the police outside the Vatican bank. Telling them to bring Christopher Zimmerman's files to him.

"Dr. Lynch," he says on a dazzling smile, one suggesting that he would be open to breaking his vow of chastity for her. "I'm Bishop Paul Hughes, Undersecretary for the Section for Personnel of Diplomatic Role. Which simply means that I manage our diplomatic talent. Without the 25% commission."

Maddie laughs, as charmed as she should be. He has a British accent, and looks like he played rugby, as his nose zigs a bit to the left. He also has thick salt and pepper blonde hair, and hazel eyes with heavy lids that give him the look of a gangster, which might not be a bad thing around this place. As they take the elevator to the third floor, he asks her about her Roman mission, and she tells him.

"Ah, that might need the help of St. Jude," he says. "To which I understand you have a connection."

Maddie smiles to cover her sense of being watched. They have all done their homework on her. "Yes, St. Jude's Oxford. It has its own lost causes."

Bishop Hughes crackles with a small laugh. "I was at

Corpus Christi," he says. "Right in the Body of Christ. Before your time."

She clocks him as being in his early forties, which is very young for a bishop. He must be a star in the secretariat.

"What did you read?" Maddie asks, using the Oxford term.

"PPE. Did better in politics than philosophy."

"And in economics?"

Bishop Hughes turns on his great smile again. "Nothing to prepare me for this place!" He throws out a big rough hand as if he was showing off his simple country church. But this corridor in the 109-acre city-state is made grand by portraits of saints in gilded frames hanging over velvet chairs, like an art museum turned into a king's waiting room.

Maddie suspects that he is well prepared if he is the one to whom Bishop Christopher Zimmerman's bank files are to be delivered. So what is he hoping to find?

They come to a wooden door, carved with cherubim, and Bishop Hughes knocks. Another British voice booms back "Come forth!"

The medieval summons breaks Maddie's stride but the Bishop gestures for her to go ahead of him, and so she does. To be greeted by Cardinal Bernard Otley, another Englishman, this one seventy years old, and who has been the Pope's right-hand man for three years now. The photos that Maddie checked online do not fully show the girth of the man who clearly enjoys his food and wine. She read that his mission is large, too, crossing the globe in pursuit of peace and Vatican politics, putting out theological fires that erupt when your office is the entire planet, and heaven, too.

Cardinal Otley welcomes Maddie with a hearty handshake and offers her a seat opposite his desk. It's a surprisingly simple office, with its uncluttered desk, and cataloged bookshelves—Aquinas to Zen, left to right—and a comfortable meeting area supplied with a sturdy oak table and four leather armchairs.

Bishop Hughes sits to the side. Whatever they want, this is not a private meeting.

"Your Eminence," says Maddie, "it is a pleasure to meet you."

"Well, Dr. Lynch," Otley replies, "the pleasure is ours that you deigned to visit our little shanty town on the Tiber!"

"Yes, I have not been back in a while," she says, and right now, she sort of feels that to be true because she now has a purpose.

"You grew up here?" Bishop Hughes asks.

"I spent part of my childhood here," Maddie says. "As for the growing up, that's still in progress."

The Cardinal laughs. "Where are you stopping?" he asks, with the bouncy cadence of his Cockney accent. "With family?"

"No family left here I'm afraid. I'm staying at *Il Convento*. Met a great old nun there yesterday. Sister Nuala."

Maddie notices on the mention of the nun that Otley's eyes glance at Bishop Hughes, and then back to her.

Then he smiles at her as if she is his favorite niece.

Maddie is far more luminous than in her photograph, Otley thinks. When the Vatican was James's beat, Otley knew the father to be a rugged and charismatic Irish brawler, but Otley thanks God that Maddie has inherited her mother's Italian *bellezza.* The tall young woman opposite him is a work of art, whose soft black curls and emerald eyes and strong nose and full mouth make her look like one of those angels Michelangelo enticed from blocks of Carrara marble.

Otley likes women, but he is in no denial about his own sexuality: he loves men. And as part of the Pink Mafia inside the Vatican, he could have used that preference to have more sex with men than even he could imagine, such is the jockeying for promotion on the Vatican's casting couch. But he has taken a vow of chastity and he takes that vow seriously. So instead, he channels his sexuality into a love of food and wine, and politics. It makes for a ruthless reputation, and an ever-expanding sash on his crimson cassock.

From Maddie's point of view, the portly, jolly cardinal, with his Churchillian half-glasses and lively blue eyes seems like the kind of don whose company she has enjoyed so much in the pubs of Oxford.

"Normally we would sit and speak, and enjoy these exceptionally comfy chairs," says the Cardinal. He runs a plump hand across a leather armchair, upholstered in the same shade of red as his zucchetto, the yarmulke-like hat worn by the princes of the Church. "But it's such a fine day that I thought we might take a turn around the gardens."

Maddie is surprised again. She just got here, and now he wants to leave.

"Bishop Hughes, I will let you attend to the affairs of state," he adds.

The Bishop stands, and Maddie notices a flash of annoyance in his eyes, which he quickly disguises with a bow to them both. "I am sure we shall meet again, Dr. Lynch."

Maddie suspects that if the Secretary of State is inviting her for a walk alone in the garden, it is because what he has to say to her is something he doesn't want to say in front of Bishop Hughes. She realizes that she has power in this story, too.

Otley leads Maddie from his office out into a common area, a rabbit warren of desks, where priests, and a couple of women hunch over computers and talk on landlines.

"This is the glamorous department of state," Otley says, "working our faith on the world."

He punctuates that statement by making a discreet sign of the cross aimed at his staff, sweeping his hand up and down and then cutting across left to right in a blessing for their work. The workers keep working, oblivious to the blessing. Then Otley gestures to Maddie that they will go onward, into the hallways of the Apostolic Palace.

And a palace it is, with tiled walls, frescoed ceilings, and marble everywhere—on the floors, the walls, the pillars, and the statues that they pass as they make their way down the staircase, lit by the sunlight filtering through the stained-glass window which features mosaics of Saints Peter and Paul. The view dazzles Maddie with its opulence, and raises questions as to whether the divinity that this place imagines is more about display than devotion.

The gardens are tranquil and lush, from rocky grottoes to bountiful African palm trees, and it is easy to forget the teeming human scene on the other side of the walls, in St. Peter's Square.

"I like to come here to escape," says the Cardinal.

"I can see why," Maddie replies. "Though I would imagine that when you take a vow as a priest, there is never a true escape, is there?"

It is a bold question, but Maddie reckons that if she wants to get what she needs, then she cannot be shy. And if she is going to be sent packing back home with bad news for Teddy Wright, and likely on the "what the hell do I do next?" hunt, she might as well enjoy a civilized exit with a man she only expects to meet once.

Cardinal Otley tips his round head back and laughs again. "I don't mean escape in the way you might," he says. "I mean it as a kind of spiritual escape. Let's me clear my noggin. I can imagine that your job in television has its share of pressures as well."

"It has its few moments. But I'm not Secretary of State for the Vatican."

Otley stops in front of a grotto, with a statue of the Virgin Mary standing on a perch. "This is a replica of the grotto of Lourdes," Otley says. "Exact size and everything, donated by a French cardinal. Wish he'd thrown in a case of champagne and escargot, but it would be unseemly to pray for the same here."

"I have seen the original," Maddie says. "No champagne there either."

"You looked?" the Cardinal asks playfully. So Maddie tells him that her mother had gone there to pray for her ailing mother, Maddie's Nonna, and she had gone with her.

"Your mother is a holy woman."

"You've met my mother?" Maddie asks in surprise.

"Just once, which was not enough," he admits. "I knew your father much better. And he was definitely not a holy man." Then he bursts out with his croaking chortle.

Maddie steps up to the Cardinal, feeling the gravitational pull of someone who knew her family. Her father. "You knew James Lynch?"

"Indeed," says the Cardinal, walking on. "I was taking the waters in Jerusalem before I became what I am now. At the Pontifical Institute. Your father became a fixture in the old city, covering the darkness of the place by day, and bringing lights to the night. I remember having a drink with him once in the Cellar Bar at the American Colony hotel, and he said, *'I like to time my arrival here so I can raise my glass of Irish to the call to prayer at the mosque next door'*." The Cardinal crackles with laughter again. "And he did." Then he looks like he's lost a brother. "It was tragic, his death."

Maddie knows that tragedy with every breath she takes.

"I am very pleased that you followed in his footsteps," the Cardinal continues, shining a light toward the future. "The world needs people like you and your father, doing what you do. Looking where others fear to look. You look into the abyss."

"My father maybe, but not me," Maddie says, deflecting this flattering catapult into her father's journalistic orbit. What he was doing and seeing and saying got him killed.

The Cardinal touches Maddie on the forearm, as if he is about to impart a great secret. "Would you like to look into the abyss?"

Maddie suddenly realizes that Cardinal Otley is not going to kiss her off but that he is going to invite her further into the story. And into a dark place.

For the first time in a long time, Maddie feels that same rush she felt when she first kissed Cosmo, one filled with the heat of a future filled with infinite possibility, and one much more interesting than her present. It is an odd conjunction, she realizes, to think of a sexual moment when faced with a churchman offering her temptation, but it is temptation to which she must give in. For the sake of her own story. So, she says, "Yes. I would."

Cardinal Otley doesn't blink his blue eyes. "Do as has been suggested. Find someone who has influence with the Pope. That would be the Holy Father's former secretary, Father Victor Franchi. I have a feeling that things will work out in your favor."

"And where is this Father Franchi?" Maddie asks.

"We don't quite know. Somewhere in Israel, I think, was his last point of contact, but he is quite the world traveler. The Pope still has a soft spot for him, so…"

Maddie now feels a chill. She has yet another test: Father Franchi, GPS unknown.

"And I would like you to do me a service," he continues. "Of course, one that you're in a particularly good position to do, whereas I am not. And as it's a particularly sensitive matter, what you find out would be for us alone."

So, the abyss is not only dark, but secretive.

Maddie considers where she stands: in the privacy of the Vatican gardens, with the Roman spring blooming under cloudless skies, and the Vatican's powerful Secretary of State giving her a test and now asking her to do something in secret. If this is what it takes to get a possible interview with the Pope, then she has underestimated the Vatican's reputation for political intrigue. Or maybe something else is up.

But she longs to step through this door that has opened, so she says: "What is it you would like me to do?"

Cardinal Otley looks around to make sure that they are truly alone, then asks Maddie for her cell phone.

Maddie hands it over, curious as to what the Cardinal wants with it. He's relieved it's not an iPhone, and he can just pop out the battery. "You never know who is listening around here," he says. "And they can't hear this: I want you to help us find out why Bishop Christopher Zimmerman is dead."

Maddie feels as if her entire body has been zapped by some electric current running beneath the freshly cut lawn. She knew Zimmerman was dead, and told no one. But now Otley knows. So she had better confess.

"I was told he died by heart attack by a source back home," Maddie says.

Otley's eyes flash with a mix of surprise and admiration, but he does not ask her why she knows this, which surprises her. Instead he says, "He was a healthy man. Surprisingly so, I am told. I'm more likely to drop from a dodgy ticker than he ever was."

Maddie realizes that Otley thinks the Bishop is not dead because God called him home. He's dead for another reason.

"I understand you are looking for him," the Cardinal says.

"Yes, I am. My old college, St. Jude's, asked me to look him up in Rome."

"Do you know why?"

"Sir Geoffrey said they hadn't heard from him for a while."

Otley utters a soft, sad moan. "They must have had money with him in the IOR. You know, the Vatican Bank. Which is missing 250 million Euros."

Maddie takes in this number. More than a quarter of a billion dollars? How much money is in the Vatican bank?

"Since we made our reforms a couple of years back," Otley says, "business has dropped. We have about five billion Euros on hand. But Zimmerman knew how to move money."

Maddie does the math. The Cardinal is saying that Zimmerman has displaced 5% of the bank's cash assets of all of Christendom. She would normally curse but instead says, "With respect, your Eminence, this is all a little bit…" She pauses, hoping that Otley might fill in the blanks. But the Cardinal just looks at her expectantly, like a good journalist or a cop would do, when waiting for more. "I mean, an interview with the Pope has now become a massive theft and an investigation into why Zimmerman died. Isn't this something for the Swiss Guard?"

Cardinal Otley's round face broadens as he smiles at the obvious. "The Swiss Guard are, of course, involved, but they are an army. The police force is the Corpo della Gendarmeria, and they are very good, but their brief is, shall we say, rather local, and I'd like to keep it that way. He died in New York, and you live there, so I am hoping you can give us some answers."

The Cardinal doesn't want the Vatican cops out in the world asking questions about a priest who has stolen money and who, Maddie now realizes, was murdered.

"But who would want to kill him? In an abandoned church? In Manhattan?"

"That's what we'd like to know, too. And we'd very much like to find the money he stole."

"I see. But then I don't. I mean, if I hadn't shown up here, what were you going to do?"

Otley's plump cheeks redden, radiating a kind of relief that Maddie is still here, still talking. "Let us say that you are proof of God's divine mercy."

Maddie cocks her head, as if to suggest that's nothing she would ever claim. But her father used to say, "*Timing is often luck, and luck is often timing.*" She walked into a moment that needs her and that she needs in a way that she didn't imagine. Is that luck? Or timing? Or something else?

"We need to be seen as hands off, here," the Cardinal says. "The truth has a clearer path to come out if it's not being blocked by busybody clerics. Of course, we'll cover any expenses above and beyond your own work in securing this interview with the Holy Father and Teddy Wright."

She nods. Keeping cool on the outside, while inside, she's burning with the story to come.

The Cardinal fixes his soft blue eyes on her. "Find Father Victor Franchi. And go where the clues lead." Then he hands her back her phone, and smiles. "Remember, all of this is just between us. Too much oxygen will make whatever flames are coming our way much worse."

Maddie promises him that. She knows at once that it is a promise she will have to break.

12. Rome.

The Roman sun warms the bright marble columns of St. Peter's Square, in reality a grand oval that is Bernini's colonnaded marble embraces before the great Basilica itself. Maddie quickly threads through the columns to the Basilica even though she's a few minutes early to meet Sister Nuala. She's hot with energy. In the meeting with the Secretary of State, in the Vatican gardens, Cardinal Otley sent her on a mission. To find what happened to a murdered priest who stole 250 million Euros. For that she will land the interview with the Pope.

Her thoughts spin around how she will tell Teddy Wright about the off-road route she's taking. As for the "why?", well, Sir Geoffrey primed that quest, and now another Englishman, Cardinal Otley, has put it in motion.

Maddie thinks on that as she strides toward the metal detectors outside the Basilica. Otley knew her father. So did Sister Nuala. So, it seems, did Christopher Zimmerman. And he's dead. Murdered, Otley thinks. Is Maddie doing a murder investigation for the Vatican?

No, she's just gathering some facts in exchange for keeping her job. Quid pro quo.

Still, she feels fueled, urgent, the way her father told her that he felt when he got the whiff of a story that no one else had. Now she has a story. But who else might have it? And how could they hurt her, running this errand for the Church?

The Church has enemies everywhere. Pope Pius XIII

is angering a lot of people within his own faith. His endorsement of Muslims to at least live free of persecution from each other and the West, causes hellfire sermons in Maddie's own country. The Pope's commitment to science, as a divine gift, is equally provoking, angering multinational oil companies and flat-earthers alike.

And the fact he has spoken out against the madness afflicting America and Europe, one which says white people need to do everything possible, including murder, to stop non-white people from enjoying full stomachs, and roofs above them and a chance to express their hopes and dreams and talents, and maybe even find happiness, has exploded.

Maddie zips through the Basilica security and bounds up the stairs, the way she used to do when her mother Francesca would take her here to see "the finest piece of art in the world."

She enters the Basilica and stands at the top of the nave, taking in the sheer size of the place. The Basilica encourages this by placing markers along the floor showing the lengths of lesser cathedrals. She has not been here since she was little and she walks a few feet to see where the second largest cathedral in the world, the Basilica of the National Shrine of the Immaculate Conception in Washington DC begins. Of course, nothing could be bigger than the Catholic Church's HQ.

She turns right and walks straight up to sorrow itself. The Pietà. When she was younger, it carried no sadness for her at all. Maddie stares, through the protective glass, at the miracle in marble depicting Mary. Yes, she can see that the sorrow in Mary's young face crushes her beauty and protests her destiny, as she cradles her crucified son Jesus in her arms. Maddie now knows sorrow, so now she sees it.

She tips her head back to dry her eyes and lets a scrum of Polish tourists crowd around the Pietà. When she checks her phone, the nun is five minutes late. When the nun is thirty minutes late, Maddie hurries back to the *Il Convento* hostel. She is just in time to see an ambulance parked out front, its rear doors open. Then she sees two ambulance attendants wheel out a gurney. On it, under an oxygen mask, is Sister Nuala.

Maddie runs up. She knows that Sister Nuala had something for her, then didn't show up with it and now is being loaded into an ambulance. The attendants wave her away and the ambulance, its siren silent, pulls away. If this was urgent, Maddie is sure there would be a siren blaring.

She climbs to the rooftop terrace of *Il Convento*, thinking, hoping the nun has left her something there. Maybe in her room? Suddenly, the nun she met with Nuala yesterday, the one with the suspicious eyes, appears like a ghost on the terrace, so quiet on those rubbery nun shoes.

She hands Maddie a manilla envelope, then says in Italian, "Sister Nuala wanted you to have this."

Maddie takes the envelope and quickly feels the seal. Smooth, it has not been opened.

"How is Sister Nuala?" she asks.

The nun's glaring eyes drop to stare at the ground as she shakes her head. Then makes the sign of the cross. "This killed her," she says, looking at the envelope. "No matter what they say." Then she is gone.

Maddie steadies herself on a deep breath, reeling from the news that Sister Nuala is dead, and that she might be holding the murder weapon.

She retreats to her room and opens the envelope. Inside it is a very old document on thick and yellowed paper that bears a red wax seal that looks very official. It's dated 1944, and it shows a deposit of $1 million in gold from a man named Josip Babić. The deposit is to a Swiss bank, Zimmerman Freres, Zurich, SUI. And it is signed for by Joachim Zimmerman.

Maddie is looking at the signature of Christopher Zimmerman's father. She had read about Zimmerman's father in a profile of the priest, which mentioned how he came from a banking family, how there were no brothers, but it just sounded a better, safer, richer name for a bank. And also how the son, Christopher Zimmerman, had abandoned the family business for the life of a Roman priest.

Or maybe he hadn't abandoned it at all.

Maddie feels blood rush to her head. This is what the dead nun wanted her to have; this is what her father knew. That the Zimmerman family had taken an awful lot of money from a man with a Croatian name near the end of a terrible war. How is Bishop Zimmerman connected to this old certificate?

Whatever his ties were, the nun is dead because of it.

And now Maddie has it.

She opens her phone and Googles “hospitals close to Vatican”. There’s the Bambino Gesu, which the Vatican sponsors, and which only treats kids, and the Gemelli, just north of Vatican City. That’s where the Pope had his appendix removed. That’s where Sister Nuala would be, and Maddie needs to find out if she is, in fact, dead.

She punches in the hospital’s number. “This is Sister Maria Corvina from the Vatican Communications office,” Maddie says in her best Italian and deepens her voice. “We have learned that a nun, Sister Nuala from *Il Convento*, was admitted earlier today. Can you please tell me how she is doing?”

Maddie listens as the clerk punches information into a computer terminal. Then the woman returns and asks Maddie again who she is. Maddie pulls out Sister Maria Corvina’s business card and reads it out, including the address. There is a pause, then the woman at the hospital replies in Italian, “I am sorry, Sister, but Sister Nuala did not survive.”

“Dio benedica la sua anima,” says Maddie. God bless her soul.

Maddie does not think the timing of the World War II certificate that the nun gave to her and the nun’s death are a coincidence. She knows that if she wants to live long enough to tell the story, then she must leave Rome at once.

She checks flights to New York, and sees that the only plane out tonight is at 12:30 AM. Maddie books it. She will head to Fiumicino now and be early, but she will be alive. And she might even say a prayer. After all she just did an impression of a nun and it worked. So she says the first Hail, Mary she has said in a very long time, that the mother of Jesus will pray for her now and at the hour of her death. Which she prays does not come before midnight in Rome.

13. New York City.

Maddie would have loved to have devoted her business class sleeper seat on the nine-hour flight between Rome and JFK to rest up and be 'ready for Teddy', as she and Aretta would joke. But the bed pod becomes her desk as she works to help Sir Geoffrey and Cardinal Otley, and Teddy. The jobs are strangely converging, and coming with corpses.

Maddie shakes her head "No" to the flight attendant offering her a glass of Italian red and maybe himself as well as he stares out longingly from under a tumble of black curls. But she'll take another cup of his strong coffee. She turns to her notes so as not to see him walk on with his wine, and gracefully shift his lovely broad shoulders so he can navigate the narrow aisle.

She has to keep her head clear and fueled with the caffeine from a hot and smoky Italian roast. Typing notes on her laptop, she stops to read the news feed. She has put "Vatican news" into Google's News engine and now she sees a piece pop up from *L'Osservatore Romano,* the Vatican's newspaper begun in 1861 by another Pope Pius, the IX. In it she scans the obituaries—which her father called the Irish Sports Pages—and sees one for Sister Nuala. The short piece proclaims that during her long life of prayerful devotion, she had indeed served Bishop Zimmerman for decades, and after a short retirement, her time on earth ended with a heart attack.

Not long after her former boss's life ended with a

heart attack in an abandoned church in New York City. As far as Maddie knows, heart attacks are not contagious.

She feels a fist of ice turning her guts. Because now she's dealing with a possibly murdered priest, Christopher Zimmerman, and a possibly murdered nun, Sister Nuala. And the killer, or killers, have a clever, heart-stopping knack for offing people in the most natural way.

If the nun was murdered because of what she gave to Maddie, then Maddie knows she is now in the killer's crosshairs.

So, what's next? Report the pair of mysterious heart attacks to Cardinal Otley along with the also mysterious Zimmerman bank certificate? But that's not news, only a pile up of coincidences. So, she digs into those mysteries. The dueling coronaries could be some kind of signature, she thinks, and how they were done might reveal the whodunnit. As she scans Mr. Google, the internet instantly obliges her with hundreds of ways to discreetly off your special someone with an aorta corker. Maddie would laugh at the homemade killer recipes, but the icy grip on her stomach is growing tighter. The killer was a pro. And discovering how they did it will take another pro.

The Why keeps taking Maddie back to the same place. The past. She needs to connect with her past, to find her future.

The handsome flight attendant gives Maddie a fleecy blanket and a look as if to say, *I could keep you warmer than that.* Wrapped in her blanket, she huddles over her computer and rides the internet. Maddie types in the name of her ex-boyfriend at Columbia, the former poet Patrick Farrell, who she knew became some kind of cop. She types in "FBI" and "NYPD" and she hopes to God not "Homeland Security". A hit comes back on LinkedIn: Patrick Farrell is a special agent with the Bureau of Alcohol, Tobacco and Firearms. Based in New York City. And that's the pro that Maddie was hoping for.

She sends Patrick Farrell a "hello after a long time" message on LinkedIn. It's a shot in the dark, but Patrick was her first serious boyfriend, and she adored him. He was as sensitive as a poet should be, and funny too. He was also a good cook, which was so important on his college shoestring budget.

They parted on good terms when she won her scholarship to Oxford. It was as if that life event was a kind of deliverance for them both. It freed Maddie from telling Patrick that they had become more of a habit than a couple, and he was grateful that she showed her hand first.

Maddie is about to log off when she receives a ping from LinkedIn. It's nearly two o'clock in the morning in New York, but Patrick Farrell is awake. And he'd be delighted to buy Maddie a pint. Assuming she hasn't fallen off the rails and become a vegan teetotaler.

Maddie grins. She always did like his sense of humor. *"It's a date,"* she writes back. *"How about today after work, say 6?"* He is right back with an instant *"Yes"*.

Six PM Eastern time is not that far away for Maddie, being six hours ahead on Roman time and landing in New York at 5 AM. Since Teddy and Aretta are not expecting her back in town, Maddie has some time off. She can use it to build her files on Zimmerman and his family's bank, and see what she can find out about this priest Victor Franchi.

When at last six o'clock rolls around, and Maddie has planted herself at the bar near Union Square, she doesn't immediately recognize Patrick when he walks in. Maddie hopes she is a bit unrecognizable herself in her 'now we are grownup' work uniform of jeans, heels and power-jacket. She daubed on extra eye-cream to mask the effects of that long, caffeinated flight from Rome, and warmed up her lips with deep red lipstick which Patrick used to kiss right off. So, she flinches when this tall, broad dude in black shiny hair and sunglasses stops at her bar stool and says "Of all the gin joints in all the world..."

Maddie smiles to see him again. "Patrick! So, this is your gin joint?"

He leans across the table and gives her a kiss on the cheek. "It is tonight, Mads. And you know I hate surprises."

Patrick Farrell is the dark to Cosmo's light, at least physically. Looking at him now, he's no longer the scrawny college kid. His thick black hair crests his shoulders and a trim goatee frames his strong chin. His black wardrobe of black leather blazer, black jeans and black Doc Martens is ready for a funeral or a crime.

Maddie thinks he looks like some kind of Mexican drug boss, and not the poet whose words she loved—eventually more than him, really—when they were both at Columbia.

"I know," he says, as if reading her mind. "Who'd believe I'm a Chirish kid from Queens looking like this? But hey, anything to keep us all safe these days from the bad guys. And bad girls, to be fair."

She smiles even more because he whips off his sunglasses when he says, "And bad girls," and she knows the poet's heart still beats despite the fact he's doing whatever he's doing for the law. But even so, this Chinese-Irish guy from Queens is a long way from Slam Night at The Heights on Broadway.

His brown eyes take Maddie in, not like a cop, but like a poet, his imagination shining backward in time and not in judgment. He seemed relieved when she left for Oxford, because he believed that distance would take care of whatever he still felt.

Maddie knew, by applying to study on the other side of the Atlantic, that she had started all over. She just wasn't good with endings, until she realized that her father's end had ended everything. And when Cosmo wanted everything to last forever, she was afraid she had nothing, not even herself. With Patrick there was no fear. Just youth and a short calendar.

He raises his glass of soda water and clinks against her pint of Stella. "Here's to old friends."

"Not really that old," Maddie says. "Still in the twentysomething time zone."

He smiles. "I turned thirty last week."

Once upon a time Maddie knew that date like she knew her own birthday, but now it surprises her that forgetting it surprises her. "You sure you don't want something stronger? It's my birthday treat…"

He shakes his head Yes and No. "I'd love a bottle of bourbon and a straw, to be honest, but I'm kind of in the middle of something and have to keep my wits about me."

There's a pause, and then Maddie says, "Only tell me what you can."

There's a longer pause, and Patrick says, "That's about everything."

She laughs, tossing her head back, her deep, throaty laugh bounding straight up through her red lips, her black curls bouncing with joy.

He can't help but look at her as he once did, as if she was his muse. And in those days, he fed her with his words, but now he has gone silent in the interest of a different kind of art form. And yet it is one in which seeing her has awakened memories of what he has lost in the transition.

"That's a pretty short everything." Maddie gets her laughter under control and feels the heat of his memory. It fuels her story now. "You know I'm competitive but not even I can beat that. So, here's my grateful second place..."

And so she begins with her father's death, her return to New York and new incarnation in Teddys Wright's newsroom. And then there's Rome.

"Wow," he says when she has finished delivering news of her mission to Rome, and now her mission to find out what happened to the nun and dead priest.

She takes a sip of beer. "I know. One day I'm a chase producer, and the next day I'm on a chase for real."

He grins. "Sounds pretty cool, actually. But I gather you're not here to impress me."

Maddie appreciates that Patrick's new incarnation as an enforcer of laws has made him much more direct. So, she responds in kind. "I want your help. Please."

"What do you want me to do, exactly?"

"I need to know if there was an autopsy on the dead priest, the one found here, and what it says."

"You think he was murdered?"

Maddie thinks so, but she can't be so sure if she wants to follow the story, and not lead it. As for the Vatican, they think foul play, and she wants to understand why they think that. "I hope not," she says carefully. "But the people I spoke to in Rome are concerned about him and want to tie up any loose ends, if there are any. A dead priest is one thing, but…"

"A murdered one is another."

"Yes," she says. "And then the Vatican can deal with whatever you find out. If you in fact can find out anything?" She hopes that she has pitched the mission just right, appealing to his own Catholic boy sense of obligation.

"I think I can," he says. "So long as what it says doesn't wind up on Teddy Wright's show."

Maddie smiles in relief. "This is between me and the

Vatican."

"Secrets of the confessional," he says.

"Yeah, something like that." She doesn't ask him to help her find Victor Franchi. She isn't sure yet if Father Franchi is even alive. Online files about the Pope's old secretary flash back on screen with a nasty 404 error code, and so Maddie will have to dig very carefully. There are two buried already.

Patrick takes in her worried look, which had once been all too rare. "OK, I know a guy who knows a guy."

"Thanks, Patrick."

Now he's worried about her and cocks an eyebrow theatrically. "Sounds like you are suddenly living the Catholic life."

Maddie remembers Patrick to be much more of a believer than she was, and though he's joking, he's also not. She cannot tell him about her turn as a godmother in Oxford, as that would just hurt him. So she says, "Well, all roads lead to Rome, so…"

He feels his phone buzz and he looks at it. "I have to go Mads." He rises and smiles. "I will see what I can find out and get back to you."

She lights up a smile. "And maybe I can buy you that birthday drink." He gives her that old Patrick grin of hope in return. But in his eyes, she sees the strain of the dark world in which he lives. And she knows that she has already stepped into that world herself.

The Vatican has asked her for a favor. But Cardinal Otley mentioned that the flames could be much worse. As Maddie's father always told her, the flames can destroy, or they can bring more light. It all depends on your perspective. Right now, Maddie is looking for the light.

14. Houston, Texas.

Brett Muenster has been summoned to another meeting, this time an audience with the Admiral, and he's sweating. That's even before he's dipped into the mole sauce that accompanies the brisket tacos and smokehouse nachos and the three pounds of BBQ pork ribs that the Admiral has ordered as appetizers. The plate, which looks like a small animal had slipped on a pool of BBQ sauce and died on a pile of nachos, sits on a table in a shady corner of Miguel's Tacos & BBQ in Houston's Greater Third Ward.

Brett Muenster eyes the plate, grateful for the diversity of Houston's cuisine, but Tex-Mex is not on his list. He hates Tex-Mex food, if you can call it that, all goopy and doughy and meaty. And after you eat it, with sauce dripping all over your face and shirt, you look like you dined at a Satanic ritual. He would also prefer a stiff bourbon to the iced tea on offer, but that's a move that would get the wrong kind of attention from the teetotal Admiral C. Parke Stranch III. Since Stranch is paying the freight on both the food and Muenster's job, he knows that keeping his head down and his mouth not too full is the smart play here and now.

The Admiral is in his early 60s, and he's easily 300 pounds on a six-foot frame, so he's fat. But it's the broad and solid kind of fat that makes him look more like an immovable obstacle than a supersized addict. He has a full head of thick silver hair, and his long, pale face is clean-shaven. If you take off the sunglasses and add a goatee, the Admiral would look like a close relative of the Colonel, famous for fried chicken.

He wears a crisp white shirt, but in place of the bolo tie, he has a large crucifix on a gold chain, the way a bishop might. And he moves his hand from his nachos to his heart, onto the cross now. One simple gesture, connecting everything he believes.

"Brother Brett," he says to Muenster, slipping off his sunglasses and lasering into him with blue eyes so clear they look Photoshopped, "Tell me about things."

Muenster takes a sip of tea. He knows what things the Admiral wants to know about, and he knows he doesn't want details that could be the kind to derail everything.

"Things are good, Admiral."

Stranch picks up a pork rib and quickly, in two big bites, chomps it to bone. Muenster also knows that the Admiral became one of the richest men in the known universe through his company Bellerophon, which he built with ex-military guys to provide "security to the world". He has to look after his own security, here and now. He has to be careful.

Muenster knows Stranch has financed his own private army through the billions he'd made as a "stripper and tipper"—buying undervalued companies, stripping off assets, firing the employees, firing all the fathers and mothers and sons and daughters who had now become too expensive, and then selling the denuded companies. The best bit was in collecting a fee on both ends of the deal.

And before that he'd been in the Navy. Rumor has it that he had even been a SEAL, which is hard to believe looking at his girth now. A whale is more like it, Muenster thinks. Stranch is also not a real Admiral, but because he was in the Navy and has a yacht and a ton of money, he considers this nickname is his right.

"Did you take care of the thing that was in our way?"

Muenster feels that he should eat something, but his mouth is so dry even with the iced tea that he can't risk it without spitting up on the Admiral's gold crucifix. "Yes sir, we did."

Stranch demolishes another rib. "And you're sure there's nothing else out there to bother Reagan?"

Muenster is not sure at all. Jane Jones was sure, but she would be, as she wanted her million dollars. "I am sure. I saw the evidence that our friend Jane provided."

Stranch swipes up some mole with a brisket taco. "How is our friend Jane?"

Muenster catches a forced casualness in Stranch's question, one that suggests he knows very well how Jane is. But Muenster says, "I think she's fine. I saw her a couple of weeks ago, and she looked good."

Stranch runs his tongue over his teeth, and stares into Muenster again. "Well, then Brother Brett, I guess what I have heard is in no way true."

Muenster now feels that what Stranch has heard could well be fatal, and he feels the sweat form on his forehead. "What would that be, sir?"

Stranch keeps those clear blue eyes beaming into Muenster. "I heard that there's someone asking after the trash."

Muenster hates this fucking code, but he also knows that if anyone is listening, and who isn't these days, then the code is what's going to save him. Someone is asking after the dead priest who wanted to destroy Reagan Clark.

"I heard this news from friends that I have in the family."

Muenster parses this to mean that Stranch's buddies in law enforcement helped out. Or maybe they're his own spies. Muenster is careful about what he says to anyone, and even more cautious here and now. "I see," Muenster says. "Do we know this someone?"

Stranch shakes his head. "No, we don't know the asker, nor the ATF guy who is asking on her behalf." Then he extracts an old-time fountain pen from inside his jacket, and scrawls a name on a napkin. "The asker," he says, then hands the napkin to Muenster, who realizes he does know this someone. Maddie Lynch.

Muenster has two choices. He can come clean, or he can find out more, and so he pulls his best poker face and looks at the napkin. "No, can't say I do. But I can see what I can do."

Stranch stares at Muenster, his cold look pile driving into Muenster's gut, then he grabs another rib and gnaws the flesh off one side of it with such vigor that the BBQ splatters Muenster in the face.

The Admiral's nose flares in disapproval as if it is Muenster's fault he's a mess and shoves the stack of napkins at him. "Fast way is the best way," he says. "It's what I pray for, and the Lord has been most gracious at hearing my prayers." And then he goes for the other side of the rib.

Muenster wonders what fast way? A thought the Admiral reads in an instant. "I want you to determine if we have missed anything when we took out the trash. And, to ask our friend Jane to finish the mission."

Muenster would really like to ask Stranch if he means to find out if they have all the dead priest's goods on Reagan Clark, or if he wants him to get rid of Maddie Lynch. The Admiral cuts in.

"I mean both, Brother Brett. Both. I don't want any of the trash to get kicked to the curb. I want it all clean gone."

He grabs another rib and takes a chomp. "What's your favorite piece of scripture, Brother Brett?" he asks, surprising Muenster with this shift. The question sends him back to childhood Bible camp, which was really an excuse for other Christian ten-year-olds to waterboard him in the shower, but he summons up the lines that will save his atheist soul.

"Now the Lord is the Spirit, and where the Spirit of the Lord is, there is freedom..."

The Admiral smiles. "Second Corinthians, 3:17. 'And we all, who with unveiled faces contemplate the Lord's glory, are being transformed into his image with ever-increasing glory, which comes from the Lord, who is the Spirit'."

There is a moment of prayerful silence, then the Admiral looks into Muenster as if he can see his gravest sins. In the next second, he grins, enjoying his chat as much as the ribs. “You keep your foot on the gas of the trash truck, Brother Brett. And you don’t stop for anything.”

It is then that Muenster knows the future as well as he knows his own crimes. Murder is the campaign strategy that’s going to get Reagan Clark into the White House.

15. Chelsea Piers, New York City.

It's the last Saturday of April and Maddie's hockey team, the Columbia Chiclets, is down a goal with three minutes left in the quarter-finals game against the Hofstra Hellcats. The winner moves on to the semis with a real shot at the title of the New York City Senior Women's Hockey League. The rink at Chelsea Piers is full for once, packed with Fordham's Fallen Angels, the Barnard College Blasters, and other losing teams who've eaten their sour grapes and are here just to watch the game they love.

Maddie wants to win. A win would give her that trophy of a cheesy bronze hockey player, with the obligatory ponytail to signify 'female', bolted onto a plate of wood, something to plant on her fake fireplace. It would give her real evidence that she can still summon victory at will.

The Columbia team catches a break when one of the Hellcats runs the Columbia goalie, Lulu Chang, hard into the net. Lulu goes down like she's been shot. Maddie and Emily and the other Chiclets swarm the Hofstra player. When she doesn't back off, Maddie drops her gloves, ready to throw a punch at the woman who tried to kill their goalie. It's not just for show. "Let's go," Maddie snarls at the offending Hellcat. "Let's see how tough you are."

Emily grabs Maddie back by the shoulders. "We got a fiver," she shouts.

And so they do, as the referee is good, and she loudly announces that it's a five-minute penalty to Hofstra. The Chiclets hang back and Maddie picks up her gloves. She still wants to pummel the skinny Hellcat, who plays hockey wearing a full-face of makeup, and who tried to injure the goalie. She will find a way to get her revenge.

Even though there are only three minutes left in the game, the Chiclets will have a one player advantage and can score as many goals as they like until the final buzzer, and still keep their advantage.

And Columbia goalie Lulu finds new life in their renewed hope. She gets up from the ice, and after conferring with Hannah, one of their teammates who is an ER doctor, is good to go. All she has to do is keep the puck out of their net, and all Maddie and Emily and the Chiclets have to do is put two in the Hofstra net.

They get their first when Karla, their fearsome defender, lets rip with a slapshot from the point. Maddie is in front of the Hofstra net, screening their goalie, and the puck rockets past her to tie the game. Maddie figures that the painful cross-checks to her back from the Hofstra goalie trying to get Maddie out of her eyeline are worth it.

"Let's go, Chiclets! Let's go!" she hollers, slapping her stick on the ice. They respond by slapping back. It sounds like firecrackers bursting in Chelsea Piers.

Emily, strong and fast, wins the face-off at center ice and circles back, to set up the play. She starts skating up the left wing, so Maddie crosses over to center ice. Once Emily has drawn the Hofstra defender close enough to her, she dishes a perfect saucer pass to Maddie.

Maddie is in alone on the goalie, and sees daylight between the goalie's pads, in the space known as the five-hole. Maddie fakes a shot, and the goalie squeezes her pads tight, and now, off-balance, can't cross her crease fast enough to stop Maddie's back hand, which puts the puck into the top shelf of the net.

The Chiclets go berserk, jumping on Maddie and showing how the word "fucking" can be used for high praise. There's still a minute left, but Hofstra, down a player, and now down a goal, has lost heart. The Chiclets are into the semi-finals.

When the team, showered and dressed, steps into the sunny Saturday afternoon, powered up from their win, it's so good they scream, "Chiclets win! Chiclets drink!" New Yorkers passing by take it in and keep going. Tourists notice and wonder if Chiclets are some cult.

As they all settle into their places at the Westside Tavern, Karla looks around and finds Maddie and Emily missing. "Hey, why are you guys sitting over there?" Karla shouts at the pair who have taken a table for two away from their teammates.

"Emily has to tell me how much money I've lost," Maddie says. "After I have a good cry, we'll join you!"

Emily tells Maddie to dry her eyes: she has actually made a lovely 27% return on her $1,000 investment, which is not bad at all for a couple of weeks in the market.

Maddie clinks her glass of Jameson's against Emily's glass of white wine, then quietly tells her that this is not the reason she wanted to sit away from their teammates. She shows Emily the photo on her phone of the document that Sister Nuala had given her, revealing that Josip Babić had given a Swiss bank $1 million in gold in 1944.

Emily whips out her own phone and does a quick calculation. "Wow," she says. "That $1 million would be worth $15,792,500.00 million today. And that's just if it had been left alone. If it had been invested, it could be worth ten times that much. Or more."

Maddie fortifies herself with a sip of whiskey. "So, a lot of money then, and a lot of money now. My question to you, as a money person, is… why is this Swiss banker taking ownership of all this money from this guy, whose name suggests he's Croatian?"

Maddie expects Emily to get out her phone again to check sources, but she grins. "I had to do a class on this very thing when I did my MBA."

"What very thing?"

"Ethics. About how the Swiss banks did business in World War Two with the Nazis and the Allies, and also with the Jews, who were looking to escape the Nazis."

"What does that…" Maddie says and then flashes the bank document on her phone, "... have to do with this?"

"What you have there is a deposit to the bank by this man, Babić, as Switzerland was seen as safe in a world war. The Nazis thought so and so did the Vatican."

That's what Maddie was waiting to hear. "What do

you know about the Vatican?"

"Me? A devout atheist with a lapsed Lutheran mother and secular Jewish father? Just that there are, shall we say, continuing issues with the Vatican and Jewish money looted by the Nazis. You're the historian, Maddie. Go get 'em!"

Maddie pulls her friend into a hug. "Thanks, Emily. I just wanted to know if this document was real."

Emily hugs her back as she whispers, "Is this what you were doing in Rome?"

"Something like that," Maddie says quietly. "Is it possible to find out what happened to that money?"

Emily keeps an arm around Maddie and can't help but see her green eyes stare hot and intense. As if she was finally her old Maddie self.

"I can try to find out."

For that, Maddie throttles her in a tight hug.

"I mean," Emily goes on to say, "with crypto investments, that's money that's not really there. With this Swiss document, I'd get to look for money that was once really there. And which is somewhere else now."

Maddie hugs her again. If Maddie could find out where that Vatican money is, then maybe she had the next clue to solving the story she now needs to tell. The question bubbles in her head: needs, yes, but does she want to tell it? She takes a sip of wine and looks out at the lovely afternoon. "No one gets out of this alive," she always heard her father say, and raises a glass to his ghost. She will keep going until she finds the truth. Or until someone stops her.

16. New York City, Upper West Side.

Every Saturday night Maddie dines with her mother at Risorgimento, a candlelit rosewood-paneled Milanese trattoria near Francesca's apartment on the Upper West Side. It's a place where the owner, Renzo Romano, treats Francesca as if she is still a sitting Contessa, and the food is worthy of a queen. It's a Saturday ritual that Maddie has kept with her mother except for last Saturday. And now, Maddie's explanation of why in the name of Teddy Wright she missed their dinner last Saturday is causing Francesca Lynch distress.

She shoots Maddie a pained look as if the lush red wine suddenly turned into drain cleaner. "That woman is outrageous! Why would the Pope want to talk to her? She hates him!"

Maddie has her mother's temper, and here they are together. It could get ugly fast. "She doesn't really hate him," Maddie says. "But since the Pope preaches love for all humankind, it would be good for him to have a sit-down with her, maybe even for the world."

Francesca fires back. "The Pope doesn't need to do that! He has an audience already!"

Maddie lowballs it. "I thought the same thing until I asked the Vatican. They were interested. And besides, Papa taught me to never take 'No' for an answer before it really was one."

Francesca's aristocratic disdain melts into a smile. "Yes. It was his strategy in getting me to the altar."

It was his strategy in everything. And it was why he wasn't with them tonight. He would never say, *"No. I won't go to war again."*

Renzo Romano slides into their brief chill to refill their wine glasses. "*Tutto va bene, contessa*?" he asks Francesca, with the kind of look in his liquid brown eyes that Maddie recognizes as puppy love, even though Renzo is older than her mother by a decade.

Francesca sighs. "*Mia figlia non mi ascolta.*"

Renzo, short and broad and built like a bricklayer, looks at Maddie as if Francesca has just said her daughter slipped poison into her dinner, rather than saying she doesn't listen.

"Allora, lei è tua madre!"

"I know she's my mother, Renzo, and I always listen," Maddie replies. "I just don't always do what she wants."

Renzo gently puts the wine back on the table, and gives Maddie a little bow. "*Un giorno, si impara,*" he says, then glides back into the shadows.

One day, you will learn. Learn what? Maddie wonders.

"Cara Francesca!" a deep voice suddenly booms out from behind Maddie. Francesca instantly turns her look of disappointed mother into one of serene content. "Ahh, Giacomo!" she says, extending her hand so that the Apostolic Nuncio to the United Nations, Archbishop Giacomo Marinelli, can kiss it.

She has known the Archbishop since he was studying

to be a priest, and she, a nun. Marinelli, a year older than Francesca, has not aged like she has. His waddling of an extra 50 pounds and thin gray hair make him seem a decade older, but his blushing smile on seeing her brings back his bloom of youth.

"Cara Francesca," he says, adding a gentle pat to the hand he kissed. "How lucky am I to see you looking so gorgeous." He takes her all in, just as he did as a young man. Then he turns to Maddie, and shakes his head in wonder. "Magdelena, where did the time go?"

"Nice to see you again, Your Grace."

The Archbishop laughs. "Please! You are now grown up enough to call me Giacomo!"

Francesca clears her throat for her announcement: "Maddie just returned from Rome. She is telling me all about it."

The Archbishop holds up his hands in mock surrender. "Ah, that is a long story. You will need another bottle of wine, I think."

Maddie laughs and watches Francesca give Giacoma her patient smile. "Maddie has made it short. She's still jet lagged." And that is Maddie's cue to stifle a yawn.

"Yes, of course," the Archbishop says, reading the message. "Please, call me anytime. I am at your service. Good night to you." He bows, and exits the restaurant. Just as Francesca wanted.

"I like him," Maddie says. "And he really likes you!"

Francesca shrugs. Of course. Then she smiles at her daughter. To anyone watching in the restaurant, the pair of them might look like sisters on girls' night out, as

Maddie's mother was just 24 when Maddie was born. Maddie will be 30 next March, and her mother looks barely 40. With her head of soft black curls tumbling elegantly to one side, and her brown eyes, her rose petal lips and pale sculpted skin and her tall, elegant frame, she is a head-turner still.

Maddie is grateful she has inherited her mother's looks, mainly, with her emerald eyes coming from her father, who looked more like an Irish pirate on the wrong end of the plank than a celebrated journalist. It's what her mother fell for. And hasn't let go of, and Maddie knows this mention of the Pope and Rome brings back what Francesca herself lost: her life, her family, her husband, her future, in the Eternal City.

"The Pope does not need Teddy Wright and you should be doing better things with your gifts, Maddie." Francesca's voice is a rich alto, and still bears the seasoning of her native Italy. She can, of course, turn on the accent when she wants, but she can also turn it almost completely off. Maddie has concluded that Francesca uses her voice, like she uses everything else, to keep the balance in her favor.

It is one of the reasons why Maddie, an only child, had hightailed it to Oxford. Francesca was hoping Maddie would follow her B.A. at Columbia with more Columbia, but Maddie wanted to escape the stifle that came from being the center of familial attention, and the listener to her mother's angry venting over the too-busy father. It is a strategy for self-protection. Now, though, she will allow her only surviving parent and family member to be her mother for as long as she can, however she wants.

And so Maddie takes a bite of her lamb cannelloni, and listens to her mother's Full Roman on "Pope and Teddy". It is an argument she cannot win. But she doesn't want to. She wants her mother's help. So, she carefully edges the conversation toward the priest who died. She needs to release information in a way that will get her help and not be shut out by some strategic Italian sulk.

Leaving the Pope-Teddy argument, Maddie rounds the corner saying, "Here's the thing, Mama: the Vatican… they asked me to help them."

Now Francesca's face softens. "I know you are a very accomplished woman, but what help can you give to them?"

Francesca was never one for a full out compliment. But this time she might have a point. Maddie has asked herself the same question, and she has not yet found the reason. But she knows that she will, once she finds what they really want.

"They want me to find out how a priest died."

Francesca leans forward, interested. "Which priest is this?"

"One who died of a heart attack, so they say, on the altar at some deconsecrated church in Midtown."

Francesca doesn't blink. "What do they want you to do?"

"They want me to find out how he died."

"Murdered?" Francesca whispers.

Maddie wanted her mother to say that, not her, and replies with an Italian shrug – why not?

On the topic of murder, her mother tops up their wine. "If the Vatican thinks he was murdered, then he was murdered. What is his name?"

"Christopher Zimmerman. He was a Swiss bishop who worked at the Vatican bank."

Her mother leans back as if Maddie has slapped her. Maddie realizes her mother knows the name. And maybe knows the priest.

"Your father knew him."

Maddie also wanted her mother to say that, not her, so she would not be blamed somehow and a new argument inflamed. She goes on to tell her mother the story about the Irish nun, Sister Nuala, who also knew Maddie's father, and left her a prayer, then left her a very interesting document. "The nun also died," Maddie adds quietly.

"Do you think this nun was murdered?" Francesca asks.

"I don't know," Maddie says carefully. She is glad at least the priest's heart attack is being revisited, thanks to her old boyfriend, Patrick. But the nun, while quite ancient, seemed in good health. She also seemed to be waiting for Maddie to come into her life to deliver the truth. She risked her life to do it. And Maddie ran for her life to get out of Rome.

"We must leave," Francesca says. The look on her mother's face is not one of fear, but of purpose.

Maddie pays the bill quickly and assures Renzo the

meal was superb, as ever, but that she is still ailing with jetlag. Then Maddie and her mother walk arm in arm up Amsterdam Avenue in silence on the crowded sidewalk of a Saturday night, toward 84th Street, where Francesca lives and works.

"Why did we leave, Mama? Was there something you wanted to tell me?"

"It's not for me to tell," Francesca says, and walks on.

"Then who will tell me!"

"Well, I'm not sure what to say… You have an Oxford doctorate and I am just a humble Italian schoolgirl, but I suspect there is more to your story."

Maddie sighs in frustration; her mother has played along so far, saying exactly what Maddie herself did not want to say. So she tries the truth. "Mama, you could easily think rings around most of Oxford. And you're the reason I went there. You made it possible."

"St. Jude's Scholarship made it possible."

That was true, but Francesca Lynch is also comfortable, if not downright affluent. Her family might have lost their noble privileges in Italy, but they had held on to some of their money, their silverware and their art. And now if Francesca sold those bloody illuminated manuscripts in her apartment, they'd have a lot more money. But instead she sells Italian art from *Arte Sacra*, her small gallery in front of which they now stand. Religious art, mainly, with some contemporary American to keep a hand in with the locals. There's a small, ornate sign, *Arte Sacra*, above the shop and girded steel covering the shop's front window like every other store in the city.

Francesca punches in the security code to the door beside the gallery, which leads up to her apartment. Maddie peers at the security cameras staring at her from above the gallery door, and above the entry to her mother's apartment. Francesca Lynch is watching the world for danger.

Inside the sleek, tasteful apartment, with its burnished wood fixtures, leather chairs, flowers everywhere and art on the walls, there is also, behind the bar, a safe.

Francesca swings back the bar gently, so as not to smash the bottles of Amaro onto the marble floor, and then enters the code to the safe. She reaches inside and extracts a battered leather satchel. Maddie feels a rush of emotion. She last saw that satchel on her father's shoulder.

Francesca hands Maddie the worn brown satchel. "In there," she says, "are your father's notes. On the story you have already mentioned. The one the Irish nun gave you a hint of, but just a hint."

Maddie holds the satchel as if she is taking her father's hand. "Have you read them, Mama?" she asks, tears in her eyes.

Francesca has tears in her eyes, too. "Just enough to know that you might need them. That's why your father left them with me the last time I saw him. When he came back here to see if I would come to Jerusalem. I told him, after reading the papers, it was too dangerous…" She pauses, remembering his plea, and her refusal. "He said one day, this story will be told. You will know when."

Maddie clutches the satchel to her chest. “I promise I will tell it.”

Francesca cups her hands around her daughter’s tear-stained face. “The Vatican wants your help and you do not know where that story will lead. I think your father would agree that it is best to go in armed. And now you are.”

17. Brooklyn, New York.

Maddie hurries back to her apartment, and as she does, looks over her shoulder and crosses the street a few times, in case she is being followed. It seems silly and maybe she is flattering her ego, but she is not going to drop her guard as she races on.

Back in her apartment, Maddie opens the old satchel gently. She inhales her father's spicy Aqua di Parma aftershave along with the musty old leather of the bag. Inside there is a notebook, and a flash drive, maybe a decade old, and an INN hard drive. Things her father has touched, and which she now touches. Maddie opens the notebook and feels her heart speed at the sight of her father's handwriting. He wrote in black, always, and in block capitals. He wasn't shouting. He was explaining. He said it was so everyone could understand.

Those black block capitals now tell Maddie what she has. Information about Christopher Zimmerman that her father felt important to hide away until the time came to reveal it. That time being tonight.

Her heart beating fast, Maddie plugs the flash drive into her laptop, and it comes to life.

There is a folder on the drive called "*The Vatican's Nazi Money*". Inside is a collection of articles and papers on the subject. The one that catches her eye is from *The Guardian*, and has Bishop Christopher Zimmerman in the sub headline.

In the piece, her father writes about the allegations

that the Vatican has profited from Nazi gold, which had been stolen from Jews. Zimmerman says, *"We are very interested in opening the windows on what the Istituto per Opere di Religione—which you would know as the Vatican Bank—was doing during World War II. We are not afraid of history. Especially when history will prove that we were on the side of the angels."*

Christopher Zimmerman was the man in charge of opening those windows, Maddie knows. So her father doesn't care about Zimmerman's 21st century reforms. He wants to look further into the past, and now he wants her to look there. To that dark time in the Church, with scholars still combing through the archives to see what exactly Pope Pius XII was doing to help the Jews.

Or was the Pope helping the Church at their expense while the Nazis were murdering Europe to install their Thousand Year Reich?

That is the question her father would have asked. Maddie can almost hear him now, the deep Irish song of his voice poking at power.

Maddie now carefully extracts the World War II certificate that the Irish nun gave her from a ZipLoc bag she had stored in her refrigerator.

Had her father seen this certificate, too, for a lot of gold to Zimmerman's Swiss bank? Is that the lead he was following?

Maddie clicks on another file called "Zimmerman in Action". It's a collection of photos of the priest that her father has compiled from various sites. There's one of a younger Zimmerman, maybe 40, dressed in a smart black pinstriped suit with a purple tie and matching pocket square. He's standing on a terrace overlooking some Swiss lake, the snow-capped mountains in the background. He has a glass of champagne in hand.

Maddie thinks he's handsome and dangerous, his deep blue eyes conveying intelligence that can help or hurt. He reminds her of Captain von Trapp, in *The Sound of Music*, vigilant but always on the edge of violence.

Her father has typed a note beneath the photo: "Zimmerman, Zurich, 1989. Last day as a civilian."

The next photo is of Zimmerman as a priest, looking less dangerous now, and more at peace. He's outside a building, whose sign reads "Hospice of St. Gildas." Her father's note identifies it as a residence for the dying poor, in Los Angeles. A long way from Zurich.

The following photo shows Zimmerman standing on a beach with palm trees flanking him, and a look of amusement on his face, as if he is hiding a great secret. "Zimmerman in Hawaii," says her father's note. He adds, "See Zimmerman bio file".

Maddie clicks on the file and reads about this human chameleon, how one-time Swiss banker Christopher Zimmerman decides to answer his vocation and become a priest, at age 40. Wanting no more than to work with the dying. Then, one summer early in his priestly ministry he is seconded to a financially troubled parish in Honolulu, Hawaii. There is a photo of Zimmerman standing outside Cathedral Basilica of Our Lady of Peace, looking happier than Maddie has seen him look.

The next thing he knows he's in the Vatican Bank,

waving his magic wand and making them money. Pure money, not from arms dealers and polluters and launderers. Or so he says: "*The Vatican Bank is not like your bank on Main Street. Our Main Street is heaven, and our investments are made with heaven in mind.*"

There is also a photo of Zimmerman in St. Peter's Square, his face fleshier, but confident, even arrogant. His stance suggests that the great basilica behind him could just as easily be a bank he owns.

Maddie plugs the hard drive into her USB port, and waits for it to boot up. She looks at the files. They are all video files. She knows that when she opens them, she is going to see her father again, alive and at his best. She takes a deep breath, and then clicks on Zimmerman 1.

The screen is black, then up pops the blunt title in white bold caps: "Swiss Sleaze: Washing God's Linen". She laughs: her father was always daring.

And when Maddie's father, James J. Lynch, pops up, Maddie feels the tears pool in her eyes, and wipes them away with her sleeve. Her father is with her again, and he wants her help to finish what he began. So she needs to let him help her. Tears will only blur her vision, and she needs it to be clear.

"*Christopher Zimmerman's Vatican bank reformation project could be looked at as an atonement of sorts*," James Lynch says to the camera. He's wearing a gray-blue Harris tweed blazer and a pale blue shirt, and jeans, as he walks through St. Peter's Square on a lovely Roman spring day.

The time code running along the bottom of the screen

tells Maddie her father made this video two years after she and her mother left Rome. So fourteen years ago. Her father would have been 45. He has a full head of auburn hair, and his face is firm and tanned, and he's so very cleft-chinned handsome that Maddie sees what her mother saw all over again.

His voice rolls, full of Irish music, ready to joke, but his eyes flash with rage as he speaks.

"His great-grandfather, Joachim von Zimmerman, had immigrated to Zurich from Berlin after World War One, to set up the family bank, Zimmerman Brothers International. There were no brothers, but it made the bank sound more solid. For him, Switzerland provided much more congenial surroundings, free of Communists looking to murder him in his bed, and then, of the Nazis, looking to nationalize the German banks, which they did in 1934."

The video cuts to images of Nazis rampaging through Europe, and shots of gold bars stamped with swastikas as her father delivers a voice-over:

"A flood of money—much of it American and British, which had been invested in Nazi Germany's profitable re-armament—now flowed south to Switzerland, which had changed its own banking laws to welcome the infusion of German, or otherwise, cash. And after a little hocus pocus, by creating German shell companies, the Swiss banks re-invested the money back into Nazi Germany."

Now Maddie sees a photograph of the Zimmerman Bank in Zurich, whose marble columns flank a high bronze door and make it seem like a temple.

"ZFI, a moderate-sized bank, did particularly well during the war, helping British and American interests to profit from the massive industrial push the Nazis made before embarking on their quest to launch the Thousand Year Reich."

Then the video cuts to Rome after the war, and to the thin, bespeckled, academic looking Pope Pius XII. Then she sees some of the Nazis who got away— and some who started working with the Allies.

"When the Allies won the war, ZFI was a major force in helping the Americans and British get their money out of Germany, using gold—and the help of the Vatican's mighty international network. They not only shipped war-profiteers' bricks of gold, but the very Nazis the Allies had been fighting were sent off to live lives of comfort in North and South America. Some of those Nazis even began working for allied intelligence agencies who had recently been their enemies."

And then James Lynch cuts away to an interview with him and Christopher Zimmerman, sitting in a sunlit room that looks like a rich man's parlor, with leather sofas and burnished wood and the glint of brass. Both very much alive again, with Zimmerman in his black cassock with its purple bishop's trim and purple sash and a purple zucchetto on his head, his gray wavy Baron Von Trapp hair flaring from beneath it. He still looks like a cool, calm banker, tolerating an annoying client. And James Lynch, in his tweed jacket and jeans, smiles like your best friend until you see the glare in his green eyes. He is about to pounce.

"It was this crime that made me want to become a priest," says Bishop Zimmerman. There's not even a hint of his Swiss accent in his perfect English. "*We did not know,"* he says, holding his hands out in the universal plea for forgiveness. "*But once I found out, I decided I could no longer ignore the call from God. And yes, I appreciate the irony that I was called back to Rome, to be a banker. This time, though, on the side of the angels."*

"Really?" James says. "*Tell me more about what these angels were doing in World War II? With the money of the dead."*

Zimmerman smiles at James as if he admires the effort, but he is not going to get anything from it. And says, *"I don't know what you're speaking about. Our work is for all the children of God."*

The video ends with James shaking his head and drawing a finger over his own neck, signaling for the camera to stop. James is not getting what he wants about money from this man of God.

And Maddie sits back, breathing hard. Seeing her father again so vital and telling her such a story has made her feel as if he is still with her. But he is not. She starts to cry.

Then her phone pings. She glares at her phone, insulted—who could be calling? It's from her ex-boyfriend, Patrick Farrell, the ATF agent. "Mads, have some info. Meet tomorrow? Outside?"

He must have received the autopsy results for

Christopher Zimmerman. Maddie wipes her eyes, blinks for a second to calm herself, and replies "Yes. High Line? 30th Street entrance. Name the time."

"High noon," he replies. "Keep a lookout, Mads. Just in case we have eyes on us."

Maddie knows that if he wants to meet outside, just like Cardinal Otley did, he does not want anyone to hear what he is going to tell her. And he thinks there might be someone watching and it is his job to see who. He thinks Maddie is already someone's target. Maddie knows she is.

18. New York City.

"I'm betting there's stuff in the Vatican Secret Archives about Zimmerman," Maddie tells Patrick Farrell, as a stiff and cold wind off the Hudson River buffets them as they stroll south on the High Line. "The years 1939-1946."

He has brought coffee for them, and she takes a warming sip from her cup. Pretty much half coffee, half cream. He remembers.

"Secret Archives sounds like a problem," he says.

Maddie shakes her head. "No, because Pope Francis opened them up to the world. Then Covid hit and only a few scholars could get in to review what's there. Pius XIII opened the thing all the way. Now they can all come take a look."

Patrick lifts his shades to look at her and scratches his drug-thug goatee as thinks about this, his black hair rippling in the wind as they walk. He's still dressed like some kind of cartel kingpin, but his dark, dreamy eyes are still those of a poet.

"It's dangerous, Mads. I mean there's always someone watching."

"I know. But I can't turn away, you know?"

He shakes his head like she's crazy as he smiles. He knows. He loved her drive. He still does. He walks her over to an empty corner above a noisy overpass.

"Zimmerman was murdered," Patrick says quietly.

Maddie shudders. She is now on the trail of a killer.

Patrick's dark eyes flicker around to see if anyone is listening to them. "Injected with two drugs, midazolam, to sedate him, and potassium chloride, to stop his heart. The official version from the coroner's office is a heart attack due to his age, 73, and severe coronary artery disease."

"Sounds like a very professional hit."

"Very. The heart attack was a total fiction, my guy says. He had another thirty years left on him."

The version delivered by the media was that Zimmerman came to New York to look at buying the deconsecrated church for the Vatican Bank. The real version is the one Maddie wants to know.

"Mads, if someone wanted him dead, then they could want you dead for trying to find out too much."

"I want to find out the truth."

He gives her arm an affectionate squeeze. "I understand that as a poet. But as an ATF agent, let's just say there's a lot of people who don't want the truth to be told."

Maddie grins to mask her fear. "Exactly my point. I want to know who they are and why they want to tell their lies."

"I thought you wanted to get an interview with the Pope."

"I do. And that's my cover story."

Maddie realizes as soon as she says this that she has now become an agent herself. But for whom? Her dead father? The Vatican? Both? And she has put Patrick in danger.

"This information," he says, "it's totally off the record."

"Don't worry, Patrick, I'm not going to bust your cover."

He laughs. "You're talking like you're on the inside, Mads."

She nods. She is on the inside now. And to know the truth about Zimmerman's death makes her feel terribly alive. She wonders how many more murders it will take to find the truth? Or will her own search end with a fake heart attack like Zimmerman's?

"Keep in touch, Mads. Please? Keep an eye out."

"You, too. And thanks." She gives him the kind of grin her father would give, full of confidence despite the stakes. Then she kisses him on the cheek and walks down the stairs to 34th Street, thinking of what her father would do now. He would start at the beginning and see what he had missed. Maddie takes a deep breath, sure she has to do the same. She knows exactly where she has to start.

19. Oxford.

The next day, as the sun sets, Maddie is walking along St. Giles on to Banbury Road, a wide and wandering street that cuts through Oxford north to south, lined with trees trimmed with bright green new leaves. Passing pubs and churches, she feels sure that here she is not being followed. Students hustle by, all with important destinations, carefully stepping over the piles of the soggy spring petals on the ground mixed with the bright dots of confetti tossed at grads, a messy celebratory tradition known as trashing.

She passes St. Jude's College and its Cotswold stone walls, holding the secrets of five years of her life. She will find out more about Cardinal Otley, suspecting he is somehow in league with Sir Geoffrey. But the secrets she really wants belong to Bishop Zimmerman. And her old mentor, who set her off on this mission, will know those as well. If Sir Geoffrey is the keeper of others secrets, maybe he is also wise to the whereabouts of the pope's mysterious and so far invisible friend, Victor Franchi.

Rain has begun by the time Maddie arrives in Park Town, Oxford's smaller version of Bloomsbury's circle of town houses. Stopping at the door of the grand Georgian townhouse where Sir Geoffrey lives, Maddie braces herself: Cosmo and Elka and her goddaughter Mathilda also live here, in the basement or 'garden' apartment in the house. When she called to say she was coming, Cosmo told her he'd be at home too, that is until

Elka's royalties get fatter and they can buy a house in London, as Elka wants, and Cosmo commutes to Oxford for work, which Cosmo does not.

So, Maddie is welcomed into the house and has her arms around Cosmo, greeting him, and then into those arms goes the cooing baby goddaughter. Elka, as Cosmo explains, has heard the muse and kicked him and her own child out of the garden flat and upstairs to join Grandpa. Maddie, who has still not read Elka's first novel, does not gloat. In fact, she wonders how Cosmo could have gone from her— knowing he loved her, and maybe still does – to this self-absorbed Valkyrie whom she can't figure out how he does love.

She looks at him now, pouring whiskies, as she rocks the wide-eyed Mathilda in her arms. It is almost the domestic picture that could have been hers. When Sir Geoffrey walks into the living room to see it, his usual world weary look lifts with a smile.

As he collects a kiss from Maddie's cheek, she asks, "Where is Lady Penelope?"

"In London, hearing *Tosca* at the Royal Opera House. Stopping at our flat in Islington," Sir Geoffrey says.

"A perfect opera for our times," says Maddie. "Lust, corruption, secrets, murder."

Cosmo beams at her, still adoring her edgy wit.

"I am glad you are here, too, Cosmo," Maddie adds. "I'd like a witness here when I ask where I am on my… mission. In case I get run over by a bus. Or get injected with potassium chloride."

"Nasty stuff," Sir Geoffrey remarks. "Can stop your

heart."

"I heard that, too, when I asked what happened to your friend Bishop Christopher Zimmerman," Maddie says. "He was murdered by that chemical which was injected into his blood, and made to look like a heart attack." She takes a long, warming sip of whiskey and lets that sink in. "So why did you want me to find him, really?"

Cosmo sits back and watches; he has seen his father go after ill-prepared students, but now Maddie is going after him. And there is a look on Sir Geoffrey's face that he rarely sees. It's one of fear.

"We had money invested with Christopher Zimmerman."

"Tell me about that money in the Vatican Bank." Maddie is well aware that the college is proud of its Catholic identity, but is pretty sure that they prefer landowning in the Home Counties to papal intrigue. She needs to know why.

"You see, only the Holy See and religious entities, charities, members of the clergy and Vatican employees are supposed to hold accounts there," Sir Geoffrey says, as if explaining a quirky old St. Jude tradition. But then he leans forward, and almost whispers, "What made Bishop Zimmerman a friend to us is that he agreed to manage some of our money through the Vatican Bank, and onward."

Maddie sees where this might be going. "You mean like a secret offshore bank, where no one is looking?"

"Yes. And when no one was looking… £15 million of Jude's money has just gone..." He snaps his fingers to punctuate the loss.

Cosmo looks at his father with a mix of awe and anger. He never shared with him, his own son, the dark pools into which St. Jude's money flowed.

"So where could it have gone?" Cosmo asks, an edge in his voice.

A silence hangs in response. That is the question.

"I recall St. Jude's endowment is about £300 million, right?" Maddie says, and Geoffrey nods. "Losing 5% of the college's money isn't a loss you can hide. Still, that solves one mystery."

"What's that?" asks Sir Geoffrey, his caterpillar eyebrows arched in hope.

"You didn't kill him."

Cosmo laughs at the idea, and his father shoots him an offended look.

"But who did? And why, and, as my son so pertinently asks, where's our money?"

Maddie tops up her own glass and takes a good belt. "You're in luck. On my quest to get that interview with the Pope, I am going to try to find out."

Now Sir Geoffrey looks worried. "Shouldn't you leave that to the authorities?"

"The authorities seem to be the problem, Daddy," Cosmo says, and Maddie gives him a wink.

She then looks Sir Geoffrey in the eye. "If you want me to tell you what I find out," she says, her emerald eyes hot, "this would be the time to tell me if there's anything more that I need to know. About Zimmerman? About Cardinal Otley? Maybe Victor Franchi?"

The names wash over Geoffrey as he settles back in his chair, and looks at the ceiling. Or maybe he's praying, Maddie thinks. Then he speaks, with the weight of history in his voice.

"Before the Second World War, St. Jude's had some money invested in Hitler's Germany. They were re-arming like mad and our president of college at the time, an economist, saw an opportunity to invest in German armaments. So, we took it. Made about £12 million, which would be worth nearly £700 million today. Once I found out about it, we wanted to make amends."

Maddie feels as if she's been slapped in the face. St. Jude's College invested in Nazi Germany, invested in armaments, guns and bombs and bullets used to kill the very students whose names lined the War Memorial Wall next to the Chapel. Weapons which certainly were used to slaughter English students and European Jews, and everyone else who the Nazis wanted dead.

"So, you made amends by investing the money with Christopher Zimmerman?" Maddie asks.

Sir Geoffrey nods with vigor, his wild gray hair flopping. "Zimmerman spoke on Vatican financial reforms at a conference that I attended in Rome not long after the Berlin Wall came tumbling down. One thing led to another, and suddenly we had fifteen million quid in the Vatican Bank. With it, I set up a fund to help Eastern European Jews get to England, but I didn't want—for obvious reasons—the college to be attached to it publicly."

"So, you're investing money in the Vatican to help

Jews after the Wall comes down. Why?"

Sir Geoffrey sighs. "My paternal grandparents died in the Holocaust, Maddie. They were Jews. My father became a Catholic in France, married a Catholic in England, and raised pious Catholic children. And you are the godmother to my Catholic grandchild. But I feel the need to honor history, not just my own, but that of our world."

It's a lot to take in, this sudden burst of family tragedy and its religious aftershock. Maddie looks to Cosmo. "I didn't know."

He smiles an apology. "It wasn't my story to tell."

"Sir Geoffrey, I'm sorry about your grandparents," she says softly. "And it's a good thing that you did. But you said that there was still £15 million of Jude's money invested with Christopher Zimmerman. He must have been quite good at what he did."

"Oh, he was very good," Sir Geoffrey says. "And you might wonder why we kept that money hidden away in that bank. So, let's just say it was for special projects."

"Ones that you didn't want on the books."

"Yes. Discretionary funds, so to speak. Of quite a size."

Maddie thinks on this. "What could St. Jude's want to do with that money? Unless, of course, you're still helping refugees?"

"We help anyone who needs it, pretty much. But we need to find that money." Sir Geoffrey rises, looking smaller, older. He rises. "I am feeling the weight of the years, children. Cosmo will fix you a place to sleep.

What time is your flight to Rome?"

Maddie has a lot more questions for her mentor, but she sees the fatigue wearing down his face as emotion drains from it. "I have to be at Heathrow at 8."

"I'll arrange a car for 5:30."

He's about to head upstairs when Maddie throws out one last question. "Christopher Zimmerman had a tattoo on the inside of his right wrist, one that read SBUIII with a cross. Do you know what that means?"

Sir Geoffrey stops and leans on the banister. "Yes, it's the Society of the Blessed Urban II. They all get that tattoo as a sign of their eternal pledge."

"A pledge to what?" Maddie asks.

"Pope Urban II is the one who started the Crusades against Islam," Cosmo says.

"Then I'll leave you to the scholarship of my son, Maddie," Sir Geoffrey says. "And thank you for your visit. Just be careful where you step. Mathilda is going to need you. We all are."

Maddie looks at the baby sleeping in Cosmo's arms, loved and warm, safe in his arms. All she needs, she has.

"The Society of the Blessed Urban II," Cosmo continues, "is a very conservative Catholic group that includes both priests and civilians who want to restore the Catholic Church to her proper majesty."

"By launching another Crusade?"

Cosmo shakes his head at the madness. "That's what people say, and that's what they deny. Pope John Paul II loved them, Benedict didn't mind them, Francis didn't like them, and Pius XIII, who loves Islam, hates them.

The feeling, I might add, is mutual."

Maddie is surprised that she hasn't heard of them, but Cosmo is not. "You're a woman, Maddie. Not allowed in their club. All very hush-hush. Almost like a terrorist cell."

"Is Pius XIII trying to shut them down?"

"It wouldn't surprise me," Cosmo says, on a yawn. "Sorry, morning comes early with this one," he says, looking at his sleeping daughter.

"And for me, too," Maddie adds. "Let's call it a night."

"Let me get your bedroom sorted," Cosmo rises.

"Sofa is fine," Maddie replies. She needs to be up before the sun to catch the car to Heathrow, and a bed might be too hard to leave. "Actually, I prefer it. Just a pillow and a duvet and I'm into the arms of Morpheus."

Cosmo turns his shy smile to the floor, his thoughts about Maddie in his own arms. Then, he puts the baby in her hands. "Do you mind? I'll fetch the bedding."

Maddie does not mind. The feel of the sleeping infant in her arms, so warm and softly breathing, so innocent of all that is around her. Maddie touches her goddaughter's soft cheek with her own. She could have been her daughter. Does she want a child? In this world?

It's a question that she needs to answer because as a child who lost a father, she learned how fast time passes, and she does not want to run out of time. Right now, the future is a mystery, and Maddie is in love with no one who could be her child's father. The realization sends a wave of warmth through her body, but not the consoling kind. It's the primal warmth of urgency.

Maddie is so deep into the thought that she doesn't hear Elka pad up the steps from the flat beneath, her eyes trimmed in red, looking as if she has just been rudely awakened from a deep sleep, and that it's all Maddie's fault.

"What are you doing with my child?" Elka asks. It doesn't sound like a question, but an accusation. As if Elka is already sure that Maddie is trying to convince the child that she's a finer person than her mother.

"Hello, Elka. I'm holding her while Cosmo fetches bedding," Maddie replies calmly.

Elka snatches baby Mathilda from Maddie's arms so roughly the child wakes and wails in startle. "Now see what you've done!" Elka snarls, and stomps down to the garden flat with the baby.

Cosmo comes down the stairs to the living room in time to see Elka's trail of vapors. "That did not sound like a sweet farewell," he says, his voice chipper but his face taught with worry.

Maddie shrugs and gives him a grin. "Dear Elka thinks I am back here like some sort of femme fatale to lure you away from domestic bliss."

Cosmo's face softens into one of remembrance and sadness. "Yes, well, you're not right about the domestic part."

Which is how Maddie finds herself two hours later sitting on the sofa next to Cosmo, riding three stiff whiskies, and his tale of woe.

"So that's in a nutshell, Mads. She got knocked up…"

"By you…"

"Yes, by me, and she's very Catholic and me…"

Maddie knows Cosmo is very Catholic, too. And so he and she became "we" and then "three". Maddie feels the need to re-establish her holy presence in their family life before Cosmo does something like try to kiss her, which she can tell he's thinking about because she has seen that look from him before, moving between her lips and her eyes. And, as soon as she thinks it, he tries to do it.

Maddie slips back and gently takes his hand. "That's not going to help anyone, Cosmo."

"No," he says sadly, "but I hoped it would feel like love once felt."

And on that, Maddie kisses him.

When she awakes in the morning, he is gone. But the kiss is still on her lips. And as she rides in the dark to the airport, she knows that she wants to kiss him again.

20. Rome, The Vatican.

One of the things that Cardinal Bernard Otley loved about St. Peter's Basilica is that every morning at 7 AM, its doors would open for Mass to take place in every altar and chapel in the building. Every ordained priest in good standing, from cardinals in the Curia to visiting parish priests from Peoria, could make a reservation with the sacristans, who assigned them a spot and a time.

But Pope Francis ended that custom, during the pandemic, and it has never returned. Now if you want to say Mass in the Basilica, you must participate in a larger group, a joint celebration, or be a bishop leading a herd of pilgrims. Francis was worried about freelancing right-wing nutjob priests turning the theological clock back to the Middle Ages, a concern Otley understood. But even so, the edict had seemed punitive.

Today the punishment is lifted. Cardinal Bernard Otley even feels the grim Zimmerman business that he's been dealing with stands in the shadows this morning because he has been invited to say a private Mass at St. Peter's. Usually he says Mass in his apartment in Santa Marta, alone, before breakfast. Yesterday, the Basilica had called him and told him he had been booked in by the Pope's private secretary. Otley is flattered and happy to oblige for whomever the Pope wants him to meet.

Probably some dignitaries from a country that is best left off the official Vatican guest list, or so the Cardinal thinks as he puts on his vestments. Green now, for the

Ordinary Time between the Church's major feasts. Tipping his head back as he changes, he takes in the elegance of the octagonal sacristy, built in the 18th century and supported by eight columns repurposed from Hadrian's villa.

Despite the room's marbled glory, its silver crucifixes on antique altars, its Old Master paintings of Jesus and Peter and the disciples on the walls, Otley always thinks the Basilica's sacristy is a bit like a very exclusive locker room, where men from around the world gather in the early morning to don the uniform to do battle.

And like athletes or warriors, preparing for a solemn task, the ten priests who vest with Otley this morning obey the command etched in the marble wall above an oil painting of the newly dead Jesus being taken for burial. "SILENTIUM" it reads. Keep silent. The Church has kept silent about a lot of things, including expressing remorse for its own crimes. Otley makes a mental note to say a prayer of healing.

Dressed and ready, Otley stands among the sunlight beams falling down in bright shafts through the windows above in the cupola. They land also on the altar boys in their red cassocks and white surplices, seconded from the minor seminary attached to the Basilica. The boys, maybe 12-years-old, stand behind a burnished oak altar, and dispense the water, wine, and wafers to the priests who are about to turn them into the body and blood of Jesus.

Otley has to smile at one altar boy, leaning on his elbow and yawning as the sunbeams light him up. Just like the work of the upstart, dramatically humanistic Italian painter, Caravaggio, of the late 1500's, Otley thinks. Then, collects the tools of his trade from the sleepy lad, who perks up when he sees the scarlet zucchetto atop Otley's head.

The boy quickly fetches the missal and a censer. Then, accompanied by a navy-blazered sacristan, they lead the Cardinal from the sacristy down the marbled corridor with its barrel-vaulted ceiling and into the gold and marble grandeur of St. Peter's Basilica.

The Basilica is quiet, save for the soft bustle of priests and sacristans, and a few pilgrims attached to bishops as they make their way to their assigned grotto. Otley relishes this time of day, when he feels that he is alone in the glory of St. Peter's, in the center of God's imagination. Or more honestly, he'll admit, how humans have imagined it to be.

The sacristan and altar boy lead him behind the papal altar topped with the large, sculpted bronze canopy that is Bernini's baldacchino. Then, they walk down the stairs to the grotto, where the Irish Chapel of St. Columbanus is found. And beyond the bronze gate into the tiny chapel, Otley can see his audience: the only priest who can wear the white papal robes.

Pope Pius XIII stands as Otley enters, and bows slightly toward him. "Good morning, Bernardo," he says. He has a deep voice, still rising with the musical scale of his Nigerian origin. He is handsome and still fit, Otley will admit, lean and taut, as if he could still make a break for goal on the football pitch. And there is still rapture in the Pope's warm gaze; to be seen by him is to be embraced.

"Your Holiness," Otley replies.

First, the Pope wants to attend Mass. So, Otley says it for him, the altar boy wide awake now and paying close attention, having the water and wine ready, ringing the bells right on time at the consecration.

The simple and austere chapel is characteristic of the Pope's personal style. Otley particularly likes the sea-green mosaic on an apse under the arch behind the altar, depicting St. Columbanus between four monks, in their symbolic walk from Ireland to Italy, with the sun pointing toward their destination, and a dove following, like a spiritual bodyguard.

The Pope is very deliberate in all he does and as he gazes at two inscriptions on the mosaic, and it is the second that tells Otley why they are here, in this chapel. It is a quotation from a letter of St Columbanus: SI TOLLIS LIBERTATEM TOLLIS DIGNITATEM. *If you take away liberty, you take away dignity.*

After Mass, Otley dismisses the altar boy, and slips him 20 Euros.

"Grazie, Eminenza!" he chirps in surprise, his voice just starting to break. He clears the grotto and heads out, mulling over a story to tell his friends, serving Mass for the Pope and getting paid for it by the Secretary of State.

Alone now, Otley sits next to Pope Pius XIII, who is contemplating the mosaic. "It is a beautiful story, is it not, Bernardo? This pilgrimage, this journey of faith."

"It is Your Holiness. But with respect, I do not think

it is why you invited me to say Mass for you here."

The Pope turns to Otley, his brown eyes lit with curiosity. "One of the gifts of the papacy is that I can find new ways to find time for myself. How great it is to have you say Mass here, in the grotto of this great church, and then to sit, as simple priests and speak about the world."

Otley has to hand it to Pius. He thinks like a spy. Finding the moment of light to shine into the darkness. They had been good friends for a long time, when they were Cardinals, but it is hard to be close these days. Otley is perceived to be a power rival to the Pope, a rumor generated by jealous conservative Cardinals. That, he thinks, is also why the Pope has picked this small chapel in the basement of the Basilica to ask Bernard Otley his question.

"Tell me, Bernardo," the Pope says, "where do things stand on the Zimmerman file?"

The Pope knows that Bishop Zimmerman is dead, and that is about it. Otley sees no need to burden the pontiff with speculation from what he would call 'friends in the Church' in New York City until he has more information. Information he wants from his 'new friend', Maddie Lynch. Until then, it is a traditional Vatican play. "We're working on it, Your Holiness," he answers.

"That much I know," the Pope replies, "but what exactly are you working on? And how?"

As for the how, the Pope also knows that the Vatican has the largest, and, so they tell themselves, the best spy service in the world. Every priest and nun, brother and deacon, every devout Catholic layperson is considered part of the network, which the Vatican spymaster deploys as needed. At the heart of espionage stands a lie, and that bothers the Pope.

It does not bother the Vatican spymaster these days, Cardinal Bernard Otley. The caustic English cardinal inherited a machine that has worked in the dark corners of history, and not always on the side of the angels. Indeed, the Vatican has been in the espionage business since Judas gave Jesus the fatal kiss, but things didn't really kick off until another Englishman took aim at the papacy in 1532, when King Henry VIII changed the faith of his nation.

"We are working on healing our bipolar world, Your Holiness," Otley says.

"Ah yes," the Pope sighs. "Rich against poor, secular against fundamentalist, progressive against the conspiracy crowd and so on."

"Don't forget those who wish us ill, Your Holiness."

The Pope smiles a weary smile. "So do we need to have a vast team of spies to fend off our enemies? Was Christopher Zimmerman an enemy?"

Otley is wounded by the question, but he remains calm. To him, it is a matter of spiritual life or physical death, the Vatican's espionage apparatus. It begins in the Pontifical Ecclesiastical Academy which rises above the Piazza di Minerva, where Church's diplomats are trained to be spies, and reaches out to the lowliest parish at the end of the earth which submits reports to Rome. It is vast and comprehensive. And it is necessary. More than ever.

"We have learned that Bishop Zimmerman is dead,

Your Holiness. We also understand a good deal of money is missing from the Vatican Bank. So, maybe he was an enemy."

"How much money?" the Pope asks.

The Cardinal can hardly tell a big lie to the Pope, traditional though that is. So, he tells a smaller one instead. "At least 100 million Euros."

The Pope winces in pain at the loss. "That's twice the deficit of last year?" The Pope isn't one to speak of cash flow and balance sheets. He speaks of the Church's ministry to the poor, but sitting here now, with the Pope's brown eyes narrowed in agony, Otley feels that he must watch out. If he alarms the Pope any further, he could trigger all kinds of house cleaning in the Vatican that could upset the very thing he is trying to do: find out who else is involved in Zimmerman's financial sleight of hand.

"We are confident we will recover the funds," says Otley.

The Pope nods, encouraged and encouraging. "Do we know where this money might be?"

"Not yet. But I trust that we will get to the bottom of it."

"I fear the bottom is deep, Bernardo." The Pope hangs his head, not in prayer. "As for the money, donations to the Church have fallen far because of the crimes some of our brethren have committed, and then tumbled further because of the pandemic a few years back. I am told that if we do not turn this state around, then we could be in default on our debts within three or maybe four years."

Otley wonders who told the Pope this. But he also knows that it is true. Unless a miracle happens, the Vatican could be selling all those holy treasures and works of divine art to oligarchs and tech bros and, if God is feeling particularly punitive, to social media influencers and YouTubers, just to keep the lights on in St. Peter's.

The Pope rubs his forehead, tired and troubled, but then nods at Otley. "We are in the service of the poor. The Church losing desperately needed money is a sin."

"I understand, Your Holiness," Otley replies evenly. "Which makes recovering that money even more urgent."

Otley hears someone walking near the chapel. Saint Peter's was built to carry sound. When the steps come to a stop and someone is possibly listening in, Otley puts a finger to his lips. The Pope's eyes widen in surprise as Otley rises and walks quietly to the door of the chapel. He looks left and right, and sees down the hall the back of the old priest, all in black, with thick gray hair, walking on. Aren't all priests old these days? Otley thinks. It could be any one of a hundred priests.

"I will be visiting America in the late summer," the Pope says when Otley returns to the pew. He hardly needs to remind the Secretary of State of that visit. It is consuming his entire staff every day, given the orgy of logistical detail that the US State Department requires. The Americans and their institutional paranoia about the papal trip make the Vatican bureaucracy look like a model of start-up efficiency.

"It will be a historic visit, Your Holiness," says Otley. That is certainly a lowball view, given that Pius XIII is the Church's first African pope, a son of Nigeria which bleeds hard from the atrocities of Islamic fanatics against the population, Christian or not. And with a kingdom of more than 1.3 billion Catholics, he is a Pope who will step on to the shores of the world's only other superpower—though the Vatican has a much smaller military budget, as he likes to joke. There is much that can be accomplished in this visit.

"Yes," replies Pope Pius. "But there are two types of history, Bernardo. The story lit by the sun, and the story buried deep in the vault, often never to see the light of day."

Is the Pope saying to bury the Zimmerman file deep in that vault? Otley casts out a line.

"We aim to have the story told by the time you are ready to journey to America, Holiness. You can then decide whether it lives in sunshine, or in shadow."

The Pope smiles. "And who is telling this story?"

"We are." Otley doesn't add that he has dispatched his new friend, a female American TV producer, to smoke out the story. The Pope would find that too risky. But Otley is all the more determined to keep the Pope from harm, both sacred and secular, and he must use whatever means he has. And at the moment, he has little, and he is playing a hunch that this secular woman doing the Vatican spy agency's bidding will not attract suspicion. He prays now that he is right.

21. Rome, The Vatican.

Maddie returns to Rome with an image from the video of her father walking past St. Peter's Basilica on the hunt for Christopher Zimmerman playing in her head. Head up, his quick, long strides said he was confident he would find the truth. Maddie walks along the path beside the brown swish that is the Tiber, and feels the teasing warmth of Rome, the place she once reluctantly called home. It is not home now. It is a threat.

She is dressed in a modest black suit and black pumps, hair pulled back, once again to avoid attention, as she knows that whoever put Sister Nuala into an ambulance and then into a grave will be watching her. She isn't sure who killed the Irish nun or Christopher Zimmerman, but how they did it says they were pros, and probably for hire. And until she does know who, Rome remains a dangerous place.

Dottoressa Sister Maria Corvina is surprised to see Maddie as she knocks at the door of the sister's office.

"Spur of the moment," Maddie says. "Still on my travels. But I need to see Cardinal Otley. I have some information that he asked for." She speaks quietly, and in English.

Sister Maria waves her inside her closet of a room that serves as her office, and into a chair. The nun's dark beauty is again packed neatly into a white blouse and cashmere cardigan, still buttoned all the way up. All that is different is the look on her face, and one that tells

Maddie that she is a happy surprise.

Sister Maria clicks through a file on her computer. “It is a true pleasure to see you again, Dr. Lynch,” the nun says on a real smile. “And you're in luck. He has an hour free tomorrow morning. The Hungarian ambassador has just canceled.”

“That is remarkably good luck,” Maddie says, though she thinks Maria Corvina is in on whatever the Vatican is up to and just deleted the Hungarian from the Cardinal’s calendar.

“Will an hour be enough, Dr. Lynch?" the nun asks, her brown eyes catching the soft Roman sun that filters through the blinds. She makes the question seem existential.

Maddie does not want to spend the night in Rome, but it looks as if she has no choice. Nights are always the most dangerous. She can’t let her fear play out in front of this gatekeeper, so she says, “That’s excellent. Tomorrow morning for an hour should be more than enough time.” Unless the Cardinal is going to add to Maddie’s mission.

After the meeting, Maddie walks across St. Peter’s Square, stroked by the sunshine of early May. She heads toward Il Convento, the former convent turned hotel that she stayed in the last time she was here. She wants to see the other nun who gave her the bank certificate that Sister Nuala wanted her to have.

As she enters the cool lobby of the hotel, the desk clerk looks up from his marble desk and forces a tight smile when he sees her, his eyes full of caution. But this wary look is one the clerk bestows on another guest: Bishop Paul Hughes, the Vatican's Undersecretary for the Section for Personnel of Diplomatic Role, coming down the stairs. He lays his heavy-lidded eyes on Maddie, his smile bright and his handshake strong.

"Dr. Lynch, how delightful to meet again," he says.

"As you predicted we would, Bishop Hughes," Maddie replies.

"How goes your quest?"

Maddie smiles to cover her thoughts: If only he knew. And maybe he is not supposed to know. She recalls how Cardinal Otley made sure to say nothing in Hughes's presence. She also remembers that he was also in this same place about the same time Sister Nuala died. So Maddie is careful in her answer. "I am working on it," she says, "and apparently a priest named Victor Franchi can help me. You don't happen to know him, do you?"

She sees the answer scud across Bishop Hughes's sleepy-looking eyes. The ones she thought made him look like a gangster. And still do, even more so now.

"I do know him," Hughes says brightly. "Not well, but well enough to make an introduction for you, if you like."

Maddie had not expected this help. If Cardinal Otley did not know how to find Franchi, how is it that his own secretary Bishop Hughes does?

"What's he like?" Maddie asks, playing this one out, though she would love to say, *"Yes, please and now!"*

Hughes looks up at the ceiling, as if trying to remember. "I don't know him well, but he's a Jesuit. So, he's smart and of the world."

"I understand that he was once upon a time the Pope's private secretary."

Hughes nods, looking at her with sleepy interest, but conveying nothing. "That was before the Pope became the pope, of course."

"What does he do now?"

"I believe that he's working on a book." As soon as Hughes says it, his tired eyes flicker; he realizes that Maddie must think he knows Franchi better than he has let on.

"A book about what?"

"I don't know," Hughes says quickly. "In my job as talent manager of the diplomatic corps, I hear things from all over the world. Some of it just rumors. A tiny bit of it is fact."

Maddie thinks on that. It sounds like Hughes has his own intelligence network, and then she realizes that he does. Every cleric in the Church is a source of information.

"Is he in Rome?" Maddie asks, knowing that he is not.

"I will have to check," Hughes replies. "He's a very peripatetic fellow. Always somewhere else. Will you be here long?"

"I have a meeting with Cardinal Otley tomorrow morning at 10 AM. From there, I guess it depends on where Victor Franchi turns up."

"Excellent," Hughes replies. "Are you staying here? Fine place."

"No," Maddie says. "I'm not. I just dropped in to see

a nun."

"Sister Virginie?" he asks.

Maddie doesn't know the name of the nun who gave her the gift from Sister Nuala. But perhaps Hughes has just given her that name.

"Yes," Maddie says.

Hughes smiles tightly. "I just saw her. She's not doing too well."

That's one dead nun and one ailing nun in Il Convento in less than a month. Hughes reads the look on Maddie's face.

"She is old and frail."

Maddie nods solemnly at this morbid turn. The nun who gave her the folder from Sister Nuala was not frail at all. Her glaring look of suspicion could cut your eyes out and her rage at the deadly bank document could set fire to your fire.

"I am afraid she is the last old nun left in the place," Hughes says. "End of an era."

The way he says it gives Maddie a chill, making her think that there are more eras to end on the agenda of Bishop Paul Hughes. But he smiles now. "I will see what I can find out about Victor Franchi and his GPS," Hughes says. He throttles her hand again in a handshake, his own hand with its amethyst bishop's ring glinting in the filtered sunlight.

But it's not the ring that has Maddie's attention. It's the flash of tattoo she spots as the Bishop's black sleeve rides up. She cannot see all of it, but for the letters "II" and a cross. It must be the SBUII tattoo that Zimmerman had.

That means that Bishop Paul Hughes is more connected to Christopher Zimmerman and to Victor Franchi than he has let on. If he has that tattoo, then he sees the world very differently than she does. And his view is dangerous.

"Thank you," she says. "I will see you in the morning."

"Until the morrow." Then he strides out of Il Convento and into the Roman sun, toward the Vatican.

Maddie heads up the stairs, to the top floor. She walks to the room at the back where Sister Nuala and Sister Virginie lived, and knocks. Nothing happens, so she knocks again. She hears shuffling feet and the door cracks open. Sister Virginie seems to have aged a decade since Maddie saw her last, her tanned face looking gray, her dark hair spilling out of her habit. Her keen brown eyes are glassy as she stares at Maddie.

"Hello, Sister Virginie," Maddie says. "We met not long ago when I met Sister Nuala. You gave me an envelope from her."

The nun stares at her, as if she doesn't remember, or understand. Maddie tries again, in slower Italian.

"I do not recall," the nun says. Maddie sees the look in her eyes is not the killer look of suspicion, or one of forgetfulness, but of cold fear.

"Sister Nuala became ill, and she gave you an envelope to give to me."

"What do you want from me?" Sister Virginie says, the door still cracked open.

"I just wanted to say hello. Bishop Hughes tells me that you are not well, and I am sorry to hear that."

On the mention of Bishop Hughes, Sister Virginie curls inward like a turtle into its shell. "I am sorry. I cannot say anything. I will pray for you."

And then she shuts the door.

Maddie's stomach lurches as she thinks the nun, still young, who was full of anger and suspicion, who probably adored her fellow sister Nuala, has been poisoned. She has never seen anyone poisoned, but when she was a child, her grandfather had chemo for his stomach cancer. And the toxic treatment gave him a waxy pallor until he died. It is the same look she saw in Sister Virginie.

Rushing to the main floor, Maddie hurries to the desk clerk, who delivers another uneasy smile.

"I just saw Sister Virginie," Maddie says in Italian. "She seems very ill."

The clerk angles her head. "You mean Sister Patrizia? On the top floor?"

Maddie feels her cheeks flush. "I mean the nun who lived with Sister Nuala."

"Yes, Sister Patrizia. I am afraid she has declined since the death of Sister Nuala. She has taken it hard. "

Maddie realizes that Bishop Hughes fed her a name, Sister Virginie, to see how much she knew. And she fell into his trap. He's shown himself to be a trap-setter, so he's more dangerous than she thought. "Does Bishop Hughes come here often?" Maddie asks.

"Every day to see Sister Patrizia. He is very good to

her."

Maddie doubts that. Sister Patrizia is terrified of him.

"And she is the last old nun you have living here?"

The clerk nods. "Yes. Bishop Hughes does not think she will be here by summertime."

Maddie thinks about that. Whatever he is doing to her will take her two months to die. July is two months away.

Maddie reaches into her bag and extracts her INN business card. "What is your name?"

"Paolo."

"Can you do me a favor please, Paolo? If Sister Patrizia gets worse, as in close to death, can you please let me know? I would like to say goodbye." She hands the clerk her card, and a 50 Euro note.

"Of course, Signora Lynch," the clerk says, his smile warming into something real as he pockets the cash. "You will be the first to know."

Maddie doubts that, but now she has sent a message to Bishop Hughes. If he is here every day, he will soon find out that Maddie has bribed the staff to keep her aware of how Sister Patrizia's health goes. She has not yet reckoned how that message will matter to Hughes, but the feeling in her gut says she might have just bought Sister Patrizia a little more time on earth.

22. Brooklyn, New York.

Jane Jones curses Maddie Lynch as she empties out another drawer in Maddie's apartment and finds nothing. She had told Brett Muenster that Maddie was the type of person who took her secrets with her. If they want those secrets, they need to have eyes and ears on her everywhere she goes. Since Maddie travels a lot, it is going to take a lot of work.

And Jane's training means she must thoroughly search the place, before she plugs in those eyes and ears. The drawers bear nothing unexpected. There's nothing in the fridge. There's only an old desktop computer on a wobbly Ikea table, leveled up with wads of take-out menus. Then there's Maddie's bookshelf, groaning under its weight, and expanded to stacks on the floor beside it. Jane curses again as she goes through every book, but none have hollowed out middles, containing whatever secret Brett Muenster thinks Maddie has.

She does have some pretty heavy-duty books, Jane thinks. Stuff that she would expect someone who has done a doctorate at Oxford to have. When her cussing stops, Jane remembers how she had longed to go to graduate school herself, and study more chemical engineering. But after West Point, she had to go after the money and that took her straight into Afghanistan. And that was an education she didn't want but couldn't ignore. It was in the mud and poppy fueled mess of that savage place that Jane Jones learned to kill. With stealth and cunning and without being seen.

Brett Muenster doesn't want her to kill Maddie Lynch. Yet. After she poked her journalistic nose into Zimmerman's death, thanks to the nose of her ex, Patrick Farrell, Muenster has to know what else she knows, first. Jane Jones has half a dozen mini-HD cameras, the size of after dinner mints, inside her bag, but there's really nowhere to plant them so that Maddie won't spot them in this very bare bones apartment. And besides, they won't get inside her head.

The solution is obvious to Jane. Maddie's desktop computer will be the spy device. Of course, killing is Jane's thing, but Muenster talked her through it and said if need be, they would start off with "plug and play". In fact, he said, "A child could do it."

That was insulting. But even looking at the lumpen, smug Brett is to be insulted, Jane thinks.

"Here we go, kids," she says, mocking Brett's idea that her work is child's play as she plugs a USB stick into Maddie's desktop, and boots it up. The stick contains a RAT, or remote access toolkit which will allow Muenster to see what Maddie is doing. Jane then powers up her laptop and connects to the USB on Maddie's desktop.

She enters the three codes she needs, and just like that, she has cracked Maddie's password—lostcause001!. Jane is inside. Once Maddie logs on from wherever she is, she will infect that login device, as well. Her phone, and her laptop will be speaking directly to Jane.

She zips through Maddie's world and sees the files

connected to her INN mission, and opens them up.

"OK, kids, what's this?" she whispers when she finds the file "The Vatican's Nazi Money." She opens it and even Jane gets a chill as she sees the collection of articles on Zimmerman.

Moving fast, Jane opens the video file named for Zimmerman and sees that Maddie's own father was after Christopher Zimmerman for his family bank's connection to Nazi gold. But actually, that's good. If Maddie follows that trail, she won't find the other one, the one that she and Brett took care of when Jane took care of Christopher Zimmerman.

Even so, Brett Muenster is paranoid that Zimmerman has not deleted all his blackmail. He insisted Jane scour Maddie's files to see if she has anything connected to Reagan Clark. The only contact Maddie has is Brett Muenster's contact details.

Next, Jane hacks into Maddie's Gmail, then pokes around her Google docs. Nothing about Zimmerman there, either, or about Reagan Clark, which could come back to haunt them.

Jane sits for a minute and plays it all forward; Maddie is smart, very smart, and as a journalist she has digging capability. If Maddie is following the Zimmerman money trail, anything can happen. And she must be watched. It's what they're paying Jane to do now, and she likes it better than having to kill people. She doesn't want to kill Maddie Lynch. Looking around the spartan apartment, nothing there signals to Jane that someone is starting a big new chapter in their life. It's the lair of a woman who is bright, alone, not exactly following her heart's desire, and stubborn.

Not so different, she thinks. But of course, if she must, then she will have to kill. She saved Brett Muenster $250 million. He can send a little more of that her way.

But she doesn't trust him. He would love to sleep with her, but that is not in the cards, not in any way you deal that deck. Jane is well aware after being in the army and working with thousands of guys, that if they are fucking stupid then they are stupid. And that is dangerous. In this assignment, she needs to leave herself an escape hatch. Just in case Muenster goes stupidly sideways.

What kind of escape, Jane is not sure, but she will know it when she sees it.

For now, she leaves Google docs open, to see if Maddie Lynch notices. And what she'll do if she does. Jane has learned that you can never have too many options, and that Brett Muenster will sell her out if he needs to. She's not betting on Maddie Lynch, but she feels something she never usually feels. She kind of admires her. And she is going to give Maddie a chance to prove that she is right.

23. Rome.

It's a little before 8 AM in Rome when Maddie, fresh from the shower and still in her fluffy cotton hotel bathrobe, pours herself a frothy cappuccino from the coffee machine in her room, and then logs on to her computer to check her email. But she can't. She is locked out.

She tries again, thinking there must be some glitch with her password, but again, she's blocked. Could INN have shut her out? No, they wouldn't do that unless they'd fired her, and they wouldn't fire her in the middle of her Pope quest.

It's the middle of the night in New York, so she can't get any help from Aretta until noon in Rome at the earliest.

She feels the blood heat up in her cheeks. This is the last thing she needs, so she tries one more time. She types in her password, and she gets in.

She goes to check her Gmail, and sees that her Google docs are open. She did not open them. Maddie freezes, as if she has just been held up at gunpoint. Someone is inside her computer.

Her Google docs contain her Pope Pius XIII file, and some of her father's material. Plus there are the articles on Zimmerman, and the first of his videos about the man as the young banker, even pictures of him on a Hawaiian beach, looking far too appealing for the priesthood. But she stopped copying them when Patrick pinged her phone, to set up a meeting about how Zimmerman died. It had been a feeling. One that now seemed like fate.

Maddie learned in the basic hacker training that INN taught them that there are a few signs to see if you're hacked. Battery drainage, slower speed, strange web pages, the webcam turning on randomly, and items in your search history that you didn't put there.

To be sure, Maddie goes into Google to check her history, but then realizes that if she's being watched, they will watch her do that. So she closes her laptop but doesn't power it off.

Maddie dips a biscotti into her coffee, but she cannot eat anything as her stomach feels packed with ice. All she can do is sip her cappuccino and try to make sense of what she just saw.

Who would want to look into her life?

It could be someone at INN, looking into what she's found, but that could open up all kinds of HR issues. Aretta would just call her if she had a question, and Teddy wouldn't know how to hack her. Asking someone to do it would be a very bad move, even for Teddy.

The Vatican. No, they want her help, and she wants their help, so there's no reason to spoil that equation by spying on her.

Patrick Farrell? He could do it, but why would he? Besides, he probably had more powerful ways of spying on her than she could ever imagine.

Or maybe it's a mistake. Maybe she's so stressed by recent life that she forgot that she left her Google docs open.

Maddie likes the last option and that is the one that she will accept until she can contact Aretta, and get INN's tech nerds on it.

Maddie relaxes. Until she knows who, if anyone, is following her digitally, she will go back to a style of journalism that her father promised her would never be obsolete. Pen and paper. The only way that anyone spying on her can find out what she is thinking or doing would be to steal her notebook. She had already been writing notes in a book, on her phone and her laptop. She promises herself to be much more monogamous to that notebook. And in these days of high-tech spyware, she is pretty sure that no one would think to look there.

"Good morning, Dr. Lynch," Bishop Paul Hughes says about an hour later. At least Maddie didn't have to bump into him again lurking in the lobby of the hotel. But this time, he is waiting for Maddie in the doorway of the Secretary of State's building.

"Vescovo Hughes, buon giorno," Maddie replies. Seeing if she can draw the priest into Italian, where she can judge him through a different lens, but he sticks to English.

"Ah, very good." And with that he dismisses her excellent Italian. "How was your visit with Sister Virginie?" he asks.

"She was in fine form," Maddie says, not letting on that she has the nun's real name. "Couldn't stop her talking about the old days with Sister Nuala. Working for Bishop Zimmerman."

Hughes's ruddy cheeks flare up at that news. Which

is what she wanted to see. That could be his 'tell'. Her father taught her to look for a giveaway tick or blink in people who you think are lying to you, a response that they cannot control.

"Good," he replies, more calmly than his face looks. "She has good days and bad days, so glad that you caught her in a good spell."

"I will keep a close eye on Sister," Maddie says. "She is very dear to me."

Hughes nods at that promise as if it is a challenge. She has sent her message, so if another nun turns up dead anytime soon, he'll be her prime suspect. She waits to see if Hughes will finally step aside, but he still hovers at the door.

"We're meeting Cardinal Otley out of office, as it were." Bishop Hughes leads Maddie back outside, then walks briskly to another ancient marble building, through a heavy and ancient wooden door, and suddenly, into the Sistine Chapel.

"One of the perks of being Secretary of State is that I have my own key to this place," Otley booms, shaking Maddie's hand. Looking at her over his half-moon glasses, his blue eyes shine. Even Otley himself is surprised by how glad he is to see Maddie Lynch.

"Good morning, Eminence," she says, relieved to know the chapel is safe, but her eyes are all over the majesty of Botticelli and Ghirlandaio and Michelangelo surrounding them in the otherwise empty chapel.

"Do you have a favorite?" the Cardinal asks, gesturing to Adam and Eve, and to the angels and God himself in the frescoes on the ceiling, as if they were old friends.

"Hard to argue with that one," Maddie says, pointing to the first of the nine panels in the ceiling, where Michelangelo has depicted a burly, bearded God dramatically thrusting apart light from darkness.

Otley crackles in delight. "Ah ha, mine, too. The beginning of it all, light from dark, day from night, good from evil."

Then he turns to Maddie and looks at her with that air of an Oxford don, expecting a snappy reply to the mention of evil.

So she says, "Yes, and about evil.... Bishop Zimmerman was murdered."

Otley touches his pectoral cross, and Bishop Hughes looks at Maddie as if she just confessed to the crime.

"Do you know how?"

Maddie glances at Hughes, and Otley catches the look. "Bishop Hughes is working on this as well, Maddie. That's why I have asked him to stay."

Maddie nods as if this is totally normal, but she wonders why, at their first meeting, Hughes was banished, and now, at their second, he is here and listening in. That, and one dead priest and a dead nun and another one on the way out. He clearly plays for another team, and either Otley is wise to this and wants to play him. Or, he wants to play her.

"He was injected with drugs to make it seem like he had a heart attack."

Otley considers this, and glances at Hughes, who

frowns.

"Any idea of who'd want to do that to him?" Maddie asks.

A silence hangs over the vast room, perhaps the kind of silence when the cardinals assemble in the chapel to elect a new pope. Otley remembers he had cast his vote here for Pius two years ago, almost. Right now he says, "Well, it wasn't me."

Maddie looks at him to see if he's joking, but he's not.

"Do you have any ideas, Dr. Lynch?"

Maddie does, and she has to tease them out to get what she wants. The phantom Father Victor Franchi, for one, whom people seem to know but don't know where he is. And an interview with the Pope for two. And she has to think that Father Franchi connects to Zimmerman and also to her father for three. Her own holy trinity.

"I think he was involved with some shadowy characters," she says, "besides the ones who killed him."

Otley hangs his head as if to digest the large size of this killing conspiracy. "Do you know who they are?"

Maddie thinks about trying out her Father Franchi theory, as he shares a tattoo with Bishop Hughes. So, she keeps her eyes on him, watching for his 'tell'. "I need to speak to Victor Franchi," she says, smiling at Hughes. "I gather Bishop Hughes has an idea where he is."

Otley turns to Hughes with curiosity. "Did he finally turn up, then?"

Maddie thinks the question is sincere, by the note of hope in Otley's voice. He also had no clue where Franchi was, who had been missing for a while. If Hughes has any information, maybe he'll cough it up now to his superior and under the eyes of God above, in the fresco.

"He's back in Jerusalem, Eminence," Hughes reports, another blush heating up his craggy face. "He had gone off the grid, but he's surfaced at the Biblicum."

"Maybe that's where he was writing his book, as you were saying," Maddie adds.

"Dr. Lynch, you would know the spot as the Pontifical Biblical Institute," Otley says.

"I do." Maddie knows it too well. A weight of memory hits along with the half ton of photocopied papers she had to drag around the Biblicum for her D.Phil. Nothing at that old library was ever online, not from the second century, the century she studied. The place does research and teaching on biblical and ancient Middle Eastern subjects, and it is run by kindly Jesuits – who even helped cart away the ton of photocopies.

"Do you know how long he's there for?" Maddie asks.

"I do not," says Bishop Hughes.

"Thank you, Bishop Hughes," Otley says. "I will not keep you any longer."

Hughes's heavy-lidded eyes flutter a little, and then he nods. "If you need anything else Dr. Lynch, please just ask. Otherwise, give my regards to Father Franchi." He hands her his business card, and then flips it over and writes on it Franchi 's Jerusalem location.

"I will, and thank you."

Bishop Hughes gives her a curt nod, and then he leaves, taking slow steps. Listening as he goes, Maddie thinks.

Cardinal Otley seems to relax. “Thank you for your information, Dr. Lynch. And for his,” Otley adds with a nod to the back door of the chapel, where Hughes vanished.

“Please, call me Maddie,” she says, as she feels that any kind of breakthrough that she is to have in her quest will require a breakdown of barriers.

“Well then, please call me Bernard,” he replies. “When we’re alone.”

Maddie’s eyes land again on the back door Bishop Hughes just exited, as she says, “I take it that you had a reason for wanting to be alone. Here in the Sistine Chapel.”

Otley sits down on one of the chairs reserved for the chapel attendants, and wipes his brow. He has been sweating, even though the chapel is cool. “Yes, the place is jammed,” he says, and Maddie looks around at the empty space, then back at the Cardinal. “By jammed I mean that they installed gear during the last conclave to prevent any Irish bookmakers from hacking us and making a fortune off the papal odds.”

Maddie wants to tell Otley that she thinks she has been hacked, as well. It would be a confession to see if she gets one in return. But she does not; she can’t seem weak in any way. Instead, she turns back to the murdered priest.

“Do you know if Zimmerman has any connection to Father Franchi?”

Again, he bows his head. “You have done good work,

Maddie. There is indeed a connection between them, but I know not what. All I am sure of is that they worked together in Rome when Zimmerman was installed here as a bishop."

"Franchi worked at the Vatican bank?"

"He did." Otley looks up fondly at Maddie over his half-moon glasses. "It would seem that you are your father's daughter in more ways than one."

"And I think there is more to the story," Maddie says.

Otley surprises Maddie by pulling up his sleeve and tapping his arm where Hughes and Zimmerman had their tattoos, where he has none, then nodding to the back door. Maddie is sure he means those two men, but he says, "I think you have poked a bear, that you might not have known you poked. And now you must keep the bear from…"

"Killing me? And all I wanted was an interview for my boss with the Pope." Maddie smiles with sweet irony.

"Be very careful around Victor Franchi," he says, his eyes unblinking, serious. "He was close to our Pope, but he is… an unknown commodity these days."

"But he can get me my interview."

"I do believe that he can. But be careful of what he asks in return."

"You're not saying he's the bear."

"I'm not saying," Otley now smiles. Then, he reaches into his cassock and produces a card. It's his business card; just his name, and his title. However, he has scrawled his cell number on it, to make it bespoke for her. "I keep late hours, Maddie. If you need me, call me.

Anytime. Any reason. And after you meet with Franchi, send me a flare, if you don't mind."

Maddie takes out her phone to put her number in his, but then realizes the place is jammed and she can't get a signal. And that maybe whoever is watching her is watching her phone, too. She needs to get a new one. But she can't tell Otley that, so she scrawls her own cell number on a piece of paper and hands it to the cardinal.

"Same with you. It will be on Signal. Encrypted."

Otley perks up. "Encrypted is what we need."

It's at that moment Maddie realizes that Otley's use of the "we" refers not to the Vatican, but to them both.

So she takes a breath and asks, "I am working for you, Bernard?"

Formulating his reply, Otley turns to take in the first mural, the one he loves, of God struggling to separate light from dark, as if they were street brawling. He pauses, thinking how Christopher Zimmerman and James Lynch and his daughter Maddie have all come to this point. He needs Maddie to say yes. "Not for me, Maddie. But for the good of the Church. Is that something you can accept?"

Now long ago she would have said "No". She can't say "No" now and expect to get the story she needs. But she is also aware that she doesn't know what she will find on this mission from the Vatican. So she joins Otley at his side and studies their favorite work. "Separating the light from the dark. If it was good enough for God, well then…"

Otley's hoot of laughter, booming through the chapel,

takes Maddie by surprise. And Maddie laughs. And in her light, bright laughter, she hears a long-lost voice of the devout Catholic schoolgirl she once was.

Faith is the one thing she needs now, but not the kind that turns bread and water into flesh and blood. Faith that the story which she is chasing is the one she will find. And that it will not be the story that ends her own.

24. Rome.

Maddie walks over the ancient cobblestones of the sunlit piazza in front of St. Peter's Basilica, embraced by the rounded marble colonnades. The crowd has grown with the good weather and fills the piazza today, chatting, stopping for selfies, blocking her way. Maddie slaloms across the piazza and realizes that she's suddenly hungry.

This morning, she couldn't eat out of cold fear that her life was violated by a cyber intruder. Now she wants a heaping bowl of pasta because she feels something she had lost has returned. Faith. And it's a faith in herself.

She follows her memories of Rome, of dinners out with her father and mother over steaming plates of pasta and bumpy walks down the cobbles of Borgo Pio. She steps into the first osteria that she encounters, the Italian version of a tavern. She orders some bruschetta, and a bowl of spinach ravioli. As much as she'd like a glass of wine, she sticks to water. Instinctively, she pulls out her phone to check her messages. She opens her Gmail, knowing that if anyone is inside her computer, they are going to see what she sees right now.

So she sends a note to Aretta, her colleague at ITT, to update her with a lie. Maddie begins to weave a thread of lies that will reveal just who broke into her life. And why.

Hi A, Or should I say "shalom". I am in Israel, chasing down a lead for the Pope interview. Looking great. Will call later. Hope all is well in your world, M.

Maddie scrolls through her other messages, most of them asking for money by various progressive action groups. Her Columbia Chiclets hockey team has a practice for their semi-final game in ten days, and she will have to miss it. And there is a note from Luke Macclesfield, her fellow godparent. He's in Rome, right now, and hoping for prayers and a pint.

Maddie shakes her head at herself; she should have read her email first and not just wrote Aretta that she is in Israel. But then Maddie nods to herself as she recalls Luke works at the Vatican Apostolic Archive. After she gobbles down her lunch, paying in cash in case anyone is watching, she makes the six-minute walk to the library in four minutes, tossing a few looks over her shoulder as she goes, if anyone is still watching.

Of course, the gatekeeper at the library entrance has other plans. Maddie does not have a permit for the archives, which were once secret but now are public—sort of. A peek of the archival glory opens up for Maddie behind the gatekeeper, looking like a stunning cross between a giant Renaissance art gallery, as painted by Raphael and friends, and an eternal library stuffed full of every document about the Church from year one to now, including a few secular items like the original folio of *Hamlet*. The academic in Maddie would love to go in, but maybe at least she can try to have Luke brought out. To do that she produces Cardinal Otley's card, like the ace in a royal flush.

The library attendant, a man in his plump fifties,

glowers in suspicion. Maddie suggests, in impeccable, academic Italian that he can call the Cardinal should he not believe that the Secretary of State has asked Maddie to meet a scholar who is working in the library.

"What is his name?" asks the attendant.

"Dr. Luke Macclesfield, of University College Dublin," Maddie says.

The library attendant sniffs at this as well, and reaches for the landline phone on his desk. He whispers into it, and Maddie hears Luke's name and Cardinal Otley's.

"I have delivered the message," he says, and Maddie thanks him. He never asked for her name, so Luke probably thinks he's meeting the Secretary of State.

Which is why he emerges about a minute later on the run, and when he sees Maddie is there and not a cardinal, he grins at her as if he just won a bet. "Maddie! You're here!" Luke steps forward to embrace her.

"And I am very glad that you are, too," Maddie hugs him back. "Do you have time for a coffee?"

Luke pulls back from her as if she's somehow forgotten that she's in Rome. "A coffee, sure, but a drink would be far better!"

Maddie agrees that it would, and the library attendant understands enough English to give Maddie a paternal smile, now, as she and Luke exit into the parking lot that is the Cortile de Belvedere, and out on into the piazza.

Luke knows a bar just on the southern side of the piazza, and it's warm enough to sit outside and clink together two cool glasses of Italian white Pinot Grigio.

Though it is warm for May, Luke wears his worn

tweed jacket. He flattens his auburn tangle of curls with his left hand, as if to tamp down his surprise. Then he takes off his glasses, sure he looks better without them. But then he can't see Maddie and slams them back on. "I have to say this is a wonderfully unexpected reunion, Godmum."

Maddie has to smile, knowing all the hair and glassses fuss is for her benefit. "Well, Godpa, you did say that you were going to be here when we last met."

"I did. A month ago in Oxford, fending off Satan for Cosmo's kid."

Maddie thinks of Cosmo and his kid now. She can still feel the pure heat of that last kiss. And wonders, does she want it to be their last kiss? He's married, and she always said she would never fix love for a married man. But what if she is still in love with him? He's emailed and texted with hot promises and she's replied in short with her own placeholder promises of more, later.

"You look like you just saw a ghost," Luke says, catching her thinking of Cosmo.

"The mention of Satan always does that to me, Luke."

"Sounds like you've met the dude in person." He seems so concerned for Maddie, his big bulge of a forehead furrowed in worry. She has to trust someone, and she is certain that Luke is not the one who broke into her computer. So she tells him as much as she can. About the Vatican mission, including her back door visit to the Sistine Chapel, with updates on Hughes, Franchi and the possible intruder in her computer.

When she is done, Luke is silent, staring at his glass.

"Wow," he finally says.

"Spoken like a true Oxford scholar," Maddie jokes.

Luke laughs, and then gets them two more glasses of wine. "It sounds as if you're the Vatican's Jane Bond." He even looks around the bar, at the herds of tourists filling the street, to see if anyone is watching.

Maddie laughs now. "I don't think they go in for that sort of Bond thing, Luke." But then she thinks about her recent conversation with Cardinal Otley. He did say they were working together. And she is on a secret mission. Without, so far as she knows, a license to kill.

Luke leans forward quickly and whispers, "Oh, but they do. There have been spies in the Vatican for centuries. I'm working on something in the archives now that connects to the Vatican's intelligence work in World War II."

Maddie slides her chair right close to his. "So you're in the part of the Secret Archives that they opened up? The part dealing with 1939-1958?"

"Those are my years. They call it the Apostolic Archives now, but even so, they kept that stuff hidden for a long time."

"Can you tell me what you're working on?"

Luke looks around again, as if there might be other scholars looking to poach what he's going to tell Maddie. He leans closer. To passersby, they look like a young couple having a romantic moment in the Eternal City. To Maddie, it looks like some mysterious force might have just landed on her side.

"I'm working on the ratlines," Luke says. "You know,

the ratline is the rope that rises to the mast on a sailing ship. The last point of refuge when the ship goes down."

Maddie has heard about them. "And the Vatican had ratlines, which were escape routes for Nazis fleeing justice after World War II."

Luke lifts his glass and toasts her in scholarly admiration. "That's the one."

Maddie then adds to her story. She tells him about her father's files, and the gold deposited into Christopher Zimmerman's bank by Josip Babić .

"Who is he?" Luke asks.

Maddie shrugs. "He has a Croatian name, and gave the Vatican money in World War II, so I am guessing he worked with the Croatian fascists. Or he did not and was trying to finance some kind of escape."

Luke smiles in delight. "Wow again. I'm working on the American angle, and you're working on the Croatian. It's destiny, Godmum! Maybe we could collaborate on a book?"

Maddie wants to keep Luke enthused, and she has to keep that possibility alive. "Sounds great, Luke. The thing is, I have to go to Israel on the first flight I can get."

Luke shudders. "Be careful there, Godmum. Their war in Gaza has made them even more enemies."

"I will," Maddie says. She knows that the enemies of Israel have multiplied and will use whatever they can to extract their revenge, and wherever and on whomever, on soldiers or civilians or American visitors. She also feels herself deeply conflicted about a place her father loved. She does not love the ruin that its self-serving prime minister and his rightwing thug of a cabinet inflicted upon Gaza and Lebanon, and ultimately upon Israel itself with his crimes. But she has to go.

"So, Luke, if you could do me a favor while you're in the Secret, sorry, Apostolic Archives, that would be amazing."

Luke grins like a schoolboy about to be rewarded. "Yes. Of course. I'm here for another week. What do you need?"

"I need you to find out as much as you can about Josip Babić, and who he was working with inside the Vatican. Because I want to find out where that gold went."

Luke nods enthusiastically, his auburn curls bouncing along. "Excellent plan! Happy to do that. I'll make notes and email them to you. Or maybe create a Google doc and we can correspond that way."

Maddie sees the hope in his eyes that now, they finally have a connection that doesn't pivot on Cosmo. "Thank you, Luke," she says, "and I have one more favor. Don't send me anything electronically. I can pick up a copy of the notes when next we meet."

Luke gives her another sorry look of concern. "Right, the prying eyes in your computer and all. It's pretty easy to get that stuff out of your machine, you know. I can take a look if you like."

Maddie does not want Luke in her computer. He's a history scholar, not a techie. "That's OK, Luke, I'll talk to IT back in New York in a couple of hours."

"What are you going to do if they have broken in?"

Maddie has thought about this all morning.

"Nothing," she says. "That would give them an advantage. I will see if their spying on me can lead me to them."

Maddie's cool remark seems to blow Luke back into his chair in alarm. To warm up, he sips his wine. "Well, all I can say is that if you're not the Vatican's Jane Bond, you should apply for the job."

Raising a glass of wine to herself, Maddie trips her head back to laugh. But she knows Luke might be onto something.

After a hug and a promise to be extra careful, she bids farewell to Luke and then goes in search of a shop that sells cheap cell phones. She needs one to call Aretta, because whoever might be watching her will also be in her phone.

And she can't use her phone to look up where a cell phone shop might be. She spots a group of Italian teenagers hanging out in front of the McDonald's on Borgo Pio, and they tell her there's a cell phone store a ten-minute walk away on Via Candia. $200 later she has a new cell phone and an international SIM card, good for a couple of months.

"Aretta, hey," Maddie says when she calls her producer as she steps into a quiet doorway on the Borgo Pio.

"Maddie! Great to hear from you. How is Israel?"

"I'm not in Israel. I'm in Rome." Maddie tells her the story of why she said was in Israel. Because someone is watching her computer, and her phone. She thinks.

"Yikes, Maddie. Who would want to do that?"

"I don't know. But I need to know if I've been hacked. Do you have someone in tech support that you trust?"

"I have just the girl. Are you near your computer?"

"I will be in about 30 minutes."

"Great. Call me then, and I'll have her with me, and we'll figure it out."

"Thanks, Aretta. And until we know, this phone is our only way of communicating the real stuff, OK?"

"Got it. Talk soon."

Maddie hustles back to her hotel in Trastevere. She picked this modern lodge far from the nun's hotel because she figured they'd have excellent security. And that Bishop Hughes would not be here.

Sitting at the hotel room's gleaming glass desk, she opens her laptop, and things are as she left them. Then she downloads WhatsApp for her smart Samsung Galaxy. She finds Aretta in the contacts list and calls her on video.

"There you are!" Aretta says, smiling at Maddie. Next to her is a young woman Maddie has seen around, but thought she was a camera girl because she has that air of genetic calm that all camera people seem to have. "This is Paula Martino, from IT, Maddie."

"Hi Paula," Maddie says, and waves.

"Hey Maddie." Paula, in her 20s, is tall with lively brown eyes hidden behind thick glasses. She waves back and smiles. "So Aretta filled me in. You saw a document open on your computer that you don't remember opening?"

"Yes. In Google docs."

"OK," Paula says. "If someone is watching you, I don't want to email you a link to let me in via remote." She chuckles. "But I will walk you through some options so you can do a self-check. We'll make it seem normal."

Maddie feels relief. Paula instructs Maddie to open a website that won't reveal anything unusual. Restaurants, or gift shops or art galleries or anything that will seem like she's planning the rest of her day.

"I'm not in Israel, Paula. Not yet, but I want the watcher to think that. So you're going to see Israeli locations because of that and not because I'm crazy!"

Paula frowns. "They probably know you're in Rome. If they are watching your computer and phone, they will have your IP address. Or maybe they can trace your phone. Take the battery out, OK?"

Maddie takes the battery out of her hacked phone. "What should I look up then?" she asks Paula.

"Maybe check out flights home."

Maddie opens Kayak on her laptop. And types in a search for flights to New York.

"OK, now that it's open, open your Task Manager."

Maddie does and then Paula asks, "OK, what's your CPU usage at?"

"66 percent," Maddie says.

Paula whistles. "And that's with one website open? Anything else?"

When Maddie tells her just Word and Gmail, Paula nods. "OK, look down the list of processes. Is there anything that you don't recognize?"

Maddie gives Paula a pleading wince. "How about

you look? I don't recognize most of it." She aims the phone at her Task Manager screen and scrolls down.

"OK, got it," says Paula. "See that process called Service Host: Service?"

"Yes."

"No such thing. See how much CPU juice it's using? Nearly 60%."

Maddie feels like she wants to strangle whoever did this.

"So do you want to know how to remove it?"

Maddie has weighed this outcome all day, and now that it's here, she knows what she must do. "No, I'm going to leave it where it is."

Aretta looks at her with concern, and Paula asks, "Really?"

"Yes. I don't want them to know that I know. Because that's how I'm going to find out who did this. Thanks, Paula. Aretta, just keep the same tone in your emails to this address, OK? You don't know any of this."

"OK, Maddie." Aretta's dark eyes are hot in concern for her friend. "Where are you going now?"

"This time I really am going to Israel. I will call you from there. Oh, and use my old phone for all work calls, otherwise they will suspect."

"Cool!" says Paula. "And I promise not to tell. OK?"

Inside, Maddie is a furnace of fury. She has inherited both her mother's temper and her father's sense of control, and while they aren't always in sync, they are now. "Not as cool as you might think, Paula. And when I find out who did this, not cool at all."

25. Jerusalem.

Jerusalem is a timeless golden maze of stone, where time itself seems to have been invented and touched by the hand of God, along with the hands of many ghosts. Even more now, she thinks, after the attack by Hamas on the country, and the lethal rampage by Israel in response. However, there is only one ghost whom Maddie sees as she sits in the Cellar Bar of the American Colony Hotel. There in her mind's eye is her father, auburn curls smoothed back, green eyes giving a wink to her as he raises his glass of Jameson's when the electronic muezzin calls for prayer at the mosque next door.

The Cellar Bar is not a big place, but it's in a palace built for a pasha. Its intricate tiles and smooth stone corridors beneath white vaulted ceilings and its fragrant gardens of mulberry and olive trees conjure the Ottoman days of this city that has seen so many rulers. Now it and the bar are run by United Nations officials and journalists. Thankfully there are none from INN's Jerusalem bureau, or she would smash a bottle of whiskey on their heads and feed them the glass shards for having let her father die on assignment.

She even took her father's favorite old room, the last one at the top and back, so the long trot to the door would expose any snoop that was following him. She slept there like she had escaped Rome with her life, a dreamless sleep that was six hours long but felt double that. Maddie didn't even need her face cream to calm the edges of her eyes where tiny wrinkles are already staking their claim. She slipped into a cool cotton dress and came to the bar.

Maddie nurses a cold Taybeh, one of the popular Palestinian beers, as she thinks over how this place is made both for secrets and conspiracy. So very true now with the afternoon sunlight dappling its ancient pink stone floor, and the nooks and low ceiling that make you feel as if you are hiding out, or making an escape.

In the outdoor pool beyond the bar's glass doors, Maddie watches the swimmers. There are two Muslim girls, maybe 10 and 12 years-old, wrapped up in black t-shirts and black Capri trousers and watched over by an unsmiling older sister wearing a hijab, struggling to keep her eyes off the man that also has Maddie's attention.

He is tall and lithe, just cresting six feet, when he bounces on the diving board. His hair is the color of flax, and his tawny skin is exposed to maximum effect by his white Speedo. His face is as fine as any on the cover of a fashion magazine, sculpted and clean, his aquiline nose bridging full lips. With one more bounce he dives from the board in a gentle arc and slips into the water without making a splash, then surfaces into a forward crawl that Maddie recognizes as one of a competitive swimmer.

Then Maddie recognizes that she has not stared at a man she didn't know like that for so long.

"Is that your young man?" asks Father Victor Franchi, his voice raspy, his blue eyes sharp as he gazes at Maddie's vista. "Nice form."

"No, I'm a single woman!" Maddie says, and then stands to offer her hand. "Father Franchi, very nice to meet you." She shakes the priest's strong hand in both of hers. His tanned, lined face seems to find more wrinkles as his cheeks fold back and he beams at Maddie.

Franchi's hair is still black and swept back, his nose is thick and solid, but his blue eyes sparkle with life and a liking for women. True to his Jesuit order's ethos, he has come in civilian clothes, though in his case, it really amounts to removing his Roman collar, as his worn loafers, rumpled black suit and white shirt pretty much scream "priest off duty".

"You look so much like your lovely mother," Franchi says, taking Maddie in. "With your father's eyes."

Maddie takes a sip of beer to hide her surprise. Victor Franchi has just dealt her a very surprising pair of cards. He brings up her father before he's even had a drink, and he has also met her mother. She takes his measure, because Google gave so little. Franchi must be sixty-five years old, stringy but strong. His light blue eyes are lit up with wary intelligence. "I didn't know you knew my parents," Maddie says.

"Oh, we were all in Rome together," Franchi responds. "I even met you when you were a *ragazza*."

Maddie doesn't remember meeting Franchi when she was a kid. "Oh? Where was that?"

"Ah, I thought I was memorable to everyone, even a babe!" Franchi chuckles, and orders a large Jameson's whiskey. "We met after Mass one Sunday morning. At the church of Sant' Anna de' Parafrenieri."

"St. Anne of the Grooms," Maddie says. She remembers going there with her parents once, or twice.

It's the parish church of Vatican City, just inside the Santa Anna gate.

"Yes, your father took us all out for lunch afterward. Pizza joint on the Borgo. To celebrate my sermon, and as he put it, the fact it was over."

Maddie smiles at the line that could only be her father's, and has a flicker of memory at eating a few pizzas with her parents on the Borgo, but not with Victor Franchi.

Franchi takes a slug of his drink and closes his eyes. "Your father, God rest his soul, now he was something."

"He was," Maddie agrees. She feels she has never missed him more than at this moment. "I take it you knew him pretty well?"

"He wanted my help on a couple of stories. One about some dubious financial dealings in the Vatican, and I knew one of the players. Good story, most of it true. Too bad it never took off."

Maddie feels her stomach lurch as she thinks about her father's work on Vatican money laundering. "And you said most of it was true."

Franchi chuckles. "If the truth were the only governor of public discourse, then most of our lives would be swathed in silence."

A cold thought cuts through Maddie. Maybe someone wanted to silence her father? To keep Franchi talking she orders another beer. She learned in Oxford that, thanks to her Irish genes, she can drink three times as much as most people to no ill outcome, or at least, not one she notices.

Franchi is Italian, and they can drink too, so he pounds back the rest of his whiskey, then waves to the waiter for another. “Now that's a taste of the divine, as well. But you didn’t come all the way to Jerusalem to hear me tell you that.”

Maddie would love to tell him that she knows he belongs to a right wing Catholic society called Blessed Urban II, after the pope who started the Crusades against Islam. But he’s also the guy that can help her get an interview with the Pope. She can’t rip his covers off and scare him away.

“It's a pleasure to come back to Jerusalem,” Maddie says. “I spent time here with my father.”

Franchi raises his glass of whiskey in the direction of the mosque. “*Cin cin,*” he says, just as James loved to do. The mimicry is chilling to see. He takes a sip, still looking at the mosque. It’s as if he wants to draw Maddie into a conversation about the deficiencies of Islam. So she shakes off the ghost of her father and takes the bait.

“Perhaps they find their cheer in other ways.”

Franchi grins at the idea. “They certainly do. Murdering each other, along with Jews and Christians seems to be their chief pleasure.”

“Really?” Maddie is ready to swat that anti-Islamic blast off the table, but she knows she can’t spit out the bait and hook just yet. She takes a long pull on her beer, pretending to think on the merits of that statement. Then she says pleasantly, “Pope Pius is very keen that the Church repair its relationship with Islam.”

Franchi sighs, annoyed. “I know. I used to work for

him. And I used to agree with him. But now I think it's best if we just make the Church smaller. And in that way, make it bigger."

Maddie spots the SBUIII tattoo on Franchi's wrist as he takes another sip of whiskey. According to the philosophy of that group, as Cosmo told her, the way to make it bigger is to eliminate all progress. "How do you mean make it smaller?"

Franchi pauses, forming his delivery to her. "The Church is here to advance the message of Jesus Christ. He wasn't concerned about Islam or climate change. Just his own perfect philosophy. That's it."

Maddie wants to kick back at that extreme redaction of the message of Jesus so she changes the subject. "Bishop Hughes says you're working on a book."

"Yes, it's a study of the Knights Templar. A much-misunderstood group." Franchi downs his second glass of whiskey, stares at the empty bottom of the glass, thinking of a third. But then he says bluntly to Maddie: "So, you're a busy woman and I don't want to keep you. What is it that you want from me?"

Maddie tells him with a straight face: "I'd like your help arranging an interview with your old boss and Teddy Wright, my current boss."

Franchi wheezes with a laugh, as if the request is news. "The Pope doesn't exactly call me up for advice, these days. And if he did, advising him to talk to Teddy Wright would not be top of my list."

Maddie is ready for that one. "I'm sure it wouldn't be on the top of a lot of people's lists, but that's the point. It will give Pope Pius XIII an audience for his message that will be diverse and large."

Franchi shoots her a hard look, going from summer to winter in a second. "I suppose he'd be grateful for what, a few million privileged Americans hearing his views on, uh, ecumenical life."

Maddie lets out a soft laugh. "You're absolutely right. Teddy Wright looks at this interview as proof of her power, and I am sure she wants to get into it about Islam with the Pope. And I look at it as proof of the Pope's smarts about the media in letting her have a go. Either way, the message gets out and people embrace it, or they do not. And everyone I spoke to in Rome says that the Pope listens to you."

Franchi smiles warmly again at Maddie in a way that lets her know he likes women in general and her in particular. "Flattery always works on me. Who made such grand claims for my humble self?"

Maddie is sure Franchi already has the answer, so she tells the truth. "Cardinal Otley, the Secretary of State."

Franchi chuckles. "That great old queen!? Otley's one of the leaders of the Pink Mafia."

Maddie opens her eyes, as if surprised.

Franchi smiles. "Oh yes, he's on the team of gay bishops and cardinals who wield uncommon power at the Vatican by virtue of their homosexuality." He snorts a little laugh. "And that in a Church which considers them intrinsically disordered. It is one of the many contradictions of the place."

"He has been 'straight' with me," Maddie replies

wryly.

Franchi nods, enjoying the pun. “Don’t get me wrong, I admire him, insofar as one can admire an Englishman. He's slippery though. You need to be wearing ice skates just to talk to him.”

“You worked with him?”

“When you spend as much time as I have in Rome, it quickly becomes a small company town without the steel mill, though it does belch smoke from the corporate chimney every few years.” His lined face folds like an accordion, as he enjoys his own joke. “You get to know everyone, at least by reputation. And despite the fact he's queer as a nine-dollar bill, he's a bigger player than anyone in that crowd. Smart enough to play on the house team, and of course, that lands him where he is today. Running the show.”

“I thought the Pope runs the show.”

“That's what Otley wants you to think,” Franchi says with a touch of impatience. “Now you have to ask yourself, why would he want you to talk to me if he could wave his fairy wand and make the Pope do a TV interview with your boss?"

Maddie has asked herself that. Otley, for whatever reason, wants her to meet Victor Franchi. She needs to find out why. So she serves up the one name that might open the bank. “Do you know Christopher Zimmerman?”

Franchi's eyes narrow, as if looking for the trick in the question. “Our paths have crossed. Why?”

“Well, he's dead. Murdered.”

Franchi doesn't blink. "I'm surprised it took this long."

It is hardly a priestly thing to say, but Maddie senses that Franchi is not an average priest.

"He had a lot of enemies?" Maddie asks.

"He was a banker before he became a priest. Maybe his past caught up to him. The man himself was a pompous git. Your father knew him. I did not, really."

Maddie's stomach lurches again. Her father connects to Franchi and Zimmerman.

"That's what your father was working on when I met him in Rome. Zimmerman had just joined the Vatican Bank, and your father was turning over rocks to see who crawled out."

"My father came to you?"

"All roads do, apparently," Franchi says. Then, as he cocks his head from side to side, he adds, "The walls have ears in this place." Taking the cocktail napkin, he writes down an address. "This is me. Tomorrow, any time after high noon."

And then he is gone.

Maddie sends a quick WhatsApp message on her new phone to Cardinal Otley: *Met with Franchi. Seeing him again tomorrow. New phone. Explain later. Maddie.*

Maddie hits send and casually glances around the room. No obvious spies catch her eye. Two guys in yarmulkes are having an animated discussion about something amusing, given their laughter; a quartet of TV Brits are planning logistics for the next day's shoot, which, owing to the amount they are drinking, is going to start late; and a couple of UN types are ostentatiously reading official documents and nibbling on their large salads. And the guy Maddie admired in the swimming pool is now dressed in faded jeans and a loose turquoise sweater and sitting alone at the bar.

He turns his head at just that moment to catch Maddie's eye. He smiles, just a little. Not sexual, but friendly, two people of the same age in this place. So Maddie smiles back, and before this becomes more than an exchange of smiles, she puts the drinks on her room's tab and leaves. There is much to think about with a clear head before tomorrow comes. And she has the feeling that Victor Franchi is more than a few steps ahead of her.

26. Ein Karem, Jerusalem.

Late on the following afternoon, Maddie sets out from the lobby of American Colony and into the soft sunshine, off to the address that Father Victor Franchi has given, to a private house in Ein Karem. It's a district in western Jerusalem, with abundant trees filtering the sunlight over curbside cafes, onto hipsters drinking exotic coffees. The area is one of those treasures the ancient city serves up: you can find the hand of God pressing down on the Peoples of the Book as they tramp the ancient stones of the Old City, or you can find mysterious priests living in charming limestone villas at the top of Ein Karem Street, with views of the valley where John the Baptist was born.

Maddie walks to the front door, which is barred by a heavy iron grill. Above it is a security camera. She pulls on the bell, which has a chain, and Franchi opens the inner door. He straightens the rumpled collar on his white shirt as if that is all that needs to be done. Then, he flashes her a mischievous smile, like he's having fun. "You'll have to come around the back, I should have said. I don't have the key for this thing."

Maddie goes around to the back of the house and up the stairs, where there is also the snow cone sphere of a dark gray security camera looking at her. Father Franchi is clearly careful about who he admits. He greets her at the door with a warm handshake, and ushers her inside.

The look on Maddie's face makes the priest smile. Her

eyes are wide at the opulence before her, the cool blue and white Palestinian tiled floors bearing the weight of elegant oak chairs and tables near open French doors leading to a vine-trellised Garden of Eden, and beyond it a private orchard of lemon and pomegranate.

"Don't worry, it's not mine. Just a loaner from a wealthy friend."

"You have good taste in friends," Maddie says. She wonders if the "wealthy friend" has the stolen gold that bought this place. But she says, "The question is why, when I look at the paradise valley where John the Baptist hails from, would he ever want to leave?"

Franchi shares a grin of agreement that only gets bigger when he unbags the bottle of whiskey Maddie has bought him from the American Colony, on her own expense. She doesn't want the vultures in INN's accounting department picking at the flesh of this visit.

"Ah, bless you," Franchi says, cradling the bottle of Jameson's Gold Reserve. "Damned hard to get a decent dram in this part of the world, unless you have your own bar. Care for some?"

Franchi goes to fetch two glasses and Maddie takes a look around to see who this wealthy friend might be. A rich gun-runner? A well-funded politico? No framed family photos, no mail. Nothing personal. Even the books in the cases climbing the walls are about the Christian history of this part of the world, as Maddie would expect.

She's not surprised either by the two fat shots Franchi has poured. He brings the bottle with them out to the filigreed iron table on the terrace. The perfume of the garden is sweet and spicy, like the air has been sprinkled with cinnamon.

"Some people call religious psychosis the Jerusalem Syndrome, but I think it's the smell of the place that does it," says Franchi. "Nowhere that I have been smells quite like it. Smells like... paradise." He raises his glass and clinks it against Maddie's. "Here's to your father."

It is an unexpected toast. Maddie blinks away the tears in her eyes that rush to fill her eyes, and then drinks deep.

"He's the reason you're here," says the priest. "I didn't haul you out to the rustic suburbs to wax on about John the Baptist. It's your area of study, no?"

Maddie is on alert. First, Franchi brings her here because of her father, and now he reveals he's checked her out, too. "I did my thesis on the second century's Jewish soldier, Simon Bar Kokhba, and his war against Rome. But yes, I am fascinated by how an obscure rabbi from Nazareth wound up creating this religion long after he was dead."

Franchi chuckles at the "obscure rabbi" line. "It was either because he truly was the son of God, or his followers were under the Jerusalem Syndrome way back then."

Maddie laughs, but Franchi's humor doesn't put her at ease.

"I think the whole story is a sequence of the miraculous," says Franchi, suddenly serious. "'To me every hour of the light and dark is a miracle. Every cubic inch of space is a miracle.' That's Walt Whitman by the way, but I agree with him."

Maddie does not reply; she does not believe in miracles.

"In any event, it's the never-ending story, isn't it?" says Franchi.

"My father always told me that all stories end. It's the telling of them that goes on and on."

"And do you think his story ended?" Franchi asks.

Maddie is startled by the question. "Yes. But he is with me here," and she taps her head, and her heart. She's angry now. What does Franchi mean?

"And that is why you're here," he continues, "enduring the deceptive fragrances of the Holy Land, is it not? To continue the story?"

She holds her drink two handed to calm her urge to wrap her hands around Franchi's neck. He is playing with her, so she plays back. "In a way, yes. We always want the ones we love to live on. But my main mission is to get your help to have the Pope speak to my boss on American TV. And I can keep my job and keep my own story going."

Franchi dry laughs crackles at that. "Yes, nothing like the prospect of being hanged at dawn to focus one's attention. But I am here to help you. I will call Joe Okonkwo, who you know as Pius XIII, and put in a good word."

Maddie feels a swell of relief pulled back by a chill of suspicion. "Thank you."

Franchi smiles, his grin bracketed by hard lines, and reaches under the table. Maddie is prepared for anything, even for the priest's hand on her knee. When he comes back up it is not a gun, or a bomb, or a Bible. But instead he hauls up a scuffed leather briefcase, one that he must have lugged around since he began his priestly mission. Maddie wouldn't have been surprised to see moths fly out of a skull when he opens it, but inside are neatly stacked file folders, yellow at their creamy edges. And inside them, another story waiting to be told.

Franchi shuffles through and removes a folder in the middle. It is labeled "*Incompiuto.*" The Italian for "Unfinished."

"Bishop Zimmerman, even as a priest, had real talent with money. He put right the finances of his first parish in Hawaii, got a new roof on the church, started a soup kitchen, and a youth group. A miracle in itself. The Vatican took note. They wanted him back home to help run the bank. But he said 'no'." He then slides the folder over to Maddie, who angles it into a patch of sun that has become a spotlight on the table and opens it.

On top is a typewritten letter, dated March 8, 1997. It is addressed to none other than Father Christopher Zimmerman, c/o Cathedral Basilica of Our Lady of Peace, Honolulu, Hawaii, USA 96813. And at the top of it is the letterhead from the Vatican's *Istituto per le Opere di Religione*. The Vatican Bank.

Maddie looks up again at Franchi. The pupils of his light blue eyes are like laser dots. "Zimmerman said 'No' to the Vatican. I'm sure that didn't go down well."

"You're about to find out."

The letter from The Vatican is to the point.

Dear Father Zimmerman,

We look forward to your presence at our next board meeting on 2 April to take up the position that His Holiness John Paul II has chosen for you. A representative of the IOR will contact you shortly to arrange your passage to Rome.

Yours in Christ,

Archbishop Joseph I Okonkwo, ✝ *Secretary, IOR*

Maddie has to catch her breath. The Vatican muscle is pretty clear, and the muscle belonged to the man who would become Pope Pius . But she cannot imagine the might of the response that will be launched by this wandering priest on an island in the middle of the Pacific Ocean.

Dear Most Reverend Okonkwo,

Thank you for your clarity, which I feel it is only responsible to reciprocate with. I will come to Rome to take up the post I have been most generously offered on three conditions: I am promoted to bishop, I am given freedom to manage the financial affairs directed to me at my discretion (or why bring me there at all?), and I am given accommodation in a Vatican apartment worthy of my office. I do not think priests living in a residence need to be troubled by my banker's hours.

Lastly, I enclose a photograph that has come into my ambit, and which has shocked me as it will no doubt shock you. If it is as easy to take such a photo of the Holy Father, it would be just as easy to shoot him.

I look forward to your response. Yours in Christ,

Father Christopher Zimmerman

And beneath the letter is the photograph of Pope John Paul II, sunning himself by his swimming pool at his summer residence of Castel Gandolfo. Naked as the day he was born in Wadowice.

At that moment, the spotlight of sun that lit up the letters and the photograph disappears behind a bank of Jerusalem pines. Maddie is stunned. This is not only a naked Pope, but naked blackmail.

"Quite," says Franchi, reading the look on Maddie's face. "And Zimmerman got what he wanted."

Maddie studies Franchi, who seems amused by it all like a middle school boy flashing naked girlie pictures in the locker room. "But I thought you didn't know Zimmerman?" she says, testing.

"I don't know him when I'm in the American Colony," Franchi replies, with an Italian shrug. "The place is a den of spies. Present company accepted. Maybe?"

Maddie goes for wide-eyed wonder. She is a spy of sorts, one of her own making, and one of the Vatican's. "How did you know Zimmerman?"

"I was the secretary to Archbishop Okonkwo at the time, as my provincial—that would be my Jesuit boss—thought I would be a good money man. I was OK, but I was much better as an archivist. I kept everything." He turns his lined smile on his stack of files and gives them a loving pat. "I should have given it to your father, when he came looking."

Maddie follows the logic. "And you thought if you gave my father this stuff, it would come back to bite you."

"Yes, and it would bite him. But I'm giving it to him now, through you. It was a sign from God to me when you got in touch and wanted to see me, and then asked after the late Bishop Zimmerman. And I don't care if it comes back to bite me anymore." He sits back and his smile having fled, and with his flash of mischief fizzled, he looks old.

Maddie sees this as an opening. "What do you know about Christopher Zimmerman and Nazi money?"

Franchi is not surprised by the question. With another sigh, he heaves himself upright and pours them both another fat shot. "I don't. But he's from a Swiss banking family, and it would not surprise me if they had a hand in washing some of the gold stolen by the Nazis during the war."

Maddie tries not to smile at her win: she asked Franchi about money, and he answered with gold. "And that laundry wound up in the Vatican?"

"We'll find out now that the archives are open." Franchi rubs his face and thinks again. "Of course,

Zimmerman might have done some of his own archival research and retrieval before the Pope opened the archives to the public."

"So, anyone who thinks the Secret Archives relating to the wartime papacy of Pius XII is a pristine and faithful record is naïve."

"And an idiot," Franchi adds, naughty smile back in place.

So, she looks at what she has, the letters and the photo of the still healthy mountain climbing Pope John Paul II sitting in front of her. God had brought them together, as Franchi said. And Maddie has to admit that she wouldn't have been here unless she'd pursued an interview with the current Pope. Now she is being offered the chance to finish the story her father couldn't tell. It is a kind of destiny.

"There's another thing," she says. Franchi leans closer, as if they are in the confessional. Maddie feels her heart thudding as she summons up the right order of words.

"An old nun in Rome gave me a document. A Croatian guy transfers a million dollars in gold to the Zimmerman Bank."

"Did she now?" he says. "Interesting. Who was the guy?"

"I don't know yet. But we do know the Vatican had ratlines and helped Nazis escape after the war."

Franchi looks at Maddie with a sudden fury in his eyes, then he smiles. "We are all sinners, but we find redemption in our faith. Which is one of forgiveness."

But forgive what? So she asks, "And is that why Christopher Zimmerman also became a priest? To be forgiven?"

Franchi nods solemnly. "So he said."

Maddie strikes quickly now. "So why would he steal 250 million Euros from the Vatican Bank?"

Franchi reacts to that with alarm. "He did what?"

"He took their money and then he was murdered, and they don't know where the money is. I don't suppose that you have any ideas?"

Franchi cocks an eyebrow at her. "You ask that of me as a keen observer of humanity and not as a potential accomplice, I assume."

Maddie smiles back; it is a challenge. "Just asking. The Vatican would like to know."

"I am sure they would. So would I. That's a helluva lot of money. You could start a revolution!"

Maddie laughs at the joke, but in it, sees that indeed Zimmerman could start a revolution. But what kind? And with who?

"I know you'll be able to handle yourself if the beast tries to clamp its jaws on you," Franchi suddenly says, surprising her with this violent image. He frowns into his empty glass, pulls the briefcase shut, then he stands.

"I thought you wanted me to take those documents," Maddie says.

"I want you to take what they reveal. I can make you copies. Tomorrow, at the Biblicum. You know it?"

Maddie had been herself to the large teaching institution that specializes in biblical and ancient studies.

"I do."

"Come when it is quiet, after 3, and I will give them to you." Then he moves closer to her, like some kind of biblical sage. "I'm keeping the originals with me. After all, when the beast comes to bite, it has to find something. And doing this might just keep you safe."

27. Jerusalem.

Maddie hurries away from Franchi's house and west, down Ein Karem street. She sees a mini-market up ahead. Ducking inside, she buys a bag of pistachio nuts, but really, she is watching the street to see if anyone is watching her. She steps outside and looks both ways. There's a guy on a motorbike opposite who checks her out, but he's just being a guy, Maddie thinks.

She downloads the app for Gett, Israel's version of Uber. The driver arrives inside of two minutes, and Maddie gets in and hangs on as he drives through the labyrinth of Jerusalem so fast it's as if he's trying to cram as many fares into the hour as possible. Maddie turns and looks out the rear window, but there are no guys on motorcycles following her.

When Maddie arrives back at the American Colony, she needs a drink. Not the kind she just had with Franchi, but one to clear the noise that has swirled in her head since she left him. He showed her blackmail from Zimmerman, and that's what he had not shown to her father. To protect him, he said. But now Maddie thinks Franchi has put her in danger, because he wouldn't give her the documents in case the beast came back to bite. The beast he protected her father from is still out there.

She orders a cold Taybeh beer in the Cellar Bar, which is surprisingly empty, save for the British TV crew still here and still drinking for England, and opens her Gmail on her phone. She glances out at the pool to see if

Mr. Olympic Swimmer is cutting the waves, maybe in a Speedo-show-all backstroke.

No luck. So, Maddie checks her old phone, knowing whoever is watching will watch what is on her phone, even if she's not sending, just reading. Catching up on what they already know.

There are nineteen new emails in all, but Maddie clicks on the message from Aretta that has as its subject line "Are you still in Israel?" And when Maddie opens the message, Aretta says: *Please call me.*

Maddie sees on the old phone that there are seven missed calls from the INN office. She knows that Aretta will have kept that news from Teddy. Maddie also sees that she has a WhatsApp message from Cosmo, much shorter than the others. *Will you ever speak to me again?* he asks.

She will, but when they are in private. She types back, *Yes. Soon,* and winces. She hates to be so brief when her heart swells to read his text, so full of things to say. But she must be brief, to protect him and to protect her goddaughter.

Then she calls Aretta's cell phone on her old phone's WhatsApp.

"Maddie, thank God," Aretta says. "I was so worried when I couldn't reach you that I thought, well, you also had a heart attack."

"I'm so sorry, Aretta." Maddie curses herself. She wants to say more but cannot. "I am getting closer to our Pope interview for Teddy. I've got the Pope's pal to back us."

"OK, great," Aretta says, her voice low, as if Teddy might be nearby. "Look, I have a favor. I need you to do a recce for us. Reagan Clark has made a surprise visit to Israel. She's holding a kind of revival meeting at some Christian theme park tomorrow morning."

"The Land of God," Maddie says, trying not to groan.

"You know it?"

Maddie wishes she didn't. Her father took her there the last time she saw him to witness what he called yet another fraud committed in the name of the rabbi from Nazareth. As James Lynch had said, "It makes Disneyland look modest in its brand promotion."

"Won't the Jerusalem bureau cover it?" Maddie asks, having no desire to visit The Land of God.

"They'll get the news angle. But Teddy wants the intel on Reagan's agenda. She still wants that interview badly and she wants stuff that she can use, you know."

Maddie knows. Teddy wants all the ammunition she can get. "OK, what time?"

"I just emailed you the details, and your media credentials. It kicks off at 11 AM. I don't think you'll need a hotel for the night. It's under a two-hour drive from where you are to there, so says Google maps."

"That's good as I have a meeting here at 3 PM tomorrow. And I need to get a car. I can ask at the front desk."

"Thanks, Maddie. I really really need to give Teddy some good news, you know?"

"Yeah, I imagine all her toy throwing. But yes, getting Teddy and the Pope in the same room is looking very possible."

"Should I tell her yes-ish?"

"Yes-ish. And keep your head down when she throws the Tonka trucks."

Maddie ends the call and finishes her beer. Then she sees the handsome swimmer who she saw here the last time in this bar, smiling at her now as he enters. She smiles back, and just like that he's standing by her table.

"Hello," he says. "Do you mind if I join you?" He looks over at the loud and loaded Brits. "I don't think I can catch up to them."

Maddie laughs. His accent is a mix of the Mediterranean and somewhere else.

"Gabriel de Almeida Schmidt," he says, offering his hand as he sits.

"Maddie Lynch," she says, shaking hands.

"You have a strong hand."

"It's from ice hockey," she replies.

"You must be a professional."

Maddie laughs. "Only as a hobby. I work in television. In New York."

"Ah, you're a journalist!" he says on the whitest smile Maddie has ever seen. Up close he's even more beautiful than at a distance. But her interest is aesthetic. Cosmo has her heart, or at least, is closest to it. But she is happy to look. He orders himself a Taybeh, and Maddie explains to him what she does for Teddy Wright.

"*I'm Wright*! Yes, I have seen that show. She is real?"

"Sometimes too real."

Gabriel laughs with a voice that is surprisingly deep.

"So, her views are not just acted for show? She seems so angry at everything all the time."

"No, that's really her. I have the marks on my back to prove it." Gabriel laughs again. "It's a strategy that plays to both the left-wing and the right, since everybody is angry about something. Teddy unites them in rage."

"What are you angry about?" Gabriel asks, seeming to mean it.

"I'm angry at the past," Maddie replies, surprising herself by giving voice to the rage inside her. "Angry that I can't change it."

He smiles sympathetically. "So, then you have to change the future, no?"

"Are you a philosopher?"

"I'm a journalist, too," Gabriel says, then smiles a little sheepishly. "I'm from Brazil. I'm a travel writer, so not a real journalist. But I get to cover places like this."

Maddie offers her own sheepish smiles. "Most people don't think TV is journalism. So I think the idea of what's 'real' just means how true is your story? Now that anyone with a cell phone can be a journo."

Gabriel laughs again. Maddie feels a burst of pleasure as he seems to truly appreciate her. Maddie has had enough guys try it on with her that her antenna is acute, and Gabriel just seems to be friendly. Or maybe gay. Or both.

"So what brings you to Israel?" he asks.

Maddie takes a sip of beer as she ponders her two answers to that one, and she gives the short one. "I have to interview someone for Teddy Wright. And I just found out that I have to go to the Galilee tomorrow morning for an event. You don't know where I could get a rental car around here do you?"

"Yes, I do. You can have mine."

"Really? That's incredibly kind, Gabriel."

"You know what," he says, his brown eyes alight. "I could drive you up there. I have never been, and I could do a piece on where Jesus walked and so on. Timely, all things considered."

"That's really generous. But I have to be back in Jerusalem by midafternoon."

"Not a problem," he says on an easy shrug.

"That's wonderful of you, Gabriel. I really appreciate it. The thing I'm covering starts at 11 so I need to be there by—"

"10 AM," he says. "Galilee is about two hours away. And we give ourselves an hour of safety. So why don't we leave at 7:30?"

Maddie smiles at this genteel Olympic swimmer who has turned into a journalist and now a chauffeur. She'd love to have another beer with him, so she breaks that magnetic current by standing up quickly. "I will meet you in the lobby then. I have to prep for tomorrow. I just got the assignment."

Gabriel graciously meets her, standing up and shaking her hand. "How exciting to be a real journalist and get these late assignments. *Bons sonhos,* as we say in Brazil."

"And to you," Maddie replies quickly, leaving the bar and aiming for the elevator, already looking forward to tomorrow. Of course, her Irish genes kick in and she knows that whenever she feels that feeling, trouble is just around the corner. She smiles to herself. What more trouble could she be in than she already is? And she hears her father's voice inside her head: "*Trust yourself. Trust the story.*"

28. Near Tiberias, Israel.

The Land of God Christian theme park sits on fifty acres of lush green Galilean land, more like the rugged Scottish hills than the parched sands of Israel of biblical imagination. Built about ten miles to the north-west of Tiberias, one of Judaism's four holy cities, it is close to a nearby hill on which Jesus delivered the Sermon on the Mount.

Maddie is surprised they could get that much land and not have to plow under a temple or church to do it. And she can't help but think that Reagan Clark has chosen this huge place to deliver her next campaign speech to become the President of the United States—not because she wants to bless the meek, but because she wants to anoint the strong. Herself. With a large and friendly audience who need friends like her, especially now.

The Land of God is garish, as if its architects found the landscape around it—the verdant hills, and the glimmering sea of Galilee—to be inconveniently subtle. So, they surrounded it with a twenty-foot-high wall built from the pale limestone of which so much of Jerusalem is built, and they closed nature off.

"Wow," Gabriel says as he stands with Maddie at the entrance. "I couldn't have made this up."

They try not to laugh out of respect for the other visitors. "Maybe you should write about it," Maddie says. "I'm sure your fellow Brazilians will think you have a talent for fiction." She has done her homework as always, this time on her new phone, and found a healthy online presence for Gabriel. He has a few travel pieces up on South America about food and wine, and a couple on France and Spain about football and beach holidays. She knows he likes flying business class, but there's nothing that reveals his preference for men or women, or anyone.

They laughed a lot on their drive up to Galilee from Jerusalem. Maddie found his company easy, and he asked thoughtful questions about her life. The only odd thing she noticed was that when she responded with questions of her own, he always found a way to redirect it back to her. Either he was some kind of old-world gentleman, or he was hiding something.

"Do you think I could get into the event?" Gabriel asks.

"I don't know. I need a media pass. But you can pay and get into the grounds and take your chances."

"A bargain at $50 American!"

The main gate, featuring a massive arch with its two faux ancient wooden doors now open for business, is guarded by a couple of Arabs dressed up like Roman soldiers, so that the neon 'Land of God' box office sign and computerized turnstiles are out of sight until the visitor has passed into first century Jerusalem.

Arabs playing first century Jews peddle their wares—cedar crucifixes and Palestinian pottery—along Jerusalem Street without any irony as far as Maddie can see. There are no winks from the vendors to her that they are in on the joke. One shop, next to the site's synagogue, even features plaster statues of Jesus.

"If the rabbi from Nazareth returned to claim his kingdom in this place," Maddie says, "he might become an atheist."

"Or if he spotted this from wherever he is, he won't come back at all."

Maddie stifles a laugh with a cough. This place was built with American dollars from evangelical Christians in the belief that they have to convert all the Jews before Jesus will return in glory. The Israelis, badly needing friends at the time, and even more so today as much of the world is wary of their revenge on Gaza, leased them the land for free. The result is a place that only those with a special kind of faith could love. One that takes the Bible, Maddie thinks, as literal.

There are more tourists here today than Maddie expected, and they are from all over. She hears French, Spanish, and a lot of English. These aren't people who came to travel through Israel, and walk where Jesus did. They are time traveling back to their Bible.

Maddie feels that time flip herself as she flashes her QR code to a Roman soldier in a silver breastplate and a red bristling Galea helmet. He is armed with a shiny black QR reader at the entrance, and instantly, she is inside this strange world.

Even odder is the young woman waiting for her, breathing hard, in her early 20s. She wears a plaid skirt, stockings, and a white blouse under a blue Land of God blazer. Her teeth are large and fill out her big nervous smile, and there is a pinch of anxious blush on her round cheeks.

"Dr. Lynch, I am so sorry. I was delayed in greeting you," she says, extending her hand. "My name is Beth Jeffers, and it is my pleasure to escort you to the venue."

Her accent, to Maddie's ear, is inflected with Georgia, and she grins when Maddie ventures a guess. "Yes ma'am, I am. From Marietta. I'm here for a year abroad from Georgia Christian Tech."

Gabriel catches up to them and smiles at Beth. "Hello," he says, "I'm Maddie's assistant, Gabriel." He offers his hand to Beth, and she shakes it.

"Nice to meet you, Gabe. I'm Beth. Please follow me."

Maddie is impressed and a little alarmed by the way Gabriel has so easily slid into her world. And he can lie, as well. But she gives him a welcoming nod, and he nods a thank you back, and they follow their guide along 'The Way of the Prophets', past a white-haired guy dressed in a simple brown tunic, leaning on a staff, his eyes closed.

He startles Maddie by suddenly bellowing in English, "A voice is calling, clear the way for the Lord in the wilderness; Make smooth in the desert a highway for our God!"

"That's the Prophet Elijah," Beth Jeffers says. "Let's nip down here."

She hangs a right down the Via Dolorosa. Even though it's twice as wide as the one in Jerusalem after which it is named, Maddie and Gabriel and Beth have to squeeze against a wall to make way for a troop of grim looking Roman soldiers, carrying spears, marching past with purpose.

"The killers on parade?" Maddie says, and Beth Jeffers looks at Maddie with quiet astonishment. "I just mean that they look efficient. Like the Roman squads were. Very authentic, Beth," Maddie says, and Beth gives her a smile in return. So does Gabriel, liking her comeback.

They move on, past the 'Raising of Lazarus' exhibit, and the 'Loaves and the Fishes' cafeteria where you can buy a grilled fish sandwich and a carafe of wine, all for $20. Maddie thinks the fact that the Evangelicals allow booze on the premises could be a miracle in itself, but then, profit is ecumenical.

"Great place for lunch," Beth says. "It's vegan friendly!"

"I'm looking forward to the wine," says Maddie, feeling far too sober.

"Me, too," whispers Gabriel, staying close to her side.

Beth Jeffers smiles tightly, unsure of this pair, then heads toward the golden dome of the venue where Reagan Clark has chosen to speak.

"The Temple of All Nations is designed to look like the Colosseum in Rome," Beth says, nodding, impressed by the building.

It is an odd choice, Maddie thinks, given that venue's hospitality to Christians. It served them up as lunch for lions, and practice dummies for gladiators, or tarred them with pitch and set them aflame to light the arena's nocturnal entertainments for Nero.

The Temple can hold two thousand people, and today

it does. It has thoughtful modern updates from its Roman Empire ancestor: a glass domed roof and air conditioning. Beth escorts Maddie and Gabriel to the guard at the gate, a burly Arab wearing a blue Land of God jacket and Gucci sunglasses. She shows him Maddie's media credentials, and he processes Maddie and her assistant Gabriel on a QR reader. The guard directs them to the standing room section to the left of the altar, where Reagan Clark will speak.

"Thanks very much, Beth," Maddie says. "I can take it from here."

Beth Jeffers looks confused, as if this is not part of the script that she has prepped. "It's no problem to stay with you."

"That's generous of you, but I have Gabriel here to help me. I'll be fine."

Beth now seems relieved. "OK, well, here's my number if you need anything. Always happy to help our friends in the secular media!"

She hands Maddie her card, and Maddie slips it into her jacket pocket. "Thanks, Beth," she says. Once Beth has vanished, Maddie says "Let's mingle among the flock."

"I can leave you to it," Gabriel says. "I just wanted to get in…"

Maddie is grateful for the offer. She feels suddenly better about Gabriel. "OK, thanks. I need to focus. How about we meet back at the entrance at 12:30?"

"Sounds good," he says. "And you have my number if you need me."

"Will do," she says, and he's off. Maddie makes her way into the crowd, one made up of evangelical Christians, Orthodox Jews, and a few VIPs from the Knesset, along with the Minister of Tourism, sitting in the first row of blood red velvet seats, waiting for their American messiah.

And then Reagan Clark herself, with no fanfare or introduction, bounds from behind the red velvet curtains and on to the altar. A quick clatter of applause rises, to which Reagan bows humbly. Then she starts on in.

"I am, as you know, pro-life," she says, her voice a pleasing confident alto, coming from the chest and not the nose. "In our throwaway culture, where we shelve the old and the infirm, and speak about murdering the unborn as a 'right', it can make you lose your faith in your fellow human being. It can make you wonder if we are living in the End Times."

The crowd screams in agreement and cheers. Maddie marvels at how Reagan has worked abortion and the apocalypse, twin fetishes of the far-right conservatives, so quickly into her opening to have her audience cheering already, just thirty seconds in.

She is also certain that this opening will not be followed by a condemnation of the child abuse at the Mexican border. Or the millions of kids who went to bed hungry because of poverty, or because their undocumented parents died in the pandemic along with hundreds of thousands of Americans which the government so badly bungled. These people only care about people they can control, Maddie thinks, but then

Reagan Clark surprises her.

"And I say to myself, we will be living in the End Times if we fail to recognize that we are under attack. And that we are heading to our doom, like the Jews of Europe under Nazi Germany."

Reagan Clark stares at her worshipful audience unblinking, eliding from Armageddon to the Holocaust as her opening gambit before an audience in Israel.

Maddie is struck by the contrast between her Old Testament oratory and her scrubbed American image. Reagan Clark looks a decade younger than her fifty years, and she's tanned and fit as one would expect the Governor of Hawaii to be. She wears a cobalt sheath dress and cream jacket, slyly playing on the national colors of Israel. And on top of it all she wears a confidence that rises above that usually found in female politicians, based on gender and equality, defying a challenge to either. This one is based on an almost messianic belief in the righteousness of herself.

Reagan Clark's confidence is also based on a fairly shrewd political calculus. She is betting that so many of the silent majority are tired of the craziness and lying and old male leadership. And she knows just what they want: power to make money, to keep the country more white than not, and in Reagan Clark's case, to keep America and the Western world Christian.

"We have survived much, through the grace of God," Reagan Clark continues, "but we are still under attack just a few miles from where we sit, by people waving the bloody banner of Islam, but who have little to do with that religion of peace. They slaughter men, women and children, slaughter them in the thousands with their sadistic serial killing."

There it is, Maddie thinks. There's the setup for Teddy Wright to go for the "gotcha" on Reagan Clark.

"And yet, I ask myself," says Reagan Clark with sudden heat, her eyes glowing with something like tears. "Why is this religion of peace doing nothing to stop the carnage? My hearing is pretty good, and I don't hear anyone from the 'religion of peace' condemning the murderous attacks in Afghanistan, or Iraq, or Syria, or on you every single day here in Israel."

A growing wave of applause ripples from the crowd. It has Maddie marveling at how Reagan Clark can pivot into policy from this harangue against Islam—and into human emotion. From the enraptured look on the faces of the Orthodox Jews and also the Christian evangelicals, they want to hear more of it.

"And the great State of Israel is our bulwark against those who would destroy us," Clark says, as if she is channeling Israel's first female prime minister, Golda Meir. "Not only do I not hear anyone from this 'religion of peace' condemning the kidnapping and murder of the innocent, but I hear from the perpetrators how they are disaffected, they're disadvantaged, they're lost. Like their savagery is our fault! Well, I can tell you from my own experience as the child of a single mother, who worked two jobs just to keep me fed and schooled, the default option of those outside the so-called power structure is not to attack Israel!"

The applause rises again, and again Reagan Clark smiles, just a little, patiently acknowledging it, and then raising a hand to show that she isn't finished.

"In my country, the United States of America, the country that will see me as its first female president, our default position—or I would say, starting position—when you're disaffected or disadvantaged or lost is to find a way to change your situation. And that is through your hard work, through your family, and through your faith. It's also the starting position of the great state of Israel!"

There is more applause, and Reagan Clark basks in it for at least half a minute. Maddie looks around, taking in the audience reaction, and spots Gabriel. He is talking to a guy who looks like Israeli security, a stocky, swarthy man in his early thirties in dark, wraparound sunglasses and a security jacket that is cut short so you can get your gun out fast. Odd choice for an interview, but then maybe the guy stopped Gabriel for some reason. If there is trouble, it looks like Gabriel can handle it with charm or a solid right hook.

The applause suddenly dies down and Maddie turns back to see Reagan Clark holding up both hands like a revivalist preacher. "I can tell you that my own faith has not been a straight line," she continues, her voice softer now. "I was born and raised a Roman Catholic, but through the grace of God, I found myself born again into the faith of a Christianity that spoke more clearly to my heart and allowed my heart to speak to the world. It is the faith that descends from the Jewish people, the one that

Jesus proclaimed within his own tradition as he preached up and down this wonderful land. And, it was not far from here that he preached the words that resonate most with me still, the Sermon on the Mount."

She pauses, and then looking up to the domed ceiling, adorned with a blue-eyed Swedish Jesus rising to heaven, she cherry-picks *The Beatitudes*:

"Blessed are those who hunger and thirst for righteousness, for they will be filled.

"Blessed are the merciful, for they will receive mercy.

"Blessed are the pure in heart, for they will see God.

"Blessed are the peacemakers, for they will be called children of God."

Reagan Clark, eyes shining, looks out at her audience, who are clearly moved even by the power of a redacted Sermon on the Mount. She nods her head, as if its message is self-evident. And then, with her blue eyes hot, she launches into what Maddie knows will be the idea that she rides to the White House on the first Tuesday in November.

"The thing is, ladies and gentlemen, we have been like the Jews of Nazi Europe for far too long in the face of these killers who want to wipe us out. Like the Jews of Europe who believed such evil that would come to befall them was not possible, we, too, have been poor in spirit. We, too, have been meek. We, too, have thirsted for justice. We, too, have been merciful, pure of heart, and Lord knows, we, too, have tried to make peace!"

At that, Maddie thinks the dome is going to lift off the roof and allow painted Jesus to escape into the blue

Galilean sky. Reagan Clark lets the rockets of applause burst around her for a good forty-five seconds now, and then holds up both hands, laying them on the applause to bring it down to silence.

"But we are still reviled, reviled for being Jews, reviled for being Christians, and marked for death because of it by people from the 'religion of peace' who want to destroy us in a holy war, or by people with no religion at all want to destroy law and order with their anarchy and their anti-Semitic attacks on this country, the only country in the Middle East where they would even be allowed to air their blasphemy in public!"

She steps from behind the podium now and paces the stage like a preacher making the pitch as the crowd cheers her on.

"Well, let me remind you that we have an obligation to protect God's creation, and that means giving it life—and yes, it means protecting our planet from the things that science tells us are happening, I see it in Hawaii—and protecting it from those who want to do us, and it, harm. Be they wielding swords, or throwing bombs, or working to build nuclear capabilities and lying about it, like the Iranians are doing just over there—"

Maddie is surprised by the roar of approval Reagan Clark gets for that line as she points to the east.

"And when we have the State of Israel, the only true and free democracy in this region, the only true friend of the United States, condemned by the anti-Semites of the world for defending themselves from constant attack, I promise you this: when I become president of the United

States, we will say enough meekness, enough peacemaking, enough thirsting for justice. For we shall deliver you from evil."

She raises her right hand as high as she can now, her index finger up in the universal Number One sign. But Maddie doesn't think she is referencing her campaign, or her country, or the other exporters of democracy to the benighted countries of the world, which have imploded into civil war. No, Maddie thinks dryily, she is pointing to heaven, the place where she is prepared to send a lot of people.

The audience rises in a kind of rapture, the Israelis for her pledge to them, and the Christians for her promise to bring on the salvation of the Jews, by provoking the Palestinians—if not the entire Muslim world—to launch Armageddon. Reagan Clark smiles, her blue eyes blazing on the distance—on the future in which she ascends. And then, she raises both hands in acknowledgment of her own power, and exits, disappearing behind the red velvet curtain.

Maddie feels a hand on her shoulder, and sees a bald man, in his late thirties, wearing a blue blazer and red tie, smiling at her. She has seen him somewhere before, and he is saying something, but the tumultuous response by the audience to Reagan Clark's vision of a Muslim free future makes hearing anything beyond it impossible. While he speaks, the man offers Maddie a business card. "Brett Muenster, Communications Director, The Next President Reagan," it reads.

Maddie lets herself enjoy a satisfied smile. This is the

other guy she has been trying to get to say "Yes". And here he is now, looking worse than he does on Zoom, sweat rolling down his bald head, mud-brown eyes blinking in the light, shirt sweat-stuck to his chest and armpits and ample belly. Then he smiles, his chiclet gum teeth point in every direction.

"Brett, really nice to meet you in person," Maddie says, now that they can hear. "I'm sorry I missed drinks with you in New York, but I had to leave town."

Muenster returns the smile as if he couldn't be happier to see her. "I would say you owe me one, or maybe two, since Aretta who came in your stead is a dry county." Then he turns his crooked smile over the crowds, still reeling from Reagan's speech, some still clapping at the empty stage, others hugging each other. "What better place than to meet here in The Land of God? I don't even think Manhattan could beat it."

Maddie smiles, speechless in shock. And Muenster grins, thinking she too is just overwhelmed. "Shall we have that drink?"

Maddie looks at her phone. She has an hour. That was a short speech.

"Yes. They even sell wine here."

Muenster honks with laughter. "Heaven on earth. Isn't it so?" He leads on. And as Maddie follows, it hits her: how did he know that she was going to be here? Aretta would never let Reagan and her crew know what Maddie was doing.

And then it hits Maddie even harder: maybe he's the guy who is spying on her. She feels her chest grow hot with anger. But she cannot give anything away if he is spying on her. She has to spy on him to find out what he is looking for. And then find a way to stop him and the murderous gang he is working for.

29. Levi's House, The Land of God, near Tiberias, Israel.

Brett Muenster insists on paying and Maddie insists on coffee at 'Levi's House', because she wants to keep her wits about her, even though she could use a double Jameson's after listening to Reagan Clark's call to arms. That, and her suspicion that the man with her is the one spying on her.

The place is a rustic first-century cafe, made from a combination of rough stone and woven tents, outside the 'The Temple of All Nations'. The male baristas are dressed like tax collectors with pouches of gold coins hanging from their necks. The female baristas wear extravagant make-up and colorful cleavage-enhancing tunics in magenta and purple, so Maddie guesses they are supposed to be prostitutes.

Maddie never would have guessed Brett Muenster to be anyone's top choice for a presidential candidate's political wrangler. In person he is even more awkward and slippery, his bald head gleaming a sunburnt pink, like a ham about to go in the oven.

"Jesus ate with the sinners at Levi's House," Muenster says. "Nice to see them working for a change."

Maddie manages a tight smile, but Muenster squeezes out a laugh that sounds like relief coming to the constipated. "Just kidding, Ms. Lynch. I know what y'all in New York think of us grassroots conservatives." Then he pauses. “Kidding on that, too.”

Maddie will smile and nod, and play the role of the New York TV producer as she tries to win over him and his candidate for Teddy Wright’s hot seat. She suspects that if Muenster is trying to throw her off balance as part of his spy game, to see what he can knock loose, she can play that game, too. She’ll find out how much he knows about her and her computer life.

“That was a pretty amazing speech that the Governor just gave,” she says. “I hear she writes all her own speeches.”

“It was and she does. Makes my job so easy.” Muenster tips his head to the side as he smiles. Is that his tell that he’s lying? “What are you working on now?”

“I’m trying to get the Pope to come on Teddy’s show, when he’s in America.”

“Isn’t the Pope in Rome?”

When Maddie hears that, she is sure that Muenster knew that she was going to be at the Land of God. So he’s really asking what she’s doing in Israel. “Yes, but the Governor was in Israel. I was here already, on research, so…”

He nods. “You’ve been here before, I take it.”

Maddie thinks about her emails to Aretta. Has she mentioned anything about coming to Israel again? No, but then, her computer probably has. “I have. My father worked here.”

“Oh right,” Muenster says, dutifully subdued. “He was a journalist, right?”

So Muenster knows her father is dead. “Yes, he was

working on a big story, and he got killed in Lebanon."

"I'm sorry," Muenster says, the default response. "Maybe you can finish his story?"

He says this with the kind of neighborly warmth you'd expect when delivering a condolence pie to the recently bereaved. But it's exactly what Maddie is doing, and she doesn't see Brett Muenster running that deep to come up with that angle all by himself.

"There's an idea," she says. "But I have a few other things I need to do first."

One of them now is to figure out what she's doing that would make her of interest to Brett Muenster, and so, for Reagan Clark?

"What made you choose this venue for the Governor's extraordinary speech?" she asks, zeroing in on his work. "It's a long way from Hawaii."

Muenster grins at her as if this should be obvious. "People of faith want to believe in a holy president. They see in her a leader who makes no bones about the fact that those who are the enemies of the state are the enemies of God. She wants to bring on our own holy war."

"Oh my…" Maddie wasn't expecting Muenster to call for an American jihad. "My thought," she goes on to say, covering her shock, "is that voters are not going to find this idea of a holy war attractive. Not after decades of so many 'endless wars' in foreign lands."

Muenster leans in, as if about to deliver a secret. "We think that the voters want America to stop pretending that we're living in a world where Christian testimony wins the day. It's us or them, now, and we're counting on good old self-interest being for us."

This, the evolution of the Us and Them argument, has fractured her country, Maddie thinks. From elections to race to abortion to immigration to what America means, it has been an Us versus Them polarity for a long time. And Brett Muenster has just reformulated this into theocratic self-interest, one nowhere to be found in the Constitution. Just hearing it out loud makes her want to smack him in the head. For the time being, she'll just imagine it.

"So," she says, "if a holy war is the central platform of Reagan Clark's campaign, what are the others?"

Muenster opens his palms, presto. "It's the only one. Reagan Clark has boldly decided to tell the only truth that matters to the American people, and to the world, and that's why she's here today. With a massive bullseye now painted on her, I might say. But she believes, as do I, that all the other issues connected to our way of life in America will be meaningless if we don't confront the very thing that is trying to kill us."

"And exactly how does she plan to do that?"

Muenster leans his pink domed head to the side again and gives another aw-shucks grin. "Well, I reckon if you get her to come on *I'm Wright,* she'll tell Teddy and America quite a bit more."

Maddie feels a surge of hope. "And what do I need to do to make that happen?"

Muenster sits up and suddenly looks very serious. "There's one big condition."

Maddie has a flash of all the conditions a man like Muenster could make, and none of them are good. But he surprises her by saying, "You beat me at one of those arcade games out there, and we have a deal."

Maddie looks out at the arcade, spinning with colored lights, clanging with fake-online sword fights, then back at Muenster. "Really? What if I lose?"

"Then we'll find another game," he says with a dangerous smile. "I'll let you choose this game, now. But be warned. I spent my Georgia boyhood in the arcade."

Maddie nods. Muenster has no idea that she can shoot. Her father taught her on regular Saturday mornings at his gun club in New Jersey. He would do it to keep in practice for tough assignments. That was his reason. And his reason for bringing Maddie along was because since America has more guns than people, he wanted his daughter to have a fighting chance.

The dozen rows of video terminals feature three games which fit the theme of an American-funded Bible park. There's *Gladiators for God*, where the Christian gladiators try to kill the Roman ones, and there's a tabletop game called *Just Like Jesus* where history is turned upside down and Christians can see how many Roman soldiers they can crucify before the clock runs out, and then there's *Eye for and Eye*, which is a shooting game, that looks like the modern Israeli army at war with its Islamic enemies. At least, the flashing neon bar above the game shows an IDF tank blowing up a building with a yellow Hezbollah flag on it. Maddie shudders. This game is too much like the reality that the world has just witnessed, when far too many times there was a school or a hospital underneath that flag. But she takes a breath and pardons her own hypocrisy to say:

"Let's go for the guns. And you can go first and show me how it's done."

Muenster easily selects the "Christian sniper" option, which is odd for an Israeli Defense Force game, but then, this whole place is crazy, Maddie thinks. She watches as Muenster, the Christian sniper, has to pick out a target as it pops up. Then kill the villain and not the civilian. So not true to anything when it comes to armies invading civilians.

A Bedouin shepherd with his flock comes round the corner of a mud building, and Muenster chuckles. "Lucky day, dude." But hard on his heels comes a bearded sun-glassed guy shooting an AK-47 at Muenster. Muenster fires back with a ferocious burst and kills the schoolgirl who has wandered out onto the street. The video screen flashes a violent bloody red, and Muenster is now facing "Court Martial" the text on screen informs. Game over.

And, Maddie thinks, a game that bears no relation to reality. Court martial? More like a medal.

Muenster rises and smiles at Maddie. "Good game this one," he says, but she can see the anger in his eyes.

Maddie settles in and selects "IDF firefight." The screen shifts to the verdant hills like those outside the Land of God, but again, there's that yellow Hezbollah flag, with its depiction of a hand reaching up to clasp an assault rifle. She feels heat flow to her cheeks. This game must be set in Lebanon. So this game is for her father.

By the time she's done, she has wiped out a battalion of Hezbollah fighters, and four mortar sites. The screen flashes green. "You have been promoted General of the Army" the message proclaims.

"Beginner's luck," Maddie says and rises. Muenster tries to put on a brave face by giving her a salute, but she can see that anger is even stronger than when he lost. Because now he has been beaten. By a girl.

An arcade attendant, dressed like a Roman gladiator, approaches Maddie and hands her a red baseball cap with white letters across its peak, proclaiming Land of God in King James bible font.

"Congratulations," he says, and shakes Maddie's hand.

"Thanks," she says, and slides the ball cap into her bag.

"You sure do know how to shoot…" Muenster says. In a way that tells her he didn't know that.

"Yeah, I did some shooting with my father."

"I didn't think they allowed guns in New York."

"They don't," Maddie says. "That's why God invented New Jersey."

Muenster laughs his grunting laugh, and Maddie wonders about this guy who could be the next press secretary in the White House…? And he could. Reagan Clark, governor of Hawaii, is holding her own in the polls and could be the next president.

And then Maddie sees it. Reagan Clark is governor of Hawaii. Christopher Zimmerman was working in Hawaii when Reagan Clark was still Catholic and still at college. Could there be a connection between them?

"Are you OK?" he says. "You look like you just saw the devil himself."

"The sun is quite something here." Maddie ducks into the shade. "Why don't you let me know when the Governor of Hawaii can come on Teddy's show, Brett, and we'll sort it out? And hey, if you come with her to New York, we will have that drink, or two."

If he's inside her computer, Maddie will also keep him close. And then she takes a selfie of them both, smiling as if they mean it. He will appreciate seeing it in her photo files.

30. Jerusalem.

Gabriel insists that they take Highway 90, "Israel's most dangerous highway" back to Jerusalem, which adds another half hour to the trip. But they have time, and he says he wants to see the Palestinian side of the country. "The highway cuts right through the West Bank."

For Maddie the danger is not the West Bank, but the reckless driving on this highway, evidence of which are the skid marks on the road and a couple of blown out tires on the shoulders. Besides, she has more dangers to think about than a highway.

Brett Muenster is now the prime suspect for being in her computer based on the fact he just wandered up to her at the Land of God as if they were supposed to meet. But the fact the Georgia aw-shucks boy has no idea that she suspects this, and even shoots better than he does, with his boss Reagan Clark set to join Maddie's boss on Teddy's show, is all to her advantage.

"You seem distracted," Gabriel says, overtaking a trio of Army trucks at top speed. "Are you thinking about those handsome Roman centurions, brooms on their helmets, sheets tied over their scrawny bodies?" He throws her a teasing smile.

"I can't say they caught my attention," she replies. "But Clark's speech sure did. What did you think of it?"

"Well, in Brazil, we are used to exaggeration from our leaders."

"So do you think she's exaggerating, or a leader, or

both?

Gabriel laughs in reply, then he tests the Toyota Corolla's cornering powers, along the Sea of Galilee coastline, the highway curving south. "I think she's American, is what I think."

Maddie shoots him a glower, and he laughs again. "And so are you, and it's such a diverse country! What did you think of her?"

"I think she's crazy," Maddie says. "She wants to start a holy war in the Middle East."

"Did she say that?"

"She said as much. And then when I met with her communications guy, he confirmed it."

"Wow," Gabriel says. "How is she going to do that?"

"I would expect the usual American way. With money and high tech weapons."

Gabriel considers that glumly and they drive in silence for a while.

"Did you get any good interviews?" Maddie asks. "I saw you talking to one of the security guys. Hope he had some soundbites."

Gabriel's smile comes right back. "He wanted to talk to me because I wasn't wearing media credentials. He wanted to know what I was doing talking to people. They're very twitchy. Don't want anything bad to happen to their American friends."

They approach Beit She'an, where the Jordan River Valley and the Jezreel Valley meet. Even from the highway Maddie can see rolling hills, palm trees shading turquoise ponds, and lines of tall white pillars from some of the best preserved temples and archeology sites in the world. "The Garden of Eden was thought to be here," she says.

"I can see why," Gabriel responds. "The hills are as green as Ireland."

"Where the Garden of Eden definitely was not," Maddie says. "I'm half Irish. Half Italian. It wasn't in Italy either."

"Nor Brazil," he says, pretending to pout. But his brown eyes are watchful, and they cling to Maddie, studying her, before he turns back to the road.

For an easy going guy, Maddie thinks, he keeps a close watch.

Suddenly, up ahead they see the flashing lights of an army checkpoint. "What's this?' Gabriel asks.

Maddie thought he would have known that there was a checkpoint at Beit She'an before he had chosen this route. She points out there's two permanent checkpoints on this highway, and they will want to see their passports and all will be fine.

"Not so fine if we were Palestinians," Maddie adds, then explains to Gabriel that she understands the complexities of the place from living here and also studying here. "But I just wish people like Reagan Clark didn't make it such a target after the War of Gaza, and all that has happened." More darkly, she adds, "I mean, does Iran need any more provocation to attack again?"

"No, I do not think they do," he replies.

The checkpoint moves quickly. The soldier is still a teenager, surrounded by other soldier teenagers holding their impossibly small, light Tavor 95s whose slender muzzle makes it seem like the gun shoots bullets through a black straw. The young soldier leans into the window, looks at them both, then asks in Hebrew for their passports.

Maddie responds in Hebrew: “Here they are.”

The soldier doesn’t react to an American speaking Hebrew. He just says, “Toda,” and looks at the passports. Then asks in English, “Where are you going?”

“To Jerusalem,” Gabriel says.

“Have a good trip,” the soldier replies without a smile, and hands them back their passports.

Gabriel slowly drives through the chicanes of the checkpoint. “You speak Hebrew?” he says, surprise in his voice.

“I read it better than I speak it,” says Maddie, glad to impress him. “I had to learn it for my academic work.”

“What other languages do you speak?”

“Italian, French, and Greek,” she says. “I know a bit of Arabic, too. You?”

“I come from a German family, who have been in Brazil since the 19th century. So, no escaped Nazis. But I spoke German as a kid. Portuguese, Spanish, and English.”

“Must be useful for travel writing,” she says.

“It is. I have a great piece on the Galilee in the works.”

“Who’s it for?” Maddie asks.

Gabriel angles his head toward her and flashes his perfect teeth as he grins. “The highest bidder. I am freelance.”

Maddie thinks about that and also about his flirty smile as they speed toward Jerusalem. He must have an inheritance or something, because freelance travel writing doesn't pay the freight for zooming around the world.

"I can send you some links if you want to read some of my pieces," he says, as if reading her mind.

"Ones in English, please," she says eagerly, not letting on that she has already read some of his stuff online. But now she wonders if Golden Gabriel de Almeida Schmidt is really who he says he is.

He drops her in front of the Biblicum in Jerusalem at exactly three o'clock in the afternoon. It's a handsome, three-story limestone and brick building on the western side of the old city's walls.

"I can walk back to the hotel from here," Maddie says.

"Great. Will I see you later in the bar?"

"You probably will," she says on a promise of a smile, "unless they keep me here late."

He pouts on her behalf for the long day ahead of her – without him. It is the kind of pout in which his large, soft lips pour down over his strong chin, which lets Maddie imagine kissing him. "Are you doing research?"

"Sort of," she says. "I'm meeting a priest who is helping me get my interview with the Pope."

"*Boa sorte*!" he says, and drives off.

Maddie enters the lush courtyard, its sweet date palms and neon pink bougainvillea giving it the full air of an Italian villa, and not an academic building in the center of Jerusalem. Walking on into the lobby, she sees presiding over the room, the photo of the thin, black-clad Saint Ignatius Loyola with the dark, woeful eyes. He's the founder of the Jesuit order, the one that educated her in high school, and the one to which Victor Franchi belongs.

Reception is attended by a Franciscan friar, wearing the brown robe and sandals of that order. Maddie asks him where she might find Father Victor Franchi. He directs her to the library, which she knows is to her left. Walking along, Maddie recalls her first impression of the Biblicum which remains her impression today: with its tiled floors and ornately carved wooden fixtures and its air of solemn, ancient scholarship, it could be any building in Oxford.

She enters the library, and an elderly priest, sitting guard duty at the front of the room, asks if he can help her.

"I am here to see Father Victor Franchi," Maddie says.

"He has not been in today," says the priest.

Maddie feels that surge of chill. "Does he keep a daily schedule?"

"Lately, he has been here every day."

Maybe the beast that he warned her about has found him.

Maddie exits the Biblicum and calls Franchi on her new phone. No answer.

She opens Gett on her new phone and punches in Franchi's address in Ein Karem.

The Gett driver shows up fast and twenty minutes

later, Maddie has zigged and zagged across the city. Pulling the red Land of God baseball cap from her bag, she puts it on, and tugs it down over her brow. Buttoning up her jacket, she then wipes off her red lipstick – maybe it will help disguise her as she remembers all the CCTV cameras that are watching this place, and if harm has come to Franchi, she wants to be as anonymous as this goddamn ugly baseball cap will allow.

The gate is unlocked, and she enters the back garden, where she and Victor Franchi sat just last evening. And where he revealed the blackmail that Christopher Zimmerman had used to get his position in the Vatican. It was a stunning picture of Pope John Paul II naked in the sunlight.

Maddie keeps her head down as she passes the security camera, and walks up to the back door, one made of wood with stippled translucent glass windows. Good for letting in light, but bad for trying to see inside, which is what Maddie wants to do. She's sure Victor Franchi is within. He would have called her if there had been a change of plan.

She turns the door handle. It's unlocked. She looks around to see if anyone can see her, but the garden has been built for privacy. No one is watching. She opens the door and stands still. Before her on the floor is a pool of blood.

It looks fresh from what Maddie knows of blood, having seen it spilled on the white ice of the hockey arena. It's fresh because it's bright red. The high level of oxyhemoglobin makes it look almost unreal, so the medic at Chelsea Piers told her when she arrived for practice once and there was bright red blood on the ice.

Maddie has a choice. To enter and find the source of this blood, or to leave. And do what? she thinks. Call the police? She can imagine that conversation. "*I entered a house that doesn't belong to me to see the blood of a priest I just met who might be part of a blackmailing scheme...*" No, if the beast has come for Victor Franchi, she needs to know this on her own terms.

She steps into the kitchen and looks left and right, to see if the blood has traveled. Drops can be seen near the entrance to the sitting room off the kitchen. She listens first, before she moves. All she hears is the sound of her own breathing.

Slowly, she steps forward into the room. Suddenly, there is an arm around her neck, trying to choke her. Maddie knows it is male, and strong. It could be Franchi himself, though this guy is taller and thicker. She also knows from the hockey fights that she has been in, there's only one way out of this and that's with a punch. She makes a fist and swings a punch backward as hard as she can, aiming for her attacker's groin. The blow strikes its target because she hears the man gasp and his grip on her neck relaxes as he doubles over in pain.

Maddie spins, and sees he is wearing a balaclava. Even so, she raises her right knee hard into the man's face, and he goes down, out cold. He has a pistol that clatters on to the floor, and Maddie picks it up. It is cocked and ready to fire. But the guy didn't shoot her, he tried to strangle her. Why?

Another masked guy appears in the doorway at the far end of the room, and he also has a pistol in his right hand. Aimed at Maddie.

"Put the gun down," he says, in an accent that sounds as if Arabic is his first language.

If Maddie lets go of the gun, she has lost whatever chance she has of escape. So she begins to crouch down as if to place the gun on the ground. Halfway there, she fires, sideways, striking the man in his right kneecap. He screams and crumples, falling to his right. The gun in his right hand spins away on the hardwood.

Maddie runs for it, through the kitchen, on the bloody floor. Skidding out the back door she smacks her knee on the door jamb. She can hear the footsteps now, and maybe the knocked-out guy is up again. She has to get into the street and into the public eye if she has any chance of escape. She has hurt her knee. She staggers to the side of the house, and out the gate.

Sitting in front of the house with the car door open is Gabriel de Almeida Schmidt.

He wipes his hand in the air—the universal gesture for "let's get out of here". Maddie's knee hurts, and she's breathing hard, and she turns to see where her pursuer now stands, but he has vanished.

And before her is the golden boy she now knows is not a Brazilian travel writer. But he is an escape, and she needs that, and so she rolls into the car and slams the door.

He looks at her, and the pistol in her hand. "Give me that," he says.

Maddie does not. “Who are you?” she asks.

“Soviet. Makarov. Reliable pistol,” Gabriel says, looking at the handgun. “We need to get rid of it.”

Maddie now hands him the gun. His moves are calm, professional, as he untucks his shirt and uses the bottom edge of it to wipe down the gun. Getting out of the car, he drops the gun in front of the house. Then they speed off into the Jerusalem afternoon.

Maddie’s brain is going full tilt: whose blood was that? Was it from Victor Franchi? And who were those guys in balaclavas who wanted to do what, kill her? Scare her? Fool her?

And who is Gabriel de Almeida Schmidt?

“So, is rescuing me going to make a great travel piece? Or was it Victor Franchi you were trying to save?”

Gabriel ignores her questions, taking a left, then a right, then a left again to lose whoever might be following. His easy smile is gone, and even the soft light in his brown eyes has hardened. His handsome face is now tough and unforgiving, one she has only seen on the guys who used to drive her father. He’s a soldier or a spy.

Without taking his eyes off the road, he says, “You hurt your knee. Rub it and flex it until you get it iced, or it’ll be fucked.” His accent is now crisp with an upward inflection at the end. An English spy? A friend of Sir Geoffrey? Maddie could use a friend. There seems to be no one on her side, and now one seems to be what they are. Not even Maddie.

31. Rome, The Vatican.

Cardinal Bernard Otley enjoys watching Manchester United, for the beauty of the sport and that of the men who play it. It's all the more glorious to see them in his private room behind his office, with his old leather chair from his seminary days, its seat worn into comfort, and with his massive 4K television, a gift from a Californian Knight of Malta. He rarely if ever takes gifts, as he would say, only those that left no evidence, like a fine meal or bottle of rose. But then he would chuckle at his own rules and the evidence would bounce along with his laugh in his growing belly.

He is not amused at all when the game gives away to INN news parsing clips of Reagan Clark's speech at the Land of God. Otley sees her speak fire and brimstone, and he hears her edits to the Sermon on the Mount, turning his ample stomach in disgust.

"I gather she's not getting your vote, Eminence?" Bishop Hughes enters the private office without knocking, and catches a glimpse of the Governor of Hawaii promising blood in the land of milk and honey.

Otley is too upset by Reagan Clark to remind Hughes yet again to knock on a door. "She's going to defend the faith, Bishop Hughes. The problem being, Christianity is the faith she wants to defend by attacking Islam at the expense of Israel."

Otley clicks the remote again, and the screen fades to black. "As if Israel hasn't been a bullseye for some time," he says, with a weary sigh. "But who is the biggest bullseye of them all?"

Quickly, coolly Hughes replies, "Our Pope."

Otley reminds Hughes that during their time here, Vatican intelligence 'interrupted' three attempts on the life of Pope Pius XIII. The last one, Otley admits, came even as a shock to him, during the Pope's trip to the Philippines. Al Qaeda had planted an IED along the route of the papal motorcade through Manila.

Hughes remembers; "We sniffed it out in the church's vast network of informers and the faithful in Manilla, and changed the Holy Father's route."

He neglects to add that the Philippine National police managed to corner the bombers, then of course lose them in the chaos of twelve million faithful followers. So, they are still out there, Hughes is sure. But he doesn't say that either.

So, he asks, "Are you thinking that we should cancel the Pope's visit to the United States?"

Otley would love to say yes. "No. The Pope would go ballistic. So to speak."

Hughes bows in deference to the Cardinal, who is, he knows, as powerful as the Pope, at least when it comes to Vatican bureaucracy. Then he turns to his own bureaucratic business. "I have to inform you, Eminence, that we've lost contact with Maddie Lynch."

Otley steps out of his private room and into his office, dropping his weight into his executive chair—customized in cardinal red just for him. He looks over his glasses at Hughes like an Inquisitioner whose mind is made up to make the torture last long and end badly.

"Victor Franchi says that she never showed up for a meeting with him."

Otley wonders if he means the second meeting that Maddie had referred to in her text.

But then, he never told Hughes about her new phone and the second meeting.

He watches Hughes carefully for a moment, and if he has any doubts about the man, they are coming together, joined by suspicion. "How is it that you knew where Victor Franchi was?" Otley asks. It's a test.

Hughes blinks his dozy eyes. "It's my job to know these things. Or to find them out."

Otley is on edge as he gets this empty remark from his own spy. "What did you tell Maddie Lynch about Victor Franchi?"

"Just his contact details. What else is there to say?"

Otley has a few responses to that. That Franchi is up to something, and it would be something very bad. And also that he suspects Hughes has more information. Much more.

Otley aims his unblinking blue eyes on Hughes. "We gave Maddie Lynch a task to see if she is cut from the right cloth. And it would seem as if she is. So now we wait." He pauses, swallowing the angry bile, and sweetening his tone. "She will contact me."

"You sound certain, Eminence."

"Should I not be?"

"It is possible that she has met with foul play."

Hughes and Otley eye each other in silence; with

Franchi anything is possible. Otley tries to hush his fears and looks out on the rain, which slicks the golden and creamy travertine stone of St. Peter's piazza below into a weeping gray blur.

Still, Otley's thoughts return to Maddie. He has grown very fond of her. Though she might not exactly have the brand of faith he was looking for. She was not the usual trusted but cloying associate. Or the dully devout. Her principles were just right, high and mighty and maybe too liberal. Backed up by smarts and quickness.

Given her great personal losses, she needed something to believe in. And Otley needed her. He hopes he has not manipulated her too much into joining his ranks. If Maddie has been murdered it will multiply the dangers that the Pope faces, and the Church, and any freedom of any faith in this world.

He turns to his own cloying associate, whom he trusts less and less. "If you speak to Victor Franchi again, I want to be on the call."

Hughes bows and exits.

That night, Cardinal Otley retires to his small but comfortably appointed apartment in the Domus Santa Marta just behind the Basilica. Its main resident, on the top floor, is the Pope. When Pope Francis retired and moved to a monastery, Pius took his old apartment at the top of this hotel for visiting clerics. To keep him company, and to keep an eye on him, Otley is right below him.

When Cardinal Bernard Otley says his prayers that

night, his eyes moisten with tears as he prays that Maddie Lynch is still alive. He is tempted to try her new phone and text her. No, the communication can only go one way, from her. As a priest, he is expected to be a father figure, though he rarely feels it. With Maddie, however, he actually feels the grip of paternal protectiveness. It hurts not to hear from her, it hurts to not know.

Bishop Paul Hughes suggested that she might have been hurt. What else does he know?

The Cardinal turns his prayers back to God, on Maddie's behalf, and for his own, praying to find out all that Hughes, who is not the devoted dud Otley which took him for, knows about what the hell is going on.

32. Israel.

Maddie is still hearing the gun blast and feeling the force of the door jamb on her knee as Gabriel drives. He put her in his car while with icepack while he checked them both out of the American Colony, swapped vehicles and found her a blue burka.

"You need to leave now," he said simply as he ushered her, limping, into the back seat.

Maddie wants to leave. The hotel. The country. Her heart is pounding like she is on a breakaway on the ice rink, and has been racing like this for the last two hours. And everyone who looks at her, even glances at her, is after her. She wants to find out what happened to Franchi? And who Gabriel really is?

"You can't depart via Tel Aviv. They will be looking for you. You cannot be seen."

"In the burka, I can't even see me." She wriggles as they drive, her knee stinging with pain, into the giant cloth baggie and peers at herself in the car's vanity mirror. It is humbling; all she sees are her own green eyes through the woven visor of the burka. "And what about you, Gabriel? Is it really Gabriel?"

"I will get you to Amman, Jordan, where you can fly out safely."

Maddie's mouth is dry. The ambush at Franchi's house must have been meant for her. And whoever left the blood on the floor might want to spill her blood still. The Israelis, on the other hand, will want to know why she was at Franchi's house, and shot a man. Her explanation that Franchi is helping her get an interview with the Pope will not seem like the truth.

"We have our eyes on Victor Franchi. So when you show up, we have our eyes on you, too."

"You sound British. But you are Mossad?" She tries to see him through the visor. Even hearing him is muffled by the burka.

"I studied in England when I was young. And because I want to stay young, at least for a while longer, that's all I can say."

Maddie's luminous green eyes are the only part of her that is now slightly visible to the world to satisfy the moral cosmos of the believers who like their women invisible. She suddenly realizes how useful a simple piece of cloth can be. It hides her emotions. This guy can't see her cheeks fire up and her fists clench. He might have helped her out with a ride from the crime scene, but he lied to her.

"Why do you have your eyes on Victor Franchi?"

Gabriel restores his magnificent smile. "Why do you?"

Maddie shakes her head; she is not going to be taken in by a smile. "I told you, he was supposed to help me get an interview with the Pope."

"I see. But he is more than that, no?"

Maddie plays him right back: "No? Do you think so?"

Gabriel speaks gently as tips his hand again; "But the Vatican sent you to find out."

"But I don't know who sent you. You owe me that,"

she says, louder than she meant to.

Gabriel drives in silence for a half mile, a half mile of burning sun and eternal sand. Maddie thinks she has turned off the tap of information with her fury.

"Do you know of the Society of Blessed Urban II?" Gabriel finally says.

Maddie knows a little bit, and says evenly, "I have heard of it. Why?"

"Franchi is one of the leaders of it."

He lets that hang as Maddie sees the signs for the Jordanian border, bright blue over the golden sands.

"It's a conservative Catholic society," Maddie says, remembering the conversation with Sir Geoffrey and Cosmo. "*Pope John Paul II loved them, Benedict didn't mind them, Francis didn't like them, and Pius XIII, who loves Islam, hates them. The feeling, I might add, is mutual.*"

"Do you know what they want?"

Maddie meets his gaze in the rearview mirror. "They want to start another Crusade."

He shoots her an appreciative look. "That's what we think, too. The question is, how? When? Where? And who? The 'why' we know."

"Do we?"

"You tell me, the Vatican sent you."

Maddie realizes he can't see her cheeks under the burka fire up again in rage. "They want to restore the Catholic Church to her rightful majesty."

"By getting rid of the Muslims and Jews?"

"I don't think so," she says.

"Well, we have to think so."

Maddie feels he now includes her in the "we". We Mossad? We Vatican? And all of this because she was asked to get an interview with the Pope.

Gabriel drives them under a tall white plaster arch that says "Welcome to Jordan" in both English and Arabic, one with a guard post in the middle featuring a huge portrait above it of Jordan's rugged-looking King Abdullah II, painted a few flattering years earlier.

"I guess that's Shalom, Israel," Maddie says with an edge in her voice if Gabriel can't see the cutting look in her eyes.

"Oh, you'll be back." Gabriel says. To show he means it, he holds out both hands to shake hers. Which she does, wrestling in the burka to find a small side vent for a woman to put her hand out into the men's world.

On a whim, she had hoped this golden swimmer was following her. Luckily, he was and saved her, or at least saved her knee that smacked the door in her escape. How much will Gabriel be involved in her return? Because it is soon apparent as they drive up to the Jordanian border, and cross the creek that is the Jordan River, that he is already in it up to his ears.

She watches as Gabriel hands the Jordanian border guard his identification, and some American cash. Then he says something to the man in Arabic, and he immediately returns Gabriel's ID and waves them on. He keeps the cash in a bottom pocket with a big smile.

"I'll send INN the bill," Gabriel jokes. But Maddie knows that crossing into another country—a Muslim country from a Jewish one—on a fistful of cash is not a joking matter.

He drives them about 100 yards into Jordan which, given the sudden shift to shabby buildings and dowdy guards, seems like a greater distance from Israel than it is. He pulls up next to a black BMW X5, Bavarian Motors' family-style car, but with tinted windows.

There is a guy in his 30s leaning against the driver's door who looks like a darker version of Gabriel, with slicked black hair, in crisp jeans and a white shirt and black blazer. His retro cool Ray-Ban Aviator shades are perched on his deeply tanned forehead.

"OK," Gabriel says, not turning to Maddie, but looking at her in the rearview mirror. "You don't tell this guy anything. About where you have been, what you are doing, Victor Franchi, nothing, understood?"

Maddie nods. "Who does he think I am?"

"A friend of mine," says Gabriel. "And that's all he needs to know. Let's go."

They get out of the Range Rover and Maddie stands five paces back while Gabriel is the smiling guy again.

"As-salamu alaykum, Daoud," Gabriel says, shaking the man's hand.

"Shalom, Gabi," Daoud replies. "This the package?" he asks in easy English, looking at the burkaed Maddie standing next to Gabriel.

"Yes," Gabriel says. "She's going to need postage."

"Sure," Daoud nods. "Then let's go. The flight to Rome leaves at 11."

Maddie hasn't said anything about going to Rome and

yet that's where they're sending her. She tries to keep her eyes as neutral as she can, since they are the only uncovered part of her that can be seen. And so, they say even more to those who are paying attention.

"*Buon viaggio*," Gabriel says. "See you soon."

Maddie is about to ask when and where, but knows it is not a question that will be answered. She will just have to expect him.

Gabriel hands over Maddie's carry-on case and briefcase, climbs back in the Range Rover and does a U-turn toward Israel.

"Passport?" Daoud asks.

Maddie, who has her purse beside her, fishes out her Italian passport. She now wants to keep the Rome fiction going.

Daoud takes it, leans into his SUV, stamps it with a Jordanian entry stamp, then hands it back. "Postage," he says.

Then he drives Maddie to Amman at speed, passing through hillside villages on winding roads. Maddie notices that in each village there is a man standing at the roadside, with a cell phone in hand. The BMW zooms past and the man makes a call. Maddie decides that while Gabriel might want her to remain silent, that's not what she wants, and this gives her a chance to see what Daoud is willing to reveal.

"Who are those guys?" Maddie asks. "The ones with the phones."

"Local color," he replies. His English is almost as smooth as Gabriel's.

"Do you work with Gabriel a lot?" Maddie asks.

"We're friends," Daoud says. "We help each other out."

Then he turns up the volume on the radio. Daoud likes classical music, and Mozart's *Requiem* blasts out of the surround sound.

Maddie gets the message. The driver doesn't want to talk, but he has already said a lot. So, Maddie rolls the question around in her head: who is Gabriel really? Mossad most likely, so that's where he'll stay in her mind. He's risked a lot to help her, with a pair of armed hitmen at Franchi's borrowed villa for starters. Why didn't those guys just kill her? Because they wanted to know what she knew. Just like Gabriel does. Could they both be connected?

Maddie must be very careful about where she goes next. There are people watching her and have been watching her ever since she first set foot in Rome when someone, Muenster and Clark's people, breached her computer.

A flutter of doubts knocks her about. She could change her ticket and fly to New York. And stay there—assuming she even gets out of Jordan. With her head down, producing segments for Teddy Wright on right-wing and left-wing nutters who just won't shut up. Play hockey. Fall in love. Start a family. Grow old. Disappear.

Or she can go hide out in Oxford.

Or she can follow even more deeply and darkly the story that has landed upon her, the story she has opened up and which has put her in a burka in the back seat of a vehicle speeding through Jordan.

That is the option that is in her blood. It's what her father would tell her to do, now that she's come this far. Because the story, as she sees it, has already tried to kill her. And it failed. She wants to tell the story, to defeat it and save herself.

33. Rome.

Maddie casually shoulder-checks the street as she walks along Via delle Fornaci, a curving canyon of a street, lined by tall villa-style buildings on either side. No one moves with her, no one is following, but these bright days in June, in the sun-loved city of Rome, everyone's eyes are hidden by sunglasses. It puts Maddie on edge, and she picks up her pace.

Suddenly, she sits down on a bench. No one stops with her, the crow around her ambling on in their own Roman haze. Safe for a moment, Maddie digs into her bag for her new phone. Nothing. Maybe that's good. Then, in the small back pocket in her bag, Maddie finds the nun's prayer from Zimmerman, or about him. She retrieves it now and reads it again.

> "*O Divine Saviour! I thank Thee for having perpetuated Thy humble, obedient, self-sacrificing and recollected silence of Nazareth in the* ***tabernacle****. How Thy example puts me to* ***shame****! Forgive me for my bold, self-seeking, and superficial talkativeness.* ***Teach me to understand*** *the words: "In silence and in hope shall your strength be. Bishop Christopher Zimmerman.*"

Tabernacle. Shame. Teach me to Understand.

Zimmerman was sending a coded message to the nun, and the nun was trusting Maddie to understand it. The prayer is coded in the same way as the Bible, in which the word of God is in bold. There's an ego for you, Maddie thinks.

She slips the note back into her purse and checks her old phone. Nothing still from her friend Emily about the document proving Zimmerman's bank accepted Croatian gold during World War Two. Gold likely stolen from Jewish victims. Maddie hopes the long silence from her best friend is the old kind, the kind in which no news was good news. Not the dangerous new kind.

She scrolls through the old phone again and is startled to see a text, one from the clerk at Il Convento, where the aged nun Sister Nuala had lived. She bribed the clerk with 50 Euros to let her know if Bishop Hughes returns.

He has: *Bishop Hughes has been to see Sister Patrizia. She has taken ill.*

Maddie shuts off her old phone. Bishop Hughes has a bigger part of the story than she thought. She knew he might be the enemy. And now she is sure he is. But who, she needs to find out, is on his team?

She slips off her bench and, watching the crowds, deliberately walks past her hotel, the Albergo San Giacomo, a four-star lodge near the Vatican, and looks in the window of a publisher, Edizioni di Storia e Letteratura, a little further down the street. Nice to see books, handsome leather books, so beautifully arranged in a window, thinks Maddie. Much better than anything online. But looking at the glass itself, what she is really looking to see is if she has been followed. No one there, so it seems.

So, Maddie swings around and walks back to an internet café. It's quiet and there's a corner seat. She can't use her own computer, but she can use this safe one, as she just needs to do a search that can't be seen by her watchers. Carefully, at a corner table, she casts an eye around the cafe where international students sip espressos, and let their coffee-fueled fingers fly over computer keyboards. Paying no attention at all to her. She's safe.

She is soon speeding through the Google-verse to find out more about Reagan Clark's life in Hawaii. And if in her Catholic days her priest might have been Christopher Zimmerman.

Zimmerman's ego found a reliable photographer, Maddie thinks, because there are dozens of images, even from early Google days, of him in Hawaii. From his beaming arrival with a pink floral lei to his departure, several pounds and gray hairs later, in silver shades. There is one of a Catholic youth group picture in Hawaii with a strapping younger Zimmerman, his regal features softer, his shoulders broader, that catches Maddie's eye. The priest is with a much younger Reagan in that photo. So they did know each other.

Reagan is a true beauty, Maddie has to admit, as she stares at the picture. Her long silky blonde hair parts in the middle, her wide eyes are bright and her smile is easy. There really was a time she was happy. So when did the darkness come? How did it banish the beauty so completely?

But clearly, as Maddie takes notes in her book, Reagan Clark and Christopher Zimmerman have a long history. Going back more than 30 years.

After Maddie wipes out her history on the cafe computer, she hurries out of the coffee-air of the internet cafe, and inhales at last the life on Via delle Fornaci. Turning back, she stares in the cafe window. Like a mirror, it shows no one is following her, no swimmer, no priest. All clear and Maddie strolls along the old street back to her hotel. A sturdy man who could have been a priest in mufti passes behind her, but he doesn't seem interested in Maddie, so he could be a real priest. She keeps going and doubles back, then finally enters the hotel, standing seven stories tall like the villas on the street, but more welcoming, with a beaming clerk at the door, flanked by tall vases of flowers.

She heads right up to her room—no bar and no swimming pool to gaze at. When she steps into the room, she notes it is more like a closet. It is just large enough for her to step out of bed and straight into the wall. Go the other way and she'd fall out the window. It is a small room on a small budget; her own. She made it out of Israel and Jordan with her life. If she wants to keep living, then no one, not even Aretta who holds the INN credit card, can know she is here.

She checks her email to see if anything has rolled in from New York. Just a couple of updates from Aretta, which Maddie responds to with short bursts back that reveal nothing, except that she is closer to getting the

Pope to say "yes" and also sealed the deal with Muenster over the Reagan interview.

Now, if her hunch pays off, she will be as close to the Pope interview as she has been to unraveling the story of Christopher Zimmerman. It is a hunch that came quite by surprise when she met Muenster in Israel and put her in mind to think Reagan was the Zimmerman connection. But now when Maddie goes into her documents file and opens the search box, she sees that she has searched for Christopher Zimmerman and Reagan Clark.

She didn't do that here, but on the cafe computer.

No one followed Maddie into the cafe, and no one saw her search. She even wiped out her browsing history.

She stands up like a shot, head racing, heart pounding. But she has to think fast, and she has to think now. Dunking her head under cold running water, she comes out spluttering. It has just the kind of sobering effect that worked all through Oxford on rough Monday mornings. Then, pacing the small room she lets her thoughts run.

Someone was checking to see if Maddie had made that connection on her own computer, from Zimmerman to Clark, which she had only just done minutes ago. Is it a gift? Is it a threat?

This check-in most certainly is a chilling act. And that convinces Maddie that the danger to Zimmerman came from Clark, and that is where the story goes.

She takes two steps to starboard and is in the bathroom again. Catching herself in the mirror, she looks like she lost weight, which she is not trying to do. Her cheekbones are just a little sharper, her long curls drooping, the black gloss of her hair tarnished and dimmed, and her eyes, weary, as if she has pulled an all-nighter checking footnotes for a conference paper that will not be well-received. Her black wool suit is a little roomier than she'd like it to be, but she's still the type of woman you would notice walking into any room.

Once she removes her makeup, and the stubborn dark stubs of mascara on the base of her eyelashes, she puts on the wire-rimmed glasses that she bought at a farmacia. And with the crucifix that she snagged at a Vatican gift shop hanging from her white collar, she looks just like a very serious and devout young woman. She puts her phone and handbag in a cloth shopping bag, then kicks off the black stilettos she loves and puts on a pair of cheap black lace-up shoes she picked up at an outlet at Piazza Navona. And when she puts on the black and white headpiece, she looks just like a woman who is a nun.

It's exactly how she wants to look.

The burka taught her how useful a disguise could be, and let a woman pass unnoticed into a man's world.

When she looks in the mirror again, she hardly sees herself; she has vanished under the habit. She realizes that Rome has truly given her the way forward to solve her own mystery.

Head down, Maddie walks quickly toward St. Peter's Square, as the last thing she wants is for some American tourist to buttonhole her and ask her for spiritual advice. But no, any inquisitive tourist would ask a priest, and not the real power in the Church, the nuns who have devoted their lives to service, to the people. And so, as a nun in Rome, she can pass utterly unnoticed.

Donning an earnest smile, she walks up to Christopher Zimmerman's apartment. The middle-aged concierge, who was on duty the first time she was here is on again now, is playing another game on his cellphone, punching the screen, and reacting with sharp bobs of his head. He clocks the nun coming in the door, and quickly puts down the phone, as if getting rid of evidence. But he shows no signs of having seen Maddie before, which she appreciates. No, her lack of make-up, her wire glasses, and her nun's habit have made her a different person than when she watched the cops carrying Zimmerman's boxes out of the building.

Maddie gives him a tight smile, and tells the man in colloquial Roman that she is from the Secretariat for Communications. Then she extracts Sister Maria Corvina's business card from her black briefcase, and hands it to him. She tells him she needs to take a few photos of Bishop Zimmerman's apartment for an important meeting with the Secretary of State, Cardinal Otley.

"The Guards have sealed it, Sister," the concierge says apologetically, his hands spread out in the Italian gesture for "*what can a poor fellow like me do*?"

Maddie nods, then produces a wad of red ten Euro notes—100 Euros worth, that she doesn't care if INN reimburses. If the equivalent of a little more than $100 USD gets her inside, it is a bargain. "Will this help open the door?" she asks.

The man's thick brows fly up in shock to meet his hairline as he looks at the money and does a quick calculation—a nun is offering him a bribe. Is this some kind of Vatican trickery, to implicate him in whatever they are looking for in Zimmerman's home? He glances around the lobby, then holds up his hand. "You misunderstand me, Sister," he says. "I am always happy to help the Church."

Maddie can see that this is not completely true, as his eyes linger on the notes in her hand. He takes another look, but that is all he takes. Then, he fishes out a master key set and bids her to follow him.

The Swiss Guards' idea of sealing the apartment is to put an orange notice on the door in Italian, explaining that the apartment is off limits due to an ongoing investigation. The concierge unlocks the oak door, and slowly pushes it open, as if fearing what might be on the other side. Maddie already knows, as she recalls her father's description of the place when he visited Zimmerman in the second video he left for her to see.

Her father's Irish tenor plays in her head.

"God's Banker lives in the kind of lavishness that God herself might envy, his massive apartment filled with Roman light, and showcasing the fine art and photographs lining his ochre walls, all of them somehow connected to him..."

Maddie's father had been generous in his take on Christopher Zimmerman's vanity. Maddie reckons that once Zimmerman had come back to Catholic power town, he figured that he might as well live like he was here.

And he lived well. The apartment is a testament to taste, with soft pastels on its walls—peach and terracotta and Mediterranean blue. Its Georgian windows frame a photographer’s view of St. Peter’s Basilica, its neighbor to the south. The furniture is not exactly what you'd find in a Medici palace, but it is expensive and sleek: black leather and cherry wood and here and there a shot of brass. It lets the visitor know that the resident at the top of the Palazzo San Carlo knows how to live here.

The concierge asks Maddie what photos she needs, and Maddie smiles her tight nun smile, and takes out her phone. “A sense of the place,” she says. “I’ll be fast. You can stay here.”

With her Galaxy phone she clicks a photo of the living room. She gives the concierge the kind of nun-nod that he surely remembers from grade school, one that suggests she knows all of his impure thoughts. It works, and he sweeps his arm forward, in a gesture for her to go forth until the end of time, if she wishes.

To Maddie, Zimmerman is the kind of man who likes to keep things that he could use later. After all, it was his photo of a naked John Paul II that had sped him back to Rome and to this penthouse. She hopes that she will find something in Zimmerman's personal possessions that might help her crack the mystery that she is now working on for both her father and herself.

But the Vatican cops have been thorough. Zimmerman's desk has been emptied. All that is left are a pack of pink post-its and some paper clips. She clicks off a photo and thinks about her father's visit here. What did Zimmerman show him?

And then she thinks about the coded prayer that Sister Nuala had given her from Zimmerman, the one with **"tabernacle, shame, teach me to understand"** in bold.

Maddie lights up with the answer to the puzzle. It is Zimmerman's prized possession—a tabernacle made especially for him in Hawaii.

The large wooden chest is in Zimmerman's bedroom, which is dominated by a king-sized bed, unusual for a chaste priest, Maddie thinks. The Pope himself sleeps in a camp bed.

On an end table, by the window overlooking St. Peter's, sits the tabernacle. It is made from Hawaii's Kamani tree, whose reddish-brown wood features a dramatic stripe when cut.

"It is fiendishly difficult wood to work with, but once mastered produces exquisite cabinetry," Maddie's father had said when they filmed it, *"and Bishop Zimmerman's Hawaiian parishioners had presented it to him as a farewell gift as a symbol of his 'fierce devotion to them', so he says."*

The ornate tabernacle is beautiful, its wood warm and supple, its door an elegant Romanesque portal with a dovetail lock, so different from the brass and red velvet tabernacles Maddie remembers from her time in the pews. The tabernacle is where priests store the eucharist, the body of Christ, and so, the holiest of holy places.

Maddie doesn't expect that she'll find anything inside it except maybe a chalice of stale eucharists, but she doesn't even find that.

She picks up the tabernacle and examines it in the afternoon light. It is a touch heavier than it should be for an empty wooden vessel. And then she spots the seam on the lower portion of the tabernacle. To the casual observer, it looks like a line of design. But Maddie sees a drawer.

She presses one of the dovetail joints and the drawer slides open. Inside is a black leather folder, bound with leather bands. Maddie unties it, and opens the flaps. Within the folder is a manilla envelope, sealed in a ZipLoc bag. Inside the envelope are two silver DVDs. And a photo.

The photo spikes her pulse higher, and it is already high enough having broken into Zimmerman's apartment. Maddie instantly recognizes that beauty in the photo nearly thirty years ago. It is Reagan Clark, and maybe the next President of the United States, on a tropical beach. She could be 21 years old, and aside from the silver crucifix around her neck, she is naked.

She smiles at the photographer with the kind of look that suggests she wants the picture-taker naked as well. And on the back of the photo, someone has written "Reagan and Me, first time… Kahuku Beach, Christmas."

Maddie knows at once who the "Me" is: the same guy who blackmailed the Vatican with a naked photo of Pope John Paul II. It's Christopher Zimmerman. And she is willing to wager that this photo is just the beginning of his blackmail of Reagan Clark.

34. Rome, The Vatican.

Cardinal Otley is very happy to see Maddie on this gloomy June morning in Rome, the gray clouds outside the grand windows of the Secretary of State offices shadowing the Cardinal's smile.

"Ah, Maddie Lynch!" he says, trying to hide his great rush of relief, as he shakes her hand in both of his. "You have returned to us. What news?"

Maddie appreciates the Cardinal getting so quickly to the point, and she responds in kind. "Indeed, your Eminence. I need to know what it is that you want from me?"

Cardinal Otley sits back down onto his cardinal red desk chair and looks at Maddie as if she is a mildly puzzling exam question. "You mean, what do I want to know about Father Franchi?"

"Well, that's part of it," Maddie says. "And I can tell you about him. But first I need to really know how I'm working for you, and why"

Otley smiles, not as if he has been found out, Maddie thinks, but musing to himself like a card shark holding an ace. "Working for me? Unless you've become a nun since I last saw you..." he stops there to let the innuendo land.

"It's a thought. Like the offices, steady work, not sure about the nun dress code …" Maddie replies with humor.

He smiles. "As I said, we're working together on a mutually beneficial project."

She replies by taking the battery out of her phone, signaling it's time to take a stroll in the garden.

"Shall we take a turn in the garden on this fine day?" he says, even though the day is a drudge, and rain could fall at any minute. But that's not Otley's point.

As they arrive at the garden, the sun begrudges them a ray of light. Otley walks on past a trail of wisteria. Maddie stops and Otley turns back to look at her to make sure she is all right. He is exactly where Maddie wants him, in sunlight, so she could see his face when she speaks. "My father produced a long piece on money laundering at the Vatican Bank," she begins.

Otley stares, giving her nothing. "A very good piece," he relents. "Too bad he never finished it." A look of genuine sadness shadows his round face.

"He left that to me," she says,

Otley looks back at Maddie, his blue eyes peering over his half-moon glasses, lit up with what? Anger? Possibility? She wonders if she will be swiftly thrown out of paradise, out of the Vatican garden.

"Your theory is wrong," Otley says, his English accent now clipped and efficient. "Wrong about it being a theory, that is. Zimmerman was actually doing it. He was, shall we say, strongly encouraged to stop."

"If you know that, then why do you need me for our 'mutually beneficial project'?" Maddie asks, risking being blunt.

"The thing is, Maddie," Otley continues, "the world likes to imagine many things about what goes on inside the walls of this place, and I can't say I blame them. I mean, the simple philosophy of the rabbi from the back of beyond didn't quite prescribe all this, did it?"

He waves his hand at the lushness surrounding them, palm trees, lilies, statues of the Virgin Mary. On his hand, the diamond cluster in his bishop's ring sparkles like some kind of magic is about to be revealed.

"But history did. History made us, because people believed, and belief builds power. And we are more than a billion Catholics on the planet. But there are people who will also believe that we are not about caring for the poor and vulnerable, and preaching the good of salvation of mankind and the defeat of evil. But that we are, in fact, up to something else which begins with 'No' and ends with 'Good'."

"Christopher Zimmerman was up to a lot of 'no good'. What did he do when you asked him to stop?"

A look of sorrow weighs on his full round face. "He took our orders to stop as our ignorance, and his reason to go faster. He was trying to start a revolution. Against us, and against everyone who is not us."

"You mean a new Church?"

Otley nods his head slowly, sadly. "That's what we think."

"And 'we' is the Vatican's... intelligence service?"

Otley's head rises up, finally with a smile as if to say now they are related, and he is Maddie's uncle, riding a few glasses of wine. "Ah, the Vatican's intelligence service. What a lovely idea. And you would think, after 2000 years of operations, more than a thousand of them in this town, that we'd have engineered a pretty sophisticated intelligence service, wouldn't you?"

"I do. And I'd venture that's why Zimmerman wanted to start another one."

"You would?"

"Yes. Because he found the one that you had somehow lacking."

"And that's where he was mistaken," Otley says, still smiling like a slightly drunken uncle. "How can it be lacking if you are now inside it?"

He lets the information sit there in mid-air like a portal, watching if Maddie will go through the door, or swat it away.

"I am inside what?" Maddie asks, surprised. "*Prefettura di Informazioni Cattolico.* But we call it Omega. And you are Omega now, too." He reaches into a pocket in his black jacket, and extracts a small, oval medallion. He drops it in Maddie's hands and cups his two large ones over it as if to seal the deal. When he withdraws his hands, she looks at the medallion, and Maddie expects to see some saint that he's going to tell her will help her on her quest. But instead, she sees the symbol for omega, the "Ω" on one side, and on the other, a number: O-944.

"If you ever need to reach us in a, shall we say, in a quiet way, you transmit that number however you can to us."

Maddie feels heat rise in her gut. She thought she'd been drawn into Otley's 'mutually beneficial project' in return for a papal interview. It would guarantee her job at INN, and she'd no longer be a sorry charity hire tied to the whims of Teddy Wright. Maybe along the way she would find out about her father, the far-away, hard working, famed journalist, who seemed like a ghost in life.

"I didn't agree to be a Vatican spy," she whispers

"Of course you didn't. Nor did we ask you to become one." Otley pats her on the back. "You did that all on your own with your crowning moment coming when you disguised yourself as a nun and paid a visit to the sealed flat of Christopher Zimmerman, which showed both imagination and initiative."

Maddie nods to herself; of course the cardinal has spies at Zimmerman's residence, and the American Colony, and everywhere.

"We already knew you were smart. We just wanted to see if you were resourceful." Otley steps back and smiles at Maddie up and down like a proud parent. "Impressively so. And I take it you found something?"

"I did," she confesses, feeling almost relieved.

"Thank God," Otley says and closes his eyes as he crosses himself. "Well, that in itself is a lot more than others who tried the same thing. So, tell me, please."

Maddie turns over the medallion in her hand, giving her time to think. Does she tell Otley what she knows, and in that sign a contract, the kind which you can never break. Or apologize with elaborate courtesy for the misunderstanding and for the trouble to them both, and to get the hell out now. But that way she betrays herself and her father.

The Cardinal's face is once again that of a poker

player, this time with a full house. Maddie won't walk away from the story that her father has begun.

She starts to speak. But she doesn't know what to say. And she certainly is not sure what the pictures mean and the contents of the disk inside the black leather folder she has found in Zimmerman's tabernacle. "I will tell you when I know what I am telling you," she says.

Otley stuns her by smiling, real and warm; he is not angered by her mysterious non-reply. Then he surprises her again. "You'll get your Pope interview, by the way. You have my word."

Maddie feels as if she has been knocked around in a kind of ecclesiastical cage fight. Everyone has been playing her in the service of the Vatican's glory. "I just want to get this straight, Your Eminence: has anything that you told me been true?"

"It's all true, and you have been using those truths to probe for another one." Then the Cardinal smiles warmly again, like a true pastor. "Ask me anything."

"Was it Omega who broke into my computer?"

Otley blinks now. He does not know about this.

"On my first visit to see you," Maddie continues. "Someone broke in and has been watching me."

"That was not us," Otley says, clearly rattled by this news. "And what have you done about it?"

"I have been careful," she says.

"Good. Now I get a question. How did things go with Victor Franchi ?"

Maddie realizes that Otley doesn't know. He's not the kind of man to pretend. So she starts at the beginning.

"He showed me how Christopher Zimmerman blackmailed the Vatican."

"How did he do that?"

Otley blinks and waits. From that, Maddie can tell he does not know that either.

"He had a photo of Pope John Paul II sunbathing naked and said, in so many words, he'd show it to the world if they didn't do what he wanted."

Otley's eyes widen. "And he got what he wanted. Did he give you copies?"

"He said he was going to do so, but when I went to the Biblicum for our second meeting, he wasn't there. So I went back to his house, and someone attacked me."

"At Franchi's house?"

"Yes. two of them, armed. They could have killed me if they wanted to. I think that they were sending a message for me to stop what I was looking for."

He pats her arm, glad she is safe---and brave. "And what are you looking for?" the Cardinal asks her.

Maddie smiles like she now has the aces, three of them. "Missing money. Who killed Christopher Zimmerman. And what Victor Franchi is doing, if he is still alive."

"You have doubts?"

"There was blood on the floor."

"Could be real, or a diversion," Otley says quickly. "And you think all of what he showed you and possibly more would be in his flat?"

"I don't know," Maddie says. "Yet."

Otley beams at her. "You were born for this, Maddie

Lynch. Call it your vocation."

Maddie feels a ripple of electricity run up her spine. The Cardinal is right. She is good at 'this'.

Cardinal Otley tilts his head, as if to say tell me more, but Maddie just nods. "I will investigate. And when I know it, you'll know it."

Otley grins at her, then hands her back her cell phone batteries. The interrogation is over for now. But then he grabs her by both hands again. "Just remember, Maddie, the story never ends. Neither its pursuit, nor its achievement, because there is always evil trying to pull it back to that dark place."

As Otley ushers her from the garden, he says, almost as an afterthought, "By the way, when it comes to Omega, we're all atheists. We don't exist. Never have. Never will."

Maddie walks briskly to Il Convento after leaving Cardinal Otley. She wants to check up on Sister Patrizia. She received the message that the nun was ill, and Maddie suspects that's because of what she has discovered in Israel.

She quickly slips on the medallion, feeling its gold warm her, and hoping it brings her luck.

She is not so sure as she steps into the comfortable old lodge, and the same clerk to whom she gave the 50 Euro bribe is on the desk. He looks up in surprise as Maddie enters.

"You got my message, Doctor Lynch?" he says before Maddie can speak.

"Yes, that Sister Patrizia was doing poorly. Thank

you for sending it."

The clerk lowers his head and raises his eyes. "Ah. I have sent you another, just this morning. Sister Patrizia is now in heaven."

Maddie feels heat rush to her cheeks. "Was Bishop Hughes here to see her?"

"Right to the very end," the clerk says. "He gave her last rites, thanks be to God."

"Thanks be," says Maddie, though she thinks Hughes was there to make sure that no one found out what Sister Patrizia could reveal. Could she have done anything? Should she have warned Cardinal Otley?

A wave of sadness catches her in its undertow. It was thanks to Sister Patrizia she had the prayer from Sister Nuala, which helped her to find the hidden folder in the tabernacle belonging to Zimmerman.

What other part of the story might the prayer reveal?

She mulls over the thought. Then she hears the ping of a WhatsApp message on her new phone. She checks it, and it's from Luke Macclesfield: *I have found good stuff Maddie.*

She answers him at once. *Where are you?*

Dublin.

Maddie leaves another 50 Euros for the clerk. Then, as she steps out into the dusk, she scrolls through her new phone. There's an Aer Lingus flight from Rome to New York that goes through Dublin. And that's the one she needs now.

35. Rome & Dublin.

That evening on Zoom, back in Maddie's tiny hotel room in Rome, Aretta proudly lets Teddy know they are in contact with Reagan Clark's people and working on a possible sit down between Teddy and Reagan Clark.

Teddy won't let the proud gush flow and jumps in, demanding to know the "dopester on the popester".

Maddie lets her and Aretta know they are very getting closer to getting the Pope on TV. She just had a couple more things to do. Teddy squeals with delight. She even hugs Aretta. If she gives Maddie any credit, it comes in the form of an even longer leash and a travel budget to go with it to get that 'Yes' from the Vatican.

Right away, Maddie enjoys the new and bigger budget for a roomier airplane seat to Ireland.

It takes her to Dublin at the start of the first week of June, and the bright and shiny blue sky over the gray Leinster granite, of which Dublin is made, is getting ready for Bloomsday on the 16th. A glass of Claret and a Gorgonzola sandwich to celebrate James Joyce and his novel *Ulysses* is what is on the menu everywhere.

University College Dublin, where Luke Macclesfield teaches, doesn't look like any part of James Joyce's Dublin, but the ultra modern cement and glass Arts and Humanities building set on a lake could be a resort, but one for college students holidaying with fat works of literature or dusty tomes of history. Its labyrinth of hallways, though, is just as winding as Dublin and so after a few minutes of passing the same classrooms over and over, and her sore knee giving her a limp, Maddie yanks out her cell and calls her fellow godparent to demand to know not only where he is, but where she is.

"Here we are, Godma," says Luke on his cell, slipping out of a classroom behind her, looking very much the professor in standard issue tweed jacket, rumpled jeans and glasses. Before leading Maddie into his room, he waves out a few straggling students from his last class. If they aren't already on their phones, they're sending flirty smiles to Luke, young men and women alike. He might be a professor, but being witty, fit and on the better side of forty, they want him to smile back. Luke quashes that hope with a reminder of their upcoming finals and sends them off without a smile.

Maddie is the one who manages to lift a grin on his boyish face. "I think you've got quite the fan club, Godpa."

He rubs his broad forehead at that, as if student crushes weary his great brain. "It's a problem. These days, admin and HR warn us to 'Don't touch and don't even look'!" He settles Maddie into one of the student desks at the front of the room. "So, I keep my eyes on my work. I much prefer history anyways."

"I'm glad you do. Thanks, Godpa." Maddie's smile fades as she gives her old knee a rub.

"Are you OK? I saw you limping."

Maddie only says that she had slipped. She neglects to say she slipped on a pool of blood, probably from a murdered priest, but she could not stop to check as she had to flee two thugs packing Russian pistols. Maddie smiles to herself, thinking how she expertly shot one attacker in the kneecap.

As she looks around the classroom, it is also standard issue, with rows of metal student desks, and a big professor desk at the front, surrounded by white boards, a bank of computers and a giant computer screen. "Ah ha, you've got some modern perks in your history class."

He nods, glad for it but then starts by pulling a fat folder out of his backpack.

"There's a lot to digest in here, Maddie."

"I'm ready."

Luke doesn't open the folder, but slides it over to her. "I created a summary for you and put it as the top sheet. The other pages are notes I took in the library. You can take them with you." He opens his computer and with a remote control in hand dims the lights. The screen at the front of the class lights up. He has done a powerpoint presentation for her, with him doing the narration beside her.

"Let me tell you a bit about Josip Babić, the guy who delivered the gold to the Vatican in 1944. He has a recurring role, as it were."

The giant screen on the front wall fills with a photo of Rome in 1946, and a photo of a church, which Luke reveals is the monastery of San Girolamo, a Croatian house. With its white marble facade, and one dark window at the top center, it looks like a place of secrets.

"Josip Babić lands back in Rome in September 1946. He stays at the gloomy San Girolamo, which is run by another Croatian, a priest named Krunoslav Draganović."

Maddie is surprised to see there's a photo of Father Draganović in a black uniform, not one from the priesthood but that of an Ustaše lieutenant-colonel.

"Yes, his 'other job' was an officer in the Ustaše… who also worked with the Nazis," Luke says more quietly. "The Vatican maintained an "Apostolic visitor" in Zagreb from June 1941 until the end of the War. So, it didn't miss the killing campaign, which started with the internment of most of the 35,000 to 45,000 Croatian Jews in the spring of 1941."

Up comes another photograph, this one of Ustaše troopers, standing armed and upright in their black uniforms, shooting Orthodox Jews, huddled together in family embraces.

Maddie's heart knocks hard as she asks, "Was this picture in the Archives?"

"Aye. They knew well what was going on. And this priest Draganović has quite the brief with the Ustaše. He oversees confiscation of Serb property by the Ustaše in Bosnia and Herzegovina. So, he's a busy man when he comes to Rome in August 1943. And like that, he's snapped up another job, that of secretary of the Croatian 'Confraternity of San Girolamo,' which then becomes the HQ for the Croat ratline. Let me add, he also had a part in the escape of the Croatian dictator Ante Pavelić to Argentina. Among many others."

Maddie takes a calming breath, but her heart is still racing. "One of them being Josip Babić, I am betting."

"And you would win the bet," Luke grins, pleased with her smarts and with himself for being able to use his archival work for her. "Josip Babić knows Draganović from their good old days in the fascist Ustaše. In 1944, Babić goes to Switzerland, and meets with Joachim Zimmerman…"

"Christopher Zimmerman's father…" Maddie adds as the Vatican history closes in on the story she's chasing. This is where the bank document Sister Nuala gave her comes in. "Next, Babić makes a big fat transfer in Ustaše gold to Zimmerman's bank."

Luke shudders to hear her say that. "I don't know how you know that, and maybe I won't ask… But, aye, Babić transfers $1 million in Ustaše gold to Zimmerman's bank."

The lost links to the dark past begin to tie into the present as the story connects before Maddie on the screen. She is anxious to see what comes next, and sits upright to get a better view of the screen, of images of young, battle-thin British troops and well-fed priests in Austria, captioned 1946, laughing as they load crates of supplies onto a truck.

"So Babić 's $1 million in gold is a lot of gold. I reckon pushing two tons, given that the price of gold was around $34 an ounce at the time. Then, I think Babić smuggles more gold into the Vatican through Austria, with help from the British. Joachim Zimmerman works with Josip Babić to keep the gold flowing; all told, the files say, more than $20 million worth."

Not something that you can hide under a cassock,

Maddie thinks. "Did Pope Pius XII know about this deal?"

Luke shakes his head. "It was a private deal between Zimmerman and Babić, with the knowledge of Draganović. But very much behind the back of Pope Pius XII."

"He was busy with other things, what with World War Two wrapping up, and about 70 million dead, and millions more without a home or country?" Maddie asks with an edge. But she is learning how millions of dollars can move around through Vatican players, or in the Church's own bank, without any Pope knowing.

"Working on that, Maddie. But your man Babić, with help from the Vatican, escapes to Argentina. With $10 million of that gold."

Maddie, quick with her gold math, says, "That's twenty tons. Not fitting in a suitcase."

"He had help for sure. He works for the CIA in Argentina, and then he moves to the United States, where he marries and starts a family. By the way, some of his ill-gotten gold goes to fund the presidential run of Richard M. Nixon."

Maddie's stomach takes a nasty turn as she thinks over the lengthening list of bad actors, now including the CIA and the defamed 37th president, Nixon.

Luke clicks through his powerpoint. "Babić has a son, Martin, who becomes a priest. Perhaps in hopes of generational absolution…"

"I suppose it would be a miracle if we had any photos of him?"

Luke sits up smartly like the kid in the front row of the classroom who has the answers. “Coming right up, Godma.” As he searches his computer file he lets Maddie know that most of the stolen gold stayed under the management of Joachim Zimmerman. The banker even came to visit Babić in DC, bringing his own son, who became pals with Babić’s son.

“And so the boys carried on the friendship?” Maddie asks.

Luke agrees while he zips back and forth through his computer file, hunting for the photo. Maddie asks if he knows the final fate of gold that remained with Zimmerman’s Bank. She hasn’t heard from her own banker friend, Emily.

“As of 1958, it’s still there,” says Luke. He’s come to the end of his file and no luck. So, he searches for Martin’s picture in Maddie’s fat file with the expertise of a bank teller counting money. As he goes, he says, “Hard to know exactly. The Bank was sold when Joachim Zimmerman dies in 1986.”

“Who buys it?”

“That I don’t have, but this I do have for you.” Luke beams, his boyish face lit up under his grand forehead as he taps a photocopied Vatican identity card.

Maddie’s heart almost stops when she sees a face she has seen before, strong, with a putty nose, and wary intelligence in those blue eyes, under slicked back black hair. She’s looking at Victor Franchi staring back at her.

Luke stares at Maddie, sitting in the dark, her face lit by the images on the front screen, her cheeks burning hot pink. "You've gone all flushed of cheek, Maddie. I mean, it's very attractive, but are you OK? I think it's time we hit the pub and I order you a double Jamesons?"

That would be the right remedy, Maddie explains, but she has to do some fact checking of her own. Pulling out her new phone, she sends a text to Cardinal Otley: *What is Father Victor Franchi's full name, and when and where was he born?*

Otley answers immediately: *Martin Victor Franchi, born December 8, 1956, in Hyattsville, Maryland. And???*

Maddie texts back her response to the *"And??? When I see you.*

Now she has the connection her father did not have. Victor Franchi is the son of Josip Babić. And that is the key to the story her father did not know, but Maddie now has the story in her hands.

Luke clicks the lights back on, keeping his eyes on Maddie as he shuffles his laptop into his backpack. She looks as if she's been hit over the head. "I'm sorry, Maddie, but usually when I give presentations my class is taking notes or nodding off. You look like you could hurl."

"I'm fine. I'm very fine." Maddie gathers herself and rises, her eyes shining, lit with a new confidence. "Luke Macclesfield, you are a hero."

"I am?" he says and allows himself a shy smile. "You pointed me to the dirt and I did some digging. It was all there."

Maddie tucks the folder in her bag, then gives Luke a

kiss on the cheek, which makes him blush. “You have cracked a code for me. Next round is on me, but not just yet. Now, I have to race and catch a flight.” She puts a 20 Euro note on his desk. “But until we meet again, the next few rounds are on me.”

36. Beirut, Lebanon.

The book shops and cafes sprawling out into the sidewalks from the first floors of the lines of handsome apartment blocks, under the kindly shade of the cover of trees, looks like anywhere in Paris. But the Dar Bistro and Books is in the Hamra section of Beirut, a short walk along the Corniche to the limestone cliffs of Raouche, in the city which was once known as the Paris of the Middle East. But turn the corner and see that many of those stalwart apartment blocks, the ones that survived the Israeli bombs, have been drilled with black holes of machine-gunfire, one that had cleaved Beirut in half, creating two solitudes of Christian and Muslim. It was a severance that had sent many young people on the run, into exile, forty years ago.

That's what Father Victor Franchi remembers, having to flee the city he loved as a young man. He isn't here today as a young scholar, nor as a dead priest as some suspect. He is here as a living conduit of revolution.

He has to keep up that living part, though he'd rather be in front of a whiskey than a dry sandwich, having lunch in Dar Bistro and Books, the commissary at Saint Joseph University. Franchi sits in a corner away from the raging glare of its whiteness, the color that seems to pass these days for newness. It's not like the old days of long chats in work leather chairs, sharing packs of cigarettes until the air was blue, when he studied Moral Theology.

That was until April 18, 1983, when it sounded as if

the apocalypse had arrived. The car bomb exploded beneath the United States Embassy in West Beirut, a building with a serene prospect of the Mediterranean Sea and the palms. The blast was so loud that Franchi's ears rang for a week afterward, sounding the death knell of the 60 souls who had been killed in the worst attack on the United States in the Middle East in history. An unknown group calling itself Islamic Jihad claimed responsibility, but Franchi understands that this bloody moment was really the beginning of Hezbollah. And today, Franchi crackles his dry laugh as he thinks Hezbollah has lost a lot of its might, thanks to its own hubris, and the Israeli army. Something needs to replace it. And he knows what will.

It has been a long time since Victor Franchi has inhaled the mulberry fragrance of the beautiful, tragic city. So he takes his espresso out to a table in the courtyard of the bistro. In the quiet, in the fruited air it's hard to believe that Franchi is a short stroll from where that flashpoint for the future had gone off. Where he sits, he could be in any of the tiled and trellised al fresco spots that he so loves—in Cairo, in Jerusalem, or better still, in Rome. And it is because of Rome that he came racing back to Beirut.

The fact that his rendezvous point is on Roma Street, and that he has not chosen it himself, makes it seem as if God is on his side. No, not seem. The Almighty knows. But it was also nice to have this ticket of knowledge stamped by reality.

The protocol had been clear. Order an espresso, have

a copy of the Camus novel *L'Étranger* open, and sit facing the entrance to the courtyard, where he could be seen. He has done all he was asked, and now waits for whomever will show up.

He knows he has made contact as soon as he sees the tall African man enter the courtyard.

"*Aujourd'hui, maman est morte*," the African says, his bass voice accented with the vowels of Africa. *Mother died today*, the opening line of Camus's novel.

"*Ou peut-être hier, je ne sais pas,*" Franchi replies. *Or maybe yesterday, I can't be sure*—the second line of the book.

The African sits down, and touches his hand to his heart. "*Al salaam a'alaykum.*"

"*A'alaykum al salaam,*" Franchi replies. He doesn't touch his heart, but he gives a polite smile, then says, "*Puis-je on parle en anglais?*" His French is good, if a little rusty, but English is his mother tongue, and a much better defense against any surprises.

"Of course. English is my favorite language to speak. It is so direct." The African is in his mid-thirties, and slender, like a dancer. He wears a crisp white shirt and a gray suit, no tie, like the Islamic scholar he is. His eyes bear the heat of something other than holy scripture.

"That it is," says Franchi, who can also be direct in Arabic and Hebrew and Italian, and French, too, though he has lied to the man about that. His native tongue and his native wit are what he needs today.

"Did you have a good trip?" the African contact asks. He is also trying to be polite, even though they are both keenly aware this is not a social occasion. No names, just a transaction.

“It's always a pleasure to be in Lebanon,” Franchi replies. “So many fellow travelers.”

“There are only a few of us. Nigerians, I mean.”

“But you punch above your weight.” Franchi’s blue eyes sparkle, an exclamation mark on his flattery.

The man tips his shaved head and smiles quizzically. “I do not know this expression.”

“You have influence greater than your numbers.”

The man leans forward, nodding in grave understanding. “Like the Jews.”

“Well,” Franchi says, rubbing his hands, “the Jews are the reason why we're here.”

The Nigerian relaxes, folding his own large hands on the table, hiding nothing. “Indeed they are.”

Franchi points under the table, indicating he is about to get something. The other man nods, and then Franchi reaches under and slides a black attaché case from beneath it. “Here's the first installment.”

The man scoops up the case as if it is filled with air, which it is. “This is very light for so much money.”

“Inside you will find a flash drive,” Franchi says. “It is encrypted. Once I am safely arrived wherever I am next going, I will send you the encryption key on Signal. That will allow you to access the funds, $10 million Euros, in Austria. It will also give you direction on contacting the supplier of what you need. It will buy you a few little birds, to be sure.”

The man looks at Franchi on a blink of

embarrassment, as if he's just been schooled in the art of financing a drone jihad. “Well then, I will look forward to your communication. How long before I hear from you?”

“Soon,” Franchi says. “But don’t try to decrypt it yourself, or it will destroy the key.”

The man drops his gaze, looking embarrassed again, as if Franchi has read his mind. “Understood.” He rises with the attaché case. “We shall smite the dogs of Abraham, inshallah,” he says.

Franchi’s lined face folds back to allow a smile. But it isn’t the dogs of Abraham that he wants to smite. If he must listen to the usual hit list of Israel hate to accomplish his grand plan, then so be it. He is here to help the Jews, not hurt them, so it is a delicate game he is playing. He knows that once you get into a league with the Iranians, then you could wind up swinging from a crane hook in Tehran, or taking two in the head from Mossad.

Even so, it is a risk he has to take for the sake of the Society of the Blessed Urban II. If Israel is to survive, if the homeland of his Messiah is to continue to exist and not be turned into one giant mosque, with a bomb factory in the tunnels beneath it, then this is the course of action that he must take.

He has nothing but affection for the Israelis. Who can blame them for taking friendship from such a rum lot as the Evangelical flat-earthers? All their Christian buddies want to do is bring on Armageddon and convert the Jews, and destroy the Holy Land in the process.

The sooner they are cleared out of the place, the better. And the sooner the Jews will realize that their only true friend is Rome, which will help them see the wisdom of negotiating a two-state solution before demographics does it for them, and they are sent into exile once again. Or worse.

Victor Franchi is a crusader all right, but he is one who has learned the lessons of the past. Indeed, he had them burned into him, thanks to his former friendship with Christopher Zimmerman. The great insight that the Swiss priest had given him is that the Muslims are not just the hair-trigger enemy with an insatiable appetite for blood. They are far more powerful than that. The Muslims are the weapon that they will use to win the war.

That, and the next President of the United States. Franchi takes out his phone as he watches the Nigerian walk away with the briefcase, and sends a text to someone who will appreciate it.

It has begun: he texts in Signal, resisting the urge to add an ironic "thumbs up" emoji.

Thanks be to Allah, comes the reply. Franchi smiles. At least Brett Muenster has a sense of humor.

37. New York City.

Maddie walks into the *I'm Wright Show* floor and into the meeting room five minutes after the day's production meeting has begun, brandishing an envelope bearing the papal insignia of the keys of St. Peter and the papal tiara.

"We're in business, Teddy," Maddie says, handing her the letter.

"He said yes?"

"Open it."

Teddy Wright carefully opens the envelope, scans the letter from Cardinal Otley, and then looks at Maddie as if she has just told her the Pope is going to canonize her, and that she is about to ascend to glory without actually having to die first.

"The Pope will do a sit-down with you, Teddy," Maddie says, taking a seat at the side with Aretta and the trio of other associate producers. "Cardinal Otley, the Secretary of State, as you can see, has confirmed it."

Aretta starts clapping and a cheer goes up from the whole room. Teddy now claps her hands like a 3-year-old finally seeing their birthday cake. "Ooh, this is going to be so fucking awesome!" she trills. "A whole sixty minutes for me and the Popester!"

Maddie catches the eye of Aretta, who gives her a wink.

"Maddie Lynch," Teddy purrs, becoming the teacher to the star pupil. "You get a raise, Maddie Lynch, and now you're associate producer. I mean, of course I know the Pope would want to talk to me, but you certainly could have fucked it up and you didn't. So that counts for something in my books."

Maddie is already an associate producer but doesn't want to spoil the Hallmark moment by pointing that out. "I'm working out the details with Cardinal Otley," she says. And since she is on a winning streak herself, she says, "I think I have Reagan Clark as well."

Teddy smiles broadly, but her eyes are shifting. "Maddie Lynch, are you gunning for my job?!"

Maddie laughs and shakes her head. "I got lucky in Israel and met Reagan's manager at the Land of God. He says she'll do it."

Aretta now speaks in support. "Reagan Clark would drive the ratings through the roof, given the current climate."

"You mean because of her planned crusade against the medieval bigots?" Teddy says.

It's not a rehearsal for Teddy's opening salvo for her Reagan interview. Maddie knows it's Teddy's own medieval bigotry. She glances at Aretta, who stares at Teddy with pain in her eyes.

"We know the Pope is going to come down on the side of Islam," Maddie says. "That is a huge, new audience for you. Teddy, you could double the advertising sales budget for Clark, and quadruple it for the Pope."

Teddy is on her feet and looking at Maddie with real admiration, as if she is the daughter Teddy always sort of wanted to have.

For Maddie, that look is just as dangerous as Teddy's

backstabbing. She has seen vicious academic jealousy in Oxford in which the reason to admire you was also the reason to trash you, and so Maddie rolled with it as a function of big egos in a little hothouse. But TV-land, she thinks, makes Oxford look like Quakers on anti-depressants. The killer moves Maddie has seen as an agent of the Vatican makes the ego games at Oxford and in television seem simple in their intrigues. Like high school, but with a fat salary to lose on the table. She hadn't signed up with the Vatican, but they had signed up with her. Once this story is told, she can release herself back into the secular world and get on with her life. She'll take the Omega medallion that hangs around her neck and toss it in with her old school rosary in a jewelry box somewhere.

Or maybe she'll keep it. Maybe this now is her life, and the closing of one story will lead to another. So, she chooses her next words very carefully, as she wants to keep Teddy on the hook and buy herself some more time.

"I also found an interesting line on Reagan Clark when I was in the Vatican," Maddie says, as if casually commenting on the weather.

Teddy Wright pulls down her black Clark Kent glasses and looks interested. "What? She wants to invade Vatican City? Win the place back for her crowd of true believers?"

The three other associate producers at the table laugh at this.

"No, don't think so," Maddie says evenly. "But she had a pretty unusual relationship with the Church when she was in Hawaii."

"What kind of unusual?" Teddy asks.

"Well, she was pretty friendly with Christopher Zimmerman, the Vatican banker."

"How?"

"I don't know," Maddie lies. "But her PR guy was concerned enough to ask me about him."

"What's the angle? I still can't see the angle," Teddy says and Aretta looks to Maddie, who nods to her.

"Christopher Zimmerman was the priest found dead in that church in midtown, a couple of months ago," Aretta says.

Teddy thinks. "Really? I didn't hear about it."

There is a lot Teddy does not hear about, Maddie thinks, because she only hears herself and what she wants to hear to advance her agenda. A dead priest, one who apparently died of a heart attack, means nothing. But he means everything to Maddie.

"I think they worked together," Maddie says, which, from the look of the photo of the pair of them on the beach, was certainly true. They were about to work on a little applied physics. "But I need to do some digging."

Teddy runs her tongue over her lips, not as a cheesy come on, but in anticipation of a feast.

"Where do you need to dig, Maddie?" she asks. "I'm guessing Hawaii?"

Maddie shakes her head. "That would be nice, but I have some leads here."

"Great!" Teddy says and claps her hands. "Back to work everyone!"

The other producers trudge off to the desks to develop shows about a ring-wing nutjob who found a left-wing senator's opioid recovery diary, or about an LGBTQ rapper running as an independent. Nothing as weighty or glamorous as an interview with the Pope or would-be President.

As Maddie heads to her own desk, Teddy takes her by the arm, as if in a conspiracy. "You'll help me prep for the Pope, yes?"

"Of course," Maddie says.

"I mean, he'll be here in about six weeks."

"Right. I'd better get Reagan Clark in here soon, then."

Teddy replies with a fiendish smile. "I need no help with her. By the time I'm done with that crazy bitch, she's going to beg me for mercy."

Maddie nods, as if this is normal talk from a boss. But she knows that Teddy Wright has no idea what Reagan Clark can do. And Maddie has to find out just what Reagan Clark has done to get where she is today.

38. New York City.

Maddie has not felt this good since she was last on the ice, about a month ago. It took her a while to get her skating legs back, especially after she smacked her knee black and blue running for her life, out of a villa in Jerusalem. But her teammates are so happy that she made it, even with a slight limp into the change room, back for the big game, the semi-final against the Hunter Hotshots.

And it was a month ago Maddie asked her friend Emily to find out if the old document from the Zimmerman bank she sent from her cell phone was real. Maddie has let the question ride out into silence. Answering it could be lethal.

After the team suits up and clomps off on their skates to the ice, Emily holds Maddie back for a moment. Popping out her mouth guard, she needs to have a quiet word. "I don't want to jinx the game…" she says, her blue eyes bright.

"You can't, Em. Unless you go out and spit on the other players!"

"Mads, I wanted to tell you in person what I found out about the…" Emily whispers, "...bank document…"

"It's real?"

Emily blushes hot pink as only a person can with pale skin. "Yes…"

Maddie gives her a hug. Another reason she loves Emily is that she can't lie and if she ever tried her face would burn off in a hot, embarrassed blush.

"You also asked me to find out what happened to that money," Emily says quietly.

"Any luck with the other ask?" Maddie asks, though she dreads the danger that will land on Emily if anything should get out. But what would get out? No one is more careful, trustworthy and discreet than Emily.

"I don't know yet, but I will soon. OK?"

"OK."

Grinning, they both skate out on the ice. The other Chiclets welcome them onto the rink, banging their sticks on the ice with a clattering welcome and screaming, "Chick-let's win! Chick-let's win!"

The Chiclets enthusiasm adds a few liters of adrenalin to the mix. Maddie is still skating strong with two minutes left to go, and with her Columbia Chiclets down 2-1 to Hunter.

Maddie and Emily are out for a face off in their own zone. Emily, with her stick scraping the ice, wins the puck, and drops it back to Karla the defender. She hustles behind the Columbia net, and starts skating up the right wing. Maddie takes off along the left wing, and Karla shoots the puck between two Hunter Hotshots right on to Maddie's stick.

Maddie is in the Hunter zone with Emily on a two-on-one, and she dishes the puck to her friend. Just as Emily is about to let rip with a shot that cannot miss, a hockey stick comes flying like a spear from a Hunter defender in chase, and whacks Emily in the back. She stumbles and falls, landing hard on her back, winded. The pucks dribbles harmlessly into the Hunter goalie's glove, and the referee raises her arm, then points to center ice. Penalty shot for Columbia.

Maddie does not think that is justice enough, and she skates hard at the Hunter hockey stick spear thrower, a big redhead who reminds her of Cosmos's wife Elka. The redhead drops her gloves, but she doesn't take off her helmet, with its full face shield made of clear polycarbonate.

Maddie drops her gloves and rips off her helmet, and plows into the Hunter defender, knocking her hard to the ice. Maddie lands on top of her, and pummels her on the side of the helmet.

"You fucking coward!" Maddie screams at the defender, who just grins as Maddie's blows do no harm. Maddie reaches for the defender's neck and clasps her hands around the woman's throat, but she is pulled off by her Columbia teammates before she can commit murder.

"You fucking loser!" Maddie hollers at the defender, who is still grinning at her. "Karma is going to be a real bitch!"

The referee skates up to Maddie and says, "You got five, please leave the ice."

Maddie has a five-minute major penalty, and since there is only a minute and thirty seconds left, she heads to the dressing room. She knows she is her team's best shot, and she has let her temper get the better of her. All of the pressure of her work for the Vatican has exploded here, on the ice in New York.

So she sits alone in the dressing room, listening to the

silence before the Columbia penalty shot. She hears the referee's whistle for the Columbia shooter to go, and then five seconds later she hears a massive cheer: "Hotshots! Hotshots! Hotshots!"

Whoever took the penalty shot for her team did not score. And then, when her teammates tromp their silence into the dressing room, she knows that they lost the game. She wails an apology for playing a crap game and losing it when they could have won. She even slaps down two hundred bucks to pay for a post-game beer cure, which she's sure they want to take without her. But no, the team wants her to come out for a post-game blowout, yet she cannot.

"I have to meet someone," she tells them. As they clap and wolf-whistle for that, she assures them it is not a hot date, though she wishes. She's meeting her mother.

"I had the penalty shot. I tried to take the shot like you would have done, Maddie," Emily says, looking like she just failed every test imaginable. "But I was still winded, I guess."

"Hey, Em," Maddie says, turning the hug around and embracing her friend. "You played a great game and you would have had that goal. The scumbag knew it, and chanced the penalty shot, and then I blew it by losing my temper."

"Well, I am glad you did it," Emily says. "Besides, there is always next season."

Maddie smiles as she savors the motto of the athlete and the sports fan alike, after their season comes to an end without a championship trophy hoisted above it.

The redheaded defender is waiting for Maddie outside the dressing room with that smug smile on her face.

"You want to keep it going, bitch?" she says to Maddie

Maddie fights the impulse to punch her in the nose.

Instead, Maddie says "We're off the ice now, scumbag, and if you look up, you'll see the video cameras looking at you. So, if you want to do something even stupider than what you did on the ice, then go for it. And I will bring charges, with the video evidence. You can play for the fucking prison hockey team. If they have one."

The woman looks at Maddie, but says nothing. So Maddie just walks on, her heart pounding, her fists clenched. Hoping that she will see a next season. And she will be the karma on that player herself.

39. New York City.

Angels and saints need a regular polish. The white Carrara marble of the small statues of angels and the gold halos painted onto the wood carvings of saints are meant to shine on behalf of heaven, right here on earth and in *Arte Sacra.* In Francesca's small gallery, one speck of dust can end the connection to the divine. At least for the customer, and so for Francesca.

"It's a mortal battle we wage, dust to dust to be dusted," Francesca used to say to her daughter when she was little, as if that would encourage young Maddie to help clean the entire shop with its dozens of icons, busts, pictures and statues. That divine impulse, together with a couple of bucks, and mother and daughter would dust the gold icons and marble statues. The best part for Maddie was, when the work was done, her mother let her get out her toys and in the shiny shop, with the little beaming cherubs and Mary, and all the saints, and play dolls in heaven.

Francesca had suggested Maddie come over to help close the shop this Saturday as normal, which was not something Maddie had done for a while. She checks the security camera's red on light, the doors are locked, and the steel grid of the front window is locked shut, too. Then she hustles up the backstairs from the office to her mother's apartment above.

Behind the marble-topped bar in the dining area of the apartment, Francesca reaches inside her safe, and produces the package that Maddie has sent to her via UPS from Rome. It is unopened.

"Thanks, Mama," Maddie says.

"Are you alright?" Francesca asks. She smooths back her thick salt and pepper hair with the curls curving around her sculpted face. "You look like you want to hit something."

Maddie smiles to hear the plain truth. "Yes. Played hockey this afternoon. I am still thinking about the punch not taken."

"It is always hard to keep so much inside," Francesca says, though her eyes are on the mysterious package, about the size of a thick textbook. "What kind of punch is in there? Mafia?"

Maddie tries not to roll her eyes, as she did as a kid. For her mother, the contessa and the nun genes always teamed up to find their way to the unifying theory that the Mafia was responsible for everything. If only it were that straightforward, Maddie thinks.

"*Al confessore, medico e madre, non tenere il ver celato,*" her mother says, changing the proverb to replace "lawyer" with herself. "Don't hide the truth from your doctor or mother." She fires up a cigarette, taking a long drag and blowing off smoke. She is an Italian smoker, lighting up after a good coffee, or in the face of disaster.

"I don't know all that it is in there, Mama," Maddie says. "But I do know that it could be dangerous."

Sirens wail in the distance. Maddie looks at her mother and can see the fear in her eyes. She feels it, too. As if something terrible is coming next.

"Where did you get it?" her mother asks.

"From Christopher Zimmerman's flat in Rome. Papa helped me."

Francesca ditches her cigarette to cup her hands around her daughter's beautiful face. Her liquid brown eyes dance over the face that in its dark corners has the wildness of her husband. Francesca understands. She speaks to him all the time in the middle of the night. "I knew he would. But if it is dangerous, don't you think you should leave it here, in my safe? I mean, who else knows you have it?"

The Vatican's Secretary of State, and likely his subordinate, Bishop Hughes. Who himself is dangerous, especially to nuns.

So Maddie says, "A cardinal in the Vatican." She sounds offhanded, but Francesca is wise to the ways of the Vatican.

"That is a mafia, too. They are indeed dangerous. They would stab you in the back one second, and then look as holy as holy the next. You should look at it in my office. Keep it here. And tell no one what you find."

Francesca's office at the back of the shop is neat, the large desk growing tidy piles of paper standing in short squared-off towers, overseen by shelves full of Marys and saints. Francesca is glad for their beneficent company as she settles her daughter at her desk, to look at the Zimmerman files.

"I will be upstairs making dinner. If you need me, call me. If you need me urgently, press this switch down." Francesca touches a plastic figurine front and center on the desk. “St. Jude,” Francesca says on a smile. “Who else to sound the alarm of disaster?”

“Thanks, Mama,” Maddie says. She hopes the patron saint of lost and hopeless causes will not be needed tonight.

Sitting back in her mother’s neat desk in her comfortable ergonomic chair, the Zimmerman package in front of her, Maddie has her mother’s desktop up and running, and is ready to travel. Christopher Zimmerman's files are going to take her deep into the darkness of his long alliance with Reagan Clark.

The bishop thoughtfully organized the files into a “Regina” section and a “Zimmerman” section. The first DVDs contain scans of dozens of letters that Christopher Zimmerman as a new priest had sent to Regina “Reagan” Clark, as if he knew that one day, he would need to have them handy for whatever necessity dictated. Then, in a file labeled “From Regina” is every letter that she had sent back.

Maddie pops a DVD into her mother’s computer tower, and hits play.

Reagan Clark isn't named Reagan when she first meets the charming Swiss priest who has come to her parish church, the Cathedral Basilica of Our Lady of Peace, to help clean up the finances. Zimmerman, as Maddie’s research tells her, has descended to work his money magic on the capital campaign to spruce up the fraying temple, and bring more faithful back into the fold.

A group shot of a dozen young earnest types fills the

screen. With crosses dangling from the young necks along with guitars and ukuleles, it can only be a youth church group. Front and center is the lovely, young twenty-year old Regina Clark leading the church's Holy Spirit Young Adults mission in "Prayer, Faith, and Fellowship" every Friday night, so the caption says.

"Your leadership skills, your sense of the true path to righteousness, are a sacred gift from God," Zimmerman writes to her on a postcard when he is off on a retreat on Maui, which comes up next on screen. "*You could be the next Ronald Reagan.*"

Odd language to encourage a young woman, Maddie thinks. Her father thought Reagan was a failed actor but that his best performance was the role of president. She smiles at the memory, and clicks on, looking on screen at a very real history. There are some photos on the DVD of Reagan's march to success. From her in her soccer uniform showing off her strong young body at the University of Hawaii, with "full ride!" scrawled across the photo. To a photo of the young woman, proud in her black gown and mortar board as she matriculates into Corpus Christi College, Oxford. This time on a Marshall Scholarship, which makes Maddie sit up and take note. Other scholarship winners have brains anointed by Oxford, and go on to become judges and White House advisors. And then Regina is at Georgetown law, looking out at the camera with the steady eye of a woman who wants to bring justice to evildoers.

Marshall Scholarships and Georgetown law are not for slackers. Maddie has to begrudge Reagan Clark some respect, at least for the stunning, smart, and hardworking young woman who she was when she was Regina.

Zimmerman sent Regina money all the way through Oxford and Georgetown. He makes it clear that he is making an investment. A note written under her proud smile on her Georgetown grad picture says;

"For the Lord is the one who repays, and he will repay you sevenfold," he writes, making sure she knows he is quoting the Book of Sirach, *"and so you shall repay me."*

Not just a gift, Maddie thinks, but Zimmerman wants something back. Feeling a warm ray of compassion for Regina for having been bought, Maddie tries to shake that off. She digs into the letters on screen, real letters, hand written, composed of thoughts before they were written. Not throw-away emails.

And as Maddie begins to read, she sees they are serious letters. Once Zimmerman was seconded to the Vatican, to play with their money, he becomes a mentor to his Regina.

And he has become her lover.

> *Dear Christopher,*
>
> *I have not been able to stop thinking about you since we crossed the line that neither of us ever believed would be crossed, especially not on a deserted beach on the North Shore. Certainly not I, who had never been with a man before. And yet, the experience is one that I want to repeat again and again, for I feel only joy, not guilt.*

That is what you meant, I now see, when you spoke of divine love bringing us together, and wanting us to carry that divine love forward. I will go wherever it and you lead me.

Love, Regina

Maddie checks the dates and, yes, and it's days before Zimmerman gets summoned back to the Vatican, when Regina and Zimmerman motored up island for a little beach time, and divine love joined them.

Zimmerman's response to her love letter, though, is not what Maddie expects.

Dearest Regina,

You are correct. Divine love has brought us together, and know that I will lead you to a place of enlightenment where your gifts can be bestowed upon the world. It is true that I have taken a vow of chastity, as well as poverty, but I have also taken one of obedience, and I believe that it supersedes the others, because I am obeying the will of God. We are obeying the will of God. And I know His will is to have us join in great enterprise for his glory. I shall reveal the pathway as you reveal yourself to me.

With the love of God encompassing us both,

Christopher

PS: I have made a copy of our time on the enclosed so that we will have it for all time. Look at it when you are alone.

Maddie has to admit that it was pretty slick. The fortysomething priest invoking his special insight into the mind of God to get the winsome young student into the sack. And then, recording it for posterity. The file is labeled "First Time" and Maddie clicks it open.

There, onscreen, is the photo again of young Regina Clark naked on the beach. Maddie first saw the photo when she opened the tabernacle in Zimmerman's apartment. Regina has clearly consented to being photographed, as she smiles proudly, directly into the camera.

It's not pornographic, and Maddie thinks, not the stuff of blackmail. To be sure, the woman Regina who is today, Reagan Clark, would not want naked photos of herself splashed out into the ether. But then, she was a young woman, proud of her body, and who hasn't done things when they were twenty years old that they would not or could not do three decades later?

So Maddie goes back to the letters.

Following the different dates of the letters and places, Zimmerman's posting to Rome might have diminished their time together, but it did not crush the intensity of their encounters. He sprung, Maddie figures, for a plane ticket and Regina flies from England to Italy, or from Washington to Florida, where they have their rendezvous in tropical lushness. Zimmerman has a thing for the heat, Maddie thinks.

He also has a divine plan for his Regina, the Galatea

to his Pygmalion. His creation when she graduates is going to go into politics, his politics. That's the repayment. His letters even grill her about her studies about the Middle East and Israel.

If there is heart and passion, Maddie finds that burning through Zimmerman's letter to Regina about the need to restore Rome's influence in the affairs of Israel, the birthplace of the one true faith which he proclaims every moment of his life. To do that, Israel needs help to settle the neighborhood boundaries with the Palestinians or time and chance will do it for them. And Rome will be shut out of the Holy Land by psychopathic jihadis, as Zimmerman calls them.

He sends Regina a picture of his bishop's portrait, sitting in an armchair chair, imperious, his hair still thick but silver now, with the Vatican flag behind him. With it, he writes to his Regina, his queen of heaven, the twin story of their powerful future, one tied to Israel's fate:

> *It is all simply a numbers game, Regina. Once there are more Palestinians than there are Jews, the groups fighting to destroy Israel will get major help from Iran, who can finally see a war against Israel that they can win. The war will last a few years, and by the end of it, whoever wants the place can take it. By then, it will be a mess, with the usual factional slaughter between the Muslims leaving rivers of blood running through the date palm orchards.*
>
> *The United States will let them fight it out, and*

> *then come in and take over, for geopolitical reasons, but will not want to stay there. The birthplace of Jesus, the Son of God, will be destroyed. We will have broken our covenant with God.*
>
> *-C*

Maddie finds Regina's reply in a letter in her files. To her credit, Regina is politely skeptical. "Why would you go to such trouble with the moral and financial weight of the west allied with Israel, for the most part? And what about the Jews?" she writes.

Maddie scans the file for Zimmerman's reply, sure there must be one. His ego and his faith would insist.

The answer is in a video message. His bishop's portrait comes to life with Zimmerman enthroned in an armchair, the Vatican flag behind him. His silver hair is still thick, though his face and belly round out with his indulgence.

He is good on camera, looking out on his audience with a frank stare. Maddie thinks; but then again his has always been a kind of performance.

"My Regina, it isn't trouble," he explains. "God has chosen me to do what the Crusaders had left undone. And with your help, Regina, or shall we say… President Regina Clark's help… it will be done. Think of the good it could do in the world!" he exclaims. "Think of the power. And really, it will be good for the Jews because they will have to realize that their refuge from the anti-Semites is not permanent. Unless they make it so."

Then he leans forward as if looking into Regina's soul and says, "Let me tell you how. My Society of Blessed Urban II is going to set up Catholic outposts in both the Occupied Territories and in Israeli settlements. The Catholic Church has special privileges in Israel, and we can use them to advantage. From there it will be a kind of outreach, on the ground, not to create conflict between the two groups, but reconciliation.

"Once you are in the White House, the United States will finally be under a leader who can make peace happen. And you will set the stage with money, however you want to use it, money that should have gone to Israel in the first place, as it belonged to Jews murdered in the Holocaust, and to the gold stolen from them and processed by my own family bank, and then, by the Vatican. It is a sin that they will atone for together, helped along by trusted friends, like an American priest who has also been stained by the sins of the people. He is my friend, Victor Franchi, whom I will have the pleasure of soon introducing to you."

Maddie's heart thuds hard in her chest. But it is clear now how the players, Reagan, Zimmerman and Franchi, play out in the story, absolutely clear: the money was stolen from Jewish people. And Victor Franchi is in on this.

Maddie reads on, coming to the end of the file and the end of letters and photos between them, gripped as to what could bring finality to such a grand alliance.

It is June 2004, and Maddie checks out Regina online and finds that she has established herself as a hardline district attorney in Honolulu, eyeing a run at politics. She has been brought up short by Mother Nature.

Dear Christopher,

I am pregnant. I don't know how, but as you are the only man who has known me intimately, it's either you or God. Either way, we are going to be parents.

-RC

Not according to the divine plan of Christopher Zimmerman, they are not, as Maddie reads the letter in reply:

Dear Regina,

I must say this news surprises me. As you say, I don't know how either, since our time together has never involved high risk activity. I can say with certainty, though, the divine plan cannot work with this outcome, so I pray that you will see the way to continue our work together.

-C

Maddie gasps—what she just read took her breath away. A father of the church in Rome who plans to atone for sins and reclaim Israel for the Holy Mother Church cannot be tainted by real fatherhood.

So, this priest of Rome is telling his devoutly Catholic girlfriend to get an abortion.

This is what Reagan Clark does. Then she renounces

him, the way a sinner renounces sin.

> *You are not a man of God, and I was a fool to follow you. You are evil, and I have purged your evil from my body.*

She also attached a receipt for $350 from Honolulu Health Center for "reproductive services".

And that, Maddie knows, is the blackmail.

It is the last letter Regina Clark has written to Zimmerman. She is never Regina again, Maddie discovers. What comes next that same year, Maddie finds out through Google, is that she changes her name to Reagan that very next month in July 2004, because of a "vision from God," says Wikipedia.

Maddie can understand the new name arises from a need to rid herself of the stain of Regina and Zimmerman. While she Googles around to find the next chapters of Reagan's life, she finds a few pictures of her in her youth strolling the beaches of Hawaii with Father Zimmerman, looking innocent enough. But Maddie knows it is not.

Then, she is not Regina at all and with her new name, Reagan makes her own way, and takes a new faith. Two years later, Reagan marries an evangelical Christian–again, twenty years older than her—and becomes born again herself. Her faith helps circle the wagons when her husband dies a year later of a heart attack after playing touch football at a church picnic. Childless, widowed, ruthless and brilliant, she has become an evangelical nun on a holy crusade. Not at all the one Zimmerman had planned for her, but her own crusade, as she just announced in the Land of God. Maddie heard Reagan Clark call for holy war on behalf of the Prince of Peace, somehow funded by Vatican money. She is not calling for peace or reconciliation, but for slaughter. And it is, with an irony that makes Maddie's heart pound, all due to Christopher Zimmerman.

She took his plan and twisted it.

Zimmerman must not have seen it coming, Maddie thinks. Indeed, he had lived to see how the destruction of Gaza by Israel after Hamas attacked them only created a global sympathy for the Palestinians, and more enemies for Israel. All the more need for the Vatican's support.

But why would Zimmerman risk coming to America? He had a fierce enemy in Reagan Clark, who hated his faith, his politics, his entire being. And yet, he came back to America and ended up dead. And maybe, Maddie realizes, feeling sweat run down her back, that what he wanted was his Regina.

All of his neatly saved and organized files were always part of his plan. In case his Regina struck out on her own. She did. He must have blackmailed her – he was always ready for that. But the blackmail he dangled before Reagan is what got him killed.

This is the story that her father hunted. And this is the story that she has found.

Francesca's mother arrives on quiet footsteps, stopping to watch her daughter who has her elbows on the desk, fingers laced, head hanging, lost in thought or prayer. She takes the hot plate of pasta carbonara back upstairs. Maddie is not going to eat one bite.

Everything she read has made her sick.

She gathers the first disk and the picture from the desk top, ready to slide it back into the UPS envelope. But before she takes out the second disk from the computer, there is one more file she hasn't read. Maddie clicks on it and sees it is a letter that she's seen before that looks different this time. It's the prayer from Sister Nuala, the one that led her to Zimmerman's tabernacle, and to Reagan Clark's shame, and now, to Maddie's understanding.

This time, though, the prayer has numbers above the words "**tabernacle**," and "**shame**, **teach me to understand**." Closing her eyes, Maddie lets her mind refresh. The numbers, she realizes, correspond to the letters forming the words, with 1 for A, and 2 for B and so on. And at the very end, SBUIII, highlighted in bold.

Maddie jots them down on the journalist pad she keeps handy. Looking at them again and again, what could those numbers mean? And why highlight some?

She stares at the words and the string of numbers above them: 20125181214125 1981125 2015138 135 2015 2114451819201124. Plus SBUIII, adds on **1922111**.

The numbers are far too large for any money that Zimmerman has stolen. So, Maddie tries to see a pattern, as if this is some kind of code. But she is not a code breaker. Unless, of course, this is not a code, but an actual destination. Maddie beams as she realizes that the numbers might be the key to where that money has gone.

Emily was on that quest and struggled for weeks to find the money. Maddie texts Emily on her new phone and hopes that her banker friend fancies a nice Italian lunch on Maddie. And the quest will be solved, and by Emily: she will know what these numbers mean.

40. New York City.

It's the last Saturday in June and finally it feels like late spring, even though it's early summer. All the bright sunshine without the sticky, smelly New York heat. Maddie is finally able to get into her summer uniform: black dress, jean jacket and heels. She feels lighter still with a glass of Jameson's in front of her on two big cubes of ice.

She has picked a table outside of Risorgimento, and spots Emily getting out of a Lyft across the street. Emily has come straight from a Saturday morning in the office and is peeling off her dark suit jacket and undoing the top of her white man-shirt as she arrives with a smile.

"Thanks for coming," Maddie says.

"Hey, this is the most exciting thing in my life!" Emily says, giving Maddie a kiss on the cheek.

Over a wonderful Milanese risotto and another Jameson's, Maddie explains, as safely as she can, what she has found out about Christopher Zimmerman. Not the details of his relationship with Reagan Clark, but the fact that they knew each other, had a falling out, and that she found a sequence of numbers in Zimmerman's files that might connect to something.

Emily looks at the paper that Maddie has placed in front of her. On it are six words: **"tabernacle, shame, teach me to understand"**. And above each letter is the number which letter represents in the alphabet. So a long string of numbers.

"There are fifty-eight in all," Maddie says.

Emily stares at the numbers and frowns as if it hurts to look at them.

"What is it?" Maddie says. "Could it be bank accounts?"

Emily glances up at her. "Why do you say that?"

"Because Christopher Zimmerman stole money from the Vatican Bank, and put it somewhere."

"I see."

Maddie looks around to see if anyone is watching. Everyone at Risorgimento is intent on their meal.

"And there's another thing," Maddie says quietly. "Can you find out what happened to Zimmerman Freres Bank in Switzerland after Joachim Zimmerman died in 1986?"

Emily takes out her phone and types in a note. "OK, so now we have maybe a Swiss bank, the Vatican bank, and a bank that is a mystery altogether. What other countries was Zimmerman involved with?"

Maddie is relieved to be speaking with someone about the stories she's found, and even better that it's her best friend. "Well, he worked in the USA, he dealt with a priest whose father was a war criminal in Croatia, and he moved a lot of stolen gold to the Vatican bank."

"How did they move it, do you know?"

Maddie thinks back to Luke's seminar in the bar in Dublin. "With the help of the British, through Austria."

Emily types in some more notes as Risorgimento's owner, Renzo Romano, appears with a plate of cannoli. "Ah, Magdalena," he says in Italian, "you and your friend must have this sweetness if only so it can bask in your smile."

Maddie beams, wide eyed like a child at the dessert. "Thank you, Renzo, my mother is fine and sends her best."

"She was here just the other night," Renzo says, his brown, liquid eyes thinking back to Francesca dining at his table. "She dines alone, and it is so..." He trails off, his hand on his heart.

"No, Renzo, she dines with you," Maddie says.

His dark eyes now sparkle with delight. "Aha! That is brava! I will leave you to your sweetness."

He disappears back inside, chuckling at Maddie's wit.

"He's in love with your mother?" Emily asks.

"It's a long-standing crush. He expresses himself through food, and she lets him. Nothing more."

"Well, this food is really excellent! It has fueled me for the quest."

"What are you going to do?" Maddie asks.

"I am going to play with these numbers, and see if any banks come up. Unless there's more to the story."

"Yes. There is always more to the story," Maddie adds. And there is certainly more to this one. When she looks around again, this time she sees a tall, blond man turn away and walk on. It's Gabriel de Almeida Schmidt.

And then it hits her. Of course, he would be tracking her as well.

"You OK, Mads?" Emily asks, noticing that Maddie has lost the color in her cheeks.

"Yes, I'm fine. Just the summer joy and the

Jameson's, you know?"

Maddie grins tightly, watching Gabriel disappear up Amsterdam Avenue. "When you have some intel, Em, can you call me on this number?"

Maddie taps her new number and texts it to Emily.

"You sure you're OK?" Emily says, feeling protective.

"Pretty sure," Maddie nods. Her life has just become even more dangerous. Mossad has come to New York, and they want her to know that.

Maddie hugs goodbye to Emily and walks south on Amsterdam even though she needs to go north. She has something on her right now that must hold a tracking device.

What did she have with her in Israel that she has on her now?

She has her phones, both old and new, and her briefcase and her laptop. Her folders with Luke's notes and her father's satchel and Zimmerman's DVDs are at her mother's gallery, in the safe. Where Gabriel might just be going.

Maddie calls the police to tell them that there is a strange man hanging around outside *Arte Sacra*. She describes the tall blond guy to the dispatcher, and then calls her mother and tells her to lock the doors and close the gallery.

"Yes, Monday is fine," Francesca says, pretending to speak with a customer.

Maddie hears fear in her mother's voice. "Is someone there with you?"

"Yes. Certainly…"

"The police are on their way and so am I. Do not open the safe."

"Thank you, I will look forward to seeing you then."

Maddie opens her briefcase and feels every inch of it. She unzips the interior pockets, and then runs her hand along the bottom of the outside pocket, which clasps to the main case with a magnet. And on that magnet she finds what looks like a button battery, the kind you use for watches and calculators. But this is no battery, she knows. This is what is tracking her.

Maddie removes the tracking device, and looks around. She needs to create a diversion, if only for the next few minutes. She sees a bank of CitiBikes across the street. Perfect.

She dashes across the street and plants the device under the seat of the bike closest to the corner. Gabriel will think that she is still at the restaurant. Until the bike moves, and then he will think she has gone wherever it goes.

Then she runs up Amsterdam Avenue, to make the ten blocks to her mother's gallery before Gabriel does whatever he is there to do.

41. New York City.

Maddie comes running around the corner of 84th and Amsterdam as if she is trying to set a record. She feels a surge of relief when she sees her mother talking to two female cops in front of the gallery. Francesca, in a black dress and jacket, string of pearls, her salt and pepper curls curving around her handsome face, is fine.

"Mama," Maddie says, breathing hard as she embraces her mother. "I got here as fast as I could."

"It's all good, *cara*," her mother says. "This is my daughter," she adds for the cops.

The taller cop, a Latina woman in her late 30s, nods at Maddie. "Everything seems to be fine now, ma'am."

The "ma'am" is jarring, but part of the class system in New York City. The cops read that they are attending an affluent family who own an art gallery, and that's the script.

"Can you tell me what happened?" Maddie asks.

"Your mother called in a report of a suspicious man in the gallery," says the shorter cop, who looks younger than Maddie and is South Asian.

"I did," says Francesca. "He was tall, blond, handsome… Looking like he wanted to rob us."

"That's terrible," Maddie says, though she is sure now it was Gabriel. "Did he threaten you?"

"No, he just looked like he was, how do you say in English, casing the joint?"

The cops both chuckle. "Yeah, that's how you say it,"

says the taller cop.

"You have a good security system, ma'am?" the shorter one asks.

"I do indeed, and a caring daughter, too." Francesca beams at Maddie for effect.

"Stay safe," the short one says. Then they get into their squad car and drive off.

Francesca turns to Maddie and says, "We need to talk."

Maddie knows that telling her mother everything only puts them both in more danger. So all she says is – "I need to get my stuff out of your safe, Mama."

"Is that what the man wanted?"

"I think so."

"Why?"

Maddie has to be careful. She moves out of the way to let a man walking a boisterous Labrador puppy pass by, then gets close to her mother. "It's because of what Papa found. And where that sent me."

Francesca bows her head and thinks. "I see. You cannot say everything. But tell me this. Will these people kill for what you have?"

"I think they could, Mama."

"So then why would I let you take this information away with you? Do you have a safe, or security cameras? No! They will kill you if you have it."

"I need it."

"But how did they know it was here? They are following you?"

"Someone was tracking me. The man who came into

your gallery. But I have fixed that."

Maddie expects her mother to go into a Mediterranean rage at being put in danger, but Francesca is calm. She looks up and down the block, to make sure the man in question is not watching them now. Then she aims those black Italian eyes on Maddie like she comes from a family of assassins.

"So we have to put it somewhere else. Somewhere that they cannot know about."

Maddie smiles. Her mother is thinking like a spy. "Do you have somewhere in mind?"

"I do," Francesca says. "I just hope he doesn't expect too much from this favor."

Maddie knows the 'he' is Renzo Romano, and he will be delighted to help. And he will do everything to protect whatever the Contessa leaves in his care.

"First, I need to copy everything, Mama."

Francesca rolls her dark eyes up to heaven. As if having one copy is bad enough.

"If they come for it, I need to have something. On a flash drive is good enough."

Francesca nods at the plan. "OK, we will do this now and then we will go see Renzo."

A half hour later, as Maddie and Francesca head south on Amsterdam, checking every shop and corner for Gabriel de Almeida Schmidt. He's gone and Maddie hopes he is off following a City Bike on a trek to Queens. She notices a tall blond woman eye her, but just for a moment, before her full focus sticks hard back on her cell phone.

.

But Jane Jones has that cell she is staring at on camera mode and watching Maddie and an older woman, who can only be her mother. Good thing Maddie got a load of her mother's beautiful genes; Jane has seen the father's photos and, though he was heading up to sixty when he was killed, his craggy Irish look didn't age well. Jane has tried to make herself look as ordinary as possible in her black tracksuit and black ball cap, her blonde hair dangling in a ponytail and her blue-gray ice eyes focused on her cell.

She sees that the mother is carrying an old leather satchel. And Jane Jones can see that Maddie's mother in no way looks the type to have a bag that old and battered as a carryall. They are transferring something that they want to keep away from people like her. Because inside the satchel is something that can do damage to Reagan Clark.

Jane follows them on the opposite side of Amsterdam, then ten blocks south to 74th Street. She has made certain that no one has been following her, and now she watches as Maddie and her mother enter a handsome, old-world restaurant.

Watching, Jane pops into a bodega on the corner and buys a bottle of water, keeping her eye on Risorgimento, which actually looks like the kind of real Italian restaurant she would enjoy. Then she parks herself to the southwest of the restaurant, figuring that when Maddie and her mother exit, they will turn north to go back the way they came.

That moment comes sooner than Jane expected. She

watches the two women stand in front of the restaurant with an Italian-looking guy who keeps smoothing his hand on his bald head as if to imagine hair that he no longer has, and who looks like he's in love with the mother.

But Jane sees that the elegant mother no longer has the old leather satchel. Whatever Maddie Lynch is trying to hide is now inside this Italian restaurant.

42. New York City.

Teddy Wright and Reagan Clark face each other across the titanium and glass desk in the *I'm Wright* studio, but their eyes are on the cameras facing them, waiting for the clock to click down, and the duel to begin. It is as if any early eye contact with each other will give one of them some kind of edge.

It's the end of a hot July day and the air conditions are humming full tilt, pouring freezing air into the studio. Teddy likes it that way. It means even into summer she can wear her fitted black suit that shows all her strength. Her Clark Kent glasses are off, and her blue-eyed gaze is sharp as a weapon should be.

But Reagan Clark, in her red sleeveless dress and pumps, blond hair a golden frame to her ageless beauty, has one up on Teddy. Reagan looks comfortable with her own strength. She has the presidency within her reach. No talk show host, no matter how jumped up in the ratings, can mess with that reality.

Maddie is in the control booth with Aretta, watching the two pretend that the other one is not in the room. Teddy didn't want any help prepping, but Maddie told her to ask one question: why did Reagan Clark end her friendship with Bishop Christopher Zimmerman? And if she doesn't answer that, then ask her if it was he who drove her away from the Catholic faith of her birth.

"What do you know?" Teddy had said, her voice tight, and urgent.

A lot more than you, Maddie thinks. But she says, "I heard some stuff in Rome that they had a falling out. The Catholic vote is big. Be great to see if she'll go there."

Teddy had even scribbled down some notes, but Maddie knows from experience that once Teddy is unleashed, she will go whichever way she wants to go, no matter how much has been prepared.

As they now sit ten feet away in the control booth, Aretta covers her headset to speak to Maddie, "No handshake, not even a nod… Do you think she's going to go for the kill?"

Maddie shrugs. "Reagan's a pretty big target, but so far, the bullets just bounce off her, so to speak."

"Maybe we should just use a knife across the throat," Aretta deadpans, knowing the anti-Islam rhetoric that is about to head out into the ether from Reagan Clark's mouth.

Maddie smiles, and looks at her friend who seems so thin and stressed.

"You OK, Aretta?" Maddie asks.

Aretta sighs. "Tired. Deservedly so."

"Very deservedly." Maddie gives her arm a squeeze in lieu of a hug.

They both look out on a set that is bright with lights, a black floor and a dozen white screens waiting to light up with images as the director cues the digital. The screens blink to life in bars of red and blue and purple. Behind the table, the big floor-to-ceiling screen alights with the ten-foot sign *I'm Wright with Teddy Wright.*

The tables and chairs on either side of the stage, like

comfortable team dugouts, have been cleared of observers. It is just the director, stage manager, the sound woman, the two camera guys, and the make-up man—dusting Teddy's forehead with powder again—who are allowed in. Brett Muenster has been banished to the green room to watch it, along with nearly twenty million other Americans, on TV, or INN's streaming service.

The floor director counts Teddy down in her earpiece, five-four-three... and then they are in. The first part of the interview is standard stuff, with Teddy asking about Reagan's poll numbers, as she's trailing the incumbent President Klein by seven points. Reagan is dismissive of that number, and gets down to the numbers that matter. The people who want change in America.

"I see a country living in a shadow of its former glory, and a country that will find its way as a beacon unto nations once we stand up for the values of the men and women who toiled in our fields and our factories, the values of our great military, who have protected us from harm, and who must now, like the prayer reveals, deliver us from evil," Reagan says. "They're the values our Founding Fathers used to establish our country, and they're in danger of being destroyed by this president, and his willingness to accommodate evil. Be it from those who slaughter the unborn to those who slaughter us in the name of their God—or their lack of one."

Maddie looks at Aretta, who smiles a weary smile. "Only took her two minutes to get to Muslim bashing. She's getting faster."

Teddy leans forward and asks Reagan for her plan to

save the nation. And Reagan tells her that she is going to show the Middle Eastern bigots some American muscle. But with a twist that won't cost the American people any more tax money.

"You're going to send private armies to fight out wars?" Teddy asks, her voice rising with incredulity.

"I'm going to send the best men and women for the job," Reagan answers. "I want to send our best, to fight the worst. Wherever the worst are. If they are here in the USA, we shall fight them here. I am fighting to restore and protect the Judeo-Christian tradition that defines us."

Maddie leans forward in the control room, and mutes her headset, saying to herself, "There's your opening, Teddy, take it."

And Teddy does. She asks Reagan about her own Christianity, and her divorce from Catholicism. Was it because of her friendship with a Catholic priest named Christopher Zimmerman?

"I don't know any priest by that name."

"Bishop Christopher Zimmerman allegedly stole 250 million Euros from the Vatican Bank."

"As I said, I don't know any priest by that name."

Maddie watches as Teddy checks her notes, and then smiles. She's going to follow Maddie's script.

"Didn't you work with him in Honolulu, and develop quite a powerful friendship? Were you not in the Holy Spirit youth group with Bishop Zimmerman, then a priest, and you were yourself at the time named Regina?"

Reagan Clark raises her eyebrows and widens her eyes as if Teddy is the worst of the lying mainstream media. "I don't know where you get your facts, but this is exactly the kind of problem we're facing in America. We have the media making up stuff and sucking oxygen out of the room while we're fighting to breathe the air of freedom. We're fighting to save America from death, to bring her back to glorious life, the torch of liberty aflame with righteousness. And with it, the renewed message of Jesus, the message the Founding Fathers knew so well, the message that pulses in the veins of our great nation. As our first president, George Washington, put it so eloquently: '*While we are zealously performing the duties of good citizens and soldiers, we certainly ought not to be inattentive to the higher duties of religion. To the distinguished character of Patriot, it should be our highest glory to add the more distinguished character of Christian.*'"

In the control room, Maddie paces. She wants to let the pious answer ripple for a moment or two, and then wishes that Teddy could go for the kill with the proof about how this family values evangelical zealot aborted the love child conceived with a Vatican priest. But Maddie doesn't know how the story ends yet, and she cannot risk ending it now.

It's time for the segment to end. Teddy White smiles at the camera and wraps up.

"We hope to have Governor Clark back soon, and we can resume our discussion about the things she can't remember now, but maybe soon. Until then, I'm Wright."

Reagan quickly thanks Teddy, plucks off her mic and

strides out the studio door.

Maddie braces, thinking that Teddy will not be thanking Maddie for her work, but be hot with fury after the interview.

Teddy slides her Clark Kent classes back on and checks her notes, then purrs into her hot mike: "We have her in a lie, I think."

Maddie's heart is pounding in her chest. She wants to scream "I know we do!" But instead she says quietly into her own headset, "I am working on the proof."

"And I know you'll get it," Teddy says. She seems calm and confident as she leaves the stage.

The control room door swings open, and before Aretta can shoo the intruder away, Brett Muenster suddenly comes into the booth. Grinning, he ignores Aretta and invites Maddie out for a drink. To celebrate the success of the interview, which he knows will put Reagan a few points up in those ever so shaky polls. "Not that they matter a whit! Teddy Wright is wrong!"

Maddie would rather give up booze than go for a drink with this guy. Yet going out might give her the chance to make him tip his hand, without tipping her own.

"There's a place around the corner that's not too busy," she says.

"Oh, I'm in the mood for adventure," Muenster replies. "How about that Italian place you like?"

How does Muenster know about Risorgimento? Unless he is telling her that he knows everything.

"That Italian place?" Maddie says, as if she doesn't know.

"Yeah, you told me about it, or I read something about it. Something "mento" like the mints."

"Right, it's just up the street."

"Just up the street in New York terms," Muenster says, when they alight from a taxi some 30 blocks north of the INN studios.

"But worth it," Maddie says. "No one from INN goes here."

"That sounds as if you're embarrassed to be seen with me, Maddie Lynch."

Maddie laughs, but he's not far off the mark. She is only doing this to see if she can get inside Brett Muenster's secret files.

"Ah, Magdalena, what a pleasure," Renzo says in Italian, spotting her and Muenster sitting at a sidewalk table opposite the door.

"Lovely to see you, Renzo," Maddie answers back, then rolls into Italian, saying. "This guy is potentially trouble so if I ask you for some cannoli, please say you're fresh out and then tell me there's an urgent call for me inside, OK?"

Renzo keeps his professional smile in place, but his dark brown eyes flash with contempt onto Muenster and then back on to Maddie with assent. He bows, and hustles off to fetch their drinks. Maddie and her stunning mother have become even more interesting to him. Like international spies.

"You speak Italian," Brett says.

"I do," Maddie replies. "Do you?" She is sure he does not, but silently curses herself for not finding out before speaking it to Renzo.

"No, I'm still working on English," he says with a self-deprecating smile.

Renzo delivers their drinks, a beer for Muenster, and a glass of Jameson's on ice for Maddie. It's an evening in late July, the humidity falling with the coming of night, but still sticky enough to make Muenster sweat, and slug the beer back fast, killing half the glass.

"I don't like the heat," he says. "Even though I grew up in Georgia."

"And now you live in Houston?"

"Wall-to-wall and mall-to-mall AC!" He grunts out his laugh. "I hear it's cool as a cucumber in DC in the summer."

Maddie smiles politely. "Well, your chances are looking good."

"I think so, not to jinx anything," Muenster says, and mimics throwing salt over his shoulder. "A lot of people watch your show, and a lot of them will see in Reagan a candidate who will make America matter again."

"She seems to have a pretty robust vision of how that will happen."

Muenster temples his fingers and tries to look serious, but just looks anxious. "She does. She's not messing around. She knows that, as a woman, if you want to be taken seriously, you need to be tougher than the guys."

"Thanks for that," Maddie says.

Muenster grins and raises his hands in surrender. "So," he says, sipping his beer like a miser now, and changing the subject, "did you get your interview with the Pope?"

"I did," she says. "Teddy Wright has a sit down with the Pope."

"He's going to come into INN studios? That would be a security nightmare."

Maddie's growing headache over the security logistics comes back to poke her in the brain. They cannot have the interview in the studio. She will have to arrange it with Cardinal Otley. "We're working on it," she says.

"Where else could you go?"

"I expect the Pope will be staying with the Apostolic Nuncio. You know, the Vatican ambassador to the UN. He lives on the Upper East Side."

"Keep it all in house," Muenster says.

"We don't want anything to happen to the Pope while he's here. And he has his own security team."

"Tell me," Muenster says, leaning in, "why is he so fond of Islam? What's in it for him?"

Maddie knows that Muenster isn't really asking the question in earnest. He is fishing for some kind of information that he can use to diminish the Pope.

"He takes the message of his faith seriously. And so it's better to show love toward one's fellow humans than it is to show the opposite."

Her bugged phone pings with a text, and she pulls it out to look at it, to show Muenster that she suspects nothing. It's from Aretta, asking her if she's coming back to the office. Maddie keys in "Not tonight" and hits send.

"Nice phone," Muenster says. "That you and your dad

on the screen? Of course I know his work."

"Yes, we were in Egypt."

Muenster nods, absently, then smiles, as if a great idea has just come to him. Then he stands. "I hate to drink and run," he says, putting two twenty-dollar bills on the table. "But I promised Reagan I'd meet her in about thirty minutes."

Maddie stands. "Thanks for the drinks," she says, surprised at the abruptness of his departure.

"Keep me posted on the Pope," he says. "I want to put that interview on my calendar."

Muenster walks west, toward Broadway and a taxi, and Maddie enters the restaurant.

"Is everything OK, Magdalena?" Renzo asks in Italian.

"I need to get into your safe, Renzo," she says.

He looks around the restaurant. It's still early, and everything is under control. "OK," he says, and leads her past the zinc bar and down the corridor past the kitchen to his cramped office.

Maddie turns away as he opens the combination on the safe.

"OK," he says.

"I think it's best if you don't see what happens next, Renzo."

He looks a touch offended, but Maddie smiles like he's her favorite uncle. "So if anyone ever asks, you can truly say that you did not know."

He smiles with warmth, and clasps his palms together as if in prayer. Then he steps outside the office.

Maddie is relieved to see that what she left in the satchel is still there. She extracts the two DVDs from Zimmerman, the photo, and her father's notebooks. The DVDs and picture she slides into the inside pocket of her laptop bag, and then slips the notebooks between her laptop and an inside flap. She closes the empty satchel and puts it back in the safe. The safe door closed; she spins the lock. If Muenster even thought that Maddie had stashed intel, a photo, a letter, anything on Reagan Clark here, is nothing there now.

"It's all fine, thank you, Renzo," Maddie says as she exits.

"I am glad," Renzo says. "Anything for your mother, and you."

They walk out of the restaurant to the sidewalk.

"If that man I was with comes back here, will you let me know?"

Renzo presses a hand to his heart. "As soon as I see him, I will call you."

Maddie reaches for her phone, but pulls out the old one. "Sorry, that's my work phone, Renzo," she says as she puts the old Lumia in her pocket and extracts the new Galaxy. She gives him the number.

"You are so busy!" Renzo says with paternal pride.

"Just trying to keep two worlds separate," says Maddie—which is very much the truth.

She bids Renzo a good night, then heads outside, her head on a swivel. No Gabriel, no Muenster, no strangers loitering, looking to follow her.

She clutches her laptop bag tight, and heads into the

subway to Brooklyn. She will have to find a new hiding place for her treasure, one that the people who want to find it will never suspect.

43. Rome.

It is a sun-kissed summer morning a little past 7 AM when Bishop Paul Hughes climbs the steps to St. Peter's. He used to work out in the Swiss Guards' gym in the Guard House, two floors, everything digital, even the punching bags. But now just getting from one side of the ancient basilica to another is his daily workout, for the body and spirit. The tourists are not yet here, and it's all the better to see the glory of God. Save for one, standing inside in front of Michelangelo's Pièta, still staring at it as if for the first time.

He has a thick shock of black hair, and a black beard, and black horn-rimmed glasses, to match his black priest's suit.

"It is new every time you see it," Bishop Hughes says to Father Victor Franchi, who turns and smiles at Hughes. His lined face smooths out in real delight.

"I thought you wouldn't recognize me," Franchi says.

"I don't," Hughes replies coolly. "But I must say the dye job, beard and glasses makes you look twenty years younger."

"That is a dividend, but not the purpose."

Franchi turns and takes a photo of the Pièta with his iPhone, and then turns the phone to Hughes. On the screen is a photo of Maddie, in Franchi's bloody kitchen, in Jerusalem.

"She thinks I am dead."

"How do you know this?" Hughes says, unconvinced.

"The blood is very convincing. I have a butcher shop I like nearby… She will not bother me again. Though she did shoot out the knee of one of my colleagues." His cold eyes burn for a moment in anger.

Hughes walks on. He genuflects, then sits in a pew next to a medallion of a woman in a side view, flanked by two pink marble columns.

"Queen Christina of Sweden," Hughes says to Franchi who sits by him. "She killed Descartes. And not with a shot to the knee."

"Oh?"

"He died from a cold caught after a pre-dawn philosophy session with her. Her Swedish castle was freezing."

"He was an atheist anyway," Franchi says. "So was she."

Hughes shakes his head, no. "She abdicated in the middle of the 17th century to convert to Catholicism," Hughes says, gazing at the gilt and bronze medallion, supported by a crowned skull.

Victor Franchi looks at the medallion. "Good for her," he says.

"You see," Hughes continues, "there are three pictures; it is a triptych. The center one is where she leaves the Swedish throne for Rome, the one on the right is the scorn of her nobility when she did that, and the one on the left is the triumph of faith over heresy."

Franchi quietly scoffs at the triptych, carrying no persuasive beauty, not like the Pièta. Just Catholic brand sales. "And the skull at the bottom is the death that puts it all in perspective."

"Which you would know, as a dead man," says Bishop Hughes.

Franchi smiles serenely. "Maddie Lynch is looking for Christopher Zimmerman and his sins. She is not looking for us."

"And you are certain?"

"I showed her that old blackmail photo he had of St. John Paul II, and that set her on a course to look for his other misdeeds with money. Which she cannot find, because they have all been destroyed. When he was."

A nun who is a Vatican cleaner walks by, looking more like a doctor in gloves, a face mask and scrubs. She nods reverently to the bishop and priest, and walks on.

Hughes is glad for the interruption; the conversation is heating up the cool of the Basilica. He does not want anyone to hear what he is saying next. Once the cleaner is gone, he says, "She found something in Zimmerman's flat."

Franchi purses his lips, as if he has just sucked a bitter lemon. "What did she find?"

"We don't know. And by we, I mean Otley and me. She wouldn't say."

"And that old queen let her get away with that?"

Hughes gives Franchi a warning smile. "Now, Victor, he is not yet on our side. He is never sure of anything until he sees it. So he thinks Maddie Lynch is going to be his salvation."

Franchi nods, taking it in. "She's working for Omega then."

"Yes."

"And where is she now?"

"She's in New York."

Franchi smiles as if he is looking out on the future, and it is shining back. "And I am guessing that you will be traveling with our Muslim-loving Holy Father when he visits the United States."

Hughes turns on his big smile, his sleepy eyes lift as he says, "Indeed, I shall be doing that very thing. We're staying in the Apostolic Nuncio's mansion on the Upper East Side. Very secure."

Franchi thinks on this, and then turns to Hughes. "And this is where the Pope will do his television interview?"

"What an excellent idea, Victor. I hope you won't mind if I take credit for it."

Franchi opens his palms, as if giving a great gift. "Not at all. I am sure it will be memorable."

There is a moment of silence, then Franchi looks Hughes in the eye. "Should I be concerned about what Maddie Lynch found in Zimmerman's flat?"

Hughes takes a deep breath. "His dealings with money have been erased. But I don't know what she found, so yes, we should be concerned."

"Is she a loose end?"

Hughes lowers his head as if in prayer and whispers, "She is at the moment. But I am sure we will find a way to tie Maddy Lynch up. So to speak."

Franchi smiles. "From your lips to God's ears. So to speak."

44. New York City.

Jane Jones waits until the last guest has left Risorgimento for the night, then enters. Renzo is at the bar, conferring with the bartender.

"I am sorry, senora, we have just closed."

Jane, who has her blonde hair now parked under beret, and wears tortoiseshell glasses, smiles apologetically. "I am sorry, sir. Can I please just use your washroom? It's an emergency. I am happy to pay."

Having heard this, Renzo, big of heart, will not let a woman in dire straits pay to get out of them. "Of course, please, it's just there." He points down the corridor.

"Thank you, sir. You are very kind."

Jane walks down the corridor and enters the restroom. Then she exits, and looks to see the bartender leaving and Renzo busy and alone at the long marble bar with the night's count.

She walks further down the corridor and finds the office. No security cameras outside it, or inside it. It's cramped, and there's a safe in the corner that looks easy enough to break into, but she doesn't need to do that.

Instead, she plants a plastic lighter on the edge of the desk. And places another at the foot of the safe. Then she reaches in her back and extracts a spray bottle and spritzes the floor between the desk and the safe with isopropyl.

The lighters contain an improvised explosive called, by chemists like Jane, triacetone triperoxide. It is a highly potent combination produced by reacting acetone and hydrogen peroxide. It is almost impossible to detect. Terrorists call it "Mother of Satan."

Then she exits and walks down the corridor.

Renzo looks up as she passes, and nods to her. "*Buona notte, senora*," he says with a warm smile.

"Good night, and thanks again," Jane says.

Walking up Amsterdam a block, she crosses the street. She has a good view of Risorgimento, and she will wait until it is totally empty before she detonates. She just has to destroy the safe. She doesn't need to kill anyone.

Jane grabs a coffee from a café, and leans against the wall of an apartment building, pretending to check her phone. It takes half an hour for the two waiters to leave. There is no sign of Renzo. She is sure she didn't miss anything.

Then Jane sees a light switch on above the restaurant, and Renzo appears in the window. He closes the curtains. He lives above his restaurant, Jane thinks. She has laid enough plastic explosive to burn out the office, but not to blow up the building. After all, he was kind to her. And if he owns the building, then he can afford the repairs.

She takes out her remote detonation device, and hits the red button.

The blast shatters the windows of Risorgimento, and a tsunami of flames follows. Jane is talented when it comes to explosives, but she is angry at herself for not thinking there must have been residual gas from the kitchen stoves that caused a bang so big.

She has to get out of there fast, but she wants to see Renzo exit safely. Instead, she sees him at the second-floor window, climbing out. He cannot get down because of the fire. He's going to jump.

Jane Jones watches in fascinated horror as the man who moments earlier was about to go to bed is now gambling with his life. He jumps. He hits the concrete. He doesn't move.

Jane Jones fights the old urge to run and walks calmly to the west, toward the Hudson River. Behind her, the sirens begin.

45. New York City.

Maddie and Emily sit in the INN cafeteria. Emily insisted on meeting somewhere safe, and after everything, Maddie feels that sitting out in the fluorescent openness of this large, green and white commissary might be the safest place for now. With the fire at Risorgimento, as her mother told her along with the morning news, and Renzo in Mount Sinai West with two broken legs and a fractured skull. And Maddie also has a cold feeling in the pit of her stomach telling her that whoever attacked Renzo is attacking her.

"The coffee is not bad," Emily says, taking a sip.

Maddie is sure Emily didn't book off her demanding job on Wall Street to sample INN's coffee. "What did you find?"

Emily, usually so earnest, her blonde elegance buttoned into her man shirt and pant suit, with pearls, suddenly looks flustered. She glances around to see if anyone is within earshot. Then she leans forward, not quite knowing how quietly to say, "This is trouble, Maddie."

If Emily is rattled, Maddie is really rattled. "What kind?"

Emily reaches into her black briefcase and extracts a manilla folder. She slides it across the table to Maddie.

Maddie opens it and sees that the numbers that she gave to Emily are now linked to three bank accounts. Banque de Lausanne is a Swiss bank. The IOR is the

Vatican bank. And Bank Lienz Österreich is the Austrian one.

"How did you do this?" Maddie asks, her worry cast aside for her surging feeling of awe now that suspicion has proof.

"We have algorithms for this sort of thing. I just input the numbers and let the software do the rest."

Maddie looks at the account numbers. "Do we know who owns these accounts?"

Emily leans back, as if leaning away from more trouble. "That's something we can't do. Opens too many legal avenues of woe."

Maddie thinks. "If you were me, how would you find out?"

"You'd need some help on the inside." She gives Maddie a friendly smile. "I know, I'm on the inside, but not in the way you now need. Which is way way inside."

Maddie takes Emily's big strong hands in hers in thanks, and then clocks Aretta approaching their table. Small, but with a fast stride, she crosses the large room in a second.

"Hey Maddie," Aretta says. "Sorry to interrupt but there is some guy from the Vatican who wants to talk to you about Teddy's interview with the Pope."

"I'll be there in a sec, Aretta. This is my friend Emily."

Aretta's round face opens wide in a smile. She clearly likes the look of Maddie's friend Emily, and they shake hands. Aretta then eyes the manilla folder, closed now on the table. "You guys working on a story?"

Maddie glances at Emily, and says, "Actually, Emily works in finance. She's helping me to make mine better."

"I could use that kind of help," Aretta says, as if asking Emily on a date.

Emily, who is so straight that you could use her to measure distance, now blushes. "Our firm is private, but you can find lots of good places online."

"I need them to be ethical, and Islamic," Aretta says, now almost as a challenge.

Emily blushes again. "I bet there are lots of them. Give the list of ones that look good to you to Maddie, and she can run them past me. For you."

"Absolutely," Maddie chimes in. She appreciates the generosity of spirit, and the elegance of the deflection.

"Thanks, I will. See you in a bit Maddie. Very nice to meet you, Emily." Aretta gives Emily a broad smile.

"And you, Aretta."

They wait until Aretta is gone before they speak again. Quietly, Maddie asks, "Did you find out who Zimmerman Freres bank was sold to?"

Silently, Emily opens the folder and points to the Swiss bank. Banque de Lausanne, the Swiss bank.

"So in theory, all these accounts could belong to Christopher Zimmerman," Maddie says.

"They could," Emily says, then smiles with an afterthought. "By the way, your account is doing very well. That initial $1,000 investment is now $23,000."

Maddie shakes her head in awe. "Thanks for the magic money, Em."

"My pleasure." Emily nods to the envelope. "Will you

be OK with what I have left you?"

"I will." Maddie hugs Emily as she goes, and then gets on her phone, the new one, to find a way into who owns the accounts.

She opens Google and sees she has a few tabs still open. She clicks them closed, one by one, but when she gets to the last tab she was at, the one with Zimmerman and Reagan on a Hawaiian beach together in the 1990s, which she was just looking at again, the image is gone. She types "Christopher Zimmerman" and clicks on Images and scrolls through. There are no images of him and Reagan Clark on Google anymore. They have been scrubbed. And Maddie knows why. Because Teddy Wright asked about them. Because Maddie Lynch prepped her.

Maddie knows that if she can connect the missing money to Reagan Clark then she will have found the story. If the beast doesn't bite her first.

46. New York City.

Maddie is nursing a whiskey on ice in Flammie's, a luscious cocktail bar on Vanderbilt Avenue in Brooklyn. It is more like a speakeasy, really, with no shingle outside its brick exterior, whose windows are frosted glass cubes, chest high, and not for looking in, nor out.

The interior is the point, with red velvet curtains covering the door from curious passersby. And with its white subway tiles within and long copper bar, it has a vibe that suggests rules are something best left at that door. It is still early, just 9 PM, and the night is not sweltering for early August, but you can still get a seat inside.

Maddie has snagged a table for two opposite the bar, her face lit by the jasmine candle burning in front of her and the glow of her Galaxy phone. The first piece of the bank account puzzle comes back to her via WhatsApp.

The Vatican account belongs to the Society of Blessed Urban II, Cardinal Otley texts. *Balance: 350 Euros.*

Maddie types her thanks. Otley has come through. The SBUIII has moved their money, she is sure of it. Because 350 Euros is not what Victor Franchi had lived on in the palatial villa in Israel.

Patrick Farrell swings through the red velvet curtains, and opens his arms to Maddie, brushing his lips against her cheek. "Great to see you again," he says. "Nice of you to join me at such short notice."

Maddie laughs, as the short notice was very much

hers. She had called him as soon as Emily left and said she needed his help again. But had to ask in person. She knew that the poet in him would respond to the mystery of the ask.

Tonight Patrick does not look like a Mexican cartel honcho but more like the poet. He is wearing a blue t-shirt, linen blazer with jeans and Doc Martens, his olive skin shining underneath that flop of black hair. His black goatee is looking better for running scruffy. It makes Maddie remember how good he looks. And much more relaxed than the last time she saw him.

The inspection finishes with a small bow from Patrick, and a short explanation: "The thing I was working on, I'm not working on anymore."

So he can have a drink. He orders a Manhattan and gets Maddie another Jameson's. Returning to their table, he scans the room for eavesdroppers. From the cast of cool characters in this bar, into their drinks and each other, no one is even looking.

He sits and Maddie starts in on her story, because now it is her story. Starting with the interview with the Pope for Teddy Wright, and how that linked up in Oxford and then in Rome with missing millions and missing Christopher Zimmerman, who died of a heart attack which was not a heart attack. Patrick knows all about that.

"My father was writing about Bishop Zimmerman when he died." Maddie can finally say this without grief breaking loose and her voice wavering over the start of tears. "They knew James Lynch. Cardinal Otley did in

Rome, and Zimmerman and also his housekeeper, a nun named Sister Nuala." Maddie even explains how the nun had a regular luncheon date with her father, and they both shared their Irish love for whiskey. She also died suddenly of a supposed heart attack, but she made sure Maddie had a certificate from World War II. It shows that a Croatian fascist killer, a member of the Ustaŝe, gave Christopher Zimmerman's father's bank a million dollars in gold.

Patrick shakes his head as if it is suddenly too full. "Wow."

"More wow to come. The old nun's roommate makes sure I have a prayer from Bishop Zimmerman."

"And then she dies, too." Patrick says. It's not a question. He knows how this strategy goes: the more money, the more bodies.

"Yes, and they're both under the so-called spiritual care of Cardinal Otley's secretary Bishop Paul Hughes." Maddie goes on to explain how Hughes connects with Zimmerman and also a priest named Victor Franchi. They are all members of the Society of Blessed Urban II, referring to the Pope who started the Crusades against Islam. They now want to finish what was left undone.

"Through prayer, I hope," Patrick says.

"Oh no," she replies. "Prayers are cheap. By the time Zimmerman is gone 250 million Euros from the Vatican Bank is gone, too. It includes the Jewish gold looted in World War Two that was stashed in the Zimmerman family's Swiss bank."

"Which would now be worth several fortunes,"

Patrick adds quietly. Primed by his undercover work, he can see where this is all going into a secret pot of mega millions. But it is the poet who shuts his eyes on the horror of it all as he says, "Enough to fund another crusade? One more bloody, more final?"

He opens his eyes to see Maddie reply with a smile at Patrick in the way he remembers from when they were together. Sweet and innocent, and about to propose something dangerous.

"And your father was writing about all of this and following the money?"

Maddie nods 'yes'. Patrick can see how she has been haunted by her father. And how her father's past has become her future, now that she is ahead of the story he found.

All she can reveal is that Zimmerman's crusade had a political side to it that is now closing in on the White House.

Patrick is not saying anything now. He's just staring at Maddie as if he's meeting her for the very first time.

"But the prayer also carried a numeric code. I gave them to a friend who works in finance…"

"Emily?"

Of course, Patrick knows Emily. They were all friends together not so long ago. Maddie nods. "She ran the numbers and came back with this intel. One is a Swiss bank, one is an Austrian bank, and one is a Vatican bank, the account owned by the Society of Blessed Urban II."

"How do you know?"

"Because the Vatican Secretary of State told me. Now I need your help to find out who owns those other two accounts, the one in Switzerland, and the one in Austria. And how much money is in them."

Patrick sits back and looks up at the ceiling, not in exasperation, Maddie hopes. He is digesting the story she has just told him as both a poet and a cop. The poet gets it, but the cop then quickly scans the room, and, all clear, comes back with questions.

"Why do you need to know, Mads?"

Now she leans forward, and lowers her voice. "Because I think that the money that Zimmerman stole is going to be in one of those accounts. And whoever owns it is in on his plot to take back Israel for the Catholic Church."

"If you find the money, you can find out who else is on this crusade."

"Yes. And that money should go to the Jewish families it was stolen from, if there are survivors. And then I can finish the story that my father started. That's my why, Patrick."

Maddie knows that it's not the complete why, but that the omission of the details about White House and how she is now working for the Vatican will protect Patrick. He might even have guessed that.

He stares at her the way he did when she was all the world to him. "I care about you Mads," he says.

"I care about you, too," she replies. "But I know that I have been sent on this… quest … by my father, and by powers beyond me, and you, as a poet, know the power of that."

His smile turns tender. "OK. I'll do it. But if it's a story that I can be part of, in my job, and as your friend, then I want to be that, too."

Maddie squeezes his hand. "Thank you, Patrick. Of course."

"Nobody fucken move!" barks the man wearing a Bill Cosby Halloween mask who has just stepped through the velvet curtains of Flammie's. In his right hand he has a revolver, with a long barrel. Maddie recognizes it as a Colt .45 "Peacemaker", a gun her father had loved.

Cosby steps forward, and behind him comes another man, this one in a pudgy Al Sharpton mask, featuring the civil rights crusader and TV host before he'd gone vegan and lost half his body weight.

He is holding a Ruger .38 Special laser-sighted pistol in his right hand, and a Trader Joe's bag in his left. The third guy, in a Tiger Woods mask, watches the door. He has a sawed-off shotgun, tucked inside a black leather greatcoat, going for the Gestapo gangster look.

"Empty 'em out!" yells Cosby. "Chop fucken chop!"

"Cash, jewelry, phones, gewgaws!" hollers Sharpton.

Their Halloween masks are black, but their voices are white, and seasoned with the South. Maddie recognizes the flavor of Georgia in Sharpton's voice, when he says, "Hurry up, white people! Take this as an opp-ah-tunity to save your fucken lives!"

Maddie looks to Patrick, who gives her the barest of nods. He's armed.

She has brought cash and both her phones, the old and

the new. The robbers cannot have the new one, as they will see the story she has just told.

She extracts her green and gold Lumia, with the photo of her and her father in Cairo, the Sphinx behind them.

Cosby takes the cash from behind the bar, and relieves the bartender of her watch, phone and silver bracelet.

Sharpton works the room, holding out his Trader Joe's bag, while the patrons throw in their money and phones. "You can keep that," he says to one lady who can't get her wedding ring off.

"Can I keep my SD card?" Maddie asks Sharpton. It has the last photo of her father on it. She gets a slap in the head from a leather-gloved hand.

"All of it," Sharpton says, and holds out his bag.

Maddie could take his gun from him right here and now, and while she's a fine shot, she doesn't know if the robbers are, and a lot of innocent people could die because of her desire to thump this bastard.

So, she dumps her old Lumia with her father and herself and the Sphinx grinning out as if none of this is happening, along with $80 into his bag.

"Wallet!" Sharpton demands.

Maddie holds out her hands. "Don't have it on me. The bar is cash only."

Sharpton aims the red laser onto Maddie's chest as he fishes Maddie's phone out of his bag, and hands it to her. "Take a fucken selfie. So I have something to remember you by."

She's the only person he has asked to do this, Maddie realizes. He nudges her with the gun so she takes a selfie.

Sharpton snatches back the phone, then turns to Patrick and runs the red laser across his chest.

"Hmm, you look like you could be trouble," he says, stopping the laser on Patrick's heart. Maddie flinches. Is it about to turn from robbery into mayhem? Is it time for her to attack and grab the .38 to stop whatever is going to happen to Patrick?

Patrick sees the look in her eyes and instead grabs Maddie's hand. "It's OK," he says, and hands over his phone, a cheap burner, and his wallet. "No trouble."

"You take a fucken selfie as well, lover boy," Sharpton barks, so Patrick does and then hands him the phone. Sharpton looks at them both as if he's never going to forget them.

And then the robbers are gone.

There is a deep silence of shock in the bar.

"Call the cops?" Maddie says to the bartender.

She shakes her head. "We only have our cell phones. And now we don't."

It is as if they have all been robbed back into the 1980s.

"I'd say this round is on us," says the bartender, but Maddie is in no mood. She is out the door and onto Vanderbilt Avenue fast.

"Mads! Don't!" Patrick yells. Then he runs out after her.

Maddie is already up at the corner of Dean Street, startled pedestrians giving way to this angry sprinter in her green summer dress and sneakers. She sees the guy in the Sharpton mask getting into a white panel van double parked half-way down the block.

Adrenaline cancels the whiskey, and she hurdles off down the middle of the street as if skating in on a breakaway with a chance to win the game. The van screeches rubber on the road as it speeds off, its muscled-up engine roaring with menace as Maddie closes in. She wants to catch the license plate number of the van. Closing in, she sees that it has no license plate. It is a ghost van.

And Sharpton is leaning out the passenger window now, the laser light of his Ruger .38 aimed right into Maddie's eyes. So Maddie hits the ground and rolls behind a parked taxi before Sharpton can shoot.

But the shot comes from Patrick, and Sharpton ducks back inside the van in surprise. Patrick shoots again, and the panel van veers sharply to the left and then crashes into a construction bin. Sharpton and Cosby leap out of the van and run for it.

Patrick aims his Glock 19-M at Sharpton, the slower of the two runners, but a jogger who is dodging the bullets ducks into his sights just before Patrick can fire. He lowers his gun. And Sharpton and Cosby chug off into the dark.

"Are you OK, Mads?" he asks.

Maddie is fine. But she knows that she is responsible for what just happened.

"We need to call the police."

Patrick takes her by the hand and shakes his head, no. "They have ShotSpotter technology everywhere, and believe me, someone around here will call it in. When they come, you saw me, but you don't know me, and remember, you have no ID. Your call. I'll talk to you soon."

Then he's gone, into the darkness of Dean Street. Maddie stands there, staring at the crashed van. She can't see any movement inside.

As Patrick predicted, the NYPD are there soon, and in force, with three cars and two SUVs.

But all they find, besides a badly wounded guy in a Tiger Woods mask in the van, is Maddie Lynch.

"There was a guy here, he said he was DEA, he fired the shots that stopped the van."

The cops are keen to speak to this guy, but Maddie says she has never seen him before. Dark hair, thirtyish, she is kind of shocked and doesn't remember much. It was dark, he was passing by, and saw the robbers run out. She was running after them because they stole her phone.

The cops try not to roll their eyes at that one as they write this down, and the ambulance shows up, and the EMT's attend to Tiger Woods. The cops then split up and go into Flammie's to ask more questions.

The cop who is talking to Maddie, a Latino man whose wide, worried eyes say he's not long out of the academy, looks at his notes. "So Christine Zimmerman, we can reach you at this number if we have any more questions?"

Maddie Lynch says yes. No ID, no phone, no money, no name. Christine Zimmerman is her revenge on this moment. She can't have the police getting in the way of the story now. She needs Patrick to be safe, and this is how she'll save him.

On her walk back to her apartment, she thinks how of all the patrons in the bar, the robbers only wanted pictures of her and Patrick. They were the targets. Is this a Brett Muenster job? He saw her phone at the restaurant when they went for drinks. But why would he want her phone if they had already bugged it? Unless he had clocked the second phone, somehow.

The temperature has cooled, so Maddie picks up her pace. She rounds Fifth Avenue, and heads toward her building. That's when she stops dead, as if another gun is aimed at her head.

Standing in front of the building, a duffel bag in hand, smiling with joy is a tall, lithe man in khakis and a blue shirt, his head crowned by an avalanche of blonde curls. Cosmo.

When he sees Maddie, he drops his bag and runs to her in embrace. She can't quite believe the trajectory of this night, but she embraces Cosmo in return. He is warm and smells of ginger, and holds her so tight.

He pulls back and looks at her fiercely. "I had to see you."

"I'm sorry. My texts were short. I was away so long," she replies. "It has been busy and—"

He puts a finger on her lips. "Elka has left me. She wants an annulment."

Maddie finds she has a laugh left in her tonight. She is about to say, "*That was quick*", but instead says, "Where is Mathilda?"

"She's with my parents."

"Do they know you're here?"

"I told them I had to speak to you in person. After the last time I saw you, you were all I could think of."

Maddie knows the feeling. But after she saw Cosmo, she has had other things on her mind.

"Come up," she says.

He looks as if he is going to kiss her right there, but she grabs his duffel bag and leads the way. They climb the stairs in silence, as Maddie knows that once they cross the threshold, her life could change again in a way she cannot imagine it changing now. She has to be careful.

When they reach the door, it is open. And when she walks in, her apartment has been ransacked by what looks like a team of rabid vandals. Books scattered, the sofa slit open, holes punched in the walls, and her computer on, doubtless copied on to some hard drive.

Cosmo stands with his mouth open. "Gosh," is all he can say.

Maddie knows that whoever was looking found nothing here. So now they will want to find her.

"Good thing you're packed, Cosmo," she says. "We're going to a very exclusive hotel."

Then Maddie hauls out her Galaxy and calls her mother, asking for a room for two for the night.

Francesca listens, and then lets a moment of silence pass. "I will make a bed for your friend. And I will open a bottle of Montepulciano for us. Because it is now time for you to tell your mother everything."

47. New York City.

C. Parke Stranch III has parked his yacht in the 79th Street Boat Basin, bobbing on the waters of the Hudson River, and catching the sunset kiss over New Jersey, to the west. These days, when he visits New York, he likes the boat basin because it is more discreet. No doormen to navigate, just a derelict boardwalk to pass by as you board his vessel, *The Ship of State*.

The large, sleek 80 motor yacht's name is his little joke on all those who laughed at him when he was creating his business empire. Too rigid, too religious, too right-wing, they had said.

But they were wrong. He came out ahead, for now he has his trinity: a fortune that rivals any mid-level billionaire, and his own private army, Bellerophon, and this 95-ton, $6.5 million testament to his success. He even has a fine white linen admiral's jacket and hat, of course it has a cross on it. He will always wear it with his string tie. It's tradition.

All he needs now is the presidency, and he will have the quartet to take charge of the world's destiny. For the good of God.

And, thank God, that is also for the good of C. Parke Stranch, he thinks as he laughs to himself and settles into his chair on the aft deck.

"Admiral, sir." The arrival of a crewman lets Stranch know that his guest has arrived.

"It is good to see you, Bishop Hughes," Stranch says,

hefting his bulk out of his chair. Stranch puts his left hand over his own pectoral cross that is larger than that of the Vatican's undersecretary of state, and shakes with his right.

"And you, Admiral," the Bishop says. "It is good to be on a ship of state that is more solid, even on water, than the one I'm currently on board in Rome."

Though Hughes speaks of the Vatican, he doesn't look the part, now wearing a fine light gray Italian suit. His face unmoving, his heavy-lidded gangster eyes take in everything on the aft deck's luxurious indoor-outdoor lounge. It gleams with a large screen TV and sound system, handsome canvas couches and bar, though it only offers ice tea. The crewman who ushered Hughes aboard, with a deft nod to Stranch, returns to his post by the gangplank. But another crew member remains, keeping watch off the stern. And Hughes doesn't like that.

"Son, you keep an eye out. We're going to take a little tour of our boat," the Admiral tells his crewman. He leads Hughes through wide open glass doors into a palatial living room, furnished with a series of comfortable seating areas, a dining area that seats twenty, with an enormous galley beyond it. Staff bustle all around, dusting, arranging flowers, stopping to greet their Admiral. Stranch is gracious to them and all while Hughes is winding tighter.

"They are my two-footed security," Stranch says quietly to Hughes. "A mind is easier to wipe clean than a security camera."

He steps into a wood paneled elevator. Hughes follows, his wariness over Stranch's idea of security turning dark.

With a welcoming bing, the elevator arrives at the lower deck. Stepping out, Stranch leads the way to bow. A smile of pride grows on his wide lips as he shows off his new addition: a private chapel that seats four.

"I hate being on the road. That's why I have a boat," Stranch laughs.

As they step into the small chapel, a sensor catches their arrival and the glass door behind them slides shut with a quiet hiss.

Hughes is obliged to genuflect, though it feels almost an offense to the Lord. This tiny golden chapel is another of the Admiral's affectations.

But he seats himself alongside Stranch before the altar, which is draped in a gold cloth, with a gold cross above it.

"I thought you were coming to New York with the Pope," Stranch says.

"That was the plan, but plans have changed. I am here to make sure the security at the Apostolic Nuncio's residence is worthy of the Holy Father."

"And is it?"

"It will be," Hughes replies.

Stranch smiles. "I am glad to hear that, Bishop. We need good security."

Bishop Hughes nods. "I trust that all is well on your end?"

Stranch leans back and puts his right hand on his gold

cross. "It is, Bishop Hughes. When we are done, it will be nothing but 'red sky at night, and sailors' delight'."

"And I am glad to hear that." Hughes does not look glad. He just looks dangerous.

"Of course, the good Lord might have other plans," Stranch says, sending Hughes a message not to mess with him, "so I keep my prayers constant and loud. And of course, I have my own army if He doesn't hear me in time."

Bishop Hughes smiles in feigned appreciation. He feels disdain for this American buffoon, whom a much lesser God than the one which Hughes believes in has chosen to help him fulfill what Jesus began.

"Our friend tells me that he has set in motion 'the angels'."

"The angels are in flight as we speak," Stranch says. "Not literally. They are on a ship. They will fly soon."

"After the election."

"Indeed."

"So, you think Reagan Clark is going to win?" Hughes asks.

"Don't you?" Stranch replies, genuinely surprised.

"Well, that would depend on her getting a big bump in the polls. It needs to be a victory that cannot be challenged. Everything, every vote is questioned."

Stranch slaps his knee and his laugh rings out. "I know all about that kind of fishing expedition, Bishop. With your help, we will get her more than a bump, but a landslide. That and Reagan's policy to make America face up to reality is reality enough. The people want a leader who will not pretend that our enemies are really civilized fair-minded folks like us, who believe that a handshake is enough to seal a deal and who will keep their promises. As if Iran will ever play nice with us. As if we, as a people, will accept that we can do nothing to ensure the primacy of the American way of life, one we were both born to."

Hughes, who had grown up in a working-class Irish-Catholic family in Liverpool, knows that his view of America is about as different to C. Parke Stranch's as it could ever be. And yet, here they are in the same boat, literally.

Stranch hears the silent reply. "We're good Christian soldiers, Bishop Hughes. Fighting the good fight. And any fight that puts Americans back to work is good in my book. I am indeed glad you came to me after the loss of Cardinal Zimmerman and we could work things out. We had our differences, the Cardinal and I. But he was a loose cannon, wanted everything his own way."

Hughes drills a cold look of contempt into Stranch. Calling the murder of the Cardinal a loss? Saying he was a loose cannon? All for the good fight? That is about as true as Stranch is a true admiral.

It was Reagan's people who approached Hughes, he recalls. She knew as well as she knew Cardinal Zimmerman what the Society's mission was and how fit perfectly into her own plans. And it fit all the better for her with the Cardinal out of the way. Even better if he was dead.

Hughes leans down and opens his briefcase, and

removes a manilla folder. He hands it to Stranch. "The Apostolic Nuncio's house is large, 11,000 square feet, but the plans are simple. All you need is ingress, egress, and the first floor."

Stranch opens the folder, nodding in approval at what he sees, at the high detail of the floor plan, down to the thickness of the walls. "Very good, Bishop Hughes, very good." As he rises, the glass door sees him and sighs open. Then, Stranch leads the way back to the aft deck for a celebratory drink.

Hughes would have enjoyed a fine Italian red, but he sees the only offering at Stranch's meager bar is a tall pitcher of iced tea.

"I am a little weary from my flight, still so I will excuse myself now."

Stranch offers Hughes his hand. "We will be in touch."

Hughes takes the offered hand and as he exits for the gangplank, gives the Admiral a clerical bow. "I look forward to it."

A woman, all in black, walks out from the galley on quiet shoes, absolutely steady though the ship rocks on the tall waves of a passing speedboat. Jane Jones does not greet Stranch with his titular address of 'Admiral'. All she asks is: "He delivered?"

"He did, Major Jones." Stranch hands her the folder, and she looks at it.

Stranch pours them tall glasses of iced tea, and brings his large mouth to his glass and sucks up half.

"Speaking of delivering, Major. The event last night

went off well. Even with a little hitch. A shot in the shoulder."

"Did M make the shot?" Jane asks, half-hoping Maddie shot the fake hold-up guy.

"Her friend, I think, in the DEA." Stranch gives her a hopeful look as he says, "We have anyone on the inside where he is?"

"We don't know for sure he was the shooter." Jane feels a chill run through her body, a readiness she had felt when the enemy was close. The operation at Flammie's was not perfect, as one of her hires was shot and is in custody, and now must be taken out before he talks. But she is with Stranch on his yacht and hearing him call the robbery of Maddie Lynch and the imminent death of one of her hired guns an 'event' in an insult. And now the DEA guy is to be killed because almighty Stranch thinks so?

"And nothing showed up in Miss Lynch's apartment, which is all well and good." Stranch gulps down the rest of his iced tea. "The event at that Italian restaurant also went well. Even the owner is recovering nicely. It went so very well that no one knows who did it. I'm not even sure it is you I have to thank."

"But I am sure you paid me. For both ops."

"Anything strike you as a problem?" Stranch asks.

Jane Jones would laugh. It's all a problem, really, doing what they do, and what they are going to do. She could snatch Stranch's glass of iced tea, smash it and use it to slash his fat neck open in two seconds, then escape on the skiff that hangs off the stern. She has enough money, but she wants more than that. She wants the power that Stranch can give her. When she has enough of it, then she will look for her skiff or whatever exit is left. But that is many millions away.

He raises his eyebrows, waiting for an answer.

She picks up her iced tea. Not that she's going to drink it. "No, not at first glance," she says.

"Good," Stranch replies. "We need whatever force is going to get us a landslide."

Jane Jones slips him a wink. She has an idea of just how she can accomplish that. And to find for herself a way out of this mess.

48. The Apostolic Nuncio Mansion, New York City.

"Cara Francesca," says the Apostolic Nuncio to the United Nations, Archbishop Giacomo Marinelli, almost applauding when he sees Francesca Lynch as she stands in his doorway, pulling off sunglasses to toss her black and white curls into place. Her dark eyes, pale skin, black dress and pearls carry on the chiaroscuro of beauty.

"Caro Giacomo," Francesca replies, kissing his ring. "I am perfect, now that I have seen you again. And yourself, handsome as ever." He's six inches shorter than Francesca, and carrying about thirty pounds more than he should, but he basks in the compliment.

Even though it has barely gone 7 AM, he welcomes Francesca and Maddie and Cosmo into his residence as if they are fashionably on time for dinner.

Francesca had called him and did not invite him out for a caffe as promised. Instead, she told him the truth – and far less than Maddie revealed to her: they are being watched. They need a place to be out of sight until the Pope has come and gone, and the watching will stop. Maddie went along with it, knowing her mother is right.

"You will have good company, my dear. The Holy Father is staying with me while he is in New York. So you will know exactly when he leaves."

This one guest at the grand mansion was expected by Maddie and everyone at *I'm Wright.* And this one guest makes it crowded. The Secret Service will have their list of reasons why she and Francesca and Cosmo cannot be there, but she will sort that out with Cardinal Otley. Right now she needs to get her mother and Cosmo settled in, and then she needs to go retrieve all that she has kept safe.

The Nuncio instructs a butler to take their bags to the top floor, on the quiet side of the house, and give them each their own room.

"I am sorry," he says suddenly, looking at Cosmo and Maddie. "I did not think to ask if you are married!"

Maddie feels the heat rush to her cheeks and Cosmo's eyes flash with a look like he might just ask her to marry him right now and the Nuncio to annul his current marriage. So Maddie is grateful when Francesca says, "Three single rooms are *perfetta. Grazie*."

Her mother's connections have opened this door, and Maddie at last feels safe. And that door belongs to the UN's Apostolic Nuncio and the Vatican's embassy in New York is even better. The 11,000-square foot limestone beauty on the Upper East Side that was built for New York City's youngest ever mayor, Hugh J. Grant, a Tammany Hall Democrat, elected in 1889 at age 30, and who ruled the city for three years, will keep them safe, and in style.

Archbishop Martinelli guides them to the mansion's dining room, a large neo-Renaissance space with floral marble arches and gold-plated chandeliers and a 30-foot-long polished oak table that could seat 35 people, but is set for four.

On a rococo glass and iron filigreed sideboard almost as long as the dining table sits breakfast laid out for an army: towering thermoses of coffee and tea, and jugs of juice, baskets of croissant and muffins, bowls of apples and bananas, and three silver food warmers containing scrambled eggs, sausage and fried potatoes, next to an electric toaster and loaves of white and whole wheat bread.

"I have to go to the UN, I'm afraid," the Archbishop says. "So I will wish you *buon appetito,* and I will see you when I see you, which cannot be soon enough."

"Thank you, Giacomo," Francesca says, as the Archbishop lavishes her hand with another kiss.

"Thanks, really, Giacomo," Maddie adds, then heads straight for the coffee urn. She grabs a mug crested with the Vatican tiara and keys, pours a cup and splashes in some milk, then grabs an apple.

She wants to get out of here as soon as she can, but her mother, ladling eggs and potatoes onto her plate, and Cosmo, taking two of everything, seem to want to remind her that breakfast is the most important meal of the day.

"So," Francesca says, her eyes on Cosmo, "I believe we left the story in *media res*, as the scholars like you would say."

Maddie tries not to roll her eyes. Now is not the time to get into her history with Cosmo, but her mother is owed more than she offered last night, when they showed up at her doorstep a little past midnight.

At the table, she continues: "You are the godmother,

Maddie, you are the father, Cosmo. But where is the mother and the child?"

Cosmo nods and chomps down his egg and sausage. "Mrs. Lynch…"

"Francesca, please," she replies, opening her palms as if to suggest all formality is now bygones, given the past less-than-twelve hours.

"Francesca," Cosmo smiles. "My wife, Elka, has decided our marriage is over. She wants an annulment."

Francesca's black eyes flash. "On what grounds?"

Cosmo looks at Maddie, whose green eyes are soft with sympathy. "She says I was already in a relationship when I married her."

"And were you?"

For Maddie, diplomacy is not her strong suit. Still, she puts a hand up. "He was not, but if it helps him and my goddaughter to be happy, I will say he was still in a relationship with me."

Francesca presses a hand to her own heart and looks at Maddie as if she has taken everything but the divine from her Jesuit education. Then she smiles in measured joy for her daughter.

"It is your business, and I wish you nothing but happiness." She takes a sip of tea. "Should we survive the next week or so…"

Maddie rises. "And on that note, I have to go."

"Surely, you're not going to work?" Francesca says.

"I'll be working remotely for the next while. I have told Teddy I am 'embedded'." Maddie sweeps her arm at the majesty of the long table, the long buffet, and the

Nuncio's residence. "I told her I'm in the Pope's house. She approves."

Cosmo rises as well. "I'll go with you."

Maddie is in danger, and Cosmo has put himself there without knowing that. Maybe having him with her will dissuade anyone who wants to take another shot that they don't want to be on the hook for two. Or maybe not.

"I am happy to dine alone," Francesca says. "It has been my habit for some time."

"Then I hope you won't mind too much if I join you…"

Maddie remembers that deep and plummy English voice, and spins to see the person for whom the fourth table setting has been laid as he enters the room.

"What a surprise to see you here, Maddie," Bishop Hughes says, his gangster eyes swiveling onto her mother and over to Cosmo.

Francesca is now the one who is surprised, looking at Maddie with curiosity. Maddie flashes a look "don't ask."

"Yes, I could say the same, Bishop Hughes. This is my mother, Francesca, and my friend Cosmo Smythe. He's visiting from England."

"How do you two know each other?" Francesca cannot resist.

"Bishop Hughes is the Vatican's undersecretary of state. He was kind enough to help me to secure the interview with the Pope."

Hughes's rugged face cracks in a small smile, tight and false. "You did all the heavy lifting. And now my job is to make sure the Pope is secure while he is here."

"You must tell me all about that," Francesca says.

"Cosmo and I are working on a book," Maddie says. "We need to get to the library."

"Oh," says Bishop Hughes. "What's your book about?"

Cosmo steps up as if he's been bursting to talk about for hours. "*The Women Who Made Jesus*."

Bishop Hughes hums, as if this is a book the world does not need. "And you can get a book out of that?"

Maddie blasts him with a grin. "Maybe even two."

As she heads out the door with Cosmo, Maddie texts her mother in Italian, asking her to keep an eye on Hughes, and to tell him nothing.

Her mother responds with emoticons of a winking eye, and the yellow face with two eyes and no mouth. That is far more tech savvy than Maddie thought her mother could be. The Mafia gene is in play.

49. New York City.

Maddie and Cosmo catch the downtown 6-train at 68th Street. It is the local and at just before 8 AM, it is packed. Maddie hangs on to the pole in the middle of the train, while Cosmo has squeezed into a space by the door. He peers over the morning's sleepy commuters, looking worried for her, as if the train were full of football hooligans.

He slings his arm through Maddie's as they climb out of the subway six stops later into a beautiful day, warm but with kindly low humidity for August. The New York sky seems higher; it might be the skyscrapers that need the room, or the sky itself stands back, dazzled by the city.

But Cosmos's eyes are quickly back on Maddie, watching her as if she was a flight risk.

"Ask me anything," she says.

He is relieved by the opening. "What's happening, Maddie?" he says. "I don't mean with me, and you and whatever happens with us, I mean with you? Why are people stealing your phone? And breaking into your flat? And fire-bombing your favorite Italian restaurant?"

"I could say it was your father who started the fire," Maddie says, then goes on to explain how it was Cosmo's father who asked Maddie to find out what happened to Christopher Zimmerman, the man behind the missing money at St. Jude's. It was thanks to a nun and her own father she found out some more.

"Golly. My father? And a nun and your father?" Cosmo's blue eyes blink in shock.

"He left some information with my mother. She gave it to me. It was like a map. My own father had part of the map."

"So did you find the other part?"

"I'm still on the hunt, but I can tell you Zimmerman, who was Bishop Zimmerman, stole money from St. Jude's. And from a lot of other people. 250 million Euros in total."

"That seems rather ungodly. Why would he do that?"

"I think he was using the money to fund a holy war in the Middle East."

Cosmo scans the street to see if anyone is listening, but people are all marching along, earbuds in, eyes on their phones, managing not to fall down or collide with each other. "A holy war in the Middle East?" he says, his voice straining with disbelief.

Maddie quietly explains Zimmerman's connection to the Society of Blessed Urban II. It's a society that Cosmo is familiar with because he was the one who told her about it. They're not a hair-shirt-and-flagellation God-gang but one that prefers to inflict their torment on others.

"That's what I think their plan is," Maddie says. "In their perverted spin, they think they are going to actually save Israel, and to do it with Jewish money stolen in World War Two. But I think there is more to the story. An American side to the story. I am working on it."

Cosmo pales to hear there is more, as there is already

so much that alarms him. “And this is why Zimmerman was killed? Did his fellow St. Urbanites bump him off?”

“No, I think he was murdered because he was blackmailing an old friend.”

“Who?”

“Reagan Clark.”

Cosmo stops in the middle of the sidewalk, and a UPS delivery woman with a full trolley has to do a quick dodge to miss him.

“Sorry,” Cosmo says to the UPS woman. “Reagan Clark?” he says to Maddie, his eyes wide and unblinking.

“Yes,” she says. A wave of relief comes over her to have said it out loud. To have someone hear it who doesn’t think she is crazy. Or is trying to kill her.

He runs a hand over his head, as if this will help process what he’s hearing. “Who knows this?”

“You, me, and Patrick.”

“The guy you were with last night?”

And for a couple of years before I met you, Maddie thinks, but that’s not a conversation that has to happen now. “Yes.”

“Do you think the guys in those masks had anything to do with this?”

“I do. While they were robbing me, they wanted my phone and my picture.”

“Just yours?”

“And Patrick’s.”

Cosmo nods as he tries to take it all in. And now Maddie has become all the more precious. Linking arms, he leads her to the crosswalk and steps off the curb at 10th

Avenue. He nearly gets clipped by a delivery guy on an electric bike.

"Careful," Maddie says.

Cosmo grins. "I'd say that's an understatement."

She settles him down safely on a bench overlooking the Hudson River while she runs a quick errand.

"You sure you don't want me to come with you?"

"You've already heard enough." She gives him a soft kiss on the cheek and walks on, heading south, weaving through the morning joggers. He can't see where she is going and what she is going to get. To try and keep her safe, he will keep staring in that same direction until she returns.

Maddie weaves in and around the slow march of traffic, then suddenly hurries into Chelsea Piers and, making sure she isn't followed, takes the elevator up to the lobby. When she steps out, she's glad to see the dings on the walls from hockey games, and a few brawls in the hallways, have been touched up, ready for a new season. But the bite in the air of ammonia, used by the Zamboni to melt the rink's ice, still provides the Sky Rink's particular brand of sporty perfume.

The Women's Club room, during preseason, is empty at this hour on a Thursday morning. Maddie can take her time to get the combination on her locker right, spinning it back and forth and back again, and then pops it open. Inside the locker are the contents of her father's satchel that she extracted before it was burned up in the fire at Risorgimento. There is also Luke's folder on Secret Archives intel, and the DVDs and photo she found in

Christopher Zimmerman's flat. She loads them into her laptop bag, shuts the locker, and clamps the combination lock back on to the locker's handle and gives it a spin.

Her phone vibrates with a WhatsApp message. It's from Patrick: *Can we meet?*

Maddie texts back: *I am at Chelsea Piers.*

Stay there. I'll meet you by the Pier 62 Carousel in 20 minutes: he writes back.

Maddie exits Pier 61 and sees Cosmo, reading *The Daily News*.

"Copy was left on the bench," he says, by way of explaining why he's reading a tabloid. "Your evening's adventure made page three."

He opens the paper and Maddie sees an item about the shocking robbery of Flammie's. She reads the short piece about a mysterious DEA agent who wounds one of the robbers and then vanishes. It's the kind of mystery the tabloids love. Speculation that it was some kind of white supremacist plot interrupted by the feds, given the white guys robbing people while wearing Black masks, adds the spice of intelligence to the story. Thankfully, she is not mentioned, and Patrick is just the mysterious gunslinger, and that's all good.

"Cosmo, I have to meet someone now. I don't know how long it will take."

"Then, I'm off to The Strand," Cosmo says. "18 miles of books. There should be a few good tomes there to help me with my next book."

"You know how to get back?"

"To New York's Papal Palace?" He grins a yes. "I

take it the key will not be under the mat."

Maddie laughs. "Just text me if security gives you trouble."

Cosmo gives her a kiss on the cheek, then heads off to the safe world of books in The Strand. As soon as he is out of sight, Maddie starts walking as she calls Cardinal Otley on WhatsApp.

"Maddie," the Cardinal says, both in relief and caution.

"Cardinal Otley, sorry for the radio silence, but I have been at work."

"Where are you?"

"In New York. I am staying with the Apostolic Nuncio. Who is a friend of my mother's."

Otley's laugh echoes over the phone. "Small world getting smaller."

"I need you to clear that with the Vatican security people, and the Secret Service."

"You plan on staying a while?"

"Someone is trying to get what I have, and it's the only place that I can be completely protected."

Maddie has her head on a swivel as she walks to the carousel. There is a large French tour group to her left. But they are busy with their cell phones, checking maps and taking selfies. No one is following her.

"I will take care of it," Otley says.

"Will you be coming here with the Pope?" Maddie asks.

"No, I have business to attend to here. I sent Bishop Hughes in my place."

Maddie feels a thud in her stomach. Is Cardinal Otley in league with Hughes? "You are the one who sent him?"

"Actually, he did me a favor by volunteering. As much as I admire you, I always find my visits to the USA leave me a little shell-shocked when I return."

Maddie breathes out. Cardinal Otley's general dislike of America has kept him at home. Or maybe something else. Maybe he wants to have an alibi when Hughes begins his crusade.

"I think I might have some intel on the Zimmerman front," Maddie says.

"I look forward to it," the Cardinal replies. "Just don't tell Hughes, whatever it is."

"Why not?" she says. "Who is he?" She takes a breath. If he doesn't tell her what sounds like the truth, then she will know whose side he is on.

Otley is silent for a few seconds, then says, "Because he's not one of us."

Maddie feels relief, but needs more. "Even so, you let him come here."

"Are you saying he's planning to do someone harm?" Otley asks.

"I don't know what he's planning," Maddie replies. "The fact that he's close is good. I'll be very safe while I keep an eye on him."

She sees Patrick walking at a clip toward the carousel. "I have to go now. More soon."

"I will pray for you."

She's grateful for the prayer and ends the call to find Patrick is in front of her. "You did well last night," he says. "We're in the news and not by name."

He links arms with her, smiling as they walk on, just a happy couple making their Manhattan tour.

"Do you know who those guys were?"

"The guy I shot in the shoulder, he'll be fine. He's an ex-Special Forces guy who was drummed out of the military and worked for a private contractor until he got sacked from that about a month ago."

"So not white supremacists."

"Maybe, but nothing on his record."

"Who did the guy work for? As a private contractor?"

"Bellerophon."

"After the Greek hero who killed the evil chimera monster and rode the flying horse." Maddie sighs at the epic size ego that would take that name. "And they're a private army?"

Patrick gives her an appreciative grin. "You know your classics, Mads. Yeah, they're run by a former Navy SEAL named C. Parke Stranch."

Maddie's work keeps her head filled with news and names for Teddy Wright, and now for all kinds of reasons. It doesn't take a second to remember. "The old SEAL who now makes billions by buying companies and firing people?"

"Yep."

Maddie covers her mouth, as if saying the next part out loud would be fatal. Why would a guy like that come after her?

Patrick pulls out his phone. "I'm going to send you this scrub app on Signal. Do you have it?"

"Yes." Maddie opens the app.

"The good thing about this scrubber is that messages can be set to self-destruct. But if you want to keep a message, you can also store it somewhere safe."

Patrick finds her in Signal and sends her the document. She opens the one called Swiss Cheese and sees that he has found the owners of the Swiss bank account.

No surprise. The account is owned by Christopher Zimmerman, and has 50 million Euros in it.

The next file, called Baron von Trapp, for the Austrian bank account, is owned by the Society of Blessed Urban II and has 190 million Euros in it. Scanning the document, Maddie reads that there was a withdrawal the month earlier of 10 million Euros.

"Wow," she says. "Zimmerman fueled some of the money to himself, and most of it to his secret society."

"Who spent a good chunk of it. But on what?"

Maddie shakes her head; she does not know, but 10 million Euros could buy a lot of Crusade.

"Is there any way you can get access to that 50 million Euros in the Swiss bank? Zimmerman is dead, and the Vatican has proof he stole money from them, so he won't be needing that account."

"You'd need to have the Vatican on board with that, but yes. Just hope he hasn't left it to some awful nephew in his will."

"I don't think Christopher Zimmerman had anyone except for Reagan Clark."

"That's the White House connection?" Patrick asks.

He was aware Maddie didn't tell him everything last night and had been thinking about the missing pieces and names. So he would know who was coming after him.

"Yes. And he certainly didn't leave it to her. He gave most of the money to the Society."

"And kept a fat parachute for himself."

A young family walks by, and the father gives a friendly nod to Maddie and Patrick, sure they are a couple, and soon to join them with their own kids.

The joyful organ music of the carousel keeps rolling as the painted horses wait for children to mount them and pretend that today will last forever. Maddie remembers when she was very happy to go round and around, and even teach at Oxford the same classes year after year, and it was not so long ago.

"Thank you, Patrick," she says.

"You're welcome." He sidles up to Maddie with a one arm hug. "I think it's a good idea if we don't see each other for a while."

Maddie feels like this is the breakup that they never really had, and tears well up in her eyes. "I'm sorry," she says. "I know you're right. I owe you."

"I owe you," he says. "I started writing again last night."

She leans up an inch and gives him a kiss on the cheek.

"Be careful, Mads," he says. "Those people have already killed once."

More than that, Maddie knows. And the cold knot in her stomach tells her that they plan to kill even more.

50. New York City.

"Who's this?"

Maddie looks at the man doing the asking. He's set up his own central command in the grand marble entry to the Apostolic Nuncio's mansion, desk, computers, chair and all. He is the massive, head-shaved boss of the Pope's US Secret Service security team, a guy who calls himself "Commander", who manages to look right through Maddie at the same time as he speaks to her, as if she might have a bomb strapped to the back of her head.

"This is Maddie Lynch," replies Bishop Paul Hughes calmly, as if answering a question about the weather. He is in his bishop's cassock wrapped with a purple sash tied tight, showing his rugby prop frame, and he wears his purple zucchetto on his head. He seems even more sinister for how he corrupts the uniform. "She's a producer with *I'm Wright,* which this popular American TV show. They will be interviewing the Holy Father here Saturday morning."

Commander looks dismayed by this news. "We thought that was canceled."

Maddie blinks hard to stop rolling her eyes—these are the people protecting the Pope?

Hughes's calm snaps, and he now speaks sharply. In control. "Your intelligence is wrong. It's going forward at 10 AM on Saturday."

The Commander speaks into the sleeve of his navy-blue suit, his brow heavy with the burden of keeping the

Pope alive. He says, “We need to accelerate and reconfigure 0700 Saturday for a TV crew.”

The Commander then looks at Cosmo and Francesca, who have also been summoned for inspection. “And who are you and why are you here?”

Francesca gives him a lovely smile beneath the winter of her gaze. “We’re guests of the Archbishop Giacomo Martinelli. Giacomo is an old friend of mine and has invited us to stay here until my home can be repaired.”

The Commander looks at Cosmo. “I’m a friend, working with Maddie Lynch.”

“You all have ID?”

Francesca produces her driver’s license and Cosmo hands over his passport.

“You two related?” he says, looking at Francesca’s license and glancing at Maddie.

“She’s my mother.”

“So why are you all here now?” asks the Commander, sensing a conspiracy.

“As I said,” Francesca replies, her Italian charm turning into scary nun about to strike, “the resident is an old friend of mine, and he invited us to stay here while the Holy Father is here. It’s a big house.”

The Commander shakes his head, as if this is the worst idea ever. “Where is the Archbishop?”

“He’s at the United Nations, being the papal representative,” Francesca says. “I can call him if you like.”

The Commander looks at her if he’s trying to decide if this is an insult, or a bluff. “Give me his number and

I'll call him."

"Of course." Francesca writes it down and hands it to him.

Maddie gives him the same cold stare over a charming smile. "You can also check with Cardinal Otley, the Vatican's Secretary of State. I have his number if you want it."

The Commander's eyes dull, knows he has been overruled by this papal pecking order. But he takes the number from Maddie for the sake of form.

Bishop Hughes weighs in with his worries. "Do you think your colleagues will be able to make it here for 7 AM?"

"Sure, they need an hour or so to set up anyway." Teddy won't be happy—she does nighttime TV for a reason, and adding a 7 AM start on a Saturday will give a sharper edge to the razoredge she always keeps.

"They're not running this, we are," the Commander says, trying to convince them of what is not exactly true. "We need a list of everyone who's going to be here onsite ASAP, and then those we'll let in have to be at the door by 7 AM sharp on Saturday for clearance. That clear?"

"Perfectly," Hughes replies.

The Commander turns his eyes on Maddie for a hostile second longer than he needs to, and says, "Make sure everyone has ID—driver's license, passport, no Costco card, OK? We'll need copies of those in advance."

"OK."

The Secret Service commander moves on, joining his

team of seven men and women in dark suits and ties who are sweeping the Nuncio's house for anything that can kill the Pope. They are armed with mirrors on wands, and sniffer dogs on leashes. They probe and feel everything: cushions, curtains, chairs, the underside of shelves, with gloved hands. This means that even kitchen knives are now locked in a safe, and can only be opened by a designated security agent.

"Nice to see Pope Pius is safe from the chef," Cosmo jokes.

Francesca enjoys that and then adds, "But we are not. The rich sauces are dangerous. I must cut back."

Maddie looks at her mother, who can eat whatever she pleases and not gain an ounce. Maddie didn't get those genes.

Another team of agents are putting up long, heavy blast curtains on the windows, in case any would-be suicide car bomber manages to get past the police roadblocks that close off all the streets around the Nuncio's house. The Commander calls in to make sure no vehicles are allowed from 71st Street to 73rd Street between 5th Avenue and Park Avenue, while Madison Avenue is closed from 68th Street to 74th Street.

"How will the crew get their gear in?" Maddie asks the Commander, as the big guardian lumbers down the front hallway back to his command center.

"They'll carry it. No truck is pulling up in front of this place. OK?"

"OK."

Maddie calls Aretta and tells her the new schedule.

Adding that she will need a list of who is coming, along with PDFs of their passport photo page. It is a very lean crew, with Teddy, two cameras, a sound woman. Aretta is now directing, and Maddie producing.

"Directing! Aretta, congratulations," Maddie says, her voice low. "They're going to jam all communications coming in here, so if there's anything I need to know, tell me."

"You need to watch the video link I sent to you. And Teddy has asked if you would send her the revised question list. But watch the video first."

Maddie wants to ask her more, but Hughes has swooped into the front hall to join the Commander. "OK, will do. I am sure I can get Wi-Fi at a café around the corner if I need to."

"Yes, good. Talk to you soon."

Maddie can hear the stress tighten Aretta's deep voice. Teddy is off the charts with anxiety about the interview, and it is all landing on Aretta, with no buffer zone – Maddie. She has to find a way to fix that.

"Come now," Francesca says. "We have a few hours before the Holy Father arrives. Just enough time."

"To do what, Mama?"

"To see Renzo. He is awake."

Francesca turns her charming smile on Cosmo. "You can come if you want, or you can stay here."

Cosmo's blue eyes flare wide open as he remembers the restaurant bombing. "I'm so happy to join you."

Renzo is very happy to see Francesca, and Maddie, and even this Englishman whom he does not know. It's all he can do to smile. He's strapped into a harness elevating his broken legs in a neuroscience ICU room on the ninth floor of Mount Sinai on West 59th Street. He has a bandage on his head, like a collapsed chef's hat, and he has tubes up his nose connected to a ventilator, and a tube attached to a needle into his left arm, dripping IV fluids into his body.

"He has only been conscious since yesterday afternoon," the attending nurse says.

"We have just come to say hello," Francesca replies with a warm smile that gets one in return from the nurse.

"I can see he's glad to see you. I'll give you fifteen minutes." The nurse leaves to answer a beeping down the hall.

Renzo's eyes have teared up, and a hand slips out of his mummy wrappings to grasp Francesca's hand. Maddie aches for him, lying here wounded because of them, and yet he aches for them.

Renzo tries to speak, but his voice is a hoarse whisper, and not the booming basso that it was before the fall. "You are well?"

"Ah, dear man," Francesca says in Italian. "It is so good to see you awake. How do you feel?"

Renzo lets go of Francesca's hand to give them a thumbs up.

"This is my friend, Cosmo. He is from England," Maddie says.

Renzo gives Cosmo a thumbs up, and Cosmo returns the gesture.

"I am sorry, Renzo," Maddie says. "Did you see who

did it?"

Renzo beckons Maddie closer, and he speaks to her in Italian.

"Maybe it was the lady who came in after we closed. Maybe your age. Blonde. Eyes like a wolf. She used the bathroom. I tell you, eyes like a wolf, blue, gray, ice…" Renzo closes his eyes. As if the memory is too much.

"Questo è molto utile. Grazie," Maddie thanks him in Italian, letting him know this is very helpful. "We should go, Mama," she adds quickly.

"You go," she says. "I will just sit with Renzo for a while. They will leave me be, if I just sit quietly here." She smiles at them as if she is at peace as she settles into a chair by Renzo.

Even though Maddie sees it is guilt that is keeping her mother here, guilt that they stored Maddie's Zimmerman DVDs and photo, Luke's folder and her father's papers in Renzo's safe before Maddie hid them in her hockey locker.

But, before she leaves, Renzo whispers to her he was proud to help. His external security system was first rate. No one could break in. Maddie gives him a thumbs up for that.

"He seems to be very keen on your mother," Cosmo says, as he and Maddie walk across Central Park on their way back to the Nuncio's mansion. "Are they?..."

"No, they are not romantically involved."

"Are we?" he asks, softly, shyly.

Maddie turns to look at Cosmo. He flips his tumble of blonde curls out of his eyes to see her better. Because there is nothing else in the world worth seeing. With the August sun heading down, dappling the grove of American elms, on the boulevard, they look like two people on a romantic stroll, pausing for an embrace. And then Maddie kisses him on the mouth. He kisses her back, wrapping her in his arms, pressing her body all against his, keeping her in his kiss. It's a kind of yes.

51. New York City.

Gabriel Almeida de Schmidt feels a lurch in his own heart as he sees that kiss. Someone has the heart of Maddie Lynch. While he is supposed to be a cool, emotionless and detached intelligence operative, he has found himself thinking far too much about Maddie Lynch in ways that are not connected to the job. What stunned him was that she was a great shot, taking out the thug's knee in the villa in Jerusalem. What he can't forget is her laugh, tipping her head back, her black curls bouncing free as her deep laugh soared.

That's what he shakes out of his head, as if to refocus his view of Maddie and this guy through his cell on the selfie stick. He's sitting on a bench, about one hundred yards to the south, hidden beneath sunglasses and a straw fedora.

Ever since Maddie found the tracking device he placed in her bag, it has been a lot more work to follow her. She has a large orbit, in Israel, Rome, Dublin, and here in New York.

He has staked out that bloody hospital for days, waiting for Maddie to show up to check on Renzo, and now she has appeared with a tall, blonde, handsome guy who is definitely in love with her and stands gazing at her as if seeing her as the star character in their "happily ever after".

The guy looks British, to Gabriel's eye. He wears turquoise trousers and a paisley shirt and has the curling flop of hair that the Brits so often sport, but it's the movement of his mouth that makes Gabriel think he is a Brit. It's not that wide American mouth and lip motion when speaking, but something more pursed and contained. Maybe he's MI6.

Even so, Maddie has just kissed him. So this guy is in with Maddie further than Gabriel ever was, and that's something to note in a professional way. Who else is in on this Maddie Lynch track?

Gabriel watches them part, with Maddie heading east, toward the park exit, and the blonde guy heading north, toward the center of the great park. He has a choice. Follow Maddie, and find out where she is going, or follow the guy she has just kissed on the mouth, and see what he does.

Gabriel will follow the guy. He knows the man will want to kiss Maddie Lynch again, and he will lead Gabriel back to her. And along the way Gabriel might find out who the hell he is. It's a gamble, but Gabriel has learned in this business that you need to have the gut of a gambler and a heart of ice, because fire in the heart sends smoke to the head.

Gabriel's head needs to be clear if he is to find out what story Maddie Lynch has uncovered. He knows it is the only way he can help recover the millions stolen from his people, which survived the Holocaust when they did not. And if he does that then he can help save many many more people. Failure is something he can't even think about.

52. New York City.

The sky-blue room on the third floor of the Nuncio's mansion reminds Maddie of her own childhood room on the Upper West Side, above the shop. She'd lay on her bed at night and look at the silver stars her father had pasted to the ceiling. "You're a star, my girl," he'd say with a wink. "You'll never have a dark night, so long as you can see the stars. Shine along with them, my darling girl."

She used to dream about flying beyond the stars when she was little, to see the heaven of which her mother spoke. But now she thinks that heaven and hell are places on earth, with hell having the geographic advantage.

She turns her thoughts back to her present bedroom and paces, hunting for a bar of WiFi. She finds it by the mansion's floor to ceiling windows. Grabbing her phone, she quickly digs up what she can on C. Parke Stranch, the ex-SEAL turned mercenary multi-millionaire with the Bellerophon army, who hired the thugs. Everything online looks like PR and worship for this big bad billionaire turned good guy, raising money for his church, and feeding the local school kids.

Maddie then logs into her laptop, aware that whoever was watching her when she first went to Rome is still inside her electronic world. Good thing Aretta's new message to a link was a brief "let's talk after," and nothing more.

The bar of WiFi flickers, but it allows Maddie to click

the link, and see the serious, solemn face of Pope Pius XIII. She clicks the play arrow.

Onscreen, through the narrow window of a cell phone camera, appears Pius XIII in a private meeting with what looks like a Muslim contingent. There are two men sitting in chairs facing the Pope, and they wear the clothing of holy men, the long black robes with white caftans over top. One wears a green turban, the other, black.

This is clearly a bootleg video, as the men do not appear to know that they are being filmed, but the quality of the video is high.

There are two more men, one in the black cassock and the purple zucchetto of a bishop, and the other in the white robe and white skullcap of a devout Muslim. They are translators, Maddie thinks, and it is double the usual number of translators.

The Pope asks the men what he can do to help them stop the violence that infuses their faith against itself, and he adds, in his country of Nigeria, against Christians.

The question is quickly delivered by the Muslim translator, as if the question could harm him should the words linger too long. It seems to stun the Pope's guests, as there is a long silence. Then the man in the green turban speaks through his own translator, who says, "It is up to us to sort our differences, Holy Father."

Maddie sees the cleverness of having each side translate the other. It lessens the chance for revision.

The Pope smiles graciously, and puts his hands together, as if thinking or praying or both. "Let me be clearer, Imam," he says, "I speak not out of judgment but out of history. My own faith was cleaved in two more than five hundred years ago. And, over the centuries, rivers of blood have been shed. And we shed it against your faith as well, and against our brothers in Abraham, the Jews. For which my own sorrow cannot begin to atone. So let me say today, I am happy we Christians, though we might come from different churches, worship the same Allah."

"Peace be upon him," say the men.

"It may take us some time as well, Holy Father," adds the man in the black turban.

The Pope beams a hopeful smile and opens in arms in a gesture of wide embrace. "I understand. But the world moves fast these days, and my fear is that if we do not come together, then the speed of time can pull us apart."

The man in the green turban, who has the aquiline look of an aristocrat, says, "What is it you propose to do, Holy Father? That we embrace the west?"

The Pope bows his head, humbled by the question. "No, I am not proposing that. I am proposing something very simple. We are all people of the book, you, and us, and our Jewish brethren. Let us live in harmony together, and go forth together, under a God of love. That is my simple idea."

The man in the black turban asks, "As one kind of family, you mean?"

The Pope claps his hands together in delight. "Yes, as a family. For if we are a family, then we will live together as a family should, and try to be the best for one another.

By speaking to each other, by trying to understand each other, by loving each other, by praying to the same God. Do you think we can do this?"

Maddie watches the men stare at the Pope in bewilderment. He has just pitched them the central idea of Jesus, one that captured hearts and minds well beyond the synagogues of Israel, for nearly two thousand years.

"I think the Pope was saying that living like Christians will be the salvation of Islam," Maddie tells Aretta when they meet by the lake in Central Park. The sun is sinking in the summer sky as they walk around the lake off the 72nd Street entrance.

"It sure sounds like it," Aretta says slowly, still worn from work stress and the mounting demands of Teddy Wright. She stops to stoke up on sweets and offers Maddie some coconut candy from the bag she has brought along. Maddie is glad to see her eating, even if it is candy. Aretta has shrunk, and Maddie is sure it is not just the work but the racism blasting through *I'm Wright,* let loose by the Pope's interview, beating her down, cutting her out and leaving her all alone.

"Where did that video come from?" Maddie asks.

"Anonymous." Aretta then adds quietly she is very moved by the video, but scared that she has it, and as a producer torn by what to do with it. Her dark eyes fly from Maddie to the lake and back, not knowing where to look or what to think.

"But you can't trace who?"

"No, because it was on the back of this…" She takes a postcard of Beirut out of her pocket, and shows Maddie the link, written in block capitals in the back of the card. The card bears a Lebanese postage stamp, and was sent three weeks ago.

"But that card is addressed to me," Maddie says.

"Yeah, it is. It just got here. And it's why I sent you the link."

"It was clearly taken by someone with access. Whoever it is, they could get into the room and not be noticed filming. Or the camera could have been hidden."

"And whoever it is, is saying the Pope is dangerous."

"What do you mean? First African pope since forever, gives women in the church enormous power, loves the Muslims, has cleaned up the Vatican bank. What can go wrong?"

Aretta looks hard at Maddie to make her point. "It's the Muslims I'm worried about."

"I'm not sure I follow?"

"The Muslims don't need the Pope's love." Aretta pulls her green iPhone out of her pocket and scrolls. "Don't get me wrong. I think the dude is a breath of fresh air. But he's a Nigerian, and the majority of Muslims where my people come from are Sunni. And you know how relations between the Sunni and the Shia make the rumble between Catholics and Protestants back in the day seem like a bar brawl. In addition to the way the rest of the world feels about us. Take a look."

She shows Maddie her Twitter feed. The most recent three messages are variations on how Aretta should slit her own throat, though one from @patriotsteve shows a photo of Aretta in an oven, with a pig, and the caption

"Pork for dinner."

Maddie winces. "So, they now have a Holocaust meme for Muslims."

"Yeah, and watch some nutbar blame the Jews for that."

"So, are you saying, the Pope should stay out of the family feud?"

Aretta nods, her dark eyes wide. "For his own good. I mean, he's a Christian from Nigeria treating all the Muslims as if they are the same, and we are not. He's going to piss off a lot of them. And you know what happens when we get pissed off."

"I get your point," Maddie says, "but don't you think that now more than ever is a time for his message of unity to be heard?"

"No." Aretta shakes her head. "I think the Pope's campaign for unity is just taking baby steps. He shouldn't take it any further, not here, not now."

Maddie thinks about this. "Has Teddy seen this?"

"Not yet. I wanted to speak to you first. After all, it was sent to you."

"OK, now she needs to see it. And in the updated question list, I added a couple of questions that capture the Pope's ideas so that she can ask them." Maddie reaches into her laptop bag and extracts a folder. "I wrote them down. And I won't add anything about the 'unity campaign'. Not yet."

Aretta gawks at the file. "Paper? You going all '80s on me, Maddie?"

Maddie can't trust Aretta, not completely. Not now.

And it hurts.

"They jammed the communications where I am staying," Maddie says. "So yeah, I had to go old school."

Glancing over the handwritten notes, Aretta reads about Zimmerman. "What else do you know about this dead bishop dude?"

Maddie looks around before she says anything. Young couples share sunset picnics, stashing wine bottles in the picnic basket. Joggers chug past, wired to their earbuds. Older couples walk barky little dogs.

Maddie is grateful for the noise, and says quietly, "He belonged to the Society of Blessed Urban II. They are a very secretive and, as they like to say, a 'traditional' organization that wants to restore the Catholic church to its rightful place on top of the world."

"How do they plan to do that?" Aretta asks.

"Pope Urban II was the guy who started the first Crusade against Islam. Teddy can ask him about that."

"Do you think they sent us the link?"

Maddie shrugs, though her heart races. She certainly thought the video was sent by the Urban people. She has to think Hughes had a pale white hand in its creation. Who else would have the access?

"What does the interview room look like?" Aretta asks.

Maddie takes out her phone, the one no one is watching since she gave up the old one to the Sharpton gang, and shows Aretta a sequence of photos. "The library is where Bishop Hughes says the interview will take place."

"Who's he?"

Good question. "He's the Pope's advance guy. He says the library is the best spot for an interview because it has books, and is quiet. And as you can see, it's big enough for you and the crew and Teddy and the Pope."

"And you will be in there, too."

Maddie had planned to be nearby, listening in, feeding Teddy questions. "I can be, if you want me to be."

"I do. You know the lay of this land better than anyone. I'm counting on you."

Maddie gives Aretta a reassuring hug, then sends the library photos to her via WhatsApp. Maddie snatches one more coconut candy. "I need to go back before they lock down for the Pope's arrival. In about two hours. This will keep me going."

"How did you manage to get a berth in the Nuncio's place?" Aretta asks.

"He's a friend of my mother's. So I asked, and he said yes." Maddie continues the lie.

"Well it's a pretty awesome embed. Teddy will want to speak to you before the interview."

Maddie almost laughs. "If the Pope is nearby, I can put him on the phone and we can do a pre-interview."

"Inshallah," Aretta says and smiles back. But Maddie knows that in Aretta's smile is the worry that if the Pope pulls off what he wants to accomplish, then the result might be worse than the cure.

53. New York City.

Cheers rise up above the regular buzz of the city outside Apostolic Nuncio's mansion. The Pope's white limo is in sight. Thousands of the devout and the curious, some having waited all night, crush in as close as the police and the barricades will allow just to see the Holy Father. As the limo pulls up shouts of "Pius, we love you!" are followed by one enormous voice singing "Ave Maria", the Pope's personal favorite. Hawkers cut into the song with their own shouts as they sell bobble-headed Pope Piuses, mugs and t-shirts with I Love PPXIII. A quiet island in the screaming throngs is a group of about one hundred protestors, holding huge signs that say "Not my Pope!" and "Catholics Need a Catholic Pope" with the Islamic crescent crossed out by a red cross.

Pope Pius emerges from the limo beaming, deeply touched to see the noisy New York crowd, and blesses them all, the faithful, the hawkers, the police and the protesters.

Inside, the Pope's arrival at the mansion is announced long before the screams of the crowd. The Vatican security team had landed in a big black SUV where 5th Avenue intersects with East 72nd Street, which has concrete anti-truck bomb barriers lining the street in zigzag.

Maddie had been invited to the marble entrance foyer by Bishop Hughes, in her official capacity as the INN representative for Saturday's interview. She dressed for the occasion in a blue dress that hides knees and elbows, but curves in all the right places.

The Bishop hurries her along, keen for her to meet the Pope's house security team. Introductions start with the Vatican security boss. He's nothing like the Secret Service Commander. He is a tall, thin Italian guy in his mid-50s, distinguished from the rest of the team by his smart gray checked suit and a purple and gold tie.

He introduces himself. "I am Dottore Marco Confieri," he says, as he shakes Maddie's hand. Maddie's brief has told her he is Inspector General of the Corpo della Gendarmeria, the Vatican's security branch.

"I am one of the producers working on the interview with the Holy Father on Saturday," Maddie says.

"Ah yes, you are Dr. Lynch," he says in smooth English. He has also read his own brief. "Cardinal Otley told me about your interview. Very interesting. How long will it last?"

Now that the US Secret Service has insisted on everyone arriving at 7 AM for a 10 AM interview, it will last five hours or so. "The whole morning," Maddie says. "And morning is going to come early."

Confieri smiles warily at the news. "The Holy Father might have something to say about that." He tilts his head towards the Secret Service, who are busy combing the ground floor again for evidence of malicious intent. "Not everyone has the luxury of time that these fellows have."

Maddie finds herself laughing. The Italians are very

good at putting people at ease, which is the idea. You relax, and they can get on with their work.

With the Inspector are two Italian agents, suave, mid-30s, one with his sunglasses perched on his bald head, the other with designer stubble. Under different circumstances they could be mistaken for Roman playboys on the wander in New York City, but they move with the economy of men who know where they are going.

This is the second time that Maddie has seen them. First, coming out of Christopher Zimmerman's apartment carrying banker's boxes of his files. "Stoppia" and "Calvo" she had called them then. Stubble and Bald. And now they are here.

"*Le strade sono tutte chiuse e siamo circondati dal army di NYPD—cosa potrebbe andare male*?" says Stoppia to Calvo, on an urbane smile, his gold tooth flashing.

Yes, thinks Maddie, the streets are all closed, and the NYPD army does surround us, but there's a lot that can go wrong. She just can't figure out how. And how these guys might be involved.

"*Dove posso fumare*?" asks Calvo, pulling out a pack of Marlboros.

Bishop Hughes points him toward the rear of the mansion. "You can *fumare in il giardino*," he says. So that's where Calvo goes to smoke, with Stoppia sauntering after him, admiring his reflection in a gilded hall mirror.

"You know those guys?" Maddie says to Hughes,

fishing. "They seem pretty chill to be cops."

His rugged face impassive, his mud-colored eyes slide around behind his wire glasses, looking everywhere but at Maddie. "They're part of the papal security detail. And as you well know, especially in Rome, nothing is what it seems."

Maddie feels a cold, stabbing pain in her gut that tells her it will be the "nothing" that she misses. There's Stranch, the new player in her story, and Reagan Clark—neither of whom she can follow, being tucked safely away in the Apostolic Nuncio's mansion and with almost no WiFi. If she misses something, it will be the end of her.

Then the Commander of the Secret Service hears something in his earpiece and moves fast to the door. Maddie figures the Pope must have arrived, by the fact Stoppia and Calvo and the US Secret Service men and women have all hustled back into the lobby.

The Commander spots Maddie and barks, "You! You need to be upstairs."

Maddie raises her hands in surrender, and Hughes even gives her a smile of sympathy. "I will keep you posted," he says.

She doesn't believe him. She is sure that he killed two nuns. And that he might like to do the same to her. But she forces a grateful smile back at him, as if she suspects nothing.

Walking across the great lobby and under the diamond chandelier, Maddie goes up the spiral staircase, past the oil paintings of Popes John Paul I and II, along with Benedict and Francis. She stops on the second floor. Turning back, she quietly kneels on the polished oak and peers through the gilded banister, feeling like one of the children who lived here when the mansion was first built, secretly watching the great people of the grand city pass below from a perch on the staircase.

She watches as the security team prepares for the arrival of the man representing the prince of peace. And she is worried by the fact that if she had ill intent, she could shoot the Pope from where she knelt, as no one responsible for his entry had bothered to look up.

Except for Cardinal Bernard Otley, who was not supposed to be here, but who is now, and is first through the door. He glances up as he enters the marble foyer, maybe as a thanks to the divine for a safe arrival in America, and for getting him inside, past the vast security detail outside. As he looks up, he spots Maddie, peering at him through the banister.

He does not betray her location by calling out, but gives her a wink. She is happy to see him and rides a warm tide of relief. Otley has come to New York. She wants to believe it's because he is on the side of the angels. If she believed in angels.

The Pope then enters the Nuncio's mansion. For a man who carries such global weight, Pope Pius XIII is surprisingly small, maybe five foot six or seven. His white robes ripple like water floating over his body, and his simple white skull cap bobs with his head as he walks. And he is thin, as if he lives on holy water and communion wafers.

The fact that he is flanked by a phalanx of clerics, who all look especially well-fed, the rings on plump hands and the crosses and crucifixes hanging from their thick necks gleaming with jewels, only contributes to the contrast of the austere African pope and the bloated European clergy.

Butlers carry the Pope's luggage, and that of his entourage, through security and upstairs. And it is Maddie's cue to get up to the third floor, at least until the parade has passed by.

Maddie hustles back to her blue room. As she enters, and switches on the light, she sees that someone has left her a book on the desk.

She flinches under the feeling of an intruder, here in the mansion. But when she picks it up it's *The Sonnets of William Shakespeare*, a new edition, from Oxford University Press. Slipping it open, she sees the inscription inside, from Cosmo. "*They're all a wonder, Mads, but number 116 speaks for my heart. What's past is prologue. Cosmo xoxo.*"

The tears now run down her cheeks, for her past and her future, and following this story that she has begun all the way to its end. If only it doesn't end her first. She feels, for the first time, no pang of doubt. There is love for Cosmo. Enduring love.

And she feels the love for her father come alive, not just a memory but real and even growing. Knowing him better, finding out more about him, how he thinks, how the flippant things he said fit the truth, how he was admired by so many, but trusted no one, and the solitude that brought him. Now, she is even discovering how much she is like him: he lives on in her.

The soul company makes her feel fearless.

She had never feared for her mortal self, as she has long since reconciled with the fact that she is not immortal. If she is afraid it is because she will fail. And her failure will be to fail the truth. She can't. Too many lives depend on her. And that, in Maddie's eyes, has now become something that she twists in her soul every moment in her life as a Vatican spy.

54. New York City.

Maddie has drifted into a shallow nap when she hears a soft knock on her door. She looks at the time. It is 6 PM. Maddie expects it is her mother, trying to sneak her off for dinner somewhere. But when she opens the door, she can't hide her surprise to see Dottoressa Maria Corvina, the nun who works in the Vatican's communication office. She looks just as she did at her tiny office in the Vatican, her dark hair pulled into a bun, her handsome face set on a strong chin. Again in a crisp white blouse and blue cardigan all buttoned up. But this time her dark eyes dance with joy to see Maddie.

"Sister Maria," Maddie says in Italian. "I didn't expect to see you here!"

Sister Maria lets herself smile. "May I come in?" she says.

Maddie swings the door open, and Sister Maria enters quickly, and then offers Maddie her hand. They shake, Sister Maria clapping both her hands over Maddie's.

"It is so very nice to see you, Dr. Lynch."

"Maddie, please." Maddie gestures to her single room, to punctuate the intimacy.

She offers Sister Maria the armchair by the air conditioner, and drags the desk chair opposite.

"So you are part of the papal team," Maddie says.

Sister Maria's deep brown eyes light up. "Yes, and I am part of your team, too."

"My team?"

"Omega."

Maddie leans back and looks again and the nun. A doctor of canon law, trusted associate of Cardinal Otley. Youthful, with maybe three gray hairs. Of course Sister Maria would be a member of Omega. That's why Maddie was fast-tracked by her every time she wanted to see Cardinal Otley.

"What does Omega want?" she asks carefully.

"What you know. About what got Christopher Zimmerman killed. And where the money went. Cardinal Otley believes that you have made progress since he last saw you."

Maddie has made more progress that she could have imagined, but she isn't sure Sister Maria is telling her the whole truth. She could be working with Bishop Hughes, who has some idea of what Maddie does, but not all.

"I will give you my thoughts," Maddie says, "but I really need to… freshen up."

Sister Maria grins. "Of course."

"It's just down the hall. I'll be right back."

Maddie is taking a risk leaving her laptop open, but there's nothing on it that will tell Sister Maria anything at all about Christopher Zimmerman.

She hustles down the hall to the lavish bathroom she shares with her mother. It's a white tile room big enough for two billiard tables, with a clawfoot tub and a modern shower, and tall vases of flowers placed on either side of the large sink with its brass faucets. Maddie imagines the Pope's bathroom is even better, and she leans against the shower stall and sends Cardinal Otley a WhatsApp message. *Is Sister Maria safe?*

She waits, and flushes the toilet for the sake of form, but nothing comes back. She was assured that messages work inside the house, but maybe the Cardinal is with the Pope, advising on important matters of state. Even so, she needs his sign off on this, or she won't speak with Sister Maria.

She has two options. She can call him, or she can find him. She tries the first option, but his phone goes straight to voicemail.

So Maddie emerges from the bathroom, and walks down the hallway as silently as she can, then takes a right down the spiral staircase.

At the bottom of it, a bishop is speaking to the Commander about something, and the Secret Service boss shoots Maddie a look of imminent doom. So she attacks first.

"Excuse me Your Grace, but Cardinal Otley sent for me. He said he'd be in the lobby."

"Ah," says the bishop, "he was just in the library. Please..." And he gestures toward the grand double doors, ajar, that lead to the world of books in his mansion.

"Thank you." Maddie smiles at the Commander, who clearly hates her and this assignment. As she enters the library, Cardinal Otley is there, speaking to Bishop Hughes, next to the ladder leading up to the Moral Philosophy section.

Maddie can't ask him about Sister Maria in front of Hughes, so she pauses by the door and gives the Cardinal a friendly wave. He looks curious. "I'll be done in five minutes, Maddie."

"No need. Can you just look at your WhatsApp messages now?"

Cardinal Otley stares at her in confusion for a beat, then he extracts his phone, and powers it on, and opens the app. He reads her message, and then tucks his phone back into his cassock.

"Yes, that's totally fine, Maddie," he says, as if she has asked to join him for a coffee. Then he surprises her by saying, "Join me for Mass tomorrow morning. In the chapel. 6 AM."

"Thanks, I will," she says, and exits as Bishop Hughes gives her a curious look. Maddie wonders what Otley is saying to Hughes that needs this urgent kind of privacy. She glances back as she slips out the door and seeing the two of them, she reminds herself: the only person she can trust is herself.

On her return journey Maddie passes by the bishop and the Commander and gives them a friendly wave. "Thanks, saw the Cardinal. He invited me to Mass in the chapel in the morning." She can't help but grind it into the Commander's sense of superiority. "Where is the chapel?"

"It is just behind the great parlor," the bishop says, pointing to his right now. "I will be there, too."

Maddie beams her best smile and walks on. If the bishop and Otley are going to be there, then she bets the Pope will be there as well.

When she enters her room, Sister Maria is where

Maddie left her, seated in the chair, hands cupped. She smiles at Maddie like a nun who has just seen her best pupil triumph. "Did Cardinal Otley say I could be trusted?"

Maddie feels the heat in her cheeks. Was it that obvious? Or is Sister Maria tracking her, too? She figures that Maria can ask Otley anyway, so truth is best. "He did. So, how do you connect to all this?" Maddie asks.

Sister Maria tilts her head to one side, as if considering Maddie for asking the question. "I connect as you connect. We are all part of the same team, though team is such an insufficient word for what we do."

"And what do we do? Exactly."

"We keep the Church informed of things which could harm her."

"And if we find those harmful things?"

Sister Maria smiles like a teacher who is glad to be learning from her pupil. "I think you know. You do what you are doing. So please, tell me what you have learned. We are safe here."

On this mention of safety, Maddie has one more question. "So if I am working with you, and Omega, are you my handler?"

Sister Maria leans forward, serious now. "No, you do not have anyone to report to other than Cardinal Otley. But I am your ally."

Maddie lets herself smile back. It's always good to have friends.

"So maybe you could start by telling me why you are really staying in the Nuncio's residence. Beyond the fact your mother is his friend."

Maddie needs to be careful here, because she cannot control where the information is going. "Someone broke into my apartment. And into my computer. Someone also robbed me of my phone. And blew up the restaurant that my mother and I like. We thought it prudent to give them one less target."

"And why are you a target?"

"Because of Christopher Zimmerman. He was killed, for certain. And I am on the trail of his killers."

Sister Maria crosses herself and sits in silence for a moment. "OK, do you know where the money he stole has gone?"

Maddie finds it odd that Sister Maria goes for the money and not the murderer. "I am working on that."

"Do you have any working theories?"

"I think he is using the money to fund a holy war in the Middle East."

Sister Maria's eyes flicker in alarm. "Why would he do that?"

"Because he wants America to save Israel," Maddie replies. "So, the land of Jesus isn't overrun by Muslims. This time, it's not so much about deaths as it is about births. Israel's days are numbered because of Arab birth rates and through its terrible wars has lost so much of the world's support, so Zimmerman saw his plan as the only solution."

"And that's what got him killed?" Sister Maria asks.

Maddie is sure Zimmerman died selling his blackmail, his own sexual abuse, back to Reagan, or

Regina. But all she lets herself say is: "It could be if he changed the plan. Or stole some of the money."

Sister Maria pats Maddie's hand, as if to say she is well aware Maddie must be careful and cagey. "Cardinal Otley will want to speak to you," Sister Maria says, then rises.

Maddie realizes that they will compare versions of what she has said.

Sister Maria opens her arms and offers a hug, and is glad when Maddie steps in. "You have done excellent work. You are the best new agent we have had in some time," she says softly.

It's the kind of compliment that Maddie thinks would have made her see a neuroscientist for a brain lesion just a few months ago. But now, it makes her feel a twinge of pride. Her new life is here.

55. New York City.

The last time that Maddie has been to Mass was on a gray April morning at St. Jude's College Chapel in Oxford, more than four months ago, when she was promising to keep Cosmo's daughter safe from evil, and this pursuit of the Pope was just beginning. At that time, Maddie had no idea of the story she had entered. She innocently thought that all she was doing was making a request that would never be met with agreement. Teddy Wright would never interview the Pope on TV.

Tomorrow is the day of her astonishing success.

This morning, Maddie is at Mass with the Pope.

Maddie is grateful for the murkiness of the private chapel in this papal house on the Upper East Side of Manhattan, as she has slept maybe two hours and she looks it. Right now, the Pope is saying Mass five feet from where she sits. Cardinal Bernard Otley is sitting to her right, with Bishop Paul Hughes acting as the Pope's altar server.

Sister Maria is here as well, and Francesca and Cosmo. Maddie had asked Otley if they could come, and he welcomed them as if to the last supper. *The appointed time is 6 AM*, read his text. Which Maddie recalls is language Jesus used to his disciples at their Passover meal, with the "appointed time" portending his death.

It has barely gone 6 AM, and the Pope intones the mass slowly, with love, his movements simple, reverent. He is soon into the Nicene Creed, that ancient statement of faith which sums up everything Maddie was taught to believe, and is no longer at all certain that she ever believed. But with the Pope in front of her, and Cardinal Otley next to her, and because she is working for Omega, she loudly says the Creed's concluding words:

We believe in one holy catholic and apostolic Church.
We acknowledge one baptism for the forgiveness of sins.
We look for the resurrection of the dead, and the life of the world to come.
Amen.

After the Mass, Maddie accepts Cardinal Otley's generous invitation to take breakfast with the Pope.

"I will see you later," says Francesca as she looks on her daughter with pride.

"Yes. Thank you for the Shakespeare, Cosmo," Maddie says. She has not seen him since they said goodbye in Central Park.

"Him? I hear he scribbled out a few good ones," Cosmo says on a wink.

At breakfast, Maddie waits humbly at the dining room door to be seated at the long table for 40. Cardinal Otley arrives and beckons her with a crook of his finger into the kitchen.

The kitchen looks like a factory, all large steel appliances and white tile, not like the opulence of the chandeliered formal dining room. At a small prep table, lie paper plates and plastic cutlery in the name of Secret Service safety. There is also fruit and porridge and much-needed coffee. A room and a meal befitting the Pope's modest demeanor.

The Secretary of State explains to the Pope just who Maddie is—a journalist here to prepare for the interview. Pope Pius smiles warmly at Maddie, making her feel welcome. She takes a seat at the table as the Pope says, "But no interview yet, shall we? I need to have my breakfast and then a good cup of coffee before I can answer any questions."

Maddie glances at Otley, who gives her a curt nod. "Of course, Your Holiness," Maddie replies. "I am just here to answer any questions that you might have."

The Pope spoons up a wedge of grapefruit with a plastic spoon, and just before he pops it into his mouth, says:

"Tell me what you have learned."

Maddie looks at Otley again, but this time the Secretary of State doesn't meet her eye. Maddie is on her own.

"How do you mean, Your Holiness?"

The Pope takes another spoonful of grapefruit. "I mean, what have you learned about your father?"

"My father?" This is not the question Maddie expects.

"Yes," says the Pope, putting his spoon on the table, and folding his hands. He turns to her, the lines on his face bracket his mouth, and crease around his eyes. They are not weary lines, but come from laughing, from living. And his deep brown eyes land on Maddie. "Is not that why you are helping us? To find the truth about your father?"

Maddie feels her throat go dry. The Pope has cut to the heart of her reason for helping the Vatican, and is now talking about her father as if he, too, doesn't believe the official version of the death of James Lynch.

"I have learned that he was investigating Christopher Zimmerman when he died," she says.

The Pope's brown eyes travel over the room, as if he is watching the face of the dead Swiss priest pass before him. "And so are you, are you not?"

Maddie feels heat rise in her cheeks. The Cardinal still doesn't know what Maddie suspects Zimmerman was doing to Reagan Clark. Or what he was using the stolen money to do.

"Yes, Your Holiness. That was my..."

"Assignment," says Cardinal Otley. "One that remains in progress."

The Pope nods in thanks to the Cardinal, who had briefed him on Maddie's work, and also on Maddie. "I trust that you will have some answers soon. That money could do much good in our troubled world."

That money stolen from the Jews, and now stolen from you, Maddie thinks. When she finds the money, she will decide what to do with that information. So instead, she says, "Yes, Your Holiness."

The Pope nods, then spoons a heaping tablespoon of demerara sugar onto his porridge. "I need a little sweetness," he says with a surprisingly boyish smile. "Perhaps a lot."

In that simple statement, Maddie realizes just how alone the Pope is. And how vulnerable.

After breakfast, Maddie asks Cardinal Otley for a moment. "Shall we take in the perfumes of Manhattan?" replies the Secretary of State. He already has his cell phone battery out and in his hand.

The morning air is cool in the garden behind the house, the summer roses bushes sit flowering, giving the pocked statue of the Virgin Mary a rosy halo. Another walk in another garden, Maddie thinks.

"What's going on?" Maddie asks.

"Big question, that," the Cardinal replies.

"Am I not to be trusted?" Maddie's voice is deeper, angrier, than she has heard herself in a while.

Otley chuckles, his belly shaking as he beams at her over his half-moon glasses. "No one is to be trusted, save for the truth of God the Father, Son and Holy Spirit. The rest is human, and fallible."

To collect herself, Maddie sits down on a marble bench, next to the statue of the Virgin Mary, cracked and chipped, looking as if she's been out here too long. "Do you know who killed my father?"

Otley sits down next to Maddie. "No. But we think Christopher Zimmerman had something to do with it."

Maddie feels outraged and yet elated. She can't exactly see God, but she can see her panoramic story in startling color. "And that's why you chose me."

"Partly. But you also chose us.

That is true.

"Yet the Pope only seems concerned about the

money."

Otley smiles, letting himself hope. "The money is the tangible good that can come out of this. Do you know where it is?"

"Zimmerman moved the 250 million Euros around. Two hundred of them he moved from the Vatican bank to an Austrian bank. They are in the name of the Society of Blessed Urban II."

Otley doesn't react, just stares straight ahead, as if listening to a confession. "And the rest went to himself?"

"Yes. He put 50 million in a Swiss bank."

Otley grunts. This one is personal. "Of course he did."

"The friend who helped me find the money says that you could get that 50 million back."

"How?"

"Did Zimmerman leave a will?"

Otley smiles. "Did you find one?"

Maddie would be surprised if he did. Zimmerman, she suspects, had planned to live longer, to enjoy the money and power that Reagan Clark was going to pay for.

But she says, "No. But you can access the account from the Vatican bank."

"Excellent," says Cardinal Otley, his hope making him eager. "I will follow up."

"On one condition," Maddie says.

Otley turns to look at her now, his face serious, his blue eyes steely, as if to make her think twice.

"If I give you the account information, and you retrieve that money, then it has to go back to the people from who Zimmerman and the Ustaŝe first stole it."

"The Jews."

"Yes."

Otley frowns. "Even after what they have done to Gaza and Lebanon?"

Maddie smiles. "The Ustaŝe didn't steal from them. Besides, it should be their choice what to do with it."

Otley thinks about this, and then says, "I'll see what I can do."

"Is that a yes?"

"The Pope, as you yourself heard, is counting on that money…"

Maddie looks deep into the Cardinal's eyes, as if she is now the pastor and he is the penitent. He gives his head a humble bow, and takes her hand. "Yes."

There is a pause, as if the city has taken in this moment. It is as quiet as Maddie has never heard it be.

Then Otley gets back to the business. "Now tell me about this money in the Austrian bank. What does the Society of Blessed Urban II need 200 million Euros for?"

"They have 190 million now. Someone withdrew 10 million."

"Oh my…" Otley gasps.

Maddie is sure he would swear but he does not.

"Do we know who?"

She shakes her head. "Not yet. But that's a lot of money to take out in one go."

Otley sighs, as if to let go of his hopes. "I don't know how they're going to try to kill the Holy Father while he's in the US, but I know they are."

"The Society?" Maddie asks, her stomach hot with the

thought that the Pope could die before her very eyes.

"They certainly do not like him. And there are others."

"Who?"

"We don't know." He looks up, maybe to God, or to cool the tears filling his eyes.

"What do you know?"

Otley gives Maddie a paternal pat on the arm. "That you're safe here, and so is the Pope. It's out there that's dangerous…"

Maddie nods to him and to herself: she has to find out more about the money that was taken out by SBUII. There is only one person that she can think of to help her. To reach them, she has to get out of the Nuncio's mansion to send a text. Not across the hall, but out there, where the danger lives.

56. New York City.

"Why do you need to leave?" It's Stoppia, one of the Vatican security guys. He and Calvo are working the front door as Maddie walks briskly to the exit. Her mother hustles to catch up, slinging her leather shoulder bag in place. Maddie only gave her about five minutes notice on her fast exit, and Francesca insisted on coming. What better cover than a mother?

"Our friend is in the hospital, and he is not well," Maddie explains with just the right amount of worry.

"Giacomo, sorry, the Nuncio, knows him. We will meet him there," Francesca adds. It is not true, but the Vatican cops straighten up a bit at the mention of church authority.

Dottore Confieri, their boss, suddenly appears out of the library, relaxed and smiling. "Might I be of service?"

Maddie smiles in relief and speaks in Italian. "Good morning, Dottore. Your officers were just making sure we had a good reason to leave the house."

Francesca plays her part, wringing her hands for added effect. "Our friend, Renzo Romano, who runs a magnificent restaurant, Risorgimento, is in hospital in serious condition, and we must check on him. He is like family."

Stoppia and Calvo look at each other—they share the one brain cell, Maddie thinks.

"OK. You need to be back before dark," says Stoppia, as if he was the mother.

The two Vatican cops open the door, and Maddie and her mother hurry out onto East 72 Street, which looks like a war zone. The concrete barricades that zigzag the street are in place to prevent anyone with a truck bomb from trying to smash into the place. The NYPD trucks at each end of the street between 5th Avenue and Madison Avenue could start a war all by themselves: muscular, angry-looking vehicles bulked with armor and twitchy with antennae. Sharpshooters in black body armor and black helmets line the roof of the mansion, their black long guns at the ready. If anything comes at them from the sky, then they are protected.

At the corner, Maddie and Francesca tell the cops that they live at 20 East 72nd Street and that they will be back.

"I need a coffee, a real one," Francesca says, as they walk on.

Maddie makes a beeline for the Italian café on East 73rd. There are police everywhere, half of them dressed for armed combat, loaded down with assault rifles and stun grenades, goggled and helmeted and body armored and looking at everything that passes as trouble. Maddie thinks the Pope is as safe as he can be so long as he stays where he is. Out here, he could get shot.

Francesca orders "*due cappuccini*," and the barista tells her that they are lucky, as he has to close shop at noon. "Because of the Pope. It's wonderful and it's awful, too."

Francesca gives him a knowing nod—such is life.

She and Maddie sit by the window, and Maddie checks out the street to make sure they were not followed. Then she takes out her phone.

"Who is this person who can help you?" Francesca asks.

"Someone in Israel. I need to get him before the sun goes down."

"Why?"

"It's Friday. You know, the sabbath."

"Oh, that sabbath," Francesca says, with a kind of Catholic disdain, as if it's the precursor to the real one on Sunday.

Maddie composes her WhatsApp to Gabriel de Almeida Schmidt.

I need to speak to you. Today.

She hits send and looks up to see her mother on fire with curiosity. "I think this person can connect a dot or two."

Francesca's eyes grow wide with interest. "This person is an artist?"

"Of a sort." Then Maddie's phone pings.

I thought you'd never ask, Gabriel writes.

Francesca smiles. Success? Maddie nods.

Can I call you now? Maddie texts.

Sure, once you've finished your coffee.

Maddie sits right up, skin prickling with nerves, and looks up. He's not in front of her. Her phone pings again.

On 5th, by the Park.

"Mama, I have to go."

"Do you want me to come with you?" Francesca is worried.

Maddie gestures to the army of cops outside the

window. "I think I'll be fine. Please, if you would, check on Renzo, and then Cosmo."

"I haven't seen Cosmo today."

When Maddie hears that her chest tightens. "That's why you should check on him." She gives her mother a soft kiss on the cheek.

Francesca works her way through the enormous security detail filling the streets as Maddie walks slowly to the west on East 73rd Street. Slipping on sunglasses and a ballcap, Maddie scans the area. She quickly sees the tall blond man from Mossad looking almost comical in a floppy straw fedora, large sunglasses, with a selfie stick, like a tourist hoping to see the Pope. But she suspects that's exactly how he wants to look, and she is glad he has been waiting for her.

He takes her hand when he sees her, greeting her like an old friend. Together, Maddie and Gabriel walk along Terrace Drive in Central Park.

"How about we start by taking batteries out of our phones," Maddie says. "I mean, I know you've been tracking me, but I don't know who's listening."

"That cuts both ways," Gabriel says, then pops the battery out of his phone. Maddie does the same.

"Now then, tell me why you're here," Maddie says pleasantly, neutrally.

Gabriel smiles at Maddie like he might at a child. "You first. Tell me about what you've found on your mission for the Vatican."

"Why would I do that?"

"Because I'll tell you who is trying to kill the Pope."

The news hits hard, though it is exactly what Maddie feared. Winded by his remark, Maddie sits down on a bench. Gabriel settles next to her, pulls off his sunglasses and looks into her eyes. "First, you tell me about Christopher Zimmerman, and what was in that package that you stole from Rome."

Maddie remembers that her father had told her that it was always a neck-and-neck race between the British and the Israelis when it came to intelligence smarts. "The Israelis because they had to be, and the British because they enjoyed duplicity," James had said. "The US, on the other hand, is hampered by the fact that while it has every technological marvel the fantasy geeks could invent, and the US has a hard time thinking that it might ever be wrong about anything. And that's about the biggest intelligence failure you can have. As for the Vatican," James went on to say, "they keep running into the fact that the guys running the show think they know more than God."

As if James was speaking to his daughter not from memory but across the years, he is telling her that Maddie's life is her own to save.

"Why are you interested in Christopher Zimmerman?" Maddie asks.

"Because he stole a lot of money," Gabriel fights to reply calmly. "Because some of it even belonged to my own family. Who were slaughtered. And so their money belongs to my people, to my country. And that is why I took this assignment."

Maddie hangs her head, sorry for all that Gabriel has

said about his family, lost to the Holocaust. About their stolen money. About Gabriel himself and why he chose to be a spy. And spy on her. "Yes," says Maddie, slowly. "The money was stolen. Twice. Second time from the Vatican, and the first time from Jews."

Gabriel's controlled calm breaks. "How do you know this?"

Maddie smiles with pride. "The Ustaše stole from the Jews, and laundered the money in Switzerland through the Vatican Bank. The Swiss bank that did it was Zimmerman's family."

Gabriel relaxes. It's as if she has just proven something, and her reward is coming. "Good. We know that a lot of gold was stolen from Jews in Croatia. It was converted to cash in a special Vatican portfolio, called Profima SA." Gabriel says. "The SA means Società Anonima, which you, as an Italian speaker, will understand."

"I understand that it means 'anonymous society'," Maddie says.

"And it means dividends were paid out by attaching coupons to their share certificates. Whomever held the certificate could collect the cash. These certificates could be transferred privately, and so the management of the company would not necessarily know who owned its shares. The shareholders were anonymous. Especially those who were dead Jews."

"But then Zimmerman stole it again after the Vatican had washed it."

Gabriel nods, impressed. "Very good. First the

Vatican re-organized things in 1999, and moved the money into a general fund they call 'Peter's Pence'. Zimmerman stole it from there and we want to know why. And we'd like it back."

"I can help you with that," Maddie says. "But now it's my turn. You tell me who is trying to kill the Pope."

Gabriel leans in and whispers, "Victor Franchi is alive."

Maddie is surprised to hear this. But she says calmly, "I never really thought he was dead."

"We tracked him in Lebanon. He met with a senior member of Boko Haram in Beirut."

"Lebanon?" Maddie goes cold, her face feels numb. It's the country where her father died. The home base of Hezbollah, who had killed him. And it's the place from which the postcard with the video link to the Pope's meeting with Muslim clerics was sent.

"Yes. He then left for Dubai. A few days later the Boko Haram guy bought 10 million Euros worth of very sophisticated micro drones."

It is hard to speak, as if Maddie has frozen over. "So it's Boko Haram? They're going to kill the Pope?"

"Don't think they could pull it off here," says Gabriel very quietly. "But I think Victor Franchi might."

"How?"

"That I don't know. But I would keep an eye on anyone connected to the Society of Blessed Urban II, who might be on this papal trip."

Maddie thinks of Bishop Hughes. Her mother kept an eye on him the other day and said he was chummy with security, with Baldy and Stubble. Maddie knows he is a killer, but she didn't imagine him as one who would kill the Pope. Gabriel sees the thought in her eyes.

"So there is someone on the trip?"

Maddie nods "Yes. But we know about him."

"OK, then he knows about you. Take care of yourself." Gabriel watches Maddie keenly. "So, tell me more about this Zimmerman theft."

When Maddie talks about Zimmerman now, it's not as an extremely loose cannon, but as her father's killer.

"He transferred 200 million Euros of the money he stole into an Urban II bank account in Austria. But someone withdrew 10 million Euros."

"Victor Franchi," says Gabriel.

"Possibility. His connection to Christopher Zimmerman goes back a long way, and they were both Urban II members. Franchi worked for the guy who is now the Pope. And he saw how Zimmerman blackmailed Pope John Paul II."

Gabriel's cool breaks again "What? How?"

Maddie is not going to tell him that. It's enough that he knows.

In her silence, Gabriel puts the pieces together himself. "So Christopher Zimmerman and Victor Franchi were working together."

"It goes back even further. Zimmerman's father's bank took the gold from a man named Josip Babić. He was a high ranking Ustaŝe member who killed thousands of Jews and stole millions. The Vatican helped him escape, and gave him a new identity. Antonio Franchi.

He had one son, Victor."

Gabriel leans back and closes his eyes, as if he can see it all better with his eyes shut. "So Franchi and Zimmerman are going to use money that their fathers stole from the Jews to try to destroy Israel?"

"No."

Gabriel sits up, eyes open, as Maddie shakes her head. "This may sound crazy, but Zimmerman was planning to use the money to save Israel from destruction by the Muslims. Victor Franchi was on board with that."

"Well, 200 million Euros would be enough to start anything. As we have seen, it just takes a couple of jihadis with assault rifles and suicide belts to destroy a kibbutz. The economics of destruction seems to have acquired all kinds of efficiencies. Look..." Gabriel lowers his voice and speaks quietly, "What made me come here is something that will never change: we can never relax."

He searches her eyes, asking in silence if she understands and she does. They exchange nods. They are in the same trade, pretending to be someone in service to the good of something greater than them.

And to do that, you have to believe in something greater than yourself, Maddie thinks, so much so that you don't blink even in the face of death. But still she is not sure exactly what she believes in, save for a baby in Oxford. And the baby's father. And now in Gabriel she could have an ally, should things go very wrong.

Trusting Gabriel with the rest of the story, Maddie continues: "Zimmerman was murdered."

"By Franchi?"

"No, by Reagan Clark's people. I think she covered up Christopher Zimmerman's murder because he was blackmailing her, too. They had a long sexual relationship. She got pregnant. He paid for an abortion, among other things. And then..."

"She ran for president, and he wanted her help..." Gabriel adds. He quickly put the pieces together, trusting all the parts Maddie found. They look at each other in a way that they each understand. They are on the same page, and maybe even the same team.

"Do you think she'll win?" he asks.

Maddie very much hopes not, but all she will say is "Reagan's a little ahead of the president in the polls. But you know what they say."

"What?"

"There's always an October Surprise. One that favors the challenger."

"If they killed the Pope in the USA, that would do it."

"He is a great supporter Islam, though," Maddie says.

"Oh, they'd find a way to blame the Muslims, even if they were nowhere near," Gabriel says. Then summer intrudes and a yipping little dog has run off into the park with a young girl's Frisbee and she is crying. It is comical in how wonderfully normal it is.

Then, Gabriel asks softly, "So can you help me get the money back?"

"Not all of it. Yet," Maddie says. "But Zimmerman parked 50 million Euros in his own account. Now that he's dead, I have asked Cardinal Otley to get it back."

"For the Vatican."

"No, I said for the Jewish people."

"And he agreed?"

"He agreed."

His bright eyes shine with emotion so strong he has to bow his head. Clapping his two strong hands over Maddie's, he says, "Thank you, Maddie. I see we have a future together."

"I just started working for the Vatican. I'm not ready to be a double agent." It is a joke, but it just might be true.

Gabriel dares to look up and laugh. "No need. We work together well," he says. "Oh, by the way, who is the Englishman? He is in the business?"

Maddie realizes he has seen her with Cosmo. She needs to do everything she can to protect him and the baby from her life now, and yet he's smack in the middle of it. "He's a colleague from Oxford. We're working on a book."

"Oh, and you have a real job as an academic?" Gabriel raises his eyebrows. "A book about?"

"The women who helped Jesus."

"Sounds like you." Then he pops the battery back into his phone. "Be careful, Maddie Lynch, and we will see each other soon." Then he slips his straw fedora back on, fixes his sunglasses in place, hoists his selfie-stick. He walks off toward 5th Avenue and just like that, disappears.

57. Jerusalem.

She is a rough beauty, the Church of the Holy Sepulchre. She has stood as the centerpiece of the Chistian Quarter of the Old City since the fourth century. She has been shot at, burnt down and rebuilt. To be here, to walk inside her, is to take the last steps of Christ Himself, where he was crucified and also where he was buried.

Tourists wander around now, taking group selfies with the golden painting of St. Anne and John the Baptist on the walls. The flash of their cell cameras gives them a bright, fleeting halo, too, that reflects on the gold of the icons.

Security guards grumble about the lack of respect from the entitled horde, and they're glad the church is closing early today for a private tour.

One by one, the private tour group enters the empty church. Silent, respectful, the only sound the arriving group makes are their heels clicking on the old stone floors. They come, seven men and two women, from London, New York, Buenos Aires, Manila, and beyond.

There are nine here, but they represent hundreds of brothers and sisters. They know each other though they have never met. Today they are even strangers to themselves, no longer in their priest cassocks, or bishops robes and nuns habits. In suits and ties, flower dresses and heels, sunglasses and makeup and hair dye, they are not who they were. And yet all of them feel their skin bristle in the stunning coolness inside the church, and their hearts thunder with sin, a necessary sin.

And they all have the same tattoo: SBUIII, with a cross next to it.

That was their entry ticket checked at the door as they subtly pulled back their sleeves for Victor Franchi. He nods them in, looking good himself in his ordinary disguise, as he calls it, like an aging Mob playboy with dyed black hair, bold blue sunglasses and in a fine Italian suit, no tie. And looking very well for a dead man.

One at the time, they take their places as they were instructed to do on a notice on the dark web, facing front, spaced out. No one is to speak in this secret society. They were never here.

Victor was the one who wanted to bring them together, though Paul Hughes warned him not to. It was too great a risk. They would all be exposed. But the mission required it, Victor knew. They had to know they were not alone in sin and together they would be absolved. And if the mission tomorrow failed, and Victor had to finger someone, he would know who.

The younger of the two nuns sidles up to Victor. Nervous, she tugs up at the neckline of her pink dress that is too low. Otherwise she looks almost beautiful in the tight-fitting rosy dress and lipstick.

"Excuse me, but where is Rome?" she asks in a whisper.

Victor smiles to think how the woman sounds very lost. Is Rome anywhere near here? He knows she means Paul Hughes. When they organized decades ago, all the members were identified not by their Christian names but by their parish.

"He is helping, but he is with us in spirit."

The nun quickly trips back into place on her high heels.

Then, Franchi takes his place in front of them all, just ten now. Paul makes eleven of them in the inner circle. Christopher Zimmerman made twelve, but he was sacrificed. That's how Victor likes to think of it. He could have brought them even more money for their mission. But he tried to do it by selling his own sin to Reagan Clark and her people. Those people only play to win.

Until then, their secret society was very secret. But Maddie Lynch stole a bundle of secrets from Christopher's apartment. Probably shared them with the Pink Mafia Queen of the Vatican, Cardinal Otley. And Maddie is still on the loose. Not for long.

With that thought, Victor steels himself, then begins. "I believe in One God…"

They all join in saying the words of the Nicene Creed that they have said thousands of times. The words bring peace and comfort, refresh the worn spirit and lift up the mortal soul. This time the words hurt, rising from a sinner's lips. But they must be sinners to save the Church.

When the prayer is done, and the group intones "Amen", Franchi adds, "Thy will be done… tomorrow." One by one, he looks at the others, "Tomorrow we will have our Church returned to us all. God bless you all."

As one, they hang their heads and cross themselves one more time. One by one, they leave. The last to go is the nun in the pink dress. As Victor ushers out the door, she runs back to clap a hand on his arm. Tears stream down from her large dark sunglasses, making her look like a bug who is crying. Words broken by heaving sobs, she asks if they will be forgiven for what they are about to do.

"Will God forgive us?"

"Yes, of course. Even Popes have to die one day."

58. New York City.

The sun is setting in the back garden of the Nuncio's mansion, polishing the worn statue of Mary in a kinder light. And the heat of the day lets loose the sweet perfume of the rose bushes into the evening air.

Cardinal Otley and Maddie walk again in the garden. He was with the Pope all day, and is refreshed for it, for having spent the day with a dear friend. "We have just finished a very simple dinner of fish and salad, with fruit for dessert. If I travel with the Pope much longer," Otley says, "I will soon regain my boyish figure."

Maddie walks along beside the Cardinal more easily now, feeling something like family, or more like kindredness, a spirit they share. She also feels a sense of a future, now that she has spoken to Gabriel. One in which she can finish the story, and have help if she needs it.

"But you did not invite me out here so I could talk about food," Otley says.

"No," she says, her voice low. "I wanted to talk about Victor Franchi."

"Oh." Otley sounds disappointed.

"He was in Beirut not long ago, and he met with someone connected to Boko Haram. You know, the Nigerian Islamic terror group."

"Oh?" Otley's tone has shifted to one of keen interest. He leads Maddie to a far corner of the garden, where security can still see them, but no one can hear.

"And after that meeting, the Boko Haram guy spent 10 million Euros on micro drones. That 10 million Euros came from the Society of Blessed Urban II bank account, where Christopher Zimmerman had parked 200 million Euros."

Otley stops and looks at Maddie in surprise. "How did you uncover all of this?"

"Because you asked me to."

He looks her up and down and smiles in growing pride. "Indeed. So I did." The light in his eyes dim as he turns back to business. "Now it would seem that the Society of Blessed Urban II have their funds for a… Crusade."

"Yes. And my source thinks they might also plan to kill the Pope."

Otley's eyes flash in alarm, and he crosses himself. "A Catholic society killing the Pope?"

"They don't like his views on Islam. As you know."

"I do know."

"And your undersecretary of state, Bishop Hughes, is a member of their society."

Otley sighs. "Yes, but I don't think he plans to kill the Pope."

"Why is he working with you?" Maddie has been keen to ask.

"You know the saying 'keep your enemies close'? The Vatican might have invented it."

Maddie smiles, appreciating the humor and Cardinal Otley's buoyant charm. "Well, I would keep an eye on him."

"I am, Maddie, I am."

Maddie suddenly feels exposed, as if she is being watched. Looking up, she sees Bishop Hughes looking down on them from his fourth-floor window. A window which is open. Has he heard what they have discussed? She turns to warn Cardinal Otley, and when she looks back up, Hughes is gone.

"We spoke softly," the Cardinal says. "And in any case, if he heard, then it's nothing he might not already know."

Cardinal Otley sees Hughes as an active threat.

"Thank you, Maddie," he says. "I have much to think about this evening and on into the wee hours."

So does Maddie, as she lies fully clothed on her bed in her blue room and stares at the ceiling. The I team will be arriving in eight hours, and she has to be sharp. She runs one more mental checklist: Teddy has her questions for the Pope, but with Teddy, as Maddie knows, having the questions doesn't mean she'll ask them. Maddie reminds herself to take Teddy aside and underline the ones that she needs to ask, especially the one about Reagan Clark, and what the Pope thinks she would do to the world. Teddy needs to stay away from any questions about the Pope brokering peace with the Sunni and Shia.

Maddie then flips open the book of Shakespeare's Sonnets that Cosmo left for her. Sonnet #116 stares back at her. *Let me not to the marriage of true minds admit impediments...*

Maddie had only seen him in passing today and she wants more. Rising, she slips on her shoes, and opens her door. The hallway is clear, no security patrol, and the house is quiet. The Pope retires early, and so does his retinue.

Maddie walks past the washroom she shares with her mother, then turns the corner. She softly knocks on the door. Cosmo opens it. She holds up the book of Sonnets like a white flag in a war zone. He smiles, and ushers her in.

"I missed you," he says.

"I missed you too." Maddie has hardly seen Cosmo since they have been in the Nuncio's house.

"Would you like a glass of whiskey?"

Maddie licks her lips, suddenly parched. "You have whiskey in here?"

Cosmo produces a bottle of Jameson's. "I told the Nuncio you were a fan of this grain. So he gave this to me and said we should enjoy."

Maddie grins, happy for Giacomo's whiskey, and to be in Cosmo's company, to be warmed by both. "Then I guess I better."

Cosmo pours the whiskey into crystal tumblers and he sits at his desk, offering Maddie the armchair.

"How is Mathilda?" she asks.

"She misses me. I miss her."

"And her mother?"

"She's in Germany. I will not have Mathilda grow up so far away."

From what little Maddie has seen of Cosmo's estranged wife, he is in for a fight.

"How are you?" he asks.

"I'm OK. Tomorrow is a big day. Once the interview is done…"

"We can get out of here?"

"I hope so."

"Are you still a target?"

"I'm not worried about it," she lies. She wonders how she will live with this constant threat of attack. It can't always be like this. She drinks back the warming whiskey. It hits harder than it used to. She has been running on nerves.

"What if you came back to Oxford with me?" Cosmo says. "My father says he'll get you a lectureship at St. Jude's if you want one, and we could just…" And he kisses her.

Maddie smiles in the kiss. The idea is tempting, but she has left Oxford. She does not know if she will let Cosmo leave. "I'm here for a while, Cosmo, I think."

"I know. I was just dreaming." Cosmo takes her hands and tugs on them. "I do love you, you know. More than anything, equal to Mathilda."

Maddie feels her eyes tear up. She's tired, and she's scared, and she knows he means it. She also knows that this moment may never come again. Does she love Cosmo? Did she ever stop? She leans into him and lets him hold her. It feels so good, she rises and takes his hand. He stands and she leads him over to the bed, and lies down. He lies down. "Just hold me some more," she says.

He wraps his arms around her, leans his head to hers, fitting all around her, and she feels, for the first time, in a long time, as if she is safe. She knows she is not, but it is nice to remember what it felt like.

When Maddie opens her eyes again, the morning light is slicing through the curtains. She sits upright, and Cosmo wakes. They are fully clothed. "What time is it?" he says.

Maddie looks at her phone. It's 5:30 in the morning. "It's showtime."

She gives Cosmo a kiss on the mouth, and he kisses her back. They both taste like Jameson's.

Rising quietly, she dashes to get ready to meet Teddy Wright and her crew. And do the thing that started all of this off. What seemed like a simple but doomed thing, which now has more layers of reality than Maddie could have imagined. Interview the Pope on TV.

59. New York City.

The INN crew has managed to make it through the security maze in the early hours, after hauling their gear from the INN truck a few blocks up Park Avenue on dolly carts to the door of the papal mansion. Next, they passed it through the portable scanners and the bomb dogs that the Secret Service has at the ready to sniff out guns and drugs and bombs. The Vatican agents then physically examined all the equipment at a table in the kitchen, and marked it as checked with a red sticker on each item. The whole process took nearly two hours. The interview is one hour out.

The Nuncio is at the door with Maddie, and he greets everyone with a cheery, "Welcome to the Vatican West!"

Francesca and Cosmo have been invited to watch the interview on the monitor outside the library, along with the Nuncio and Sister Maria, who now watches the INN crew as if looking for signs of foreign agents. Her mouth is smiling, but her eyes are not.

Everyone on Maddie's list has made it through security. Even Aretta. She is out of her usual jeans and jacket, and looking like the show's director in a black skirt suit and black t-shirt. As the director, she is taking an earful about something from Teddy, but she catches Maddie's eye. She looks like she wants to talk to Maddie, but with the bustle of preparation, that is going to have to wait.

The camera men set up the room. They are the regulars who shoot Teddy's show in the studio, and so is the sound woman. They have set up in the library, with one camera positioned to get the Pope answering questions, and the other to capture Teddy Wright asking them.

Teddy is wearing a black Chanel suit, and a simple string of pearls, and looks like the picture of virginal modesty. She looks relieved when she spots Maddie standing by the library door, and quickly walks over to her.

"Maddie!" she says with unexpected warmth. "Are you OK?" she asks, genuine concern softening her electric blue eyes, her battle posture slouching a bit as she leans toward Maddie.

"I'm fine," Maddie says. "It's been good being on the inside."

As Maddie expects, Teddy bites. "Oh, what insider stuff have you got for me?"

Maddie tries not to smile. Teddy is the only journalist in the world who is going to have a sit-down interview, on camera, with the Pope, and is still trawling for gossip. "Ask the Pope my question about Christopher Zimmerman," Maddie says.

Teddy blushes in guilt. "Look, I know you told me to ask Reagan about him, but she denied everything. Would the Pope even know?"

"He knew Zimmerman personally, Bishop Zimmerman, and it would be good for you just to have the question out there." Maddie knows it is also a kind of insurance for her if the Pope answers it with anything of substance.

"OK," Teddy says. And she scribbles down a reminder on her notepad. "If he's open to it, what else?"

"Ask him about how Zimmerman influenced his reform of the Vatican's finances."

"Ah, the follow-the-money question."

"Yeah. Ask him about how they plan to repay the money they stole during the Holocaust."

Teddy watches Maddie, the cold blue zinging back into her eyes. "What do you mean?"

"The Nazis stole money from the Jews, and laundered it through the Vatican."

"Really?"

Maddie is surprised Teddy doesn't know this. But then, history is not the strong suit of the modern media. "Just asking the question will be enough."

Teddy touches Maddie on the arm, which is how Teddy hugs people. "Thanks for everything, Maddie. I mean it. I'm glad you got to be the producer of this segment." She glances over at Aretta. "And we hope you can come back soon. Our segment director over there is out of sorts. Been totally stressed out lately, but then, she's a Muslim and she hates the Pope."

Maddie smiles tightly, and watches Teddy walk off to her prep notes. If she starts in with her Muslim-baiting stuff with the Pope, it will be a short interview. Maddie has forty-five minutes to prep, and goes over her own notes so she can feed them to Teddy. If it ever comes to that.

Suddenly, there is a parade of footsteps coming down the hall.

"Ladies and Gentlemen, His Holiness Pope Pius XIII, and Cardinal Bernard Otley," says Bishop Hughes, and the Pope, in white, and Cardinal Otley in a black cassock with his crimson sash and zucchetto, enter.

The INN crew stand as if frozen, not sure what to do with this early arrival, so Maddie steps up to the front of the group. "Thank you, Bishop Hughes," she says. "Your Holiness, it's my pleasure to introduce you to Teddy Wright."

Teddy Wright is trembling as she does an awkward curtsy before the Pope.

Pope Pius reaches out both hands and holds her two hands, beaming God's love right at her. "It is a pleasure to meet you," he says in his booming baritone. "We have much to discuss."

"The pleasure is all mine, Holy Father," says Teddy Wright.

Maddie is pleased she hasn't just called him "Pope".

"Your Holiness," she says, "can you please sit here, and we'll get you miked and lit."

The Pope sits down in a scarlet antique high-backed Queen Anne armchair, serenely curious about the technology around him. "So much work to talk to me!" he exclaims.

"Aretta, mike up the Holy Father, please," Teddy says.

"Aretta," the Pope says, when Aretta is nervously attaching the alligator clip for the wireless microphone on the Pope's cassock. "Where are your people from, Aretta?" the Pope asks.

"Nigeria, sir, like you."

"You are a woman of faith?" the Pope asks, as if asking the time.

Aretta seems paralyzed by the question, as if she doesn't know where to begin to explain that she is a gay Muslim, who has lot of problems with religion but is, nevertheless, devout. So she says, "Yes, Holy Father."

"I am glad to hear that," the Pope says with a gentle smile. He doesn't ask her which faith. To the Pope, it does not matter.

Maddie catches the eye of Cardinal Otley to whom it does matter. A Nigerian Muslim in the same room as the Pope, with her hands on the Holy Father? This can't end well.

Maddie steps in. "Let me help," she says, making a discreet pleat in the Pope's cassock so Aretta can attach the microphone. Aretta shoots her a look of relief.

Maddie then holds the body pack for the microphone in front of the Pope. Someone has helpfully labeled it 'Pope Pius mic' next to the red security sticker. It seems heavy for a wireless body pack, but Maddie figures that INN is using the best for this interview, an over-engineered microphone so as not to miss a single papal syllable. "I need to put this somewhere on your person, Your Holiness," Maddie says.

The Pope smiles with an idea. "Might I just hold it in my lap? The camera will not see it, correct?"

"That's fine, Your Holiness," says Teddy. "Can we

do a sound check?" She asks the Pope to say something, so Pope Pius starts to say the Ave Maria.

"Hail, Mary, full of grace, the Lord is with thee, blessed art thou amongst women—"

"Hang on there, Pope Pius," the sound woman interrupts. They are having a problem with the Pope's wireless microphone. "That red light should be on," she says.

The sound woman fusses with the Pope's body pack, and Aretta grabs Maddie by the arm. "I've got something for you."

She reaches into her backpack stashed by the door, and returns with a small, padded envelope. It is addressed to Maddie, and bears the postmark of New York City, but there is no return address. Maddie opens the package, and inside it is a small silver bag, like a ZipLoc bag, except shinier. The kind of bag that defeats airport security.

Maddie opens the bag. Inside it is her Lumia phone. She takes it out and stares at it. It is her phone, the green and gold St. Jude's College case still in place. It looks very much like the one stolen by the men in Flammie's, the robbers wearing the celebrity masks. Who made her take a selfie so they could remember.

But who would be returning her stolen phone to her? Brett Muenster? And why now?

"Is there a note?" she asks herself, looking in the bag, but finding nothing. So, she switches the phone on, and it powers up. There is the screensaver of her and her father standing at the Sphinx.

As Maddie switches her phone on, the red light on the body pack for the wireless microphone lights up. The one sitting on the Pope's lap.

"I think the power of prayer worked!" says the Pope.

The microphone is now working. It has come to life when Maddie powered on her phone.

Maddie feels a burning heat surge through her body. She realizes that her phone is connected to whatever is inside the wireless microphone's body pack, the one that had made it through security. But the red sticker isn't on it.

It could have been switched.

Aretta catches the look on her face. "What's wrong, Maddie?"

"That's going to explode," Maddie says, her throat so dry she can barely whisper. She walks quickly to the Pope and grabs the body pack for the wireless microphone from the startled Pope's hands.

She starts to walk toward the library door, holding both the body pack and her phone close, focused and calm even though every fiber in her body screams at her to run for it. She can't run. She can't set the bomb off with a bounce.

"Where are you going with that, Maddie?" Teddy asks, surprisingly calmly, given that Maddie is walking off with the Pope's microphone body pack.

Maddie doesn't dare to speak. She just keeps walking, to the library door.

Francesca sees the look on Maddie's face and knows that she is in trouble. Cosmo steps forward to help her, but Francesca grabs his arm. "No," she says. She cannot let anything distract her daughter now.

The Secret Service team, and the Vatican security guys, Stoppia and Calvo, are sitting outside the library, making sure no trouble can get in. Maddie has to let them know that trouble is trying to get out.

"Open the front door," Maddie says.

Aretta follows her, agitated and wailing, "It's a bomb, it's a bomb!"

The Secret Service boss, the big bald Commander who doesn't trust his own shadow, looks at the body pack and the phone and pulls out his gun, as if he is going to shoot them to bits.

But Maddie shakes her head. "Just open the door."

The Secret Service boss moves fast, and runs to the front door of the house, fumbling with the grated doors.

Maddie walks as quickly as she can, while keeping the body pack and the phone steady. She notices the alarm clock icon lit up in the top right corner of the phone's screen. It was a diabolical addition by whoever set this device, for Maddie thinks that if she touches the icon to see how much time she has, she will have no time at all.

The Secret Service boss finally throws open the doors, and yells to the agents in the street. "Halo Friendly Red, Halo Friendly Red!"

The agents hurl themselves into cover behind the blast barricades, and then rise above the parapet, their guns aimed at Maddie as she walks out the door, and down the steps. She can't throw the body pack and the phone without having one of them take it personally and shoot her. So she puts them down carefully in the only place she can think of, the middle of 73rd Street.

"It's a bomb, it's a bomb!" Aretta shouts, running out after Maddie, and pulling her away from the body pack and the phone.

Maddie hears a gunshot blast out from behind her. The force of the bullet hitting Aretta knocks them both flat, with her friend on top of her.

A giant crack breaks the air, so loud it stabs at Maddie's ears as the bomb explodes. Then Maddie feels as if she has been swallowed under a giant wave as she did once swimming in Hawaii with her father. Then everything slams to black.

60. New York Mount Sinai Hospital.

When Maddie finally awakes, she is surrounded by tall creatures all in white. The angels hover above her, murmuring in their own language. Light spills in from everywhere. Two long figures slip away from the haze of whiteness and brightness to lean over her, the lights beaming onto their heads as halos.

Blinking the brilliance into focus, Maddie realizes the figures are her mother, Francesca, and Cosmo. There are three angels, she realizes, when she makes out little Mathilda, cradled in her father's arms.

"Hello?" Maddie says, more as a question, to see if she is dreaming. Or dead.

Both her mother and Cosmo start to cry. Her mother leans down and kisses her on the cheek. Cosmo leans down and kisses her on her mouth. Then, he holds his daughter in front of her godmother.

"Hello Mathilda," Maddie says, as if brought back to a fuller consciousness by being kissed. She lifts a hand strapped into an IV drip and places it on Mathilda's blonde head. With her white blond curls and easy smile, she is a beautiful child.

"The doctors say you are a miracle," Francesca exclaims, stroking Maddie's head. "A true miracle."

"How am I a miracle?" she asks.

Her mother and Cosmo exchange glances of fear, and

then gratitude. "You saved the Pope, Maddie," her mother says. "And you didn't die."

Maddie tries to force open that memory, of the Pope, her phone, of the large sound pack… but she just sees a blur.

"Yes, you did," says Cosmo. "I saw it with my own eyes."

"What happened?" Maddie asks.

Francesca Lynch takes her hand and with it, control of the room. "The doctors put you in a medically induced coma because your brain was swollen after the explosion."

"Explosion?"

Francesca looks at Cosmo. "Yes, the terrorists tried to kill the Holy Father with a bomb in the wireless microphone body pack, one to be detonated by your cell phone. You saved him. Moreover, you saved a lot of other people. And when the bomb exploded, you were only a few feet away. But you lived."

Maddie moves her limbs, to make sure that if she is alive, that she is not missing legs or paralyzed. It hurts to move them, but they do what her brain commands.

"You are a miracle," Cosmo repeats, rocking Mathilda in his arms, his eyes a watery blue, tears streaming down his cheeks.

"How long have I been here?"

"Since the explosion. Six weeks ago."

"I don't remember." And it is true. She cannot remember anything.

Maddie tries to sit up, but her mother gently stops her.

"There is a button for that." Francesca presses it, and as if by magic the head of the bed slowly rises.

"That's good," Maddie says, when she can make level eye contact with her visitors. Her brain is waking up.

Francesca moves nearer to Maddie's bed. "The doctors said your memory will return, in time. They think Muslim terrorists tried to kill the Pope. This bomb they put into the microphone, and it was smuggled into the papal residence by your colleague, Aretta Zayed."

Maddie feels like she's been smacked in the head again. "Aretta? She's no terrorist!"

A funereal silence meets that statement.

"She was killed in the explosion," Francesca replies. "So, we will never know for certain."

Maddie squeezes her eyes shut, trying to wring out memory, so she can see through the haze of the explosion.

"Who else was killed?"

"Just her," says her mother. "God protected you."

"Daddy is so proud of you," Cosmo says. "He was the one who suggested you for this work."

"This work…" Maddie says dryly. Saving the Pope?

The shiny glass bits of her memory, shattered on the pavement, start to come back together. She works for the Pope. Cosmo's father suggested it. To find Christopher Zimmerman. Who was murdered. She found out who the killers are. And where the money is. And who it belongs to. Then she closes her eyes.

Aretta is dead, her name being torched in the media as a terrorist when Maddie is very sure that Aretta saved her, but is now part of a fatal cast of characters set loose by Brett Muenster to enact his bloody plot to power.

"What month is it?"

"Almost November. In two days."

"The election has not happened…" Maddie says.

Her mother grimaces. "Not yet, but that terrible woman is going to win. The sheep will vote her in, all out of fear."

Maddie feels nausea squeeze her gut. She fights it as her theory about Reagan Clark's ascent through murder congeals into a hard and lethal fact.

Brett Muenster was the mastermind. He had killed Christopher Zimmerman and had left her alive because he needed her to be in the same room as the Pope. So her phone could blow them both to pieces. They would pin it all on the Muslims, to whip the country into a terrified frenzy. And Reagan Clark to victory. Tears stream down Maddie's cheeks. For Aretta. For herself. For the whole story she found and found herself in. And for what she must do now.

There is a dark look in her eyes. And so, Cosmo holds up little Mathilda to Maddie. The beautiful child looks at her with a mixture of curiosity and apprehension, now, as her consciousness of the world around her is starting to form.

"You protected your god girl," Cosmo says. "You swore you would protect her from evil, and you have kept your promise."

Maddie, her head pounding with consciousness of her own, tries to smile at Mathilda through her tears, and the child smiles back, bright eyed as if Maddie is the one thing in the world that makes her happy. So like her father. But Maddie also knows that while she may have protected them from evil, evil is not finished with her.

And that she is not at all finished with it.

61. Signal Virtual Meeting: Houston & Somewhere in the Mediterranean Sea.

The cold breeze flying off the Mediterranean whips at Jane's hair and claws at her face as she waits. She has her civvy jeans and sweatshirt on, but prefers to be in uniform, or at least black ops gear when she is about to go into an ops, especially one that she is leading. But the deck of the ship on which she stands also has a civilian spin, being an old freighter, at least above deck. Down below is the kind of mission and the kind of troops that are going to be part of Jane's future. And her casual look, and that of the old freighter are all part of the plan.

Then Jane Jones logs on to Signal. She looks a little weary to C. Parke Stranch, but maybe that's just the night lighting, casting shadows on her fine face. He's lit up by the December afternoon sun of Houston, but he looks anything but sunny himself.

"Is everything good to go, Major?" Stranch asks.

"Yes," Jane says. Though good is not the word she'd use, but then, she has no choice after the Pope didn't blow up. She owes Stranch one, and this is it.

"How far out are you now?"

Jane looks at a monitor and says, "Sixty-seven nautical miles southeast of Cyprus. On schedule."

Stranch allows a smile. "And the systems have all

been tested?"

"Even as we speak. We just jammed up all the defense systems in Cyprus for about 30 seconds and they hadn't even begun to figure it out before we switched them all back on."

Stranch smiles more broadly now. "That's excellent news. Though the Israelis will be a tougher nut to crack."

Jane has prepared for that statement and replies, "If we can turn off the lights, we can turn off all the lights, Admiral."

She has taken to calling him Admiral and not Parke ever since he let her keep the $2 million for not killing the Pope, in exchange for further service to him. She wants to remind him that she is doing this to fulfill an agreement. And then she's out.

Of course, Stranch doesn't know that she's leaving, and he won't know it tonight. Jane rises and lifts her laptop so Stranch can see the wonders behind her. There are four men and two women on the deck, sitting in front of gear that looks more suited to the cockpit of a fighter plane than it does to this a cyber-warship steaming south in the Mediterranean, one disguised as a freighter, registered in Panama.

They tap codes on keyboards attached to massive LED screens, and Stranch can see that this crew can see the very satellites monitoring their progress toward the coast of Israel.

"Wow, that's impressive," Stranch says.

Jane says something to one of the technicians, who types in a code, and the screens showing the ship on the sea go blank.

"Just turned off the lights, Admiral."

He claps his hands together in applause as the satellites come back on. "Well done, Major. Well done."

Jane knows it's the kind of war that she could never stomach, the one where you kill from a distance. But she obliges the Admiral with a smile and bids him good night.

"Good night and Godspeed, Major," he says.

She shuts the laptop, and stares at the Bellerophon logo on its cover, one of the ancient Greek heroes, the slayer of monsters, riding Pegasus, his flying horse. She wishes she could be on that horse. Flying away from the monsters. If she does what she has to do next, then she can make her escape. If it doesn't kill her. But she also understands death is what she deserves.

62. New York City.

It is Christmas Eve, and Maddie has taken up her mother's offer of residence while she continues her recovery. Headaches still assault her for no reason, nasty ones, like a brain surgeon was at work with kitchen gear and using a skewer to poke at her cerebellum. When that happens, her eyesight blurs like a foggy day.

She sits in childhood comfort by the tall blue spruce, their Christmas tree, decorated by Francesca with white lights, gold balls and ribbons, and an angel on top.

Renzo has fully recovered, but not Risorgimento. After being bombed out, the restaurant is getting a restoration and a facelift. And so Renzo is running a kind of classic Italian pop up which delivers meals to Maddie and her mother as sumptuous as any they were served before the bombing. This evening of the seven fishes, Maddie enjoys a delicious fish stew.

Francesca planned with Renzo this feast of the seven fishes for them as a proper Italian Christmas Eve. Francesca is surprisingly discreet about demanding Maddie's attention, and her time. It is as if she knows that Maddie must recover her strength quickly, before her next journey into the darkness.

Francesca's living room has become quiet these last few weeks since Cosmo and Mathilda went back to England. Cosmo left, telling Maddie that he would see her when she wanted to be seen. Maddie wants to see him very much. She calls and texts and sends him emails, and thinks about him all the time as part of her "emotional recovery program", as she calls it.

But she does not want to move back to Oxford. Not now. Not after everything. Even New York feels foreign to her, as if the explosion severed all ties with the idea of home. Of being safe.

They have the television on, and Francesca suggests that they watch the Christmas classic, "The Bishop's Wife," as the tiramisu chills in the fridge, but Maddie is fixed on INN's news roundup, to try to recover lost time.

"How about a romantic comedy on Netflix," Francesca tries. Anything to get her daughter, and herself, out of the day's reality.

But Maddie is dialing up INN. She got a Merry Christmas message from Cardinal Otley earlier today, which had directed her to watch the network's special coverage from Israel. He texted that it announced a kind of thank you gift to Maddie. She texted back trying to wrangle another kind of news, an update on Bishop Hughes. He vanished soon after the bombing, saying he needed to go on retreat after the shocking attack on the Pope.

Because of the failed attack, Maddie texted back.

More news when you have recovered, Cardinal Otley replied, then reminded her again to watch the news from Tel Aviv.

A CGI image of a large gleaming white building spins into view, and the building of a modern, massive teaching hospital is announced, one that will serve whoever enters its door, Jew, Muslim, everyone. The funds for building it, as the reporter reveals, will come from the millions of dollars returned through the recent Reparations Agreement with the Vatican.

The news coverage shows a line-up of local leaders and doctors and nurses, and the ubiquitous Israeli soldiers, passing a ceremonial shovel as they each turn the soil, to mark the spot for the new home of medical miracles. Maddie sees a tall blond man in a suit and sunglasses, watching as if to make sure it will happen. Maddie knows it is Gabriel.

And maybe, just maybe, all her work has helped turn the bad that was done into some good.

"Okay," Maddie says as the report ends, "Let's watch Netflix," but then the bottom of the TV screen lights up with a red crawler of INN Breaking News.

The anchor, listening to a producer on her earpiece, says "We are now going to breaking news from Israel…"

Onscreen, Maddie sees scenes that look like the destruction of a Biblical city of sin, with flames, and dead people, and walking wounded, dazed and bleeding. She feels her heart thump hard, for she recognizes the place as the Land of God.

The shot cuts to a woman who stares pleadingly, disbelievingly into the camera, her white blouse covered with blood. Maddie sits up, recognizing her as the young woman who had escorted her around the bible theme park a few months earlier.

"I have met that woman," Maddie says.

"Hezbollah," her mother replies, her hand to her mouth, staring at the carnage. Blaming the gang that killed her husband.

"A micro drone attack in northern Israel during the Christmas Eve service has reportedly killed more than 100 people, and wounded dozens more," says the reporter from the scene.

"As yet, there is no claim of responsibility, nor how the drones made it through Israel's Iron Dome security. But Israeli security forces have recently expressed concern about Boko Haram's acquisition of micro-drones from Iran. Evangelical Christians from the United States and England had gathered in the thousands to celebrate Christmas at the Land of God, the Christian theme park near Tiberias..."

Maddie feels a chill run through her body. Victor Franchi met with Boko Haram and gave them money and they spent it on micro drones. Now they attacked evangelical Christians? That doesn't make sense to her. They are not the enemy. But then, they are friends to the Jews, and if Boko Haram wants to make the Jews friendless, this is the way to do it.

The reporter continues: "US President-elect Reagan Clark, herself an evangelical Christian, could barely contain her fury upon hearing the news."

Onscreen is the woman herself, less than a month away from her inauguration.

"'In this thou shalt know that I am the Lord'," says Reagan Clark, dressed in blood-red, her face hard and angry, looking like vengeance itself as she raises a fist. "'Behold, I will smite with the rod that is in mine hand upon the waters which are in the river, and they shall be turned to blood'." She raises a fist, ready to start the fight herself.

Maddie's eyes blur, the lights all around her swimming, not from her headaches but tears. Reagan Clark got her war.

63. New York City, three weeks later.

Maddie usually runs late to meetings, and now that this is her first day back at *I'm Wright,* she definitely wants to make a low-key entrance and slip in late through the back door. It is a huge meeting this time, a kind of all-hands-on-deck with dozens of producers, technical staff and admin gathered in the glassed-in central newsroom of INN with the rest of the New York network employees.

When Maddie steps in late, she is very much noticed.

"Welcome home, hero!" Teddy shouts from the front of the room. And when she stands and claps, so does everyone else. In an instant the room thunders with applause and rings with cheers for Maddie. The front screen flashes to life with an image of Maddie, followed by a mini montage of INN news clips about the now-famous *I'm Wright* producer saving the life of the Pope. There is even a clip from Teddy oozing out a few kind words about Maddie.

The real Teddy says, "I love it when the news is the news."

Maddie presses a hand to waist and takes a small bow, hoping this adulation ends soon. The tom toms are already playing a warm up in her head, warning about a massive headache about to lay siege to her brain.

What hushes the room is when the montage kicks over

to the news that is the other news, about how another producer, Aretta Zayed, was the Muslim mastermind behind the attack.

A small smile flickers on Teddy's face to see it. Maddie thinks Teddy's ghoulish joy owes to the fact that the awful news about Aretta, that is all lies, still gave *I'm Wright* a ratings bump.

In the silence that now takes over the crowded room, the screen changes again. C. Parke Stranch III now fills the screen, looking to Maddie like a nasty cousin to Colonel Sanders. She curses herself for coming late and not knowing why Stranch invaded the meeting. But as she looks around the room, no one else seems to know. Maddie is thankful for the small bit of background work on Stranch she gleaned and that her uncertain memory and online whitewashing has supplied on this bad billionaire who owns Bellerophon, who supposedly is now a churchy do-gooder. But the clearest memory Maddie has is of Patrick telling her this is the man who paid for the thugs to steal their phones, and probably return hers as well. With a blast trigger in it.

She hasn't heard from Patrick since, except for a text while she was in hospital, saying *Thank God for Saint Mads.*

So her headache starts crashing cymbals together and Maddie trains to hear Stranch announcing that he has bought their network.

Teddy is dead still but her lazer blue eyes flicker over to Maddie, to her sound woman and to the floor director for the reaction of these trusted few to the sudden takeover. Clearly this is news even to the star of INN's top news talk show.

INN now belongs to a man who would actually destroy the very platform from which Maddie is going to battle against evil for Omega.

As a late January storm drops a heavy layer of snow on the freezing city, Stranch is up on screen, lit in a warm light atop his yacht somewhere off South Carolina, addressing the INN global network via television.

"I know that you are all wondering what will happen now that I have taken over, and I would have told you yesterday. But my dear friend, Governor Reagan Clark, was inaugurated as President of the United States."

Teddy keeps smiling for the cameras, as Stranch is watching. But her crossed and legs crossed has her body language screaming out again this batshit bitch who is going to kill them all.

Up on screen now are images of that inauguration, with Reagan Clark in a blazing red coat putting her hand on Lincoln's Bible, and swearing to all kinds of things Maddie knows mean nothing to her vision of how she wants America to go.

The screen returns to the image of the portly, smug Stranch, looking as if he is now the Pope.

"Now, I know some of you are thinking what the heck is a guy like me, who will be helping President Clark as an advisor, be doing to an organization like yours, which did pretty much everything possible short of assassination to stop her from being elected."

He pauses, apparently to allow for laughter, as this is

apparently a joke. There is no laughter as the room of a hundred people waits in steel clad silence.

"The short answer is nothing. It's business as usual at INN, and in my capacity as a member of the Reagan Clark council of advisors, I consider it proper to hand over the daily running of the network to a very talented man who knows the media well. Mr. Brett Muenster will become COO of INN until I am able to return to help out, should that day ever come."

Brett Muenster, the man whom Maddie has first seen in the flesh at the Land of God in Israel, the man who had killed Christopher Zimmerman, and framed Aretta by sending her Maddie's phone so she was shot, and who tried to kill the Pope and Maddie, now stands at the front of the room.

Suddenly, Muenster's bald head and square glasses are lit up in the wash of TV light, and a camera projects his image on screen. Then he speaks to the INN people from twenty feet in front of Maddie. Still short and twitchy, and now, Maddie's boss.

"Thank you, Admiral Stranch. It is my great honor to be part of such a storied organization that has done so much to advance the cause of journalism," Muenster says, smiling his gap tooth grin as if he is going to get even with everyone who has ever underestimated him. "I pledge that I will continue in its great spirit of progressive truth seeking, and going forward, we will keep the INN ship sailing as she was. With one notable exception. Given the importance of the Middle East to the world we live in, and to the stories we tell, we are making history by appointing a new Jerusalem Bureau Chief to follow in the illustrious footsteps of her own father. Ladies and gentlemen, the woman who saved the Pope, Maddie Lynch."

At this news, applause breaks out again in the newsroom, with Teddy Wright herself whooping as if Maddie has been elected president.

Maddie feels the heat rise from her stomach to her cheeks, as she has no idea that this move is coming. And now that it has, her aching head settles to let her think about her two choices: walk out the door and disappear until they find her and kill her, or take the hand that evil has dealt her and fight back.

So, she nods, and the cameras swing around to the back of the room to find her. She now sees herself smile and wave back from the big screen. Waving hello, waving goodbye.

"Sorry to ambush you like that, Maddie," Muenster says, catching Maddie alone in the hallway as she walks back to her office. Muenster pumps Maddie's hand like a politician, all hearty action with no meaning attached, holding on just a little too long in case Maddie tries to escape. "But INN is always keen to break news, and we didn't want this one to get out until we broke it, so to speak." He releases his grunt of laughter but doesn't really mean that either.

Maddie pulls back her hand and looks at Muenster as if regarding someone who has been human once but who now is a creature who will deal harshly with any human impulse that counters that reality. "No, I would imagine there are a lot of things that you don't want to get out," Maddie replies.

"Well," Muenster says on a nervous smile, "nothing that would make the Palestinians happy. Then we'd know we were doing something wrong!"

"What if I say 'No'?" Maddie says. "I won't go to Jerusalem."

Muenster looks at Maddie as if she is joking. "At triple your salary, in the center of the world of journalism, to follow in your father's footsteps? C'mon, this is the kind of assignment journalists kill for."

"My father died for it," Maddie says sadly. "Hey, maybe I can find who killed Christopher Zimmerman. And framed Aretta Zayed. And who tried to kill the Pope."

Muenster cocks his head in sympathy, acting as though it is Maddie's continued concussion. "The Muslim was killed by the Secret Service. She was part of it all. As for Zimmerman and the Pope…" he holds out his hands like a magician who has just fooled the audience with a trick. "That would be a major story. But you be careful. We don't want to lose another Lynch out there on the frontier."

It is a threat. Maddie can ignore it, but then, that would be reasonable. And the one thing she knows that with the election of Reagan Clark is that reason, as she had once known it, has been blown to smithereens. So, she meets the threat with one of her own. "I think if anything happens to me out there on the frontier, or anywhere, then Christopher Zimmerman happens to you."

Muenster blinks in confusion. "What do you mean 'happens'?"

"I mean that if I wind up shot in the back, or die of a heart attack. Something like that."

"That's what I mean," Muenster says with that aw-shucks smile. "You be careful."

Maddie smiles back cold and hard. "And what I mean is that Christopher Zimmerman's history of love and money and dead babies with Regina, sorry, President Reagan Clark, is safely stored in the Cloud, and in about a dozen other earthly places, and if anything bad, like violent death, happens to me, or to my mother, or to Cosmo Smythe and his family, then it all comes out into the open."

Muenster's boyish smile grows as he grins now, holding the winning hand. "She's the president, Maddie. We've already got what we wanted."

But his eyes are not smiling. Maddie sees a touch of fear keeping them blinking and that makes her feel better.

"And you thought you'd send me to the center of the bullseye and take care of another problem while you were at it. Sorry to disappoint you, Brett."

Muenster's smile vanishes. "Why do you think Zimmerman stole all that money?"

Maddie doesn't blink. "I'm working on that story. But it will be easier to tell it from Jerusalem. I better go pack. Don't want to lose any time on finding out the truth, do I?"

Then she leaves him in the hall as she walks to her office. Her corner closet office has never looked so good, stuffed with red roses and boxes of chocolates, and get well cards mixed with ones that say Welcome Home! Someone even did a mockup meme of the Pope blessing Maddie. She gives it all a goodbye smile, and one also to the empty room beside it that was Aretta's.

Coat in hand, and her laptop and briefcase, she heads for her new life.

On her way to the elevator, Teddy catches up with her.

"Hey Maddie, that's great about Jerusalem," she says. "I'm going to miss you."

Maddie wishes she could say the same, but in her heart, she left *I'm Wright* the moment the bomb went off. "You'll see enough of me on Zoom," Maddie says. "And you can come visit."

Teddy jerks her head back as if Maddie has suggested she walk into the Hudson River. "No, thank you. I think I can get through life without going there," Teddy says. "Besides, we have enough crazy here to keep me busy."

Someone calls out to Teddy, and she holds out a hand to Maddie. "Thank you for everything. You saved not only the Pope, but me, too."

Maddie shakes Teddy's hand, and Teddy even pulls Maddie into a hug, something she has never seen Teddy do. Then the elevator arrives and Maddie steps on board. Teddy does not wait until the doors have closed before she disappears. To the next thing.

Yanking on her puffer coat, Maddie walks out onto 10th Avenue, and into the blizzard that swirls around her.

The air is thick with attacking wind and snow, but her headache is gone, and her eyesight is clear. Maddie can see her future clearly. Stranch and Muenster, in trying to cut her out, have carved an entrance to the future.

She feels her phone vibrate in her coat pocket. She pulls over under a bodega awning, and looks at her phone. The vibration is a text, from Cardinal Bernard Otley.

Got the latest news from INN and it is news of you. Jerusalem is where your father began his last story. Are you still with us?

Maddie thinks about that. Otley isn't asking her if she is still an agent of Omega. That agency is something you resigned with death or excommunication. And that medallion he gave her is still hanging from her neck. So, he is asking if Maddie is prepared to go forward into another dark place. Indeed, a place to which she is being sent by the forces of evil that she once dismissed with a philosopher's nonchalance. Now she is a woman who has faced death and, for now, postponed it.

She sees her father, James Lynch, smiling at her, his eyes lit with possibility, and with love. And she hears his voice now, as clear as the fire engine sirens roaring on 10th Avenue. "*No one gets out alive, Maddie. Might as well go where the story goes. Find out what happened.*"

She texts Otley back: *I am with you. More soon.* Turning into the wind, she heads toward uptown to pack.

64. Jerusalem.

Maddie has taken a bigger room in the American Colony until she can decide where in the ancient city she should live. She will make INN pay for anything she wants: books, a new computer, and a well-stocked bar. She'll be a kind of blackmailer herself, now.

The thought makes her smile as she eats her Mediterranean salad in the Cellar Bar. She has meetings with the bureau on Sunday, so that gives her two days to inhale the perfume of Jerusalem, and think about how she will find Victor Franchi, and what she will do when she does.

She thinks Bishop Hughes is in hiding here as well. He may even have changed sides. After all, he would have been killed in the bomb blast. She makes a mental note to ask Gabriel about him when she catches up with her pal in Mossad in the next few days.

Maddie's mind rolls on, no headaches of late to stop it. The quiet of the bar even lets her thoughts roar loudly along through this sundown on a Friday. She will toast to that as she orders a second glass of sparkling water, and notices a woman sitting alone at the bar. About her age, blonde, fit. She's as blonde as Emily, who threw her a going away party. The hockey team, some old pals from high school, and Patrick and Renzo and her mother came to that affair, and even Teddy Wright came, and as eclectic as the guest list was, it all worked out. And Emily told Maddie her little 1K investment had gone up to $50,000. She leaves it alone, and lets Emily work her magic. As for her mother, she will come to Jerusalem at Easter, she says. If Maddie hasn't moved back to civilization by then.

The woman at the bar finishes her beer, and turns toward Maddie. She has eyes that pierce the room, such is their unusual blue-gray iciness. Maddie feels suddenly pinned to her chair. Renzo said the woman who may have bombed his restaurant was blonde and Maddie's age and had eyes like a wolf. Blue, gray, icy… This woman has come to kill Maddie before she even gets started.

But instead Jane Jones smiles with real delight as she sits alongside Maddie, as if invited.

"I think you know who I am," she says.

"You know who I am," Maddie replies, her throat dry.

Jane beams her bright smile. "My name is Jane. I know a lot of things."

Maddie grabs the bar to steady herself. "Why are you here?"

"Because you're here. And it seemed to be the safest place to speak."

"I'm listening."

"Our conversation will take a while. First, I need to trust you."

Maddie shakes her head: Jane has this all wrong. "How can I trust you?"

Jane looks away as if to confer with herself on a decision. Turning back she says, "OK, so when you switched your phone on, I put in a timer to give you a chance. I could have had it blow up as soon as you powered up."

Maddie feels like Jane has tried to kill her all over again, and that she now wants to strangle Jane.

"I know, it's a lot to take in. But I've also seen that you are really smart. You would figure it out, and everything would be alright."

Maddie doesn't believe that. And yet Jane has just admitted she tried to kill the Pope. And she gave Maddie a chance to save him.

"Who are you working for?" Maddie asks.

"Myself, now," Jane says. Then she rises and smiles. "I'll be in touch."

She walks out of the Cellar Bar. Maddie rises and follows, to see where she goes, but Jane turns back and shakes her head no, then leaves the hotel.

Maddie sits back down at the bar, at her salad, but she has lost her appetite. She pays her bill and heads back to her room, the Deluxe Pasha suite that overlooks the pool.

Though the doctor insists on no alcohol as Maddie continues to recover, she insists on a glass of Jameson's.

As she fills her glass, she thinks about what Jane said, about how luck and timing or maybe divine intervention saved her from being blown to bits with the Pope.

Right beside the bottle of Jameson's Maddie sees that there is an envelope on her desk. It was not there when she left, and it is addressed to her, the address typed in Courier font. It has a Lebanese postage stamp. Could Victor Franchi be sending her a message? Or Bishop Hughes?

She holds the envelope up to the light. There are no wires. She sniffs it, and there is no powder. Then, in the bathroom with the door closed, to contain the blast if there is any, she carefully opens the envelope. Inside is a photograph. It's of her and her father, in Cairo, the Sphinx behind them. The photo from her phone. Her last photo with him.

Maddie's heart is thudding in her chest and tears start to pool in her eyes. She stares at the photo, hoping, fearing, and then turns it over. On the back there are words: "The story only ends when it is told. Unlike the Sphinx, I have more to say."

Maddie knows that it is her father's handwriting because it is not handwriting. Black pen, all uppercase. Did someone psycho send an old note from her father to torment her? Or if he has sent it here, is he alive?

Her head is ringing again and she sits heavily on the bed. She was called a living miracle, for saving the Pope, but she doesn't believe in miracles. She was called a saint by Gabriel for helping return part of the stolen money to Israel. But there is more, so much more to find. No, she is not a believer in saints and angels. And yet, she feels a surge of miraculous elation run through her body.

Her father is alive.

He is her story now. And she will tell it.

END.

Our Authors:

Michael McKinley has published more than twenty books, and produced, written and directed a dozen more TV shows. He has also written award-winning magazine and feature articles in publications in the UK, US and Canada. Michael is one of the authors of this new thriller and also the CEO and Co-Founder of BookGo and YourBook and YourFlick.

Nancy Merritt Bell has developed over twenty plays in as many theaters in New York City, Toronto, Berlin, and around the world. Working in TV, she helped create and develop over a dozen series. Nancy is one of the authors of this new thriller and also the Director of Development at BookGo and YourBook, and also YourFlick.

BookGo is the next chapter in publishing for writers and readers everywhere.

Also come and visit us at YourBook and YourFlick. We are everyone and everything you need to take your book from the gleam of an idea to the best sellers list, and your screenplay to Sundance Film Festival, or Cannes, or the Oscars.

https://www.bookgo.pub/yourbook

www.ingramcontent.com/pod-product-compliance
Lightning Source LLC
Chambersburg PA
CBHW070542310726
48982CB00010B/1435/J
9798998535796